Battlefield Matrix

(Book II in the Nelta Series)

J.P. Osterman

Battlefield Matrix

(Book II in the Nelta Series)

Copyright © 2013 J.P. Osterman

All rights reserved.

CreateSpace, Charleston SC

Published by: JPOsterman.com

ISBN-10: 0615977146
ISBN-13: 978-0-615-97714-0
Date of Publication: August 13, 2014
Printed in the United States of America

Cover Photo: Bruce Rolff | Shutterstock.com

DEDICATION

To my Brother Mark, gone too soon, eternal peace.

ACKNOWLEDGMENTS

I thank Drew, my editor, and Bruce Rolff for my cover artwork.

Chapter 1

Matrix Blackout

"Sometimes, old technology, like this Canon A95 digital camera I'm holding is the *best* technology, especially now since this blackout started. It's battery driven. My parents had it before they died and I almost recycled it. Thank God I didn't 'cause now I can record what's happening when no one else can!"

Elisa's camera slid sideways, but she re-aligned it and resumed recording and narrating the scene.

"Oops! Sorry." She checked her watch, stalled at 7:05 p.m. "I'm Dr. Elisa Holton. Today is Monday, February 27, 2068. I just landed at the Richmond Clinton Airfield in Virginia. This blackout began sweeping through the East Coast at 6:45 p.m., so I'm hearing people say. On the way down here from Research Station II, I *did* see all the lights and advertising beacons gradually extinguish from the north. I was wondering what the heck was happening...now I know...but I *never* woulda believed a quantum-computer-matrix blackout could occur on a global scale, leaving everyone in the dark!"

J.P. Osterman

She pointed the camera toward the north sky. "No stars, yet. The Matter Stream sample has healed the ozone. But because of the powerful tropopause shield, we can only see light from the moon and the five space stations."

A small argument broke out behind her—two people fighting over what triggered the blackout. One man yelled, "Someone *definitely* attacked the matrix!" A group of racing scientists stopped the fight by yelling out the ground zero location. They also confirmed the attack. Those who heard the news either dashed for overcrowded exits or sprinted outside toward the lifts to catch hovercraft docking and taking off high up on lily-pad platforms. The news circulated through the crowd like the residual light trickling from LED walls and solar panels: Earth's matrix, Terra-II, was responsible for processing energy to *everything.* Terra appeared dead.

"The attack *is* coming from the North Pole," Elisa continued, recording the chaos. *That's* what experts are saying." She felt her throat dry and a bit disoriented as she stepped outside Baggage Claim leading to the hovercraft thoroughfares. With people crying and shouting all around her, she resumed recording the scene. She could see the old paved and pot-holed streets under the dead magnetic grid that was still attempting to electrify and connect to the matrix. "Everywhere, there seems to be a bit of stored energy, but only enough to keep people from dying," she said.

The latest Shiny fission-fusion vehicles were darting in-and-out of frozen guidance beams like disoriented hummingbirds. Some were stalled or burping in midair. At the end of all the sky-lane airstrips, craft were shut down in Dead-mode. The ones still in the sky, miles-high, were slowly gliding back to the airfield, where outdated emergency vehicles were blaring their horns and waiting on idle to assist them.

Beyond the sky lane thoroughfares were two biodomes and two glass towers, their sleek facades dwindling through the stored energy. People could rent rooms there, attend conferences, descend to the subways, or embark on Maglevs and L-cars to other destinations. All their virtual adds had

Battlefield Matrix

fizzled out.

Seeing mass confusion suddenly on her right, Elisa stopped to find her bearings as someone walked into her. Rubbing her shoulder, she waved for people to go around her. She was now yards from a busy crossing. Again, she re-tested her wrist device to connect to Terra. Then she noticed that *every* portable tablet and interactive accessory around her was also dead and unresponsive. "Nothing...not even an verbal app. The quantum computer seems to have lost all interpersonal capability." She began recording a woman shouting at her stalled avatar like someone yelling at a disobedient dog on a leash.

"Come on! We gotta go!" She was crying and appeared lost. "Whata I do! How do I getcha moving? Should I leave without cha?" Her life-size avatar was holographic bright in its yellow projection light, but frozen as were others alongside the curb and inside the building. People had called on them for help but weren't receiving any answers, just blank avatar stares.

One man threw down his portable tablet and stomped it into cinders. Two attendants pushed him back and doused the sizzling silicon with water.

"If Richmond is at this level of confusion...the rest of the world must be in utter chaos!" Elisa said into her camera. Noticing it shaking with her trembling fingers, she tried steadying it by zooming in on orderly places inside Baggage Claim: the ceiling processors, 3D wall-zone screens, and hub processing mounds on the walls inside the building. Then she panned the camera around places outside the building. Positioned in strategic, matrix-processing locations on the brick and stucco surfaces, and on the exterior of all the advertising and security kiosks, the matrix processor mounds appeared structurally sound and thick in their beehive shapes, but only black in their concave niches, not rainbow processing. All the high towers supplying electromagnetic and photonic matrix connections to all those mounds and wall zones appeared like dead branches with thin black fractal limbs, their green-light signals off-line.

3

Quickly panning through the scene again, she whispered: "So the difference is twenty minutes between the start of the blackout to now. It took *twenty* minutes for my ride to descend from Research Station II and disembark people here at the Richmond Airfield. Security is *really* tight! Enforcers are gunned up and running all over, targeting *everything* in the shadows."

A disheveled Asian woman nearly ran into a stalled hover cart, stopped, and then shouted: "If Matrix Techs can't resolve the blackout, I heard a Stealth Force officer just say that the nine o'clock Final Communication with the Neltans *might* not happen!"

Elisa zoomed in on her frightened expression.

"It's gotta happen!" a man stopped and cried.

"I *can't* believe it won't," said another bystander, flipping closed his wrist device. He was a Stealth Force officer, out of uniform. Elisa focused on his Stealth Force insignia on the cover of his wrist device: a gold Eagle surrounded by three stars, symbolizing Space Station III. That meant he had the latest information, and he tried to comfort the panicking woman by telling her that. "It's true, Lady! Before the blackout, I received a live stream from The Regency. Half of them are *now* inside the Press Room preparing the IMAX screen to process the quantum-communication from the Decagon."

Elisa quickly turned the camera lens back at her face to continue her 'selfie' report. "That's the accelerator between Mars and Jupiter. It receives the wormhole from Nelta and then transfers the quantum signals to the Neltan-based screen in the Press Room, where Terra-II, our quantum-computer matrix, helps translate the communication some more, and the Neltans materialize and hold discussions with *our* people."

Meanwhile, a small nervous crowd had assembled around the three arguing individuals, and the off-duty, Stealth Force officer appeared almost ready to shake the panicking woman to her senses. She screamed, "Final Communication might *not* happen! We could *all* wind up dead!" Just as the officer was about to call a *real* person for help, because he forgot that his avatar wouldn't activate when he tried calling it for assistance, the woman dashed into a sky lane thoroughfare with hover cars racing above her, but not before her statement ignited a wave of screams that seemed to ripple 'round the world.

Everyone began repeating those words as if Earth might end: "Final Communication with the Neltans might not happen!"

Arriving safely across the thoroughfare, the hysterical woman raced into line behind several other trembling people in front of a kiosk labeled neon, *Norfolk*. In front of their small loading zone, a long hovercraft swooped down and docked, its steels claws around its base clamping to struts. A door slid open, and everyone piled inside like clattering birds squishing into a bulging nest. After the door hissed shut, the hover vehicle shot up through several honks and a near hit-and-miss accident and launched east.

Another huge craft glided overhead, and Elisa pointed her camera at it. The air felt tingly as the craft's landing lights flashed blue and white. The craft's gravitational array of rods and filaments on its hull were adjusting with the atmosphere. Shouting and gasping at the close-up encounter, people ducked, and some almost dropped to the shimmering ground.

Elisa cowered then stood up straight. *"That's* sure unusual. I hope nothing comes crashing down in this blackout!"

A man ten feet away from her called out: "All large ones have been landing on stored power, just like the one that passed over us. So we're safe! Smaller ones have more stored power and can glide in for a landing, soak up a charge from one of the side stations, and then take off again."

Thanking him as he ran off with several other people who had been nervously waiting for him, Elisa turned the camera back at herself and said into the lens: "Did a Tech-No hacker group unleash the virus that's responsible for this matrix blackout? Or did a terrorist group do this? *That's* what I'm hearing some people ask right now."

The bright light was now shining far enough into the background behind her that her wide lens could capture people pointing at the craft's wafting contrail. Their faces looked like those stunned individuals on First Communication Day when the Neltans first appeared to humanity! People standing on her left side were complaining. People on her right had their hands over their mouths like stoppers, preventing them from screaming and vomiting. Still, at some point during the course of their reactions to the blackout, *everyone* was trying to access Terra, but failing to get an avatar, icon or holographic help of any kind.

"No one's sure *who* started this blackout it seems…except, usually, the Tech-Nos hack and attack the matrix, and terrorists use explosives," she said, centering the lens on her face. "Time'll tell. In either case, it's a Tech-No group that's gonna pay for this or, hopefully, Enforcers will get lucky this time and capture the terrorist responsible for this…this bedlam."

She then pointed her camera at the glaring green Entry sign over a tight archway under which she walked. The sounds of clattering footsteps were all around her, and peoples' clothes were slapping her arms and face. She jostled her camera and caught it before it toppled. "*Whew*—close call!" She could feel hot breathing on her ears and her neck as people raced past her, sprinting toward the buildings for help and directions. Then she knocked shoulders with people heading toward another thoroughfare of sky-gliding hovercraft. Above those, larger astrocraft were ascending and descending, disembarking and harvesting passengers from tubular modules leading into Arrivals and Departures. Like magnets interacting with steel, hover cab drivers were shuffling passengers in and out of their canopy doors. She stopped behind a small curbside crowd and raised her camera lens so it could capture several frustrated people who were hailing rides as angry people wiggled ahead of them to cross the glistening thoroughfare and wave down a large astrocraft that had *Off World Only* plastered in glowing orange lights.

She ducked, believing one of them might start a fistfight. "This place is nuts! Just think…the same craziness might be happening *everywhere*!"

Battlefield Matrix

The crossing lights in the pedestrian thoroughfare were flashing *all* three colors; green, yellow and red simultaneously. Automated directional icons were frozen mid-air like misplaced Christmas ornaments.

"Thank God all streets are revamping for hovercraft flight or all these people'd be struck dead," she said to her camera. "I wonder if the whole world's experiencing this blackout."

A woman stuck her face into the camera light. "No—just *us* in the northern hemisphere." She then ran to catch a hover cab after several people flagged her over to them.

"Well you heard it…the matrix blackout is *only* in the north. But it's certainly debilitating on this half of the globe! My wrist device stalled at that 7:05 mark after the craft I was riding maneuvered under the tropopause shield. *All* the matrix capability we have right now seems to be what we've already programmed into our portable devices. All interactive live-streaming capability is out. If you try activating your programs for help, you can't get a virtual connection. The matrix *is* dead. Terra is processing *completely* flat."

She re-set the camera exposure that blasted her face with more light.

"*Whoow*…I'm not very good at…at working this thing…and when I'm done recording and storing this show, I don't even know if I'll be able to transfer it *into* the matrix. Still, I'm gonna try. I want what I'm recording stored in the Neltan Archival Museum, that's is, if my interview with Regent Manning ends well. He could hire me on the spot for the Regeneration position on *Sagan*. Terra *has* to return to full processing at *some* point."

A man stuck his frightened glance in front of the lens and shouted, "Soon I hope!"

She waved him away and continued, whispering: "If my interview with Regent Manning goes well, and I hope it will, he *could* direct me to *Sagan* right after tonight's signing ceremony. I *could* be off-Earth as soon as 1 a.m. tomorrow morning! Uh-oh…I shoulda planned better."

"Planned better for what?" asked a little girl, holding her

mother's hand.

"Come on, Jennifer, we gotta leave!" her mother ordered, jerking the girl toward a long, silver hover bus loading passengers for *Underground Center A*. The living quarters in their beehive community had to be small to be only a letter designation, but their support system had to be large in the alphabetical wheel arrangement from *A* through *F* under Richmond.

"*I* just forgot to do something!" Elisa began, waving to the little girl still glancing back at her. "It's okay! It'll be okay," she called, hoping she hadn't alarmed her even though she felt so unprepared. She thought of the next, hard, six sleepless hours and remembered that she only had a protein snack in her long thin backpack. Noticing her slightly unkempt reflection in the silver casing around the camera lens, she rearranged her backpack so she could reach the protein bar. Then she adjusted the weight of her backpack so its bulges didn't peak over her shoulders, smoothed down the wrinkled collars on her thin blue jacket, and unleashed the top button of her white blouse, but not too much.

"There...that's better, but not too revealing," she sighed, but quickly tilted up the camera, hoping she hadn't let it slip for very long to record too much of the glistening fabrication of the streets. "I'm gonna look like hell for this interview. It's *still* so darn hot!" Right up close to the lens, she said, "I better catch a hover cab fast or my clothes are gonna melt right off 'o me! It must still be ninety-eight degrees...even after 7 p.m." She inhaled and coughed, a sting pinching in her trachea. "The air is humid and it's so hard to breathe, even though the Matter Stream sample healed it. It's gonna take years, forecasters say, for Earth to return to its pre-2057 state."

At the pedestrian crossway to her left, stampeding people dashed for an astrocraft flashing its *Military Space Station III* destination.

She whispered into the camera lens, "I wish, that before leaving Earth for good, I could feel *one* hour of cold weather...*and* snow...just like when I was twenty-two...the month before the ozone bombs exploded."

The faces of her parents flashed through her mind. They died from radiation poisoning eight months after her brother and sister died when one of the dirty bombs left its trajectory and exploded over Chicago during the Ozone Attack of June 10, 2057. Because she was packing up her things in her dorm room at the University of Chicago the day after graduation, she was able to survive the ozone bombings by rushing into an underground shelter. Uniting with other survivors three weeks later, after Recovery team IV cremated the remains of her siblings at one of the cemetery sites outside Chicago, she took a subway east; thereafter, she accessed several safe roads to Washington, D.C. Once there, she met up with her ill parents, began a long period of mourning, and, subsequently, received her M.S. at Georgetown, followed by her Ph.D. in Bioengineering from Duke University in North Carolina. For the past six years, she has held prestigious positions as a Lead Researcher at several labs on Earth and published several high-ranking articles in the *Journal of Nano-Robotics and Biogenetics*. For the last two of those years, she has worked for Bio Gen, Inc., a research corporation on Station II experimenting with DNA, mostly Top Secret, the later ripped from her controlled sites once *Sagan* Techs or The Regency designated the experiments as Black Ops and/or for *Regency Eyes Only*. She has lived alone, and for the past two years, worked alone, except for icon helpers and her Matrix Interfacer—her avatar, currently disconnected from Terra.

She said into her camera, "I forgot about how winter feels even though a few snowballs have hit my face!" Then she felt a bit disoriented but quickly snapped out of the haze as a line of hover cabs realigned high in the sky for a landing. If she could cut through the raucous group in front of her, she could slide into one of the huge elevators, head up to one of the modular pads that looked like a platform inside a hamster habitat. There, she could hail a hover cab.

When she noticed a tiny, red flickering light on top of her camera, she came to a dead stop. Battery power was getting low. She said into the glass panel: "Is being on *Sagan*, tonight, or any other time, and *maybe* for good, what I *really* want? Do I *really* want that? Damn!" She tapped the camera but the low-battery indicator kept flashing.

"Damn *what*, ma'am?" asked a stranger. "You all right? Need help?"

She felt red-faced. "No thanks. I'm just trying to keep this thing working."

He chuckled. "When ya get *that* right, why not offer your services to one of the matrix processing facilities. Seems you know what you're doing and *they* could use *your* help!" After touching her camera in an obvious gesture of inquisitiveness, he jumped into the elevator that three others leaped in after him. The doors thudded shut.

"Full!" she said into her camera. She felt stupid. "Ya coulda had *that* ride! Ya need to act a little more quickly next time...quit being so polite all the time," she whispered, slapping a bit of sense into the side of her head. Then she remembered her train of thought. "I don't have time to rethink my decision to leave Earth," she whispered. "Stop thinking so much and just move on. You're going to *Sagan* and then to Nelta, that is, if Regent Manning himself is willing to vouch for you, and that recommendation alters Terra, which in turn might bump you up from Wait-mode to Necessary or Vital." She huffed facetiously. "Yeah, right!"

Waiting in line for the next elevator as well, people backed away from her a bit, and she put the camera low at her waist and continued: "My decision's final."

A black woman whispered in her ear, "You keep tellin' yerself that, Sistah!"

The red battery light was now like a small strobe, soon to unleash its power dregs.

After giving her a smile of thanks from behind her camera, she turned back the lens to her face. "A camera...me and you making decisions. Is *this* what it's come to? Wow—I gotta get a life!" She saw her smiling reflection in the silver frame. "Getting on that astrocity *is* the answer...and getting the hell

Battlefield Matrix

off Research Station II!" More than ever, she felt filled with the desire to search for a purpose. She had studied to be a *real* physician, helping people, not a statistical outlier feeding pollen to a hive! "They take *everything* I do and I never see the results. I feel like honey being sucked down someone's gullet."

"I wouldn't take *that*, Sistah, nuh-uh no way," the black woman said. Then she quickly left the line when her colleague, another ticket agent, hailed her toward the Departure elevator. All the elevators at the major thoroughfares leading up to the pedestrian modules were lurched up and lunging down, their pulleys now on Emergency Manual, the wait times and transport times now twice as long.

Her near-empty stomach was making her suddenly focus on food. If the blackout wouldn't end soon, she might have trouble finding food and water in D.C. She said into the camera: "Well, maybe I can figure out a way to stall Regent Manning's fast-pace style of immediately transferring new hires. I'll have to think of something that'll buy me time for a few days. But he's a *real* mover, Regent Manning."

Then she realized that what she was recording, and planning to stream to the archives would be available for Public Viewing. She was sounding a bit too critical, especially of Regent Manning who was still giving her updates on his progress in finding out who sabotaged the *Greeter* shuttle that killed their mutual friend, Lynn Altmin. No telling *who* might access her recording at the archives. Her running impromptu dialog *could* get back *to him*.

"Well, on second thought, I might *not* stream this to any museum requesting recordings of this blackout. I don't know *what* I'll do with it. Maybe I'll just keep it to watch later. It'll be like a time capsule I'll one day replay and use as a measuring stick to see where I've come from, if I made the right choice to go to Nelta, and if I'm happy."

An elderly woman put her face into her line of sight and whispered, "Maybe your grandchildren will see your show!"

A short thin woman with frizzy brown hair jostled her baseball cap and tugged at her patched jeans that obviously

J.P. Osterman

weren't manufactured with self-repairing materials. That meant she was below the poverty level. How she ever managed to slip through airfield security was a mystery! Terra's malfunction allowed her entrance. She had a dirt-speckled expression of pungent drudgery on her face as she leaned into Elisa and said: "Happy? Who can be *happy* with attacks happening all the time? I live outside this place, under the streets, and came here to remember why I left everybody and everything." She grabbed the camera and pulled it in front of her face. "I think you're all nuts!" With her head low, she began stepping away like a young kitten terrified of human contact. If cars were still in the streets, one would have hit her.

Feeling embarrassed and *pausing* her camera, Elisa noticed that many people were eavesdropping on her camera conversations and that she was affecting *them* with her recording. If Terra were processing, one of them most likely would have streamed a *Concerned Citizen* report to Clinton Airfield Security. Smiling, she pulled back her camera gently and said: "I need this recording to learn about various intervention methods later on should a blackout occur again. I'm a physician." She showed them her small Station II insignia that appeared to quell the fear on their faces. Then she realized that her recording was for so much more: as a substitute for her disabled avatar that she was having difficulty coping without, or for necessary companionship that she hadn't had for years. Stepping into the giant glass elevator, she snuggled into the corner and elbowed for more room. She felt like crying, but pulled out a small bottle of cold water from her backpack and gulped down the empty pangs. As the elevator lurched upward toward a special sky lane where hover cabs were lining up next to modular exits with loading platforms, she peeked up and spotted the despondent young woman wedged between adolescence and adulthood. She appeared at the nexus of darkness and light at the end of what used to be a long curb. Obviously, she was heading home. Elisa realized that she *never* wanted to be like *that* woman who seemed to see herself as having no future and no hope. She took her camera off *pause* and began in a whisper, "If after my interview and Terra includes me on The List, Regent Manning will *surely* have someone pack up my things and move me into *Sagan* in a matter of hours. That's what he does. *That's* what a few of my colleagues told me he did to them."

As she exited the jerking lift and began walking through a tubular passageway over an easterly hovercraft thoroughfare, several people dashed past her, flagging down one of many smooth-gliding hover cabs. A frail elderly woman with a pale look of recovery on her face stopped Elisa abruptly. "An Enforcer just told us back in Departure that tonight's signing ceremony *is* in jeopardy!" She had a British accent, flyaway hair and misaligned teeth. She appeared so pain stricken, Elisa didn't have the heart to snatch back the camera. Dabbing away tears, the elderly woman added: "A Tech-No group caused this viral blackout! The Regents just learned the name of the person responsible."

"Who?" asked Elisa.

"The name Sender has been appearing as little signatures under *horrible* images that have been materializing on mirrors everywhere around the northern East Coast. We just saw a monster in Departure!" She about fainted but Elisa caught her and gave the jittery woman her bottle of cold water. Through gulps, the woman continued: "The Enforcer had to break the mirror to stop the villainous cartoon from shrieking and breaking all the windows. Because of this Sender person, we could *all* end up alien meat! I hope Enforcers catch 'em all!" After Elisa told her to sit down and rest, the old woman shook herself free and ran into a transport tube leading toward the large astrocraft pad. At the tunnel's end hovered an elongated, retrofitted craft with two attendants at the sliding door, hurriedly waving in passengers. Its directional indicators were pointing upward surrounded by flashing white stars. The craft had to be programmed for some off-Earth colony, anywhere out of reach of Mars. That spacefold quadrant was closed in preparation for the Decagon to intercept the Neltan/Earth wormhole at 9 p.m.

Feeling frustrated that she couldn't help the woman, she saw two cabs docking and began waving them toward her while continuing to speak into her camera. "So many people are angry at the Tech-Nos who now appear to have a *powerful* leader. Some people are as mad as hell at the Tech-Nos as they are at the terrorists! You just saw one. And this blackout's making *everything* so frustrating 'cause no one can receive help or answers from Terra. We have lights, and basic power from stored energy, even in all the fission-fusion plasma engines you see powering all these craft, but the *entire* virtual world, including our avatars and holographic aids are dead, frozen, useless."

She then directed her camera at two happy teenagers pointing into the clearing night sky. *Sagan* was shining brightly like a three-quarter moon alongside the pear-shaped Construction Station I. The tropopause shield array was occasionally flickering as various craft passed through its de-activated zones. The teenagers were debating whether the weather would really turn cold, as a forecaster had predicted when she announced the stats of the ozone layer, still holding constant and still affirming that the Matter Stream sample had healed the ozone as the Neltans had promised and was also purifying the atmosphere at the same time—a real surprise!

"There are two situations happening around me," Elisa continued. "There are people so happy that they seem about ready to kiss the ground." She directed her camera to an arguing couple. "Then there are people who're at their wits end 'cause they have *no* idea how to navigate the world without Terra's matrix."

When the door of a vibrating hover cab *swooshed* open, Elisa felt its vacuum suck her inside, and she grabbed the ceiling bar to sit up straight. Nodding at the driver and setting down her backpack, she buckled in and slid her wrist device over the interactive stage. Her pre-programmed information activated on the driver's GPS monitors that began displaying various topographical landscapes.

"Dr. Holton, it's gonna take a while for me to access Sky

Battlefield Matrix

Lane 95 to getcha to D.C. by 8:15," the driver said, taking another chew of his crackling gum. "There's real congestion goin' on up there and I've gotta navigate on Manual. See those hover vessels jamming up?" He craned his neck upward so the top panel on his canopy could scan his eyes and open.

"Yep, I sure do," she sighed, noticing the blockage.

"Every sky lane indicator and all the directional signals are blasting red!" His fission-fusion engine droned and revved as his hover cab quivered.

She exhaled, "I see." She felt helpless. She couldn't stream Regent Manning and tell him she was on her way but delayed. There might be *another* problem. Their 8:30 p.m. interview was close to the start of Final Communication. Being even a minute past 8:30 might mean *no* interview. *Surely* he'll understanding if I arrive a *little* late, won't he? she wondered.

"People're stuck *every*where, Dr. Holton," the driver said softly and snappily. Turning to her, even though two of her images were on his monitors, he gave her a long tired look. Obviously, he wasn't at all used to relating to his passengers. Wearing a V-neck leather vest with Glow patches indicating his various jobs, he had broad shoulders and a blond crew cut through which he quickly swept his thick fingers.

She noticed the time, burning green, that he had on Manual over the open panel between them. The flare stung her eyes and felt as constricting as the two cramped back seats and his small front navigation hub. The driver had renovated one of the old 2040 Smart Cars for his cab, the medium model. "It's 7:17—"

She then saw his name flash *on* in neon blue over the time. IDs and background stats were hologram-based and always mandatory for service providers, but his center hologram stage was dead like all the others she could see in cabs around them.

"It's 7:17, Ben. If you just get your cab airborne, I'll make my interview at the White House." She took out an old prepaid card she'd been keeping in her backpack for just such a drastic time as this and stuck it to the Plexiglas panel between them. The crispy card was worth *real* money at an exchange center. "Will this help get me there faster...*including* your fee?"

He opened the panel and snatched the card. "This'll sure help *ahem* Dr. Holton," he said, sticking the card on a steering module he had unleashed and locked into his otherwise virtual navigation column. All the navigation hardware seemed to bolt to life like energized blood with her topographical information. Now Ben looked like an expert video gamer about to embark on a world of aerial stunts! When he tapped on the *Vertical Take Off and Landing* icons on one of his monitors, his cab rushed upward and launched between several sputtering cabs.

"Just go a *little* faster, Ben...little," she chuckled, gripping her seat. "This cab looks stoked with plasma power...and you sure know how to keep your monitors prepared for emergencies, wow!" As he gave her the thumbs up in a proud gesture, she added, "I just *know* I'll make it to D.C. by 8:15 now. You're awesome, Ben!"

Popping his gum, he gave her a sideways grin. "Got that, Dr. Holton. Hold on!" After the cab lurched forward on a trajectory north, an Automated Steward lit up in 3D on the Plexiglas panel—a bit more fuzzy than usual. She morphed into Standard Terra per Elisa's preprogrammed preference. Then Ben called out the time that began ticking down the time on the meter and launched toward the mile-high set of directional lights entering Sky Lane 95N.

As they ascended like a shooting arrow, she noticed the stick people under them clamoring for hovercraft and cabs like lines of ants wrinkling their antennae in a hamsters habitat. Adjusting the camera lens and little eating tray so she could get a clear recording of her face, she turned the camera back on, rolled up her shoulder-length brown hair into a ponytail, and sat back, watching all the red lights elongate into lines but then return to flaring lane bulbs whenever they encountered traffic.

Ben pushed back a small monitor so she could see the stats on their journey: *7: 18 p.m. 120 mph. Arrival Time 8:13:03:998 p.m.* However, the milliseconds kept fluctuating. Arrival Time could change with the flow of air, speed, or God-awful hovercraft congestion. Ben's graceful manipulation of all the hover-metrics reminded her of last night's basketball championship that she activated for a virtual seat in her living unit on Station II. Ben was like the star player who had no problem tipping the victory in favor of the Knicks with a last minute *Globetrotter* maneuvering of the ball. Brilliant! He was skirting his cab around all the stopped and stalling hover vehicles and hedging his way up-and-down and in-and-around large astrocraft, the later igniting their fission-fusion engines in preparation for lift off into space. Closing her eyes as he shot his way over two Enforcer craft, she gasped in relief when they finally steadied.

Obviously having fun, he laughed, but she said: "If you keep up *this* pace, Ben, I'll not only make it to D.C. by 8:15, but you'll make the *Guinness Book of Records* for reaching the speed of light!"

Slowing down a bit, he enlarged the pre-screened coordinates she included in the file that Regent Manning streamed to her. "With these, Dr. Holton, I can drop ya off next to The Regency's private landing zone. Good thinking thatchya asked Manning for this a head o' time or else you might not make it to the White House until midnight due to this blasted blackout," he laughed. "I can glide ya right in for a quick and soft landing." When her camera suddenly shut down, he told her to unleash old hardware from a side pocket. Inside, she could find a connection to energize her battery. After pulling out a bundle of cords and flash drives that fell to her feet, she picked them up and found the power source under the seat for her camera. That's when she noticed how odd Ben appeared surrounded by all his cab technology. He had a few wires peeking out of two monitors that looked like exposed wallboards in need of a matrix renovation! He seemed stuck between the old and the new but an expert at stretching the limits of his old technology to its death before sending it up to Asteroid 2055 WY55 for dismantling.

He appeared to realize that she was watching him. "I'm tryin' to getcha to D.C. like ya need, Dr. Holton. Please don't report me, will ya?" He whispered: "I got an anti-detection device runnin' so Enforcers can't track my speed. If they know I've found a way to stump their radar, they'll haul me off ta Station V for sure!" He coughed, and then blushed and laughed, his cab gliding in midair overdrive! For a split second, he careened into a right-lane marker that retaliated with a bolt of electromagnetic light, and he straightened out his cab fast and jettisoned high above several slow-moving hover cars. They were all lightweight now, fully refurbished and overhauled with the newest of additive manufacturing materials and matrix interfacing.

"Just don't kill me getting me there, Ben," she said, exhaling after holding her breath. "I've got a lot of life ahead of me and I want it to go in a new but *safe* direction!" When he gave her his usual thumbs up signal, she turned on her camera, adjusted the lens, and tapped the setting to *Automatic*. When the Recording light turned green, she said into the glass plate, "I've just taken off from the Clinton Airfield north of Richmond, and my hover cab driver is taking me to my interview with Regent Manning—."

"Please don't record my face, Dr. Holton!" Ben hollered back at her in a different tone of voice, obviously attempting to conceal his identity.

Shaking her head reassuringly no, she continued in a whisper: "As I said earlier, I need to be in D.C. before eight thirty. I have a job interview with Regent Thornton Manning." She checked her holographic itinerary running over the small receiver stage next to her eating tray. Ben had the map portion alongside him, graphically depicting every intricate sky lane around them, address below them, and off-Earth networks extending above the tropopause shield. As she flipped through a virtual map of where she should go after arriving at the White House, she paused her camera when she noticed that Ben had something she hadn't seen in years: a small radio playing over one of his monitors. "Any news on what's happening at the White House?"

He turned up the volume. "This announcer on the

Battlefield Matrix

Emergency Broadcast channel—" He showed her the dial, set at WIYY 97.9 FM, "is saying that Enforcers are bandying solutions with Researchers on Station II and General Rand on Station III. I'm working to get a live show of Regent Manning in the Oval Office. That's where he and Regent Jenkens are countering the virus that's causing this blackout. He just announced that he has a prototype Terra-III right there in his office."

"Wow! I wonder what *that* powerful matrix can do!"

He shrugged, but looked fearful. "I don't know, but that's why he's hold up there. Some people have been calling him a coward for not leaving his *sanctuary*. I'm tellin' ya…the guy's got secrets!" He whispered, "Maybe the Tech-Nos are *somewhat* right, Dr. Holton. Ya ever consider that?" He had a concerned expression on his face.

She didn't answer as he knocked a side monitor that suddenly came to life with a special program from the White House.

"Got it!" He connected two small monitors so she could see the program clearly, and she thanked him as she read the scrolling ticker-tape message on the bottom: *General Rand is sending spare craft to the Skolkovo facility to counter the intrusion. …*

"From what The General has learned, this Tech-No hacker, Sender, and his followers are using a Warrior virus…a serious malware that's reading energy codes and circumventing them," Ben said.

"So *that's* how they think they'll deprive the IMAX screen in the Press Room of power and disable the Neltan-based transmission screen," she said.

"Appears so," he said.

They stopped talking when the announcer of the Emergency Broadcast Channel said: "The Secret Service has set up special barricades around the White House. Agent Jane Dirk is in charge of positioning troops. Protecting the IMAX screen from further disruption and streaming more energy to it in case the Skolkovo goes off-line due to the Warrior virus is paramount."

Elisa had friends on Station II who were the best at writing matrix code. After she told Ben their names, she said, "I know their teams are assisting in solving this mess too. I just hope this blackout resolves soon so Stealth Force can discover the place where the Tech-Nos are streaming the virus and capture the culprits."

"Me too! I sure don't want the Neltans thinking we're not answering their final quantum-call! A deal's-a-deal. We made *The Pact* with 'em, they delivered *their* part, and now it's *our* turn to start giving back. Simple." He kept driving, turning and twisting through a new traffic snarl. He spun his cab up then maneuvered in line behind a stream of fast-gliding hover cars.

Then she took another glance at his nest of technological wizardry and her itinerary. Where they would be landing, alongside The Regents' zone, would be an ideal place for a Tech-No to gain access to the White House. If Terra's matrix were streaming, Terra would have set up protocols for Ben long ago. This little glitch could become a giant breach in security, and she'd be to blame because *she* had given Ben front-and-center seats to the White House! The thought that she might be trusting and inadvertently helping a potential enemy made her plaster herself close to the window and as far away from Ben as possible. Whom to trust? She never had to think of *that* before!

Opening a small bottle of cold water that Ben handed her when she told him she was feeling dizzy, she drank some and turned her camera on. "Back to my interview," she whispered, scooting close to the window. The taxi's power cord was still supplying energy to her battery that delivered a sudden burst of light into her face. Setting it back and adjusting its angle of direction, she closed her itinerary, opened up a slow file of her Living Resume, and pointed the camera at the 3D Background page. "As I said, I've done everything to prepare for this interview. I sent Regent Manning this resume, with an attached mini-presentation from when we first met on First Communication Day. I fixed my hair...put on lipstick." She puckered up and then laughed. "It's funny! Hair, lips...I could

Battlefield Matrix

*care less…*you know *that.*"

Ben's hover cab jerked upward to miss another sidewinding car.

Gripping her seat, she said: "Yes, I'm going through all this 'cause I want the Regeneration position on *Sagan.*" She held up her hand in a self-denigrating expression. "I'm not going to change my mind. Still, anything could happen between now and after the interview. Regent Manning *could* hire me on the spot, or I'll just go back to my living cube and boring research job on Station II," she yawned, "and wait and hope for Terra to select me for The List whenever Terra comes back to life. The matrix currently has my status as, basically, in line with other physicians who are competing for those slots, so I'm hoping a personal reference from Regent Manning might influence Terra to bump me up to Necessary status. There's hope yet that Terra will include me as one of the seventy-five thousand to launch on *Sagan* in June 2070. In the meantime, while I'm on this *wild* ride, I'll continue to polish my Living Resume to perfection. Later on…after I know whether he hires me, I can record some more again…pick this up as a hobby maybe." She picked up the camera, pulled it close to her face, and smiled. She felt as if the moment might stick forever. "Bye! See ya later!"

J.P. Osterman

Chapter 2

Matrix-Shopping

Sipping his coffee while watching the effects of the blackout outside the White House, Regent Thornton Manning tried to discern the tops of all the monuments, but their facades were gradually fading. Their stored energy systems were almost void of power, and the crowds of people were frantic under the spell of near blackness. From his comfortable Oval office view, he could hear Enforcers using all their methods of emergency crowd control that appeared to be working. "All these counter terrorism drills we've implemented for the past decade are working for us now, but *this* time, against the Tech-Nos," he said to Steven Jenkens, his fellow Regent. "I never thought their group would become so powerful."

"Not powerful but smart, and under the direction of a powerful leader," Jenkens said. At the center of his office stood Steve Jenkens, tapping his wrist device, obviously trying to activate his apps. His little Jackie Gleason avatar had stalled over it, appearing like a glowing ghost stick sieving power. "Useless!" Jenkens huffed. "I *hate* not being able to do something to stop this blackout. When they capture Sender, their leader, I'm gonna kill 'im!"

"Not before I get my hands on him," Manning said.

"Or her!" said Jenkens.

Then the Lead Researcher for Algorithmic Compilation on Station II contacted him through an outdated but revamped communication relay that Agent Jane Dirk had set up at 7:10 p.m. after the start of the matrix blackout. After addressing them, she said: "The invasion of the Skolkovo facility has leveled off at a 75% infiltration rate. We're stream down to the North Pole a new set of counter codes. They're reversing through all seven, matrix processing facilities on the seven continents."

"Make sure you include the Top Secret facility on Easter Island!"

"Yes, Sir," she snapped. "We have more counter-cyphers in the development phase should this attempt fail." As she explained the counter attack in detail, he saw flashes of light strike all the monuments, biodomes, and shimmering high rises. They lit up as if dawn broke, but they quickly dimmed to Normal output. The fission-fusion engines on all the advertising zeppelin and Enforcer craft revved, and they resumed their scheduled aerial trajectories.

"We just acquired power," he told her, "but no Terra connectivity."

People around the Mall, overflowing subways and streets began clapping. High in the atmosphere, the tropopause shield was bleeding rays of light, feeding the world energy.

Then, Terra flickered on at several circular locations throughout the room. She was frozen, her holograms appearing like half-a-dozen yellow ice statues, but at least she was manifesting, yet in need of serious energy. The holographic Smart Bar over his desk activated in rapid scrolling of statistics, including the time, 7:20 p.m. His rainbow-processing ceiling hubs began oscillating in Reboot-mode, and all the wall mount processors began droning. On Wall Zone 1, Jane Dirk's face illuminated. After testing the connection,

J.P. Osterman

Manning told her to resume her intense hunt for the Tech-No intrusion in the Oval Office and increase the number of agents in the Press Room protecting the IMAX transmission screen. "Fortifying that place as well as the Decagon beyond Mars is our number one priority right now, Jane," he said, feelings his every word breathe out hot and loud into her 3D image on the screen.

"Yes, Sir!" Jane said. She had an entire force of Secret Service agents and four teams of Enforcers under her command. They began barking orders and dashing out of that Center Lobby kiosk to their designated advantage points.

Meanwhile, as his office continued to ignite with matrix processing power, and as his Terra began to illuminate and her arms and head move, the large mirror over his shiny sideboard containing drinks and food shattered. That's where Sender had in-streamed the Reflection virus that materialized in his office and then rippled around the northern hemisphere into *everyone's* portable devices. The virus appeared right at the center of his room as a villainous cartoon character from Sender meant to intimidate everyone into breaking off tonight's Final Communication and *Pact* signing ceremony with the Neltans.

As Jenkens appeared teary-eyed and about to drop to the ground and kiss it in thanksgiving, the remainder of the twenty Wall Zones flashed on, resuming their links with outside sources and, most importantly, the Press Room harboring the IMAX screen.

With the Skolkovo now secure, and Jenkens ordering a Global Matrix Scan via Matrix Security on Wall Zone 3, Manning contacted General Rand on Military Station III. When The General's image materialized next to his Terra, he sighed in relief. He reached out to touch them both. His hands moved through them. He laughed with delight. "It looks like I can almost touch you, so I know we've been successful in stopping the attack and re-establishing full-virtual processing. Thanks, General. Terra's back…the blackout's over!"

Battlefield Matrix

His face had always appeared hard and he had an unwavering personality, but suddenly he smiled. "We all worked together, Regent Manning. The Regency worked with me from several locations as did some great code writers on Station II. We now are doing everything in our power to locate Sender and his or her Tech-No band that started this mess."

"That blackout almost spread globally," Jenkens interrupted, then he closed his Jackie Gleason avatar that had given him an update on the Executive Regency election through the Global Voting Facility.

Terra had melted back into one solid holographic form at the center of his office. "I am creating pathways to receive what my matrix gleaned during the blackout and storing everything my processors gleaned to add into the matrix." Rays of colorful lights were permeating her hair as General Rand stepped forward and streamed to her what his team on Military Station II had learned during the blackout. "We're still searching for the terrorists who are heading into deep space." He had a concerned look in his steely black eyes while behind him his entire navigation crew were standing at their high-tech cubes and monitors, doling out surveillance, attack, and recon orders to avatars and captains on astrocraft and astrofighters at their stations around the Decagon accelerator system. "We did locate contrails, as I said earlier, and we're tracing the steps of their astrocraft, but they all veer off into many directions."

Manning felt frantic but fended off a display of panic by taking gulps of cold water and a quick glimpse of the election numbers that flashed over the Smart Bar. It showed him tied with several Regents for the Executive title, and then it reverted to scrolling environmental stats of his office. "Keep that Decagon secure, General. That's what we have to focus on. We know the enemy's off-Earth and heading into deep space. Why? We have no idea yet. But protecting the Decagon and the IMAX screen in the Press Room are vital!" Then he remembered his Black Ops mission he had begun on *Sagan*. By now, the mission was well under way. He could check on it later, after General Rand faded and after he could distract Jenkens.

"Yes, Sir. And I'll stream everything we do, *everything* we learn, and all the movements of *all* our astrofighters *directly* to you and the rest of The Regents," General Rand said.

Manning told Terra to continue her link to Captain Bartlet and his lunar mission on Wall Zone 2, and to receive all The General's Live Streams on Wall Zones 3 through 5. Then General Rand faded from the Oval Office.

For a moment, he basked in the quiet atmosphere as Jenkens continued whispering to his pint-size avatar over his wrist device. Obviously, he was retrieving information from his personal home holosite and The Regency.

Manning had his holosite on Voice Mail-mode with an Automated Standard Reply. In case of a real emergency, like the Skolkovo facility attack or a terrorist bombing, he had *his* Terra set to interrupt him and inform him of the disaster.

"Regent Manning?" Terra's voice was at Standard Intensity setting, and soft, each word optimizing with photonic projector perfection. She always stood pillar-straight and unblinking—her matrix processor in Wait-mode for his order.

"Yes?" he replied, turning to her life-size form at the center of his office. This time, he could see clearly her thawed out vision. He almost called her Lynn! Everything from Terra's shoulder-length blond hair to the heterochromatic splash of green in her eye, "she" looked like Lynn. He felt deadened love. Then he heard a muffled commotion outside on the Mall. Walking over to the large windows, he saw an Enforcer zeppelin with its police light whirring as it swooped down on a small crowd of hecklers shining Neltan monster icons at people. "Terra, try to get biometric IDs of those people so officers can single them out." He had her prototype Version Three, so she could easily pick up biometrics of an ant on in the grass! As her matrix processed through the building hubs and tower hubs to yield their "reads," he realized he had to do something fast and drastic to stop another full-blown Tech-No disturbance from escalating into an *Emergency Alert*. Anger

Battlefield Matrix

pulsed through him. When he saw incoming tropopause shield readings from scans several panels had conducted during the blackout of Death Valley, an idea struck him, and he interrupted Jenkens' pensive search of a 100,000 mile, conical quadrant in beyond Mars. "Steve, remember the late 1960s when a small group of people believed the moon landing was a hoax?"

As Jenkens swept the new enemy's contrail results to General Rand, he replied: "That's the same thing going on outside *now* I believe. These Tech-Nos and their Sender leader are using outlandish alien graphics to instill fear and doubt as to the Neltans' motives for helping us. They're trying to convince people to renege on our part of *The Pact* and abort tonight's scheduled wormhole. This is an actual threat against the Decagon!"

Over his wrist device, Manning activated a link to one of the Stealth Force astrofighters in space. It was streaming to Stations II, III and The Regents a Confidential view of the fleet's trajectory. A ray of whipping bright light appeared out of nowhere, on a destructive path speeding toward their fleet. Some Tech-No group had photoshopped images of the harmless Matter Stream sample that had healed the ozone and revitalized Earth's atmosphere. Obviously, they had redesigned the scene to trick people into believing that the Neltans were attacking.

"Some Tech-No group is photoshopping—I mean matrix shopping—all types of crazy cosmic particles into The Matter Stream sample." Jenkens showed a display of an orange comet tail breaking apart in Earth's atmosphere. "Can you believe this?! They're trying to make the public believe that the sample is altering…that it's going to reassemble as poison, return to Earth and blast away our ozone. They're making the Neltans appear vicious, and their faces unmasking into horrible hideous creatures! They say we've been tricked."

As Manning ordered Terra to counter the slanderous attempt with a global-wide holosite message to the contrary, he glanced into the evening sky where he saw the tiny white stripe of The Matter Stream sample that looked like the arm of a spiral galaxy in the ecliptic. *Sagan* techs with their craft were passing through it, sweeping up and containing the sample's vital remnants for the journey to Nelta. As per *The Pact*, the astrocity needed the sample's powerful particles for its fission-fusion spacefolding drive engines and its life-enhancing forces for the Regeneration procedure to keep the crew young.

He said: "An agreement's an agreement though. There's no backing out now! The World approved *The Pact*. That's what we tell them regardless of *any* Tech-No interference."

Terra stepped forward on Auto Speak-mode. *"Item 1* in *The Pact* states: *In exchange for providing to Earth a sample of the Neltan Matter Stream to heal their ozone, explorers from Earth agree to travel to Nelta and provide Neltans with human DNA. Upon arriving in orbit, the explorers will free The Matter Stream contained in its artificial sun, awaken the Neltan population, and give Ambassador Shaesar the DNA."*

"That's the plan in a nutshell," Jenkens said.

Manning backed away from Terra when he heard clanking and crashing sounds coming from the Press Room. When he activated the Wall Zone next to the door, he saw that more Regents were gathering, and the media. They were intensifying the setup of robotics, security matrixware and other projection hardware, the sounds of which were beginning to trickle into his office. He ordered Terra to add more layers of nano-organics between the two rooms—actually, a morphing partition—with noise reducers.

Then he turned his attention back to the outside Mall, where Enforcers had locked on to the dissidents with their floodlights. "We have less than *two* hours before the final transmission with Nelta. It's time we stop this damn Tech-No movement and smoke out Sender!"

"How? Whataya got in mind?" Jenkens asked. "Cause everything we've done thus far has only lead to them eluding us even more! It's like they're watching *us* watch *them*. They absorb our Security codes as we block them, alter those codes and matrix cyphers, and then use the modifications to go deeper into hiding and intensify their attacks on us."

"I'll get them to come out of hiding like this." Manning called on a few holograms of satellites orbiting Earth and activated their weapons programs. "Terra."

"Yes, Regent Manning."

"Flash me that image of that underground Tech-No commune in Death Valley you located and scheduled to surprise tomorrow after Final Communication." Turning to Jenkens, he said: "It's a small one, so The General believes, but taking out *this* group could create a sinkhole in their movement and draw out their leader, Sender. When this group transmits a call for help after we attack, maybe Terra can locate other groups. I've been trying to figure out a kind way to get rid of 'em, but given the viral attack the terrorists launched on *The Spider*, the one at the Skolkovo, and now *this* one on the Mall, I have no other choice but to resort to doing something outside the Global Law."

"What do you have in mind with those orbiting weapons?" Jenkens was rubbing his wrinkled and red forehead. "They're incendiary dangerous...not just for target practice."

"You look like I feel," Manning huffed, "sick-and-tired of playing tag with terrorists and protesters...actually fed up of *always* playing defense and getting punched in the face!"

"You've got *that* right!" Jenkens said.

"So, now it's time to act, not just track and trace 'em down."

"What do you have in mind?"

"We have to strike without consulting opinion polls and getting global-wide approval," he answered. "Damn daily vote and media bias! I don't know about you, Steve, but every reporter's opinion and poll results I dread. I keep bowing down to all of 'em and ending up like a dead flower in the wind." He believed that members of The Press, especially the famous ones, were always colluding to gain support of their various agendas. "The last vote dictates that we need treat all our captured enemies with compassion and *cognitively* convert them from their extremist ways. Ha!" He glanced out the window. "Look what's happened by us being so soft. The enemy sees us as completely weak! Enough of that."

One of the Tech-No's small, autopilot drones had just slipped between two advertisement Zeppelin, attacking a black-and-white Enforcer craft. As a crowd of people ducked and raged in anger, a large red astrocraft burst into the area, firing on the drone. The Tech-No drone exploded in a blaze of smoke, and the Enforcer craft netted the flaming parts just in time before they spiraled down into the shrieking crowd.

"Their attacks *are* getting worse, Thornton, but what are you planning to do?" Jenkens asked. "I've always heard you were a Regent with an iron fist, but it would take a heartless act to eliminate an entire community of families." He opened up an old attachment over his wrist device. The app began displaying images of two subterranean Tech-No groups that a Stealth Force recon officer on Station III had sent him. "The Tech-Nos live in these types of communes, as did the hippies in the 1960s, disconnected from society, which isn't hard to do since many spots are still uninhabitable. They clean up these zones in secret and occupy them under our radar. Some of them might be old terrorist hideouts! After establishing themselves, they begin to rear their children to hate all technological advancements *and us* for using them!" A ghastly pain spread over his face. "You'll be killing a lot of children by striking that commune from space." The outside crowd began chanting. People had scavenged the destroyed drone parts and had tossed them to Enforcers who threw the crowd monetary rewards that looked like flying confetti. He opened up a holographic model of the Tech-No drone that Terra had reconstructed and gasped. "Then again, Thornton, you're right. Something has to be done or soon we'll have a massive body count. That drone they had on autopilot was obviously, Armed to Kill."

Night had completely enveloped D.C and the small surrounding dome communities. Bright lights from processor mounds—adhered to the buildings—and matrix connectivity towers were illuminating most of the crowds, all the monuments, eateries, and subways portals. Enforcers and Secret Service were at the kiosk entrances of all historic locations and transport facilities, along with their scanning avatars that were interfacing with the matrix. Zeppelins, peoples' personal avatars, and hovercraft advertisements were adding to the lighting. High up, various types of fission-fusion engines were emitting blue or red Doppler residuals from their astrocraft. They were making sporadic landings on top of buildings and at designated landing sites, or launching to the space stations. The aurora borealis in the distant horizon was shimmering light green and yellow—not the usual, dangerous orange-red hue. On a wall zone, Manning glanced at one view of Earth from outer space.

The ozone layer was still reading *Normal* over his Smart Bar.

"Watch this," Manning said, activating his office ambiance to Virtual Grid-mode.

The walls, ceiling, and flooring hummed as they morphed into a black zone, in Wait-mode, for virtual graphics imaging and participation.

After he flipped through several images of military installations and their contents over his wrist device, he said, "Vertical Unmanned Vehicle *341* looks ready."

Jenkens breathed in obvious fright. "What *exactly* are you unleashing?! That's vehicle packs a *Volcanic Strike*, if I'm not mistaken, and'll yield a crater the size o' the one in Arizona!"

"Damn, Jenkens, you look as if you've *never* had to do a bad thing in your life for the sake of saving thousands!" He saw Jenkens shake his head a vehement no.

"I—I can't say I—I've *always* been completely honest with the public," he said, "but—"

"We gotta start getting tough, Steve, to *act* outside the box not just *think* outside the box. I learned that long ago, after *Greeter* exploded," he said, softly, glancing up a Terra. Lynn...he was continuing to see Lynn, and miss her, like a long aching hole spreading through his gut.

"Yes—I remember that moment...and I watched it all again...looked back at it as you streamed your *I Was There* show of First Communication into the Neltan Archival Museum," Jenkens said, softly, his voice empathetic. "The loss was great for you. I have my own…" He waved away something obviously painful that was still pricking at him. "No one ever did discover who downed that shuttle. Several sources still maintain it was sabotage. That a group of scientists—either inside the old military or from the private sector—colluded prior to General Bernstein ordering the mission. Some people in high up places didn't want extraterrestrial contact. Someone, maybe he or she might even be a Regent now, was afraid of communicating with the Neltans, believing the aliens would lead Earth down a horrible direction."

"That's really when the Tech-No movement increased in numbers," Manning said. "See—see!? Ya never know who's behind attacks now. The enemy could be anyone, Steve, and more will grow up and *become* the enemy if we don't act now to stop the increase. Fear changes behavior, Steve. I'm a firm believer in using fear as a deterrent and a detergent!"

After a pause, Jenkens said: "Weren't you at Duke when *The Greeter* exploded?"

A burst of memory welled into his consciousness as Manning recalled Lynn telling him over the phone that General Bernstein had selected her to stabilize the communications wormhole from Neltan. Lynn was so excited. He remembered her saying: "I'm going into space, Thornton! Aren't you happy for me? This is what I've been waiting for!" He tried to talk her out of the impromptu launch, but she wouldn't take no for an answer. She told him: "I encouraged *you* to run for the Regency, Thornton, now won't you please give *me* a little bit of encouragement? I sure need it!" Then she hugged him and ran off to help assemble *Greeter*.

Jenkens touched him on the shoulder. "Hey."

Manning flinched and stepped back. He wanted to seek refuge in one of the black areas preparing to launch a visual in the virtual grid.

"I just heard of a few theories, Thornton, that's all,"

Battlefield Matrix

Jenkens said. "Only rumors from the investigative committee that the lab might have been responsible for misaligning a few parts on the shuttle." He called open several portraits of *The Greeter*'s team mangers that enlarged over his wrist device. "Didn't you know a few people in that lab? People who might have had the ability to sabotage something and then hide behind a veil of prestige at Duke?"

He glanced at the pictures and then gestured for Jenkens to extinguish them. "I knew a few scientists, but not any physicians." When he stopped pacing, he realized he had walked a circle around Terra who was obviously waiting for his Strike order on the secret desert commune. Everything about her holographic projection—from head-to-toe—he had reconstructed from photographs of Lynn that he had found and continued to add to his Terra program. He suddenly felt surprised: Lynn, right in front of him. As the black grid bulged to accommodate an entire a scene from a vast location, he told Jenkens: "But I *personally* conducted a detailed investigation of everyone in that lab. Those scientists checked out. The people I interviewed had pretty healthy psychological profiles and couldn't hurt anyone."

Jenkens coughed. "I suppose you're right then. No one you knew from way back when could have committed such a heinous sabotage."

"I know two people who were close to Lynn and who also knew General Bernstein," Manning said.

"Who?"

"Dr. Wade Farstel and Dr. Elisa Holton. But they were Lynn's friends. They'd never hurt her," he said, firmly. He felt a throb of heartburn race into his chest. "Let's quit talking about this. There's nothing I can do about the investigation now anyway."

Suddenly, the interior of a Death Valley cavern appeared in Surround Vision on his walls. Inside the giant cave was a large colony of Tech-No protesters. In the far right section of the illuminated cavern were computer hackers seated in high-tech chairs calling out intercept commands, programming spy ware, and communicating with one another through covert Terra grids. In one small cubicle, he noticed the image of a small satellite in space that he couldn't enlarge. Obviously, this group was the source of a Shadow app that the entire group was utilizing to hide all their matrix attacks vis-à-vis the covert satellite.

"That's how they're staying undetected!" he said. "Yes!—gotcha! Terra, trace this array to all of them."

Terra's eyes flashed green, but then caution yellow. "The grid they are utilizing will burst at contact, and they will detect your presence and flee successfully before the strike."

"Then don't do that! Just keep locking on to this location!"

"Our long-range terahertz cameras in *our* satellites are seeing through rock and detecting their biometric readings," Jenkens said as Terra complied. He appeared amazed at the homey subterranean scene. "This place *really* feels like we're inside the cave along with 'em!"

"Yep, but don't get sympathetic, Steve. These people are not only threats to the matrix here, but they could also pose a threat to *Sagan*. You see how they're intensifying in hardware and hacking abilities! We have to take 'em *all* down and protect us from them…even their children of the future." He activated the Laser Channel app on the drone that locked on the subterranean desert hideout. "Now, Terra, copy a *terrorist* hideout and inject the image alongside this Tech-No's hideaway. Keep the same desert scene though."

"Why?" Jenkens asked as she began turning around, her eyes scanning the scene for a matrix-shopped presentation.

"I need to show The World that the protesters are colluding with the terrorists, that they're also to blame for the attacks on *The Spider* and Space Station I. I'll also include a large body count in the false show she's creating now. Then, after their underground hideout explodes, the media will portray us as heroes. If someone recognizes an illegal manipulation of the matrix, we have an excuse."

Terra activated an automatic countdown: "Laser strike in three minutes, fifty—"

Battlefield Matrix

"Only give me the last ten seconds, Terra."

Jenkens was watching a mother teach her small daughter to weave a blanket on a loom. "I don't know, Thornton. We'll be killing a lot of people...God—children! At least fifty children from what I'm detecting through this terahertz camera."

Manning saw a crushing sadness wash over his face. He had to act fast before Jenkens might decide to stream out a secret warning to them. He had to convince Jenkens that he was right. "You wait until we look out the window again. You'll see. Tech-No attacks should subside. We'll reap overwhelming public support. This strike should cause the Tech-Nos and their Sender leader to disband systematically. They'll realize that the Regency won't tolerate *any* interference in our communications with the Neltans tonight. They'll most likely stop all their attacks. You'll see that I'm right." Able to experience, as a voyeur, the Tech-No's cavern hideout under complete Terra obscurity, he tiptoed over to a Tech-No protester and peeked over his shoulder. "I know he can't hear me, but as real as this all looks, it feels like he can."

"I know what you mean!" Jenkens said, his back against the cavern wall, running his fingers along the shiny wet surface. "I feel the insulated coldness down here, and people are coming and going all around us, but they can't hear us. I can even smell a fire kindling."

Manning felt brimming with excitement. "Just think," he whispered, "the new Terra-III will provide us with this capability everywhere on *Sagan*. We'll be able to call up any image from Earth: smells, sounds, every sensory detail...you name it. A complete augmented existence, just like this experimental one I'm trying out in here."

Then Terra opened up an alert from one of the advertisements he and Jenkens had posted almost an hour ago.

"Could this be Sender?" he asked Terra, standing beyond the virtual window to his office.

Out of a rolling virtual ball that appeared over her hand, Terra enlarged a Most Wanted poster from a Matrix Security facility. The bearded scruffy man was about to unleash a virus into the tropopause shield. Terra showed them the targeted area, circled in red: the glowing hot panel was about to launch a strike on the Death Valley commune. The man on The Most Wanted Tech-No list had apparently intercepted the strike command or Manning's drone search and was attempting to counter the strike.

"No!" he cried. "If this guy succeeds, he'll disable that entire portion of the shield that General Rand is using as a prototype to buffer Earth against radioactivity. Stop him, Terra!"

The *0* countdown resounded in a hologram next to the image of the disheveled hacker.

Drone 341's turret burst open, and out launched a laser beam that struck the desert surface above the Tech-No's cavern. The ground began to shake; the walls buckling. Screaming and horrified people dashed into the elevator exits, but the ropes began sheering over the weight of their bodies. Dust, smoke, fire, and slabs of rock flooded the cavern.

"Take us outta here, Terra," Manning said. "I know we can't feel it, but *I* feel like I'm being buried alive!"

His Oval Office reverted to its Normal ambiance after the augmented world extinguished.

Jenkens was sitting on the floor with hands over his head. "*Ahhh*!"

Drinking water as if squelching internal heat, Manning said: "Stream the catastrophe to The World and include the new terrorist location, Terra. If anyone accuses me of misinterpreting the Use of Force Clause in Global Law VIII, or if anyone files a criminal report against me to Judicial Station V for violating that law, intercept the complaint and destroy any report."

"Can you do that?" Jenkens asked, finally standing up in a gesture of adapting to the new safe scenery of the office.

Manning showed him an advanced interception application in one of the prototype Terra-III matrix grids. "I sure can." The he said to Terra, who was following him with green eyes

Battlefield Matrix

in Record-mode: "Stream back to anyone who questions the launch or reports me for a violation that more Tech-No attacks or matrix viruses could occur. I had no other choice but to act quickly to stop a global-wide threat. The next attack could prove *deadly* to one of *them*...a neural linguistic infection perhaps...right in their own homes or business." He checked the status of Earth's fixed tropopause shield. "*Whew*—it's okay." Realizing that he had prevented a hacker from disabling the shield, he said to Jenkens as Terra streamed her matrixshopped images to holosites around the globe: "That's it. The mission was a success." He laughed as Jenkens ran his hands over his chest and bulging belly, checking his health. "Now we wait and see how the media reacts. Depending on what the polls post in the next several minutes, and the reverberations from the harm the Tech-Nos have done, we might run more Black-Ops, attacks on them as the terahertz camera discovers their locations."

"Oh my gosh—I, I—"

"Still frazzled?" Manning laughed.

"Ha—*ha*—Ha—*ha* I—"

"It's all right, Steve, just breathe." He gave him a cold bottle of water and sat him down in the chair alongside his desk. "That all looks so real, doesn't it? And Terra-III's new matrix is the best—definitely imaging real-life, experiential settings...complete sensory realities in any place and time...from *any* image ever stored, scanned to storage or streamed through any server. Just call for a date, time and place...or tell your personal Terra the person's name ya wanna see, and, voila, there that scene'll be, all around ya. It'll feel like it *really* exists! Like you're there."

"Yeah...so the techs up there on *Sagan* say." Doubt and fear seemed to be twisting into sharp lines on his face.

"You need to get a little more excited about the place!" He glided over to him a button of the astrocity. "Here, put this on your lapel. I plan to hand them out tonight...after I win—"

"*You* win..." Jenkens grimaced a little.

Shrugging, Manning rocked back in his chair and said: "Just

take it. Let it remind you of what great *new* lives we're going to begin on *Sagan*. Imagine having an augmented world *everywhere* at our beckon call…and everywhere we go. The *entire* astrocity will be that way, Steve. Keep that pin. Let it remind you of the future. I wear mine, and I prick it now and then whenever I get in the dumps about how things are progressing here on Earth. I want off here. And I'll do anything to make that happen."

"Yeah, you're right." Jenkens adjusted himself in his chair and donned the lapel pin.

Manning said: "All terrorists and protestors from here to Mars will view the disaster." Forgetting something, he added, "Oh—and Terra, stream the catastrophe alongside my conversation with Ambassador Shaesar. I'll use the accident to appear compassionate to the Neltans when I stream out a Call-For-Assistance to help search for survivors stranded in the desert." He checked the time: 7:25 p.m. "That's almost an hour and thirty-five minutes away."

"Yes, Regent Manning," Terra replied.

"You can fade," he said, and she disappeared; but her rainbow, processing light continued to cycle around the ceiling hub.

Jenkens doffed his coat and slipped it quickly behind his chair. "I see what you're doing, Thornton. Just like me, you're tired of people constantly opposing us and distrusting advanced technology that we both know is helping humanity…advancing us on our evolutionary path."

"Right!"

"I just don't know if doing all this covert and illegal stuff is going to make matters worse or better," Jenkens said, sipping water and then dabbing sweat off his balding head. "This time, you won, Thornton. You stopped an attack. But I think there'll always be a next time. It's just in our DNA to always be opposed to something and mad enough to hurt somebody when we're pushed too far."

"God—there's gotta be a way to change that!"

Chapter 3

Elisa Holton's Living Resume

From what Jenkens had said, Manning began to believe that he might be able to trust him, that he was turning Jenkens to his point of view. Then Terra flashed an important calendar item: *Interview with Dr. Holton, 8:30 p.m.* He had scheduled the time three days ago after postponing the interview several times. He couldn't cancel. "We were just talking about her."

"Who?" Jenkens asked.

"I scheduled an interview with Dr. Holton. When we update the Neltans on the construction of *Sagan*, I want all the astrocity's Regeneration Specialists standing alongside us to answer any concerns anyone might have regarding the Regeneration technology. The technicalities and medical terminology are so complex." He called up her resume and swept it onto a wall display. A picture of Dr. Elisa Holton appeared—her cover page. "I am not knowledgeable in interfacing Cellular Regeneration with Genetic Engineering, and I know you're not, but she is, and we could use her on *Sagan*."

J.P. Osterman

"You're right, Thornton, I know nanotechnology but that's it," Jenkens said.

"Not too many of us Regents do either, except physicians like Dr. Holton who are true biomedical engineers and eugenic experts. I studied Cellular Biophysics, but these docs conducted research specifically to invent biomedical agents to fight the terrorists. I also need specialists like her for another reason."

"Why?"

"To advise *me*—no *us* I mean—on how to expand the cloning experiments I'm conducting on *Sagan*," Manning whispered.

"Expand cloning into what? To where?" Jenkens asked.

Quieting him down, Manning began to explain. "A long time ago, Dr. Holton brought up the possibility of implementing such an advanced cellular construction." Lynn's face flashed through his mind, but cloning her was impossible—no biological. "But dialoguing about cloning will have to be classified as *For Eyes Regency Only*, after The World exits tonight's Final Communication." He changed Dr. Holton's holographic information. "Terra, image Dr. Holton's background."

The birthdate, May 1, 2035, flashed inside a yellow ribbon below Dr. Holton's virtual body. Elisa Holton was wearing a business suit and holding a giant briefcase against her chest. Obviously, she chose to present her resume in that visual format because her most recent positions at Duke University and Johns Hopkins began scrolling down on the tan leather fabric.

"Oh—you nominated Dr. Holton as a possible Regeneration Engineer on *Sagan*. That's right," exclaimed Jenkens. "I saw this resume that you sent the Regency a few weeks ago. I liked her educational background, job performance, and her references most of all. Ten—*ten* Ph.D. referrals. Great credentials. She'll be an asset on the astrocity for sure."

"I know," Manning said, remembering statements his

Battlefield Matrix

colleagues had made who had only impressive things to say about Elisa Holton.

Jenkens' voice turned somber. "She's also a global activist you know…and a conservationist. *Here* she says she promotes the development and use of Neltan technology but only after careful consideration and for specific purposes, such as regenerating our bodies with synthetic telomeres until we disembark on Nelta. Then she says: 'After the long voyage, I believe the crew needs to stop altered telomeres and begin to age naturally. I am a naturalist'."

Manning heard caution in Jenkens' voice. "Are you hinting that she might be a member of the Tech-No movement? No way!"

"No—not at all, Thornton," he said. "However, realize that *anything* you or the rest of us might want to implement— for example, Cognitive Relief and Repair, or Emotional Interrogation and Intervention—in other words, *anything* we might want to implement *without* a ship-wide vote or some sort of stamp of approval, Dr. Holton probably wouldn't tolerate."

"*Hmmm…*"

"And what you just did to that Tech-No commune…and then afterwards created a graphics illusion to spread *more* fear to The World, Dr. Holton would *never* sit back idly and watch an explosion like that occur without sounding off an alarm. I'm just reading through the lines in this resume. She says her research acumen is impeccable, her eye for detail is astute, and her tolerance for inaccuracy low. An IQ of 135—wow! Oh…she's the whistle blower type, according to *my* interpretation. She's a bit of a perfectionist and an approval seeker. But we could use the latter to our advantage."

Several of Elisa Holton's hobbies and her political background appeared on her briefcase resume. Her voting history was secret; but a Graph-Bar and Tally app that Manning activated and swept into her ID icon showed that sometimes she streamed 'yes' for him when she voted. On a few occasions, she voted 'no.' He wondered why her approval for him was sporadic. He recalled some of the covert technology he was planning to implement on *Sagan*: the Spy Drop Ware and Gamma pulse apps in select Terra hubs. Jenkens was right: Dr. Holton would never condone *any* type of covert activity even if the technology might ensure *Sagan*'s mission or protect the crew until their arrival on Nelta. She'd want to make sure facts would quench fears…and she'd demand transparency.

Should he hire her, as he promised her before Lynn died? Obviously, she was determined to be one of the seventy-five thousand on The List of Terra-selected crewmembers to board *Sagan*. He saw her history, childhood to the present. Nothing about her suggested instability or pathology. And she was high on the Empathy Model and Social Responsibility scales. *Sagan*'s evolving Terra-III had labeled Dr. Holton as "Necessary But on Standby." She had applied for two medical positions on Level 4 of the astrocity and had obviously toned down one section of her resume to appear employable at the Recycling Center on Level 7, as Lead Plastics Facilitator. That would be the one of the most menial of tasks. Five thousand people were still applying for that position; but as of yet, Terra had selected none. Dr. Holton appeared desperate, and serious, about leaving Earth. He wondered why.

"Well—whataya think?" Jenkens asked, waiting.

He turned away from her resume and glanced out the window to the cheering and excited crowd. People were partying and celebrating the approach of Final Contact an hour and thirty-five minutes away. As more Regency astrocraft landed and the world leaders disembarked toward the White House, people appeared optimistic in spite of the rare Tech-No attacks. Spotlights and avatars were streaking through the air like advertisers launching new businesses. There were hovering eateries, wineries, and coffee carts scattered everywhere like glowing game pieces on a board, but people appeared to buying beer, hot dogs, and small snacks the most—their wrist devices glowing as firefly lights making payments.

"What are you thinking about, Thornton? How to turn her

down?" Jenkens opened up a satellite enlargement of the asteroid belt. He was beginning his terrorist hunt, again.

"I just don't know." A collision of outcomes began churning through his mind. "We need her, and I definitely want her, but I also feel I should reject this resume and send *her* ninety degrees back to the exit! *Ahhh*, for some damn reason, I can't." He knew why. Lynn. "But if I don't turn her away, I also feel, well, that someday, I'm gonna regret not doing just that."

"I can order her away," Jenkens said. "Let me do it."

"No, not yet. Let me read more about her...what she's done in the past few years since I last saw her. I'll then meet her and see if I can get a good read outta her. I still say we need her, and Terra is now labeling her as Necessary. Look! She's only a handful of experts in those fields. If any problems arise after *Sagan* launches, she'd definitely be one of the scientists who could solve unforeseeable difficulties." He remembered his motto. "Prediction increases prevention, Steve. Terra including Dr. Holton is an advantage."

"You've persuaded me," Jenkens said. "And obviously, you've persuaded your Terra!" he laughed.

Still, after what Jenkens just told him about Elisa Holton, he realized that implementing any technology covertly would yield dire consequences for him—and anyone else helping him—if she would discover it. That would present a catastrophic problem, especially on an astrocity spacefolding through complex wormholes through the cosmos. Working on the Regeneration Corridors on Level 5, Elisa Holton would have a prominent and powerful position.

He said to Jenkens: "We ordered Terra to choose all thirty Regeneration Specialists early on. That way we can train them in the new Neltan technology, and they'll be ready to begin their jobs on Level 5 before *Sagan* launches. I just thought that she'd be great for the job, and she obviously wants to go to Nelta. We've already chosen fifteen. We need fifteen more." Then it occurred to him that a few of those he would appoint to loftier positions: Clone Techs. But he didn't want to tell

Jenkens about that secret section of the ship just yet. "Remembering our days at Duke during those first few communications with Nelta, I think I can use those events to create a bond between her and me. A bond that should help us in the future."

Jenkens glanced at the clock. "You're cutting the interview a bit close to Final Transmission though, aren't you? It's 7:30."

"Oh well," Manning shrugged.

"Obviously, you anticipated hiring her from the start, but you seem afraid of her, and that fear, or doubt, or whatever, has you stymied. But I think more is at the heart of what's rattling you." Jenkens face pinched with angry wrinkles and he let out a light growl when he couldn't locate any terrorists. He closed a Search-n-Discover grid projecting only asteroids on the wall zone. He appeared serious and reserved—stepping forward and then a bit back—as if afraid of saying something wrong but testing the boundaries of their relationship.

"And what do *you* think is making me indecisive, although I didn't ask for your analysis," he asked, folding his arms, feeling interrogation ready.

"Personal reasons, that's all. She's been close to you…knows you, or knows people who've known you. All I'm saying, Thornton, is that sometime in the future, well, you might regret the day you included her on The List. Heck, *I* might be the one to *remind* you of this moment someday. Maybe you want Dr. Holton out of guilt, or—"

"Stop analyzing me, Steve!"

"Fine," Jenkens snapped, stepping back. "Sorry." Again, he gestured at the clock. "We don't have much time for an extensive meet-n-greet session with her though. Final transmission is approaching fast. We have to continue searching for Tech-Nos, and Bartlet's *Spider* is still preparing on its way to the moon the weed out terrorists. We might have to help him and General Rand with battle strategies."

"Yep, but I only need a few minutes to talk to her. It's been such a long time since I've seen her." He listened to Dr. Holton's opening monologue on her resume:

Battlefield Matrix

Regent Manning, you told me once that if you ever needed someone of my expertise that you would include me. Upon seeing your visual posting for Regeneration Specialist, I decided to apply for the position. As you are seeing at this point in the resume—"

The hologram changed to show her working in the lab at Duke.

I have a degree in Cellular and Molecular Biology with an emphasis in bioinformatics and biomechanics. I was part of the panel discussions with Shaesar's team of Neltan scientists on two occasions."

The hologram showed her standing alongside Elizabeth Tufter—Captain Bartlet's First-Chair Matrix Technician—in front of a Neltan/Earth communications screen in London on March 2, 2067. Elisa was one of the medical helpers who had whisked Beth Tufter off to safety after her consciousness teleported back into her. Dr. Holton concluded her resume by saying:

Regent Manning, please send any response to EHolton@DukeTeam12. I look forward to seeing you again, Sir. And on a personal and sad note, I continue to remember our friend, Lynn Altmin. Each day, I think of her...as I'm sure you do, Sir. I miss Lynn.

Once again, memories of *Greeter*'s explosion blasted through his thoughts. He glanced outside in the far distance and saw an Enforcer craft fire on a Tech-No drone that exploded into shrapnel. He breathed in and out, trying to calm the fury racing across his line of vision. A debris craft swooped down just in time to magnetize the junk and net it before it could kill people on the ground. Between it and him, avatars were popping in-and-out of the air—flooding the public with their food and lodging advertisements. The nighttime sky was like a water globe of floating lights. Then he turned around and saw Terra standing in the center of his Oval Office. He recognized Lynn in every detail of her quantum-matrix projection. Jenkens was right. He would hire Dr. Holton, even if one day he might regret the decision. She was one of the few people who had known Lynn, the one person he could at least talk to over the hundred-year journey to Nelta to grasp a remnant of Lynn.

Terra announced Dr. Holton's early arrival, and Manning ordered her to his office.

Jenkens stepped in front of him as he was about to leave the office to greet her. "Thornton, back to what I first mentioned when I walked into this office. The media might confront you on several issues if you step into that Press Room."

"What now?" It felt like Jenkens was trying to protect him, not harm him. Still, could he trust him, he wondered?

"What if we can't eliminate the Tech-Nos?" Jenkens whispered right up close to his face: "What if a group of them, or maybe some terrorists, figure out how to sneak onboard *Sagan* and sabotage it, preventing us from accomplishing the mission? What are you doing to secure that ship, especially after it's apparent that the extremists just nearly exploded it?"

Manning glanced up at the ceiling at Terra's rainbow-spiraling beehive processor. Pointing at a black, button-sized cavity, he whispered: "I have a Neural-Detection Program, NDP, ready to implement *everywhere* on that ship. If any protestor or terrorist manages to trick our vetting system and get on The List, eventually, they'll set off a Hostile Cognition alarm in the private center I'm constructing on the ship. Terra's NDP facility, a one-hundred foot lab, will be the main seat of our Threat and SpyWare Security grid. From there, we can monitor everyone and track-and-trace all dangers. Then we'll arrest them and eliminate them."

"Private center?" Jenkens asked. He called open a blueprint of the astrocity on Manning's screen display of *Sagan*. Several ship levels appeared in front of them. "Where?"

Gradually, Manning zoomed in on the bottom portion of the astroship. "Here." He realized he was in murky territory by trusting Jenkens and revealing that covert area on *Sagan*.

A dark-blue domed arena appeared. The empty facility looked like an indoor football field. Along the far-eastern curvature of the facility was a small docking pad, smaller than other stations throughout the ship where Maglev cars could load and unload passengers and cargo simultaneously at the speed of one Maglev car every two minutes.

"No one knows about this section, Steve," Manning began. "I'm waiting until after Final Transmission to tell The Regency. I'll make a strong case for the Classified but necessary level when I present a potential Doomsday simulation. As you just suggested, The Regency must know the ramifications of possible inside attacks, hacks on the astrocity's matrix, or raids that could cripple the ship. We must prepare for *all* worse case scenarios. Covert monitoring and cognitive restructuring is a must, even though it's an invasion of privacy."

"Then you have no choice but to continue construction on that level and keep it hidden," Jenkens said softly.

"At this concealed level, we can receive neural scans on everyone as they pass under certain archways. I wouldn't want a saboteur collapsing a wormhole on us so that we can't catch a Schwarzschild friction-line to spacefold," Manning said.

"We'd die instantly, or find ourselves floating dead in space without a habitable planet anywhere—my God!" Jenkens hunched over as if he might shrivel.

Manning patted his arm. "Jenkens," he laughed, "I think you're over exaggerating. You haven't been watching very closely, have you?"

Jenkens shook his head. He looked lost. "You have another strategy besides everything we've been doing thus far to protect *Sagan*?"

Manning smiled. "I do!" He walked over and sat down in a plush chair next to Jenkens. "Captain Bartlet and our elite military Stealth Force."

"But Bartlet and his team are on The List," Jenkens said.

Manning opened up Bartlet's resume he had converted into a visual program alongside *The Spider*. "You must admit, Steve, that Robert Bartlet is one of a kind, a brilliant military genius...the best." He noticed that when he called Jenkens by his first name in those instances where he appeared anxious, overwhelmed or frightened, Jenkens calmed down and behaved in a collected manner. Then Jenkens changed his mind and stopped arguing. Remembering those tiny nuances would make a difference in convincing not only Jenkens but also other Regents of his plans to develop and implement all sorts of new technology on *Sagan*. "We can't have *any* sabotage or attacks onboard the astrocity, Steve, none. I'm going to see to that! Bartlet's intuitive nose can weed out dissidents just about as good as Terra. Cultivating that portion of his DNA into the clones we order the matrix to create will be an asset."

Terra stepped forward and turned her head in confusion. "Sir? Explain please, 'as good as Terra'. Did I underperform in capability?"

Manning laughed. "No offense intended, Terra. Just joking."

"Do you think we might encounter a murderous strike the likes of what took out *Greeter*?" Jenkens asked.

Manning felt a jolt of acid hit his stomach. "You mentioned before that *Greeter* exploded. Now you said, 'murderous.' Sounds like *you* know that *someone* murdered that crew on purpose." He bent down close to Jenkens who had wide doe-eyes. "Tell me, Steve, do you know something that I don't know, even when I believe I know everything...from *each* daily report of *each* daily investigation?" He had that phrase, 'Daily Investigative Report,' on Auto Activation, and today's report flared on as a small hologram he could enlarge over the Smart Bar on his desk. He pointed at it—drummed his finger at it. "I put together that Investigative Committee, Steve. I receive reports—*daily* reports, 'cause even though other people believe I've closed the investigation, I haven't. It's my investigation now. So, *out* with what you know!"

Jenkens held out his wrist device, called open an icon he had titled, *Greeter's Assembly*, and then began weeding through small images of machinery and shuttle components. "I can send you this phase-shifted electron image I received anonymously two months after your committee concluded the investigation."

"Why didn't I receive this?" Manning swept over a cipher that morphed into the misaligned part that was supposed to interface a mirror with the accelerator on *Greeter*, thus enabling the first Neltan/Earth communications conduit to stabilize when *Greeter*'s particle accelerators linked with the Neltan's event horizon.

"Fear maybe?" Jenkens shrugged. "Uncertainty? The part *is* blurry. Maybe an investigator lacked the confidence to draw a conclusion. Now at least, you have something to work with."

"*Hm*," Manning groaned. When powerless defeat curled through his mind, he felt seething rage. He didn't know whether he could trust Jenkens or whether Jenkens was just trying to trade a future position for knowledge to get on his good side. "Let me think about that for a while. Now, back to the point I was about to make about clone technology."

"What's that?" Jenkens asked.

"With the technology from Nelta and the leftovers from the Matter Stream sample that our fission-fusion craft are collecting like earthly fishing boats amassing their catch with a net, I'm managing a small biomedical team on *Sagan* that's assembling clone chambers *now*."

"Clone *chambers*? Like the subterranean Neltan *stasis* pods?" Jenkens folded his arms across his chest like rods. "Wow, you *are* making *Sagan* into a type of an experimental facility, don't you think? The whole environment feels like it's gonna be transporting three classes of people: Regents, civilians and patrolling Enforcers." He began rubbing his forehead that creased and reddened. "I can't see how this is all going to play out, Thornton…a hundred years of spacefolding, *with* strangers, and secret projects. I know the astrocity is almost as large as Oahu, but come on! If anyone discovers that you're implementing even just a smidgeon of this stuff, even now, they'll accuse us of *Abuse of Power* and *Obstructing Transparency*. We'll be ousted from The Regency. People will nail me as being *your* accomplice. We'll wind up outcasts, penniless *and* jobless. Forget going to Nelta!" He opened up the blueprint of the bottom of the astrocity, enlarged the lowest level, and with his forefinger, began tracing several secret corridors leading up to the Regents' private, Level-5, Clone-Tech facility. "I just don't understand the necessity for all these covert activities, Thornton. *God*—what am I doing here? Doing now? With you? And how'll I end up if all this—this *stuff* leaks to the media?"

Manning turned away. Next to the two-by-two-foot Threat screen were a series of several wall screens—Security imagers. On one, he spotted Dr. Holton walking through a scanner at the West Wing. In ten minutes, she'd be at his door, and he could get rid of Jenkens, for a while...stall for time for a while. If he couldn't change Jenkens' mind in the next few hours, he could eliminate him with the Gamma-Pulse app in his rainbow-cycling ceiling hub. He could call Jenkens back into the office immediately after *The Signing of The Pact* program and incinerate him in a second.

Then he had an idea that could change Steve Jenkens—a negative re-enforcement. He said: "To persuade people to allow us to use just enough technology *not* to get us into trouble before our launch to Nelta, I'll stream the Tech-No protesters' assaults, raids and hacking strikes into *every* person's home and business right now. I'm sure I can generate a positive media spin for my sudden use of technological force and convince The World to side with me and fault *you* for inaction if, *if* you divulge to anyone, *any* technology I'm implementing here and intend to implement on *Sagan*, Steve—"

"I'll lose my vote!" Jenkens cried through a scorned expression. "I'll lose my Regency position! You can't—"

"Yes, *ahem*, that will most likely happen. Have you seen the best quantum features of the new Terra-III?"

"No, and I don't—"

Terra," he called her over, "Give me five Terras out of Virtual-mode and multiply them in Augmented-mode, please."

Five various types of holographic Terras stepped out of five screens. Each one had a different appearance, height and weight.

"All these images Terra randomly selected from various

Battlefield Matrix

body types and faces in the matrix," Manning began. "This new Terra-III can create, edit or enhance *any* situation, person, or thing and plaster it below ground to Terra's farthest reach in space, which is, where, Terra?"

"Ten thousand miles beyond Jupiter and expanding, Regent Manning," she answered.

"Wow—the new Terra-III has expanded to reflect human needs and wants based on encountered conditions," Jenkens marveled. He had obviously forgotten Manning's threat.

"Scan Regent Jenkens for profile, Terra," Manning ordered.

As Jenkens huffed in opposition, six more Terras materialized and began walking around him, scanning each of his movements, studying his eyes, absorbing his verbal tones and inflections. All the while, "his" Terra remained at his side, unchanging.

"What are you doing? What's going on?" Jenkens walked backwards toward the door until a chair stopped his progress.

The walls and floor were interacting with the ten Terra's to create almost tangible human bodies. They were reading Jenkens' body language and his biometrics. One Terra opened up images of his past, another Terra activated a Voice sequence that started several scenes of conversations he had with other people from this morning onward.

"Is she sending information on me somewhere? Is she, like, copying me?" he gasped when her 3D finger touched him like the prick of a needle extracting blood. "Ouch! A laser probe!"

Manning said to his Terra: "Terra, stream the data to my holosite. Later on, I can compose a profile and make interpretations." She complied.

"But those will be *your* interpretations to use how *you* see fit!" Jenkens argued. "No—this is way too powerful and can manipulate facts and events on a global scale, not just a little one-time occurrence as you did with that Tech-No group, Thornton."

Manning gestured for him to calm down. "I ordered Terra to collect the DNA of *everyone* on The List in triplicate, Steve,"

J.P. Osterman

he said after he called off the Terra holograms. "Spy Ware technology, Clone technology...I'm trying to make a point. We *need* to develop and implement *all* the technology that we can to help us keep *Sagan* safe and us safe on *Sagan*. That's my answer to your question. You asked me: 'What are you going to do to make sure we fulfill our mission?'"

"Yeah?" Jenkens gripped the back of the chair.

"Well that's what I'm doing: continuing to evolve Terra on *Sagan* and assemble technology covertly. Next, I'm going to ask you to help me. Are you in, or out...with me, or against me." He waited through a thickening silence as Terra activated vents to cool the air. "Steve, I need your help. We have to see eye-to-eye here. If not, then we part ways right now."

Jenkens sighed deeply with an expression on his face that shone surrender. "But Thornton, Clone technology will only be legal on *Sagan*. And it's only voter-sanctioned as a back-up plan in case crewmembers start dying like flies while onboard the astrocity. It's *illegal* now, anywhere, and punishable with *life* on that prison facility." He pointed to the sky. "My gosh, Thornton. This isn't a question of *me* helping you. First, you tell me you have secret Spy Ware, then a brain-scan detection program, then a secret facility on *Sagan*, and now illegal cloning?" He gave a half-turn of frustration as he whispered harshly: "What the hell's wrong with you, Thornton? How'd you get this way? Scanning minds, tapping blood illegally—"

He rubbed his arm where Terra's laser light struck him.

"And atomizing people?!" Jenkens glanced around the room as if suddenly he might disappear. "What the hell happened to you?"

Manning spotted sweat rounds under Jenkens' arms. He looked afraid to move, yet he was still in the room when he could have ran out long ago. "Let me explain, Steve—"

"There's a watchdog agency on the lookout for illegal cloning, Thornton. Cloning is like performing Life Extension. We can't! Uh-huh, no. At some point, we'll be discovered."

He was talking so fast, Manning thought he might collapse. "*Shhh!*" Jenkens had a whiny voice. Shoving the palm of his hand into the air to quiet him, he felt compelled to itemize Jenkens' concerns. "Number one, Steve, you told me you're worried about Bartlet dying. Number two, everyone's panicked about the terrorists annihilating our Stealth Forces. And number three, you—*and me*—are afraid The World will vote us out of the Regency." Noticing that Jenkens was about to counter his list, he grabbed Jenkens' shoulder. "Listen," he whispered. "The construction of *Sagan* is in trouble. Our journey to Nelta is in jeopardy. How did I get this way? Secretive? Covert?" He watched Jenkens' plop back down in his chair. "It's called isolationism and protectionism, Steve. It's called making a preemptive strike before someone kills us first. To survive, unlike those on *Greeter*, or those three Regents who left this morning with all their stuff shoved boxes, obviously downtrodden and suicidal looking—"

"Yeah, I noticed that," Jenkens interrupted.

"*I* had to change. Long ago, I changed, Steve." He walked up to him and pounded his desk. "You better change too. Get some tough skin and start thinking 'covert' not 'transparency' so you too can obtain the element of surprise and eliminate threats." He looked out the large picture windows into the sparkling nighttime world of avatars. They were hosts' alter egos, people who had paid for advertising to display their causes or products on blimps, hovering billboards and buildings. "I lead two lives. I think you're the only person, besides Terra—who's not real...I know that—who knows me both as a person and a Regent."

Jenkens sighed and said: "O.K. Tell me what you have in mind concerning the Clone technology. I'm in."

Chapter 4

Deceased But Collected

Manning smoothed down his coat. "For over a year I've been gathering DNA on scientists, world leaders, and—well, *ahem*, a criminal or two."

"Why?" Jenkens asked.

He opened up Robert Bartlet's profile on one of the Security screens. "Take Captain Bartlet as an example. Using a tiny portion of The Matter Stream leftovers that our craft have been collecting in space combined with the Regeneration technology on *Sagan*, if Bartlet dies while fighting terrorists, we can replace him. As I said before, he's invaluable." When he noticed Jenkens' chest calmly rise and fall, he believed Jenkens was beginning to understand his logic. He just needed time to convince him that implementing Clone technology would be advantageous for *Sagan*, and maybe even now, if needed. "Cloning saves us training time, recruitment, and money." He called up the statistical data Terra-III had compiled onboard *Sagan*. "We can replace valuable and highly intelligent people who die and have died. If we can convince The World to approve cloning, we can then access all the genetic databases, procure their special DNA—even though they're not on The List—and store the DNA in Terra-III's matrix. We can use DNA splicing to manipulate features. Terra-III's neural therapy revises or restructures personality, identity and memories. Furthermore, Cloning will strengthen *Sagan*'s Enforcer pool because when we Clone an Enforcer, we can not only alter their telomeres but also their muscular system and make them stronger...even impervious to pain."

"But not hulkish," Jenkens rebuffed.

"Course not!" Manning scoffed. "All the clones we place throughout the astrocity will be human...with names and identities, with cognition, consciousness and true personalities." He closed *Sagan*'s Clone program.

"You've done a lot of work to put all this together." Jenkens touched his throat as if protecting it from a guillotine. As he let it go, he said: "Cloning is nano-robotics building DNA, stem-cell assembling with some synthetic tissues, and photon energy, Thornton. Clones are soulless, aren't they?"

He called Terra to show Jenkens him a hologram of a clone solidifying through a stem-cell spray in a body pod on *Sagan*. "You're wrong. Clones *are* human. Here's an experiment I'm working on to prove it." He showed Jenkens two craft that had launched from *Sagan* fifteen minutes ago. "Ten clones are on the way to support Captain Bartlet and *The Spider*. They're clones of those geoengineers who died last week setting terraforming rods on the Martian poles. Clone Techs on *Sagan* had Terra modify their cognition after we uploaded their minds into her matrix so that after we downloaded the minds into new bodies, they'd have selective memory."

"That's not a lifetime of memories though," began Jenkens, "so they could begin to wonder where they came from, or question reality and then go crazy."

"They're in the experimental stages, so we'll be monitoring them for those behaviors," Manning said. "Still, they're human in every way, and we altered their appearances just a little so no one can recognize them. Yesterday, when I put out a Call for

Assistance on Station III to support our Stealth Force because our numbers are depleting, these people insisted on joining Captain Bartlet. They knew who he was, his job duties...*everything* that those geoengineers remembered about their jobs. Doesn't *that* make them human?"

Jenkens called open a profile of one of the dead geoengineers. Terra had already classified him *Deceased*, and stored his death certificate in the matrix Deceased Storage grid. The man's avatar was there as a Living Archive of the diseased man for all his family, friends or inquirers to experience virtually the man's lifetime accomplishments, glean his historic data, and trace his ancestry. The clone's new avatar suddenly popped up. He had a new name, a new identity and a false life. The clone could gradually add experiences, narrations and more biographical information.

Another dead profile copied and altered in the matrix to indicate a new life. This clone was now a Program Analyst onboard the recon astrocraft *Vallarta*.

"So you're saying that these people—and that this woman—can handle the jobs you've given them?" Jenkens asked as all ten clones appeared over death certificates.

"Yep," Manning said proudly. He called open the secret site at the bow of *Sagan*'s Level-5, and the screen displayed a stasis pod. "Here's a portion of how the process works."

As scientists inside a decontaminated lab monitored biometrics of a developing clone inside a line of empty pods; Terra announced, "Clone-in-Progress." The mind-stream ceiling hub above the pod looked like a floodlight flowing with ionized particles. The red flashing bar outside the coffin-shaped pod read, 'Name Pending, Identity Formation, Stage 3.'

Manning said: "This is the cognition portion of the consciousness manipulation. Terra applies our evolved Spy Drop Ware to sift through this woman's mind and extract memories. After a mind uploads into the matrix, Terra reconfigures it, edits it, to a paradigm we specified and then streams the altered consciousness back into the clone. This clone forming here, I'll send to our London office, where under radar, a team will monitor everything about her. When they notice problems, they'll help her, and we'll adjust the matrix accordingly for future use. In a short time, we'll perfect cloning."

"*Whoa*—this seems *too* easy. We're "playing God" *so* casually!" Jenkens said.

Manning closed the life stream from *Sagan*'s Level-5 and then called open and enlarged the small *Vallarta* transporting his clone crew. "It's innovation, Steve. But when *this* experimental team that's about to rendezvous with Bartlet downs a few terrorists, I know The World will approve cloning, at least under intense supervision and for survival purposes. That's how I'll put it in order to secure the vote in a few days, after we see the successful results. On the way to Nelta, I have Terra already scheduled to clone four families."

"Four—why not five? Even ten!" Jenkens said.

"Wait until you hear the purpose before you blindly dismiss the plan, Steve."

"Can't wait…go on." Jenkens plopped back down in his chair.

"A few clones will be older people. We'll cognitively deep-wave their DNA-regulating memory with encoded images, signs and symbols—what Terra has already encoded as thoughts." He pulled up a DNA strand, and Terra began a Neuro-Jumping-Gene slide show that began displaying brain cells transmitting information to new cells. "The clones will believe they share common historical events. And we'll infuse them with positive images for The Regency. They'll help us monitor the crew and inform us if they discover any covert activity."

Jenkens tapped a dot on the NJG slide show and up popped a memory of a child riding a horse. "Whose memories are you using for the clone that's forming now? All information has to come from somewhere or someone."

"I have a team right now uploading and storing the minds of those participants who went berserk in that failed research project last week. The empty stasis pods I just showed you on

Leve-5 will replicate them someday."

Jenkens opened a hologram, and a line of gray-faced students clad in hospital gowns materialized over his wrist device. "Oh those poor people...wasted talent and lives. Oh God—I think I'm gonna be sick."

Manning handed him water and decrease the room's temperature. "I know, Steve...that's horrible to watch. But through cloning, we can recover those young people."

"Are they just bodies with brainstem functioning?" Jenkens asked.

"I'm afraid so," he replied. "I just haven't had the guts to tell their families that we're going to have to disengage them from the ventilators. Even with Vital Organ drips and Stem-Cell Infusions, those kids will be only bodies living off machine energy. They're only hope is a stasis existence inside the matrix on *Sagan* until a time when we can clone them and make them part of the crew. Then they'll have new lives. Meanwhile, Terra can duplicate a few of their positive memories to imprint in the minds of other clones to give them emotional stability."

He had Terra zoom in on their bodies lying on gurneys. All twelve of them had IVs and a mesh mind-link helmet covering their heads. With their eyes open, they were alive, but lifeless; awake but incognizant of reality. Above each of them was a tiny Terra hub, cycling a rainbow light of quantum processing. Manning traced for Jenkens the upload of their minds to the matrix center on *Sagan*, Level-7.

Jenkens scooped up a Kleenex and dabbed his eyes. "*Ahem*...they were *brilliant* young people who were on The List—damn! Well, at least with the Clone technology, they'll live again someday. Maybe the technology's not such a bad thing if we examine it from that angle."

"That's right," Manning said, realizing that Jenkens had changed his mind. Suddenly, he heard a commotion coming from the Press Room. There was shouting and then arguing. Opening the door, he noticed that white-suited Matrix Techs, holding wand instruments and photonic pads—had positioned themselves all around the frame of the IMAX transmission screen, adjusting the frequency and checking the screen's connectivity to the matrix.

The towering screen had to interface perfectly with the Decagon accelerator system beyond Mars in preparation for Final Communication. In less than two hours, the Neltan/Earth wormhole would open. The Decagon would stabilize the singularity and its event horizon forces, then transmit the quantum-communication to the IMAX screen, where Shaesar's image and those of the Neltan Advancement Committee would appear in the Press Room.

But protesters outside the White House were shining icons into the room, trying to disrupt the media by disrupting their robotic imagers. A few of the nano-photonic processors on the screen were popping on and off, their sounds like corn kernels ricocheting in a hot skillet. He and Jenkens began prying down robotic projector arms and redistributing their imaging weights. Manning called for Terra to intensify the security layer in all the long line of windows. Finally, the robotic projectors stabilized. Still, he felt something terrible was about to encroach.

With guns unleashed, Enforcers were racing through the room in search of spyware. Manning's Lead Secret Service Agent, Jane Dirk, said she was using an optics frequency detector to scan the hardware for ghastly avatars, icons, or photonic nano-atomizers that could unleash in the Press Room at any moment. She called the dangerous intruders, geocaches. "They could also be spyware. But I think they morph into sensory bombs after they infiltrate any hardware—stinky, sticky, and ear piercing," she described the virtual geocaches. "I got the name from the 2012 recreational activity where participants use GPS devices to locate fun or informational containers. But this cyber geocache we detected is coming from space…a threatening, phase-shifted electron virus, a real algorithmic monster!" She said the hostile geocache was on its way, or could be somewhere around the White House right now. No one had located the geocache yet, nor detected its trigger mechanism. Logically, she said, the geocacher had to be heading straight for the Press Room...the most plausible site for an attack. Jane Dirk was intensifying her hunt, evident by the massive Security detail.

"Stay inside the Oval Office, Regent Manning. This is clear and present danger!" Agent Dirk shouted. She stopped a ceiling scan and said: "Sir, I just received a message saying that a Dr. Elisa Holton is at the North East Security Kiosk. We show you have her on your schedule for 8:30. Obviously, she's really early. We've cleared her through her biometrics. We can have her wait until 8:30 or send her up now. Which do you prefer?"

"Yes, send her up," he said.

As Jane Dirk gave the order, a static-filled reply returned to her wrist device. "Crazy!"

"What?" Manning asked. Enforcers began checking their wrist devices and the Security wall zones in the Press Room that were also experiencing white noise.

"Security is telling me that someone's trying to stop that kiosk from functioning, as if it's purposely preventing Dr. Holton from gaining entry, Sir," Jane began. "Someone is continually trying to hack into our grid, change the clocks, and alter the Neltan/Earth wormhole connection."

Jenkens looked about ready to faint and Matrix Techs around the screen began backing away and discussing solution. "But we're working to stop the disruptor," Jane added as she continued to glance around the Press Room and then ordered a fast scan of the Oval Office. The instruments were all reading green for Cleared. All the while, she maintained a studious look and an expression of vengeance. "We'll capture the culprit or culprits, Sir, and stop any geocacher intrusion. Don't you worry."

Jenkens said in a low voice, "I suggest you hard link the White House with Station II researchers, Agent Dirk. They have experimental matrix apps and programs, and help from the military in writing counter codes for intrusions and terror viruses. We've been experiencing all sorts of attacks lately…crazy matrix-strikes the like of what occurred on *The Spider*. With them supporting you, you'll have a greater chance of stopping the incoming sabotage."

"Doing that now, Sir, thanks," Jane said. She had a look of red failure on her face. "I shoulda done that."

Patting her on the arm consolingly, Manning activated his avatar, displaying for her a hologram of his calendar. He swept the day's activities into her wrist device. "It's 7:47, so send up Dr. Holton with an escort. That should ensure her safety."

"Yes, Regent Manning." Then Agent Jane Dirk returned to her low-beeping and green-flaring tracking device to hunt down the threat.

When Manning shut the door to the Oval Office and shut the door, he heard a confusing exhale come from Jenkens who said, "I think I'm beginning to see your overarching strategy, Thornton, regarding the use of covert technology." He nodded at a cluster of security wall zones and stepped toward a scene displaying a threat to sabotage Final Communication. "I probably sound like a real blowhard sometimes…at least that's what my wife calls me when I start analyzing everything." After laughing, he sipped some water and sat down in his chair next to Manning's long desk. All the while, the hologram clock was ticking down the minutes to Final Transmission: one hour, twelve minutes. "All this application of Neltan technology you've been telling me about, Thornton, and what I'm seeing—"

"Yes?"

Jenkens had determination moving in his every gesture. "It's going to take a little time for me to digest everything going on around here. I need time to adjust to what we need to do to save that astrocity 'cause people are trying to destroy it. As you said, we need every advancement and innovation, especially after we launch from Earth."

"For sure. As I've been showing you, every application of Neltan technology I've contrived *is* necessary…no, essential, Steve."

Jenkens poured himself more water and called Agent Dirk

J.P. Osterman

to make sure that all the incoming guests had plenty to drink and hors d'oeuvres. The Press Room appeared to have return to normal, with the media vying for seats and their small projection robots scanning and gliding around the room in search of the best locations for holosite connectivity to The World. He said: "Gradually, I'm becoming convinced that your strategies to make our journey to Nelta as safe and secure as possible are right. I understand that you're trying to take *all* possible precautions to give us Saganeers—" He perked up happily. "Hey—what a *great* name for those of us who are on The List!"

"Yeah," Manning laughed, "we'll have to throw that new term to The World right after they vote me in as Executive Regent."

Jenkens' face appeared serious again. "You're trying to give us Saganeers the best advantages so that everyone will get along...so that there won't be any attacks or sabotage—"

"As happened with *The Greeter*!" Manning interrupted.

Jenkens reopened the images of those brain-dead students—a line of bodies clothed in hospital gowns. Rainbow processors in the Terra ceiling hubs were obviously working to store their minds. "Downloading people's minds prior to death looks freaky." He shuddered and took another gulp of water. "You're turning death into a permanent a state of transition, where someone's entire experiences can be relegated to a matrix for various periods of time. It's half-life-half-nonexistence, Thornton. What would you call it, Terra?"

Materializing at the center of the office, Terra smiled a bit—the system's standard friendly expression and calm gesture of response whenever someone asked a question. "I define 'reality' as a reflective representation of living in the present, Regent Jenkens. I define 'life within my contained matrix' as the following: *The non-corporeal existence inside an artificial entity during which time, reality, truth, sensory experiences, materiality, and interpersonal relationships remain intact and solid, but which I preserve.*"

"*Whoa*," Jenkens huffed, "Thanks, Terra, *I'm* glad *I'm* not

Battlefield Matrix

there!"

After a pause, Terra giggled slightly—a Response to an interpretation of a joke. She quickly stopped.

Jenkens sipped some water and set his glass down gently as if testing the space around him. "The artificial reality Terra just defined reminds me of that old movie, *Tron*, or that old series, *Cube*."

"I remember those," Manning said.

Jenkens squinted at the hologram of the photonic light through which Terra was upstreaming one student's mind into a storage grid inside the matrix. "In those story plots, someone's consciousness becomes trapped in a space-time confabulation, an artificial environment, wherein people are aware of their surroundings, are responding to a dimension of computer processing, and can't release themselves out of a human-versus-cyber reality. *This* seems like a horrible existence, Thornton." Jenkens turned away from the show and folded his arms across his belly. "I wouldn't want this for me if I were about to die."

"Some people do want that though, Steve." Calling for Terra to give them a visual of the Pro-Coning site inside one of the new medical facilities, he spotted a woman in line, signing a nondisclosure agreement to have her consciousness stored within the matrix on Earth. "This woman, who is terminal, doesn't want to die. She doesn't want everything she's ever experienced and felt, gone—*poof*—into nothingness. We also have people with severe disabilities, like multiple sclerosis, who have complete awareness but can't move one muscle."

"I know," Jenkens said sadly.

"They're beyond our stem-cell cures and in line for The World to approve Consciousness Uploading and Storage until we can find ways to safely repair their bodies—or create them *new* ones—" He was suggesting his new Clone technology.

Jenkens took one more look at the elderly woman who was hesitating about signing her *Life Into Terra* and then quickly shut down the hologram. "God—I hope she knows what she's doing 'cause there's no guarantee what her existence is

J.P. Osterman

going to look like after she dies, if she'll ever be cured or cloned to a new life." He stood up then quickly sat back down. "We're playing God at this level, Thornton. This is *way* too much power and responsibility for one small scientific hierarchy to be overlords of life and death. Unethical I gotta say. There."

Manning felt his shoulders slump in fatigue. He imagined a hundred years of such pointless dialoguing with him...on *Sagan*. It was the first time in a long time he experienced dread. Later, when they'd have more time, he decided he'd set some ground rules with him, some boundaries. The thought of spending one hundred years of Jenkens parsing his every word, idea and opinion created a mental weariness. It reminded him of a Mark Twain's phrase: "the tiresome chirping of a cricket." He said: "Actually, Steve, according to Terra-III's current but blurry visual of the inside of her matrix, after a person's consciousness quantum vaults—I call the uploading *quantum vaulting*—into the matrix, that consciousness can partake of and experience any type of scene stored inside the matrix. That person can interact with fictional characters or another quantum-vaulted consciousness. It might be a great reality and yield heavenly experiences to be inside Terra-III's artificial reality. We don't know yet. We have to accrue more data and wait for Terra-III to translate matrix-experiences and matrix-participant realities into our human reality and perception of reality. No easy task!"

"I agree...even for the *best* quantum system, Terra-III!" Jenkens said. "I bet *Sagan*'s Terra matrix is going to have to evolve quite a bit more before we'll ever see *those* images."

"I'm working on that with a team of engineers right now, Steve, but we won't see any visuals of a matrix reality until we're well on our journey to Nelta." Opening up Terra-III's new, 4D Graphics-Morph app on *Sagan*, Manning spliced out a Terra hub that copied from the mental facility on Station II. Then he inserted the hub into Jenkens' hologram of the Regeneration Corridor. The stern of Level-5 was almost complete with Regeneration stations and quantum-vaulting

Battlefield Matrix

hubs. "I want to get this ready to show Dr. Holton and the other Regeneration Specialists what their working environment is going to look like." As he reloaded Dr. Holton's resume to join the other specialists on The List, First Communication flashed through his mind, followed by a strong memory of Lynn. His chest burned. He felt heat around his blurring eyes. "People have *great* experiences they accrue throughout a lifetime, Steve."

He thought of Lynn's experiences, now gone, except for the ones he was carrying of her. And the memories of her were like happy, haunting, slide-shows. The two gulps of water he drank didn't douse the memory of her being on *Greeter* and the shuttle exploding. Immediately, Dr. Holton's face flashed into his mind. They were like sisters.

"Why should good experiences disappear when our bodies die, Steve? That's so unjust! Unfair! That we're born to *have* to die."

"Yeah, it sucks, but that's just the way it is," Jenkens said. "Rage against the dying light. You're not the only one. But then again...you're obviously working hard...extremely hard, to change it."

Despising the reality, he pounded the desk. Terra responded with her standard Wellness Inquiry, which he waved at as sign for her to stop. "Why can't we preserve our memories, access them and enjoy them whenever we want?" He walked around Dr. Holton's hologram that he asked Terra to project at the center of his office. He swiped her Living Resume to the wall zone displaying *Sagan*'s construction. Now, her number was among the crew—the matrix processing her Living Cube and cementing her in place among critical locations.

"Maybe our experiences *do* live beyond our deaths as the Neltans strongly maintain," Jenkens said softly. "They never could give us a visual of The Divine, but the evidence behind The Divine's existence is overwhelming. The big one is that both our races are so similar even though we're fifty-five million light years apart and have evolved differently through billions of years on separate evolutionary paths. Death is another proof of The Divine. We're terrified of it; they're not, even though their lifespan is twice as long as ours. They believe wholeheartedly that their bodily essence—we call our souls—live on after death." Jenkens stepped toward Dr. Holton's hologram where he joined Manning.

As part of her experience, she had listed, 'The Greeter, Cockpit Assembly Crew.'

Jenkens added a Regeneration Corridor laboratory scene to the Graphics-Morph app. Then he superimposed her image into the white Regeneration lab on Level-5. The result showed Dr. Holton inside one of *Sagan*'s Regeneration corridors and standing in front of a high-tech gurney. In obvious deep inspection of the contrived scene, he said: "Well, Dr. Holton might like working in a place like this. She definitely wants to go to Nelta. I think she'll like this realistic representation we've made for her to peruse."

Enlarging the lab and planting more technology in the scene, Manning asked Terra to generate a simulation in which Dr. Holton would appear to be working inside the lab with a patient. "She should definitely like this when I show it to her."

"And include several perks when you offer her the position. She and the other Regeneration specialists will have larger Living Cubes and unlimited Maglev shuttle access," Jenkens said.

Manning tapped him on the shoulder. "Hey—Terra just done all that!" He snapped his head toward Terra. "But don't stream her The Acceptance. I want to tell her."

"Yes, Regent Manning," Terra replied.

"She also has great job prospects once we arrive on Nelta," Jenkens said. "She's already met Shaesar and the Neltan Advancement Committee. Maybe they'll offer her a role in helping them repair their genetic mutation."

"I believe the Neltans could use Dr. Holton as well," Manning said. He thought of The Matter Stream and remembered a few genetic tests he was conducting with the multiverse creation force. "There could be other technical applications of Clone technology and Neltan technology for which we might also need her skills."

"Oh—what?"

"I'll know more once I interview her...test her sense of loyalty. Terra, create a bar graph and start profiling Dr. Elisa Holton when she walks in here."

Chapter 5

Attack Code: Galaxy Runner

Terra rematerialized. "Dr. Holton is now inside the main lobby, Regent Manning. Jane Dirk cleared her entrance."

"Have the escort bring her in here and seat her next to the transmission screen. I'll greet her when my security screen in here alerts me of her presence."

As Terra faded and left to comply, Regent Jenkens whispered, "I have another concern, Thornton."

"What?" He thought: hell what *now?* Jenkens' expressions of panic and heightened concern were becoming like automatic jabs!

Outside, various zeppelins were still flashing the faces of Regents, Neltans, and Neltan scenery. They were paid advertisements, mostly by The Regents who were still campaigning for the Executive position. Now and then, the airship lights would pierce through the laser-protection security bars and jab the Oval Office walls with a yellow glare that Terra quenched with a hushed sizzling sound—absorbing the light energy into the matrix.

Battlefield Matrix

Jenkens appeared afraid. "Can someone hack your experimental Terra-III ceiling hub in here and listen in on us?"

Manning eased up and laughed. "Nope—no way. In that cavity right there—" He pointed to a pin-sized, glowing blue button inside the rainbow cycling processor. Telling him about the gamma disintegration capability might also be an added incentive—albeit a Negative Reinforcement—for Jenkens to support him. "I installed a gamma weapon device months ago."

"Let me guess...as well as the other technology you've been talking about, no one knows about this device either."

"Correct, Steve. To detect all hackers and potential hackers and trap the intruder, I keep most surveillance devices covert. This one is special."

Jenkens craned his neck toward the rainbow processor. "How's the gamma device work? I know some Enforcers are using modified, photon-propelled laser guns pistols instead of the heavy duty guns, but a small, gamma weapon would be great. The enemy can't see the fire power or target mechanism that's about to killing 'em." Manning slightly increased the volume on the weapon's hum-upload. "What're ya doing!?"

"To call this app 'On' means the gamma weapon will disintegrate the trespasser with a well-defined and sensitively-tuned beam. Any spy in here would turn to instant ash, fall to the floor, and the nano-carpet fibers will soaks him or her up. Gone—like that."

Jenkens careened and ducked.

Manning snapped his fingers and called off the app. Laughing, he said, "It's off." He had the upper hand of power now and he imbibed that flow of energy and strength.

"Are you testing any more of these?" Jenkens gestured in relief and sat back down.

"Tomorrow I'm having one installed in the Press Room. A preemptive strike is always the best strategy. It's the same principle with the clones on their way to assist Captain Bartlet." Manning zoomed in on a small stealth fighter, the *Vallarta*, shaped like a stingray that a camouflaged satellite was capturing through etendue-in-free-space. "While these eight clones in the *Vallarta* will be fighting alongside The Captain, I re-directed two clones to become spies."

"Spies? The likes you said you'll distribute throughout the astrocity to monitor the crew?" Jenkens asked.

"One and the same," Manning answered. "The two clone spies are piloting an enemy craft we captured and reconfigured a few months ago. One of our astrofreighters secretly launched the craft, and then an astrofighter downed it within miles of where Captain Bartlet believes the terrorists are holding up under the lunar surface. We wanted the scenario to appear as if the two craft were engaged in a real skirmish. Immediately after the clones began a nose-dive to the lunar surface, our astrofighter high-tailed it outta there, making the fight appear as if the clones won but also sustained injury. They started an SOS signal that we translated as their newest cry for help when that *Tiger* virus infected Captain Bartlet."

"Yeah—The Regency received a recap of that," Jenkens said. "Glad he's recovered!"

"That crashed craft with the spy clones inside is now transmitting a homing signal so The Captain can locate the enemy's stronghold. Meanwhile, the enemy should buy the ruse and take the clones into their subterranean hideout and into their confidence. As soon as Bartlet receives a message from them, he can summon support craft, converge on the target, and take out that bad enemy stronghold." He showed Jenkens an image of one of the clones.

"That's Dr. Hendricks!" Jenkens said. "The Lead Physician on that experiment that backfired on those grad students we just checking up on. One student knifed the guy to death."

He called open another profile. "Here's the clone of the student who killed him. An Enforcer had no choice but to shoot to kill."

"These two are working *together* as moles?" Jenkens asked.

"Yep, but Terra modified their minds in the matrix. They don't know each other," he answered, enlarging Dr. Hendricks' clone. The profile flashed the clone's current job description:

Battlefield Matrix

Astropilot, Stealth Force: Black Ops. "He's not Dr. Hendricks anymore. He has a new name and new memories. He's Brent Gorham."

"From what I can see from all his likes and dislikes scrolling down like a resume, he's more than a mole. He's both them and us...from language to preferences," Jenkens said.

"Yep. His cover is Abram el Shaleki, a man with an identity that *Sagan*'s Terra-III crisscrossed with their Demon Terra as a shadow virus so as to appear as if they are rescuing their own. Both clones have modified, nano-cytoskeletal protein trackers swimming through their blood. They'll be completely undetectable as spies. With their covers solidly in place, we hope they can convince their terrorist comrades that they've been in hiding for months and finally escaped. We included a map of Aleppo and its surrounding desert. It has their symbols the use as pinpoints for some of the most recent hideouts. One of the new POWs blurted out a few locations after a hot neural remapping session. Generals Rand's team has used CBRR to extract a lot of tactical info from the enemy...fried a few brains too, accidentally, but oh well."

Jenkens continued to watch the small craft skim across soft terrain until it struck the rim of a crater and stopped with a jolt. "So now, the clones need to win the enemy's confidence."

"That right, and then contact us regarding their plans," Manning added.

Jenkens gestured in apprehension. "I hope they can do all that without getting caught. I hope *Sagan*'s matrix did a near perfect job in imprinting their minds so they can handle all this!"

"Rightly so, or I wouldn't have approved the mission yesterday," Manning said. "The reason I did this in the first place was our biggest fear. And that fear, as we learned, *could* become a reality if we can't stop the terrorist army from infiltrating the Decagon system, activating an untraceable wormhole network, and spacefolding out of the solar system."

"That's right," Jenkens said. "Last week's briefing with General Rand and our other high ranking officers showed an increased threat to the Decagon. We successfully warded off two attacks on the accelerator facility, but they believed those attacks were like minuscule scratches, like the enemy's testing our resources and numbers."

"That accelerator is scheduled to activate the Neltan/Earth wormhole in under two hours!" Manning said, noticing on a wall zone that the Decagon system appeared shield protected and troop fortified. It was a tungsten-based, giant accelerator—half the radius of the moon—with a robot crew, a military, scientists, and technicians. As a macrocosm comprised of micro-solenoids, neodymium magnets, capacitors, and aluminum busbars, the Decagon was powered by fission-fusion energy, magnetic energy, and dark matter from planetary winds and celestial pressures interacting with space—the same powers needed to stabilize the gravitational wormhole forces from an incoming spacefold location. The Decagon appeared safe and secure.

But he knew that condition could change any second. Feeling anger rage through his breath, he said: "But I'm planning a surprise that I'm sure will work to kill the enemy before they can make it half way to the Decagon." He showed Jenkens the schematics of the covert mission. "Brent Gorham, aka Abram el Shaleki, should be able to communicate covertly with us to transmit what this lunar cell and all the terrorists are plotting. If he streams the coded phrase, *Galaxy Runner*, as a cypher, that'll give us the info we need so that Bartlet can blast them before this cell can launch from the moon and join their comrades. We'll also know their exact location as they travel toward the Decagon. That's what we're waiting for now...not only positions, but also intelligence on their future plans."

"Wow—clone spies in operation—*interesting*," Jenkens said. "Does General Rand know that Brent Gorham and his teammate are clones?"

"No," Manning replied, "just you, me, and the Clone Techs on *Sagan* who did the cloning. But I better fix that!" He called Terra over to him and asked her to inform The General about the Black Ops mission. "Also tell him that when he receives

Battlefield Matrix

the *Galaxy Runner* message from Brent Gorham, aka Abram el Shaleki, that's also Captain Bartlet's signal to launch a full-scale attack on their moon base. Imbed the entire operation with a *For Your Eyes Only* prefix."

After Terra complied, Jenkens asked: "What about the clones? They'll be there too!"

Manning sighed, extinguishing the clones' identities. "Ya wanna win this war or not?"

"Yes—but give them—"

"It's the element of surprise and our edge," he interrupted. "The terrorists will never believe we have this type of clone technology and cognition/modification capability. And from our cushy treatment of them in the past, they'll never believe we'd hurt one of our own. *That's* why I believe they'll buy the clones' identities and stories. When Bartlet attacks, the two might have a way off the moon if they can access their craft. But really, this is a suicide mission."

"Our first one ever!" Jenkens said, his brow wrinkles creasing in obvious pain. "Too bad it has to come to this...stooping to their gruesome level. I guess to win this war, as you're suggesting, we must resort treating life as if *all* life is expendable."

Manning leaned across the table towards him. "The clones have that downed craft they can use to launch off the moon, *if* they can. If not, they die. The Clone Techs on *Sagan* imprinted their minds with images of peace at the point they realize they will die. They also have poisonous agents they could breathe or swallow."

"Still, I wouldn't a death like that for my clone," Jenkens said softly. "But maybe it might be a comforting gesture if Terra would appear to them right before they die and tell them that in that very spot, at some point in the future, we'll commemorate them with a statue, commending them for turning around World War III."

"Good idea...do that, Terra," he said, and then he added, intentionally changing the somber conversation: "I can show you the Clone Facility after Final Communication and *The*

Executive Pinning Ceremony holocast to The World. Come with me to *Sagan* and check it out. I really need your support of this technology that, as you said, is going to come out sooner or later anyway if we can't implement it here on Earth, after *Sagan* launches."

"*Hmmm…*" Jenkens stood up and began pacing the floor. "Yes, count me in." He seemed fixated on the show of the craft carrying the spy clones that suddenly faded into static when the satellite went into blackout beyond the far side of the moon.

Manning felt shocked. After all the heated arguing and debating, Jenkens had changed his mind so suddenly. This was the first time he had ever seen him so readily amenable!

Once jumping into Jenkens' holosite to get a good read on the competition, he noticed "young Jenkens" describe himself: "I am the Master of Moore's Law for Technical Innovation. I can predict which technology will evolve to the next level." Jenkens also had his bodily characteristics matrix-shopped with the old, 1960s Jackie Gleason persona, obviously trying to bolster his popularity in the polls by portraying himself as humorous, light-hearted, gregarious, and easy going, and a team player. Now Jenkens appeared a bit gray-haired, balding, droopy eyed, and as energetic as a snail—in person, way different. After coughing, trying not to laugh, Manning said: "Good, great, Steve. We'll board *Sagan* on a quick trajectory to Station I, where I maintain a special entrance to *Sagan*. It's a short trip there. After I give you a tour the temporary Clone Facility on Level-5, we'll head back to Earth." He checked the time bar. "We shouldn't be more than two hours."

"Yes but—"

"Or we can sleep there overnight in The Regency's new quarters. They're finished! You can call it a first-night trial in your future living space." Manning switched on *Sagan*'s holosite world that was prepared to show scenes of the astrocity for The World to view or experience. "People will eat up the footage, Steve. Virtual tours should secure donations to make construction go faster."

Battlefield Matrix

"*Hmm*, yeah, fine I guess. If my wife'll let me. She said she might attend Final Communication. I'll ask her," Jenkens said.

Manning closed *Sagan*'s holosite address, flicked on his Beethoven wrist-device avatar, and streamed the appointment to the astrocity's construction site on Space Station I. On a wall-zone streaming the image of the station, his private docking bay flashed green. "Done. They're expecting us."

Workers were still welding sections and moving sheets of nanofabric and nanomaterials throughout the giant astrocity. The materials were bending, folding, and modifying like volume adjusters synchronizing with *Sagan*'s matrix and the astrocity's specs. Some crews were suited up for intense work in space to make further repairs after the terrorist attack. "I'll also give you a quick tour of the bottom-most level, Steve: Level-10. After we board *Sagan* for good, I'll move the Clone Facility out of Level-5 down to there. Level-10 is the most exciting place! It's that football-sized facility I showed you that'll contain all the advanced security measures, everything from the newest Spy Ware, Scan Ware—"

"The clone technology might help me personally, Thornton." Jenkens' face reddened and his hands began to shake. He sat back down in his chair. He looked stiff with worry.

"How do you mean?" Sitting down, Manning faced him.

An expression of loss swept across Jenkens' face. "I should have mentioned this before, *ahem*, but I didn't." He appeared to be swallowing down tears.

"What the hell's wrong?"

"I was all caught up in the legalities and ethics surrounding cloning, *and* the fear of being ousted should we even talk about it," Jenkens said, softly.

"What's wrong?" he asked sternly. "Out with it."

"My wife's just been diagnosed with stage 4 cancer." He squirmed.

"Oh—sorry." Manning realized why Jenkens had changed his stance on cloning so quickly. Obviously, when he saw the biology fully operational and apparently successful, he saw how cloning could benefit him.

Jenkens poured a shot of coffee from the cart and chugged it. "Myra's doctors say that immunotherapy, gene therapy or Organ Growth and Transplant won't cure it 'cause *it's* metastasized beyond intervention." He said 'it' like a rancid pill melting on his tongue. "If I see that your clones can sustain themselves for long periods of time—" He sat up excitedly. "Then I can sneak her onboard *Sagan* and you can clone her…right?"

"Well…" Manning leaned back. "*Hmm.*"

"*You'll* make her all right…right, Thornton. Upstream her mind…I mean, quantum-vault her consciousness into the matrix, clone her, and then downstream *her* back into *her*?"

Manning sat at attention. "It sounds like we're making somewhat of an exchange—a deal, right Steve?"

"Exchange?"

"I mean, we *are* talking about doing something that technically is illegal."

"Yeah…I guess so," Jenkens whispered, glancing around as if searching for spyware.

"Well," Manning coughed, "you want a healthy wife, and I want a future for the clone technology. With you backing me when I present the technology to The Regency someday, I'm sure they'll approve the technology and we can implement it on *Sagan* with no reproach."

"An equal trade?"

"Yep."

"Then *that's* what I want," Jenkens said, sharply. "I keep quiet and help you promote the technology when you need me to, and you help Myra…clone her when the time comes."

"Yes!" Manning rocked gently in his chair and took another long sip of water.

"Exactly the way Myra is right now?"

"Yep… exact duplication is done in just three days," he said, showing Jenkens the elapsed time on a clone forming in a body pod. "When the new Terra-III matrix fully activates on *Sagan*, we're looking at a day."

Battlefield Matrix

Jenkens sighed and folded his arms across his chest in an obvious attempt to regain emotional ground after surrendering. "If I can keep my wife, *I'm* for cloning."

"Thanks!" Manning called on the clone chambers inside *Sagan*, and zoomed in on one, giant, ceiling-hub processor responsible for quantum-vaulting minds. "I isolated The Matter Stream sample in a dark-matter containment tank and then connected those tanks to the clone pods. The innovative tank system from the Neltans allows us to concentrate our supply of what we have of The Matter Stream until we arrive on Nelta. It's like condensing pure water from salt water. Still, the creation force will only allow us to intensify it so much. The force has a type of failsafe system built into it so that once anyone interferes or tries to duplicate its particle forces the sample of what we're working with begins to decay."

"We can't have that," Jenkens began, "'cause after tonight, there's no more help from Nelta to try to persuade them, again, to give us more. And they'll be angry that we disobeyed our agreement *not* to interfere or manipulate what's left of the sample. We only have enough to propagate and use for the voyage to Nelta."

"Or the Neltans infused the sample with something that lets them know if someone messes with it," Manning said. "We're all too afraid right now to venture further into our research...but we're working on it...working to increase, modify, and find other uses for The Matter Stream. He stood and enlarged a wall zone depicting The Matter Stream continuing to dissipate in space. As approved by the Neltans, over one hundred craft were collecting its remnants. The craft were glowing in the transfer of energy to diffused solid states.

"The Divine's pallet of the universe," Jenkens said, tracing long lines of glowing string energy with his finger as if it was laser pointer. "That Matter Stream is the creation thread that connects all universes to the multiverse. Without it, the Neltans say a universe can't exit 'cause it can't expand without The Matter Stream." He had an expression of angelic awe on his face. "It's the creative force behind all the Regeneration technology...and obviously, your clone technology. It'll energize our synthetic telomeres, and make us young and keep us young for the long journey. But the leftovers we're collecting will run out when we reach Nelta."

"If we had The Matter Stream, as the Neltans have been privileged to have, we could—"

"No way, Thornton!" Jenkens face clouded with harshness. "Don't even *consider* it."

Staring down the glare, Manning felt the silence in the room thicken. "The Neltans haven't told us everything about their Matter Stream, Steve. You *know*, Steve, that the Neltans are keeping valuable applications of that force out of our hands. I think that's criminal!"

"Huh! Even *considering* something like capturing that force is scientifically unachievable, Thornton. Not a *single* earthling has a clue as to how we could even measure that Matter Stream never mind capturing it and storing it for the long journey back to Earth."

"I'd—"

"No, nuh-uh, no way, Thornton. I'm supporting you in *everything*, but—that's just plain nuts even thinking about taking The Matter Stream." Jenkens walked around his chair, turned, and clenched his fists. "Thornton, you have no idea how many times I've wanted to walk outta this room and scream out *the details* of the illicit endeavors you've been engaged in for who knows how long. The World would call you a traitor. The Neltans would call you a thief." He suddenly plopped down in his chair. "I give up. There's no challenging you for sure!" He glanced up at the tiny blue glowing gamma app.

Manning realized that Jenkens needed him to help his wife. "I'm thinking about the possibilities for humanity, Steve, that's all...and for the future of *our* solar system."

"The Matter Stream is theirs though," Jenkens countered. "Like it or not, fair or not, right or wrong...*that* Matter Stream was and is part of Nelta's destiny from the beginning of time in *our* universe. The Neltans have the right to determine the direction of technological advancement for any society with whom they share their Matter Stream. It's *their* decision *who*—in our universe or in another multiverse—gets samples of their Matter Stream, and it's *their* responsibility to ensure that Beings use that sample according to how the Neltans design their agreement with other civilizations. *They* decide how much we get and precisely how we can use it. It's healing our ozone now, and as we travel to Nelta, the remnants of it will help us stay young so that *we*, the people who are part of this pact that we're finalizing with the Neltans tonight, can shake their hands personally upon arriving on their planet, and thank the Neltans for saving Earth." He breathed and sat back down. "That's what *they* did. They saved Earth."

"Saved Earth for how long though?" Manning asked.

"For good we hope!" Jenkens said, his voice sounding suspicious. "Now, you're sounding like the Tech-Nos we despise."

A strong silence settled between them like wax when a burst of shouting suddenly resounded from the Press Room.

Chapter 6

The Centipede

"What's that!" Jenkens asked.

A blaring warning siren activated, and Terra's holographic outline intensified. "Security is at *Stage-1 Alert*, Regent Manning. The White House is under attack."

Manning had raced to his main Security wall zone showing the five sets of double doors leading from the Press Room to the T-section of the corridors swooshing open. Government icons appeared: the arrows and signs meant to illuminate the way outside. He directed the icons and Help Avatars to guide people to several storage rooms and cleaning closets. A small line of processor mounts at the crease of his ceiling began flashing yellow lights—protective lasers that, on command, could activated down the walls and his door, killing an intruder.

"Who's attacking?" he asked Terra as he secured his desk while keeping an eye on Screen-2.

Half-filled at capacity, the Press Room had been getting crowded, and guests and Regents began panicking in the chaos.

Battlefield Matrix

The three-foot tall robotic projectors halted their Set-Up activities, activated their Auto-Emergency Response, and began gliding or stilting into corners. The androgynous robot servers, glowing in their white-and-black uniforms, congregated around their fellow robot greeters like clusters in nougat and then took their trajectory courses towards their designated glow spots along the walls. Virtual flowers in their arrangements collapsed like nighttime, and leaves and branches on artificial trees *crunched* as they folded into stalks. Screaming and shouting reporters and holosite anchors were shoving one another out the room, jamming the flow of traffic, racing through the Helping Avatars and icons like passing through ghosts. Chairs fell, the wood clattering as more guests sprinted towards various exits and locations. Waving a science team to safety, two guards were barking orders into their wrist devices and then toppled over hologram stages as they ran out of the room to answer a Call for Assistance. Four Enforcers took their places, assuring Manning and Jenkens that they were ready to defend them with the newest laser weaponry and prepared to kill anyone whose biometrics were foreign to the matrix. Down the long corridors leading to the main lobby and security kiosks, the walls and ceilings were thickening in liquid stirring sounds. They were really fortifying, preparing to absorb all energy that might strike them.

His Terra advised, "Regent Manning, the best defense and protection is in the Oval Office; hence, return there, Sir."

Jenkens asked: "If we're under a matrix attack, biometric scanners could fail. Oh no! Guards, contact Agent Dirk. Let her know about that while I order engineers on the Research Facility to work on a solution." He dashed into the office and connected to Space Station II. "But from wall-zone 2, Thornton, I don't see any *physical* assault on us," he called, and then he began consulting with two Matrix Techs who appeared on-screen from Station II.

"It's espionage, Steve, or sabotage...tell them that," Manning ordered. "Terra, fortify your matrix with the securityware General Rand copied from *The Spider*. This could be the same type of invasion."

After sending Enforcers and agents icons of two weapons Terra ascertained would best defeat a physical attack, she appeared in front of Manning and stood at the threshold between the Press Room and the Oval Office. This time, her holographic light was bright yellow like a protective line. He realized he shouldn't dare walk through it. She said, "A mechanical spy circumvented security and is using a matrix interface in the walling as cover, Regent Manning."

"So we *are* dealing with espionage!" Manning said. "How could this have happened? Terra, you've *always* detected security breaches, foreign devices, enemy signatures and countered accordingly. What's wrong?"

Terra's eyes brightened to two pools of blue as she pointed at his beehive ceiling hub cycling wildly with its rainbow processor. The indicator on his Smart Bar showed it processing three times its normal speed. It began to look like a liquid blue glow ball.

"What the hell's that!?" He shielded his eyes.

"I have detected a Cloak program that I am fighting to synchronize with, alter, and then expunge, Regent Manning." Terra's image wavered. The invasion was disrupting her matrix.

Outside the White House, he spotted the effects that weren't supposed to ripple outward, but they were: zeppelin lights flickering, and avatar and icon projections flashing. People were shrieking and shouting cuss words as cans and bottles collided in waves. Some people were cheering— obviously believing the interruption was a Final Communication promotional, and they began chanting for more.

Terra added: "I am buffering the Cloak program successfully. My matrix is staving off a global-wide infection."

"Keep it up, Terra, and zap up power from anywhere you can get it if it means stopping a global matrix meltdown!" he said.

As lights outside the White House stabilized, Manning

sighed in relief. "Terra, keep your grid-defense streaming with the energy you amassed from the tropopause shield, but don't subtract from what you need for the Decagon system to send energy into the wormhole."

"Yes, Regent Manning, I am measuring and dispensing energy commensurate to each need of each site. That is the programmed parameter of Energy Storage and Dispersal until you personally and manually alter my parameter of distribution."

Manning felt stupid for doubting her. "Sorry, Terra, go on."

"Has the attack stopped?" Jenkens asked. "Engineers streamed a solution into Security."

Meanwhile, Agent Jane Dirk and several agents had scrambled into the Press Room. Armed with weapons and other hand-held devices, they were scanning the ceiling, the high string of tiny red-flashing wall mounts, the wall projector zones, and all the roboticware statue-like in Stand-By mode.

Jane stopped her analysis and streaming of information and answered a tiny avatar that was hailing her on her wrist device. Calling closed the message, she said: "Sirs, we've discovered that this damn matrix intruder has the capability to infiltrate *all* our mechanics. We're processing a program Station II just streamed to us to fight it. In the meantime, who knows what the enemy can do once they interface with our hardware. We've got to stop this *fast*! Damn Security gridlock...what a hell-of-a-wait to interface hardware!"

"I wanna know if Terra's seven matrix facilities around the globe could still be in jeopardy of crashing," Manning said. "That would be like taking oxygen outta the air!" Feeling the intensity of another type of encroaching battle, he thought of Captain Bartlet and his near-death experience. "Wait—I have an idea." He ran to his center wall zone and brought up Terra-III blueprints and a regulatory code.

"What?" Jenkens asked.

Terra's eyes flashed green and the ceiling processor burst out another rainbow that sent a wave of bright light coursing through the office and adjacent Press Room.

Manning called on the program from *Sagan* that he had dedicated to the evolution of Terra-II to the new Terra-III. "Terra, fortify your processing sites around the globe, including the covert matrix location, now. Expand each grid to self-organize exponentially by two. Do that until you completely evolve." He whispered to Jenkens, "We can't wait for a vote, Steve." Looking at his ceiling hub, he called: "Terra, begin counting down from ten."

As she began the count, Jenkens gasped and put his face close to Manning's cheek. "What are you doing? The World keeps voting down matrix expansion! You could lose—"

"Terra, evolve," he said after Terra said, "Zero."

He stepped back, waiting for a ripple effect.

His Smart Bar displayed her expansion rate. On the Turing Scale of Processing ranging from sixty seconds to Planck Time, Terra-III was two attoseconds processing in her matrix electron stream. Her maximum capabilities and app were actualizing off the Artificial Intelligence Cognitive Scale. He wondered if that meant she'd soon manifest in some wondrous form! All the ceiling hubs began a slow drone, their nano-organic hardware layering to expand twice their normal size. They began pulsing Doppler blue as a new type of energy and capability began surging around the globe. It would take hours for Terra-III to evolve completely, but now, no one could stop *her*.

He felt the magnetic/electric hum mingling in a complex, particle, gravitational energy dance through the hairs on his skin. Static rippled across his face: the intensifying power of Terra quantum reconfiguring. "After people see Terra's evolution save everyone, they'll thank us, Steve. I believed they'll call us heroes. Wait—you'll see."

Standing at the center of the Press Room, Jane Dirk unsheathed her small laser pistol and began shooting as if the event were a the most important assessment of her life. "I can't see the damn thing but something stung me!" As Manning watched from behind the yellow barrier of his office, she fired four more blind shots. They struck several smoking hissing wall zones. Shows and images zapped off, but the tech self-repaired.

"Didja kill it?" Jenkens cried. "I can't see the damn thing either! Where is it?!"

"Spyware this sophisticated defies detection, Steve," Manning said. "It's like a nanobot swimming through blood.

Not answering, but still blasting the room with laser shots, Jane said: "You're right on, Sir. The spyware was photon based when it entered the White House but it morphed. That's how this virtual critter got by us—*fire, fire*—and it's continuing to grow. Already it's escaped the walls four times between here and the security kiosks, bit three agents and like a scorpion, stung two Enforcers. They're all in quarantine and headed for Station II where, hopefully, they can help them. Right now, they're good as dead."

"My God!" Jenkens screamed, running under the evolving Terra hub, obviously expecting shield protection. "This is just what happened to Captain Bartlet yesterday!"

Laser Fire erupted. Jane's flaming-red target site kept whining, then her gun firing, then again auto-seeking the entity. "Security's telling me from the center lobby that it's in here— *fire, fire*. They're actually receiving a visual in the Press Room—*fire*—but my scanner's useless in locating it. Don't interface with Security, Sirs! This spyware has spunk and body heat antennae. If it morphs any larger it could rip out your vocal cords!"

Manning ran to his desk, unlocked his top drawer and took out his pistol. Then he ran back to the transparent yellow barrier in the doorway where Jenkens was pacing back and forth, obviously debating whether to run out and help the agents or remain in the Oval Office under protection. After firing off two shots through the yellow barrier that almost struck two agents but that instead fried a wall zone, he realized that helping them was wasting time; and he closed the door so he and Jenkens could seek out more help and only watch the fight through a crack. "This mechanical spyware has to be nano-organic and virtual. The crew of *The Spider* encountered the same type of camouflage. Damn!"

"That's why it's invisible," Jenkens began. "Look for frequency distortions!" he called out to the agents.

"I wish I could detect an impression of the speedy intruder then I could direct the gamma hub app to fire on it and disintegrate it," Manning said.

As Jane Dirk and her agents fired off another round of laser blasts, the waves that missed reflected off a large mirror, scorching a hologram stage. Jane shouted for several officers to protect the transmission screen. That was paramount! An Elite Enforcer team entered the room, aiming their red sights on the chairs, hologram stages, carts, and serving trays. Now The Best were involved in hunting down the photonic intrusion that was morphing into a real nano-organic hardware of terror. The Press Room darkened as the string of high ceiling processors flashed red emergency lights. They extinguished, and the walls changed into PET scan imagers.

"When we get red on the wall, we know we got it!" shouted Jane. "Keep a sharp lookout all around, everyone. It's here...somewhere." Walking stealthily across the Press Room as her shiny special glasses reflected PET scan frequencies, Jane reached the door to the Oval Office while remaining behind the yellow laser barrier. She peeked inside and said to Manning and Jenkens, "Just stay grounded in there, Sirs." She sprayed the doorframe with a violet repellant developed to disable all nanotechnology. The doorframe began hissing and lightly bubbling. "We'll fix this later, but now, this barrier *should* protect you." After she left, more agents pounced into the Press Room.

"I see it!" an Enforcer cried, his pistol pointing at 12 o'clock. Falling on their knees and bellies, the teams began firing wildly at a small, silver light spinning like a top through the air. A gold cart exploded. The small chandeliers rattled and a few crystals flew off their ornate finials like darts. A Regent who had been hiding under a hologram stage— obviously staying to watch the action—quickly raced out of the room screaming. Making shrill squealing sounds, the small scuttling creature was visible now—and appearing real—biting at the Regent's heels until an agent fired at the crab-like outline, but missed. The tiny creature whipped into the ceiling—a blue light streaking behind it—the creature's contrail.

The Ceiling program activated in Repair-mode, and the multifaceted chandelier crystals sparkled like diamonds. The PET scan imagers were homing in on the invading entity.

A silver, thin, foot-long centipede with glowing eyes appeared high on the wall and began rattling, its glowing yellow pincers clattering in challenging retaliation.

Jane said into her wrist device that was linking with her team: "This organic centipede is searching for flesh. Listen up, all of you. Set your targets on it and on my word, fire."

In a sudden bright orange illumination, the centipede's torso lunged off the smoking, crackling ceiling. It began lunging and clawing at two agents who fired at it and hit it, but the silver snapping menacing centipede absorbed the laser energy. It then dove into the ceiling like a dolphin propelling through water. Jane ordered the team to stop and wait for the creature to reappear. After several moments, its small, almond-shaped eyes materialized out of the PET scan walls and flared green, its clattering noises increasing like fangs sharpening.

Jane ducked and cried into her wrist device: "It's in Upload-mode...communicating with its creator I bet 'cause I'm receiving gaps of connectivity in the com grid indicating an exchange of info. I'm having my gun update and see if that helps. All of you...do the same with your weapons." She tapped open the Voice Trap App so her com grid would soak up her words and photon-buffer the air around her face. "It sure as hell can't hear me now," she whispered to her teams. "Slip around the baseboards using the carpet's tech to help hide you. We'll create an encirclement. Then we kill it with a Parthian shot when we all retreat from those damn pincers and fangs. Don't let *them* pierce ya...no tellin' what augmented disease'll get into your skins. Two of our colleagues it struck are dead. The others are in critical condition. This thing's bad ass!"

She and her team fired at the centipede, and her laser cut off a portion of its rattling whipping tail that dropped to the smoking floor and began twisting and melting. The centipede dove back into the vibrating ceiling in cries of metallic agony. "I think the thing's got a destruct that's attempting to sync with our weapons 'cause my pistol's feeling unusually warm," Jane said, adjusting her wrist device and its connectivity with her weapon and its com grid.

The jangling centipede's head spun around full circle—its glowing blue eyes increasing in intensity. It had spotted the giant IMAX transmission screen. The frame around the screen thickened—its quantum security buffers fighting the centipede's intrusion. The Neltan Advancement Committee had quantum-streamed into the frame the one-and-only Reactive Intrusion Detection and Counter software with matrix interface. That meant the new Terra-III could help, when necessary and safe, so as to not disable Earth's matrix.

"Blast the damn thing now!" Jane screamed through the smoke filled room. Ceiling pixels were sparking, electricity arcing, and Terra's ceiling hubs began countering the onset of fire with extending extinguishers.

More laser-burst shots struck the centipede's flailing body. The shrieking intruder sounded like a mythical beast unleashed as it began twitching and dove out the room into the hallway ceiling. Jane Dirk fired again—hitting the doorframe. The force threw the agent standing underneath it into the wall that bounced him to the floor. "Damn I missed!" she cried. The she called into her wrist device: "It's moving to the southwest exit Fire when you spot or detect it. And evacuate *everyone* from the lobbies, fast." Nearly breathless, she exclaimed: "Damn thing's movin' like light, *whew*. No telling *how* much intel it's collected. Damn."

"Enough for its creator to stop Final Communications?" Jenkens asked her, cracking open the door to the Oval Office.

Battlefield Matrix

"I hope not!"

"From what I saw, you interfered with its transmission of data," Manning said to her and her team. "Good job, people. But I bet that it's just re-enforcing and will be back."

"We'll be ready for it, Sirs, if our teams in the lobbies can't take it out." She held up her scanner. "We have the creature's frequency now, Sirs. There's no way that we can miss destroying the invader." They could hear the centipede screeching and clattering down the corridor. "And, we just added one more foreign signature to our Security grid." She blew into her laser-burst pistol as if gesturing that she had won The West. "That's a great advantage."

Jenkens said: "All good and well, but destroying it won't tell us about who sent it."

"Yes, we need to know his or her identity for sure!" Manning said.

Meanwhile, in the Press Room, the doorframes were automatically reverting to their previous hardwood consistency, the PET scan readers on the walls reverted to processing 3D wall-zone images and scenes, the ceiling hubs stabilized—continuing to process Terra's new evolution—and Enforcers were replacing new Security crystals in the decorative chandeliers.

Terra hissed back on, her image static-filled in adaptation to an obviously perceived new environment. She said: "Regent Manning, the centipede's Cloak app emitted an altered quantum stream that deposited code wherever it touched. That algorithmic code morphed into a goo…a clogging agent in that is beginning to infect the entire Security grid, capable of expanding into the tropopause shield, and then beyond."

"The space stations!" cried Jenkens.

"Inform General Rand and Security on *Sagan*," Manning ordered.

After Jenkens asked her how she was countering the goo intrusion, she answered: "In response, as I am evolving, I am reconfiguring and realigning my entire matrix—all seven quantum-processor sites, including the covert site—to adapt to a new electromagnetic signature. Engineers on Station II have named the new signature, the Electromagnetic Nanotech Imaging Twister. They are now perfecting the grid against future attacks. The new ENIT program will begin to stream in twenty minutes, sixteen seconds."

"Not good, Thornton," Jenkens said, pushing open the door to the Oval Office.

Manning felt a rage boiling that he strained to contain. "God! I'm doing *everything*—everything!—to stop attacks. Nothing's working! What the hell's wrong?" He thought of *Sagan* and wished he were on it. "First, that stolen shield panel...then, that *Tiger* virus on *The Spider*. Now this. Is it all *ever* gonna stop?!" As Terra began to answer him, he added when he gestured for *her* to stop: "God—I wish I could launch the hell outta here!"

Jenkens touched his shoulder. "And trade in another problem? Get used to it...like the old saying goes: If it's not one thing it's another. Now look at who's consoling *who*," he joked.

Manning shoved him off. "Whoever instigated this attack, I want the criminal brought to my office ASAP." Glancing at his rainbow-cycling hub, he knew the culprit would never exit.

Leaning into Manning's ear, Jenkens whispered: "Take it easy, Thornton. Terra's matrix has adapted to fend off sabotage and espionage before, and she will again, especially this evolving version. Yeah, we had a problem. But look around. The robots are cleaning up, and Secret Service and Enforcers are helping them. We're all okay. We'll locate the centipede and I hope snare it, disassemble its code and track down its creator. I just wonder who'd go to such a length and launch such an attack?"

Jane Dirk looked out of breath but adrenalin had energized her. She holstered her pistol and straightened her white cuffs. "We're searching hard, Sirs. The new Terra is tracking the invader's signature, scanning for residuals, and using high-resolution imagers to retrieve any human DNA or fingerprints that might have touched that centipede spyware. Once we acquire evidence, we can generate a profile of the individual who attacked this place. That'll most likely tell us the motive behind the attack as well. We're assuming the transmission screen is the target, but ya never know." After taking a swig of water, she tapped off her cheek sweat onto her arm pads and said. "While other attacks have been happening around the globe that Enforcers have been successfully countering, nothing has been as detrimental and outright covert as this one in here. This attack is quantum-infused and a real photonic entity...definitely entirely new. I suspect it's mission is to thwart Final Communication, and I know how upset that makes you...no, I correct myself, how upset that makes us all!" She coughed, barked more orders to her teams and then gulped down more water.

Remembering that Jane never drew conclusions without substantiating them with data, Manning said: "Yes, that must be, but I'm conflicted about the source of the attack."

"How so?" Jenkens asked.

Again, he remembered the viral poisoning that occurred on *The Spider*. "We just learned that the terrorists have moved off-Earth. That *Tiger of Mysore* quantum strike that almost killed Captain Bartlet proved that. Using all sorts of subliminal images, they've been brainwashing people through their holosites. After they succeed in converting the neophytes, they whisk them off to that subterranean lunar stronghold or to various craft in space. They initiate the recruits by making them prove their loyalty and stealing technology. *That's* what we've learned. Very few terrorists are on Earth now. And never have they been anywhere near D.C."

"Yes, Sir, we agree," Jane said.

"A Tech-No Protester then," Jenkens exclaimed, "that's who's responsible for this."

Agreeing, Manning gestured at the mess in the room and said, "What kind of powerful Tech-No Protester could have accomplished *this* type of advanced espionage?"

Jenkens had a pressing look on his face, and Jane appeared overwhelmed. "Do you think the centipede was able to stream any vital information that could interfere with the Decagon? The transmission screen in here has sophisticated components—"

"Yes—we know, Steve...nano-processors that synchronize with the Decagon," Manning scoffed. He was getting tired, and his thoughts beginning to blur with his words. He realized that others were probably perceiving him as irritable, grumpy and condescending. He didn't mind that from Jenkens, but not Jane Dirk, the Gold Agent he had promoted himself. "Any serious strike to that system will take out the accelerator, I know. Without the proton/electron matter and anti-matter energy it produces, that accelerator can't activate the incoming wormhole from Nelta. The quadrant around it needs to be doubly re-enforced. I've done that, but I'll re-check our military forces." He streamed General the concern for added protection.

Jane Dirk's wrist device flared. Someone was contacting her. After the tiny Security avatar appeared over her device, it said: "Matrix Techs recovered a design stamp that the centipede left on one of its tracks after we struck it. It's dead and gone...fried. We killed it...now celebrate!"

"What's on the stamp?" Manning asked.

The tiny Secret Security caricature turned to him and cheerily replied: "Station II techs discovered the initials, *D. U.*, stamped on a residual track before we fried the invader. Actually, the centipede spyware self-destructed, but—"

"Enough, pleeeaase, off," Jane said, red faced, and her avatar disappeared.

Manning laughed gently and then said: "The initials, *D. U.*, must stand for Duke University, especially since they appear on such a technical invention as that cloaked centipedeware." He ordered Jane to activate the University's HR holosite to upstream a personal message from him to Duke's security team. He said: "This Regent Manning. Spies and saboteurs are hiding somewhere on campus. Somewhere, they've stock piled advanced technology and are using it against us. I'm streaming to you what just occurred inside the Press Room.

Battlefield Matrix

You can see that another type of attack might jeopardize Final Communication. We can't have that. So consider the saboteurs and spies as enemies to our Global Union. Take protective measures. Arm yourselves and fire on anyone you locate who is illegally using technology at the university. I'm sending you Enforcers to assist. They should be arriving at Duke in about twenty minutes, given your distance of two-hundred and twenty miles from D.C. I do want the criminal or criminals captured if possible. Oh—check Duke's Developmental and Experimental Research facility. I worked there, a long time ago. If that centipede spyware originated at Duke, that's the place from where its creator might have developed it—"

"And that location should have the creator's residual biometrics so we can stop him or her," Jane interrupted. She called up her avatar, told it to tone down its perky vivacious program, and then asked it to help her synthesize the event and process strategies for the future.

"Makes sense!" Jenkens said.

"Yep," Manning agreed, and then he closed the connection with Duke. "Several of the scientists, researchers, and professors at Duke have the intelligence and means to have launched that centipedeware. We just lack a motive and who had the opportunity."

"Terra is weeding out everyone affiliated with Duke who uses minimum holosite activity, Sirs," Jane said. Manning noticed her wrist device on Wait-mode as the new Terra-III sifted through Duke's Educational grid.

Terra said: "I show three hundred, ninety-two students and faculty and personnel who only use their holosites for research and communication." After synchronizing with Duke's Security, she added: "I am activating a link between their Security and The White House. I will search all Security feeds for visuals and biometrics at Duke during the time of the attack. Then I will compare those to what the White House Security grid compiled during the attack."

"Yes—*my* agents will probe these things to the death to

find the creator of that attack, Sirs," Jane said. She stood at attention, puffed out her chest proudly and then called, "Everyone, assemble to move out."

Manning suddenly felt violated and vulnerable. The White was The Regency's fortress that he believed was impervious to invasion, especially considering the thick, laser-reinforced windows. "Who...*who* at Duke could manage to be so far under the radar of security and create a device so sophisticated that would fool our security here at the White House?"

He thought of the Reactive Intrusion Detection and Counter (RIDC) technology embedded in the transmission screen's frame. That interacting with more advanced organic hardware, no one would dare infiltrate the space around it without it eating up the individual or virtual attacker. Anyone interested in basic knowledge on the fundamental schematics of the screen would know that by way of the Transparency Law. But that's it. The Neltan Advancement Council had quantum-streamed layers of their unique, one-and-only on Earth, Encantado program right into the RIDC. Processing vis-a-vis through a complex mix of Bosons, other elementary particles and waves; the Encantado nano-organic frame generates a shape shifter to counter any perceived foreign entity and eliminate the threat with Planck time efficiency. The long bar on the bottom of the screen acts like an arcing power of knowledge and protection. A few scientists believe it's god-like! But the Encantado is intelligentware that learns: scans, watches, analyzes, and then synthesizes people, data, and language. It can interface with Terra, which it also assists with global matrix evolutions, updates, or expansions. With every communication from Neltan, the transmission screen updates for future usage. What would happen after tonight's Final Communication, the Neltans told us to prepare for a spectacular show they had planned for humanity.

"Damn—we could use that Encantado capability everywhere to hunt down the criminal!" Manning said. "Damn that the Neltans wouldn't let us mass produce it."

Jane gave a nod of determination and said, "Sirs, I'm gonna

find out who at Duke is responsible for this. When I do, you'll be the *second* people I contact. The first'll be the Enforcer I congratulate for killing the saboteur!" She had a mean look on her face. Quickly, she self-regulated her breathing to its normal state of at-ease. "I know many of us have overcome our need to see blood spill after 2057, Sirs, but if I find out that terrorists launched this attack, my blood's gonna boil with that same ol' anger. I'm gonna wanna see 'em *all* dead. That attacked killed five of my colleagues." Her eyes were glossy pink with tears until she clenched her teeth and caught two new guns her teammates threw to her.

Manning felt the same hate rage through him when he remembered watching that viral *Tiger* morph like an exploding geyser on *The Spider.* He ordered Jane: "Continue to scout for the source of the attack. Be on the lookout for any physical evidence the centipede spy might have left behind. Use protective ware and I want the special scanners from Station II down here now." As Jane called for the support, he thought of the poisonous walls *The Tiger* had organically converted on the astrofighter and used to strike, poison and almost kill Captain Robert Bartlet. "Collect what you can around here, Jane, and keep The Regency updated. And restore the floral arrangements and trees in here...and add some inviting citrus scents." The giant Press Room looked like a tossed, sterile zone with only the wall zones as background. She turned away, unleashed her hand-held scanner and began probing the room. He walked to the center of his office and said, "Terra, put Duke University on a *Stage-1, Emergency Alert.*"

"The *entire* university ya wanna on alert?" Jenkens asked.

"Yep...maybe the alert might smoke out the criminal." After Terra acknowledged the act, he added: "Direct everyone who streams us an inquiry to The Regency's holosite. Trace all contacts to their point of origin, even those incoming from space, and compare them to the biometrics and feeds. Any sophisticated response or anomalous read you detect, stream the concern to Agent Dirk, General Rand, and the Lead Researcher on Station II."

J.P. Osterman

"Yes, Regent Manning," Terra said. Her hologram copied, and the copy disappeared. She told him that was her evolving program at work, and her future method of carrying out all orders. "I will always evidence a visual assurance to benefit all human users."

"Wow...great, Terra," he said, feeling stunned. He then felt small, but protected. "An augmented Terra for everyone." He wondered how the new matrix application would change reality when Terras would begin to manifest to everyone along with their personal avatars.

Jane tossed two new ray pistol prototypes to Secret Service agents and a Sealing stick that looked like a large tube of glue to Manning. She said: "Sir, keep this on you. Should a matrix-based intrusion occur again, even though Terra is evolving and strengthened, apply this sealant to the edges of the door. It'll interface with the nanofibers in the wood, trigger an energy foil and meld the door shut. This entire partition between these rooms will benefit too. We're working on that. Researchers are interfacing with the walls and floors and writing more applications for this room divide. Until then, with the protection in this Sealing stick, no one'll be able to infiltrate the Oval Office, except by blowing up the entire partition. And that'll take minutes, but you have the escape exit that we, uh, *ahem*—"

"Yes, Jane, I know," Manning whispered. He remembered the long secret tunnel he could escape into, but he hadn't accessed it or the L-car system under the Potomac in years.

He stuck the Sealing stick in the pocket of his white shirt. Before she left, he said, "Thanks...and Jane, I forgot, make sure Dr. Holton makes it here safely. Other Regeneration Specialists should be arriving soon as well. Give them all, including all incoming Regents, escorts." He glanced at the time. "We have about fifty-five minutes until 9 p.m. I need Dr. Holton up here within the next *two* minutes. And I have to stress again: We need to make sure this transmission comes off without a hitch...*no* interference! Please!"

"Yes, Regent Manning," Jane said, and then she left.

Battlefield Matrix

He opened up his wrist-device, called in the same order to his tiny avatar, and then streamed the order into the Enforcer holosite. "Done."

After closing the door to his office, he sat down with Jenkens who broke an awkward silence that had been percolating between them. "Thornton, do you ever worry that something—just like what happened—will go very wrong on *Sagan* after we leave Earth?"

"I could detect something was bothering you besides your wife's illness," Manning began. "I assume you're worried about a spacefolding accident occurring between galaxies?"

"Well—now ya just added more!" Jenkens' droopy eyelids appeared electrified. "In spite of all the fail-proof hardware, construction materials, and failsafe technology the Neltans have provided us to build the astrocity, I don't care how exact everything is, nothing's *ever* one-hundred solid, crack proof, matrix quantified and secure. You know that, 'cause that's life." He seemed fidgety anxious. "And what we just experienced in here tells me that anything could go wrong even that the spacefold fission-fusion technology you just mentioned."

Manning recounted to him the details of the *Safety and Security* clause for their future *Friendship Mission* to Nelta. It was part of *The Pact*. If *Sagan* malfunctioned, *The Pact* would void. The Neltans needed human DNA. The astrocity transporting it to Nelta had to be impenetrable, the matrix fully optimized, all the Regeneration technology infallible, and the hull and interior structures interfacing with the matrix to self-repair as needed. He showed him again the long scroll of propulsion technology blueprints that the Neltans had quantum-streamed to them on August 30, 2064. The new engine system would enable *Sagan* to condense a thousand years of Real Time travel into one-hundred years Space-Fold travel. One thousand years would pass for the Neltans and humanity while only one hundred years would pass for the crew on the *Sagan*. That also meant that those on The List, the seventy-five thousand people at the outset of the cosmic voyage, would have to create and maintain a society yet to be formed and run on its own rules, morality and culture—a mini-civilization that would continue to evolve and adapt.

The Regeneration Technology was allaying some of the anxiety people on The List were beginning to manifest just anticipating long voyage. But the one fear concerning The World, because the result would affect the population on Earth, was the cryo-storage vaults on *Sagan*. They contained the precious human DNA that The World had promised to deliver to the Neltans in exchange for The Matter Stream sample that was healing the ozone. The crewmembers themselves couldn't be "The Human Genetic Help" for the Neltans because the Regeneration process *could* elicit effects on those undergoing the medical and quantum-vaulting mind procedure. Thus, *Sagan*'s cargo was becoming more precious, delicate, and irreplaceable. There was no successful back-up plan that didn't call for some type of manual intervention or assistance that a matrix on autopilot to Nelta could handle. No probe or small craft would suffice. In the last dialogue with The Regency that took place on December 18, 2068, members of the Neltan Advancement Council guaranteed The World: "Nothing can go wrong on the spacefold journey to Nelta…no mechanical or matrix failures that we can detect or foresee in the various simulations we have generated. Nothing, except for what might happen among the crew on *Sagan*. Earth's travelers will have to control that, which certainly is not a minor challenge." They asked us, "Correct?"

A Tech-No Protest group hacked into the communication and a woman's voice blared through the Press Room: "When given the opportunity, people take advantage of the situation to satisfy their own desires. What can arise while living in the confines of a ship-city even if it's as big as an island? Evil comes from within. Evil—"

The Encantado program intervened, stopping the hacker.

Manning reminded Jenkens of the icy stares and hard glares they received from Ambassador Shaesar and the Committee. "Remember that, Steve? It took minutes to gather and stream to them more on human philosophy and psychology."

"Thank goodness ya did," Jenkens exclaimed. "Shaesar said that the more they knew about us, the more they could program into the astrocity...right into *Sagan*! That place is starting to become a real artificial intelligence to help us along on the journey."

In an attempt to reassure him further, he said: "See? Nothing to fear. Just remember: we're leaving home and country, Steve.   Leaving everything and everybody— cemeteries and all." Lynn's face and her gravesite popped into his mind. "No touching real dirt for a long time. I can't even imagine right at this moment being forced to say goodbye and part this place even though I constantly say I wanna leave." He bent down and swept his fingers over the carpet. "Except for the various artificial parks, ponds, sand dunes, etcetera that we're building into *Sagan*. And we haven't even decided yet whether we'll return to Earth after we arrive on Nelta." He threw Jenkens a bottle of water and then sat back down behind his desk.

"Well, yeah, we're dealing with lifespan issues, unknown cultural considerations, and a future that no one can predict. If we return, no one we know will be here, only great-great grandchildren or remote relatives."   Jenkens appeared indecisive now about the journey.

Meanwhile, Manning heard the crowds outside the White House cheering. More people were gathering like sardines in the streets in eager anticipation of the Final Communication. "We're building the astrocity according to the specifications the Neltans gave us. We should encounter no difficulties at all *if* we stay on course—on the spacefold path the Neltan engineers will finalize in *Sagan*'s Navigation center tonight. That's part of why this last communication is so critical. A one-layer, cosmic, wormhole map isn't good enough they said. They've been taking extra time to calculate, down to the second, our spacefold course.   That's how intricate each maneuver of the ship has to be.   The fact that they can calculate the minutest space/time intricacies and dark-matter, accumulation sites in galaxies we'll glide through tells us just how advanced beyond us they *really* are. *That* puts me at ease for sure, Steve. It should you too."

Jenkens' chest dropped to a comfortable rise-and-fall motion. "Yeah...I guess you're right. I shouldn't worry. I guess I should also remember that their engineers visually inspected *Sagan* each time we communicated with them. After each, intense virtual tour, they've assured us that *Sagan* is exactly how they constructed all of their astrocraft that are still journeying through the cosmos, periodically sending status signals back to Nelta."

"So *Sagan*—even though it's about as big as Oahu, ten-miles deep, and has rivulets filled with spacefold activators at the bow—should have no trouble making it to the Neltan atmosphere. There, Steve, your worries should be over," he said.

Jenkens sighed and chuckled. "Yeah...as long as we remain on course, we'll be all right...all seventy five thousand of us on The List. I guess I'm just thinking about all the families with kids."

Manning called for Terra to show them a section of *The Pact* they were about to sign in forty-eight minutes. "Here's that *Attack Clause* at the end of *The Pact* that the Tech-Nos have been ranting and raving against. Still, The World approved it. This is the Rosetta Stone version:

Deviating, severing, or veering off course of any portion herein of The Pact between Humanity and the People of Nelta will constitute a violation of our Exchange and result in a future negative consequences for Earth.

"Dangerous consequences!" Jenkens cried. "That's why I'm so damn nervous all the time. What form of retaliation do you think they mean? Any directional change we make to *Sagan* after launching from Earth will trigger an attack on *Sagan* or the people on Earth? We better find out more about this tonight, Thornton. I mean that." He gulped down some water. "Could there be forces and situations we can't control? *That's* what concerns me. Think again about that matrix-based invasion. We need to tell the Neltans about it tonight....show them."

"What specifically?" he asked. "It's too late to alter *The Pact*."

"Sabotage. They need to know it's happening. They know we're not perfect, and they know how we are as humans. The Tech-Nos disapprove of our relationship and the direction our species are heading toward in the future, and the terrorists are just plain wackos!"

"There...so perhaps it's good they have a policy of noninterference," he said.

"God—you don't seem worried about this *Attack Clause* at all!" scoffed Jenkens

"I'm not." His Terra appeared and another materialized alongside Jenkens, startling him. He didn't know what to do or ask her for, so he told her to send various programs and commands to his Jackie Gleason avatar who he'd consult with later. Manning continued: "With me in control on *Sagan*, and the covert hub technology I showed you, we'd govern unopposed. Our voyage there will not be as things are here. We'll be in control and in charge, completely." He pointed to the vote tally on his virtual Smart Bar. It touch-synched with his fingers, and he gestured for it to hover over the center of his desk. With only minutes left before the global polling center closed, he was winning the Executive title. "Furthermore, Steve, if you're worried about some type of Tech-No protest occurring on *Sagan*, don't. Terra is screening for dissidents even monitoring those she's already chosen for The List."

"What about the possibility that people could outsmart Terra's assessments or lose it mentally while we're on the voyage and go berserk—"

"The covert Cerebral Archway hubs, remember?"

Wildly shaking his head no, Jenkens said, "Or some type of mass infection that might incapacitate us all and cause the ship to divert off course—"

"Stem cell treatments will take care of that, and cryogenic stasis, Steve."

J.P. Osterman

"The Matter Stream remnant we're collecting might deteriorate, or deplete, or—"

"Steve—stop!" He reached into his drawer, took out two shot glasses and set his prized bottle of Mortlach 120-year-old scotch on his desk. Slowly, he opened the bottle. "We solve problems one-at-a-time. You're panicking about the future and making yourself a mess...all unnecessarily. I'm sure issues will come up during the hundred-year voyage, but we'll solve them," he said calmly. "Tonight, after we sign *The Pact*, I'll have our new Terra-III generate several simulations on worst-case scenarios that might lead us, or force us, to divert *Sagan* off its spacefold course to Nelta. We did that already with the Neltans, but Terra produced no bad catastrophe. Still, I'll insert this most recent attack and the virtual poisoning that occurred on *The Spider*. When the time comes for us to voice any concerns, as the Neltan Advancement Committee always asks us, I'll ask them to be specific about a possible strike against us should we accidentally...*ac, ci, dent, ally*...here that?—slip out of their pre-programmed, wormhole course on another road to Neltan." He was thinking about The Matter Stream again and securing the creation force for Earth.

Jenkens drooping eyelids shot wide open. "Thornton, you remind me of everything I once read about your father who must gave you that hundred-thousand-dollar bottle to you. You believe you're untouchable, and you have his same intimidating look that scares people into submission or inaction at the best. But nothing has worked to change the mind of a Neltan, ever. We've asked them to be specific before about that *Attack Clause*. That didn't work. They know how to turn our concerns back to how they saved us with their Matter Stream. They've mastered our language and ways of using rhetoric to put us on the spot."

He had brought out his dead father's scotch in anticipation of winning the election, but he decided that now they could use a good drink. "Yes, my dad was the best businessman since Rupert Murdock back in the early 21st century." He laughed. "He taught me everything."

Battlefield Matrix

"Well, yes, but this is 2068...and the new Terra that's evolving will be ushering in The Matrix era, where rules and laws like the ones your father, and mine, taught you and me won't apply." Jenkens replied. "A new kind of Terra just popped up right in front of me and I have no idea what the hell to do, even though I know that her capabilities will open up a wealth of opportunities for me...virtually, emotionally, and ways I can't even imagine." She reappeared, walked around him, and then faded out of his presence when he smiled and thanked her.

"A better day and age, Steve. That's what coming and in store for us on *Sagan*."

Every now-and-then, Jenkens turned a little in his seat and glanced around suspiciously. "Sometimes, I think they have ears everywhere. They're over fifty million light years away from us, but somehow—don't even ask me how 'cause I couldn't even begin to tell ya—they're all around us." He glanced at the rainbow-cycling ceiling hub that altered a bit but returned to its intensifying evolution.

Manning surmised that Jenkens was still afraid of eavesdropping spyware. "We're fine, Steve. Our surveillance would have detected a Neltan spy program if the Neltans had planted one in the matrix. After all, they gave us everything in the blueprints; otherwise, we wouldn't have her. There isn't one thing in Terra-III that could betray us, Steve."

"Really?"

"Yeah! I just know Terra isn't infected with any type of destructive strain, black hole activator, or anything so vicious that it would exterminate humanity."

"*Whew*—I hope you're right. I'm sure you are, but then again, nothing's really one-hundred-percent out in the open." He whispered: "Secrets...everyone...maybe even our quantum Terra has them. Don't' we all."

"Ha!" Manning scoffed. "Terra? No way. We would detect any harmful impulse, rogue image, or shadow projection." He called Terra to appear.

"Yes, Regent Manning?" Terra asked.

J.P. Osterman

Every little detail about Terra's hologram looked like the image photographers had taken of Lynn Altmin standing alongside the experimental fabric that had saved their lives on First Communication Day. This Terra was his Terra…not Jenkens or anyone else's—his. He walked up to her and put his finger on her cheek that looked so human and solid. His finger disappeared as his flesh entered the projection beam. He remembered taking one picture of Lynn. She was smiling as she held up the fabric he had named *Altmin Guard-L*. It was the invention that William Wallum had wrapped up Captain Bartlet and saved his life.

"Nothing ever goes unnoticed that doesn't leave a ripple behind in its place," he said softly into his Terra's face. "Right?" For a moment, he believed he could breathe Lynn.

"Relativity says that Time is a Continuum, but Mass in the Continuum is Displacing Time," his Terra answered. "Ambassador Shaesar displayed the formula as Ulam's Spiral and a closed-loop transfer function."

He stepped back and turned away from her. "Terra, is there anything—any message, program, illusive algorithm, or threat seed embedded in your evolving matrix that could destroy Earth or that the Neltans are using to spy on us?" He felt stricken by sudden numbness as of another encroaching loss of life.

Terra's pupils flashed a burst of yellow. With now faster processing time than the human brain, the evolving matrix had accessed, checked the facts and was streaming the answer through its eight matrix facilities around the globe. "Regent Manning, I have threat detectors—both quantum imagers and reflective imagers—that constantly stream through frequencies, light sources and particle energies. I detect no threat to humanity or Earth from the Neltans as Regent Jenkens is suggesting and is fearful of occurring."

"She thinks I'm scared, ha!" said Jenkens. "This *is* a new interpretive level. And?"

"On *Sagan*, however, I have another matrix under construction. If I receive data and extrapolate a statistically significant threat, I will counter accordingly, as per protocol, either by gamma disarmament, a nano-robotic counter assault, or neutralizing the neural networks of—"

Terra stopped speaking and glanced at Jenkens. "Should I continue, Regent Manning? I am sensing a threat."

"Hey—*I* didn't do anything! Tell 'er!" Jenkens took a stride back and fell into his chair.

Terra stepped sideways, her lower body passing through Manning's desk.

"He's friendly, Terra...you know that, come on," Manning said.

She returned to his side, stabilized, and retreated into the shadows. It was obvious that His Terra was in tune with him and linking with the Smart Bar, the wall zones in the room, and his biometrics to process holistically his every move, breath, and word.

"That's fine, Terra. Clear Regent Jenkens. You can tell him."

"Tell me what?" he gasped, his body shuttering.

After she gave Jenkens a light virtual touch, Manning said to him: "There are things I instructed her before not to reveal to anyone, but this new Terra just coded you, read-you-in."

"I understand...I think," Jenkens sighed, "*whew!*"

Terra then continued her explanation. "When activated inside the archway hubs on *Sagan*, the Cerebral ScanWare can stop the flow of electricity in the brain, until a cognitive restructuring re-starts the stasis shut down."

Jenkens plopped down in his chair. "I'm glad I'm on your *new* good side, Terra."

Glancing at Wall Zone 2 next his desk, Manning noticed agents spraying the Press Room wall zones with the same, special, purple Sealant repellant that Agent Dirk had given him in a tube. The special, 3D panels were removable, interactive, and stackable. They were Verbal-based and could display any global or space-oriented scene or image. Like painters dressed in white caps and suits, the agents were also blasting the corridors everywhere inside and beyond the West Wing, extending their preemptive measures to the outside perimeter. Global Intelligence agents dressed in black and beige business suits were scanning surfaces everywhere in search of residual traces of the centipede spyware.

Manning said: "See, Steve? Nothing. No Neltan death-trigger in Terra, no secret contagion or black hole activator *anywhere.*" After he sat down, he saw the outline of Jenkens' face through the smoky, amber-colored, bottle of liquor. He asked Terra to show him the current count of the daily vote for Executive Regent, and then he poured two glasses of the now priceless scotch. When the count lit up on his Smart Bar, an icon of a ringing bell appeared and rang four times. "Wow— look at the count!" The multi-million tally shone so brightly it hurt his he tired eyes. "It's well over the number to lock in the win! Yes!" He felt victorious.

"It looks like you are the first Executive Regent, Thornton." Jenkens shook his hand, congratulated him, and grabbed his glass of scotch. He had a look of eager anticipation that the drink *should* eliminate his fears.

Manning called up the next number. Jenkens' name appeared. "Well, Steve, it looks like you'll be my second in command and the one to take my place should something happen to me. You're now Second Regulate."

"Great!" As Jenkens' cheeks reddened from the obvious heat of the smooth liquor, he slammed down the glass of half-filled scotch. "I can't believe it...but that's great. Second Regulate...I can deal with that."

Manning rock a little in his chair as the scotch smoothed over all the raw sore spots on the back of his throat. "Finally...it's over...no more worrying over daily votes and whether we'll be in or out of office." He breathed deeply and drank some more. "This is everything I wanted...the position I've fought for since Day One when people posted the position."

"Now ya got it," Jenkens said. "And *I'm* Second Regulate."

"I guess you're not gonna stop that echo, huh?" he asked. They both laughed, and Manning lifted his glass and let it rock

Battlefield Matrix

between his fingers. "A toast, to us. We won." As he drank more of his scotch, he glanced at the wall zone showing *Sagan*'s construction on Station I. Sparks were flying and metal sheets merging. The astrocity with its diamond-shaped top and triple-bulged bottom was seventy-two percent complete. The builders were fusing the bow seams at the mid-ship level. Connecting the center levels to the magnetic-gravitational field flooring would take months of layering dark-matter tubing, anti-matter containers, and graviton collection coils with particle accelerators joining the fission-fusion engines that would be powering, propelling and gliding *Sagan* through the wormhole course to Nelta. They were located in the sterns of Level-4 and Level-7. The astrocity still had months before completion.

The excitement to leave burned in him like the liquor-induced peace. He almost said, "Let's get the hell outta here and leave right now!" Too early. Shaesar and the Neltans were on their way in the form of images quantum-streaming to Earth for *The Pact* signing.

Chapter 7

The Photonic Strike

Two loud bangs cracked through the air outside the White House.

"What the hell's that!" he shouted, running to the windows.

Black-and-white Enforcer craft had activated heat-seeking scanners in search of weapons. The crafts' broad, white beacons were scouring heads in the crowd that looked like a field of cabbage crowns. Clouds parted, and the moonlight illuminated a state of turmoil. People were shrieking—diving into dome-tents and dashing for the subways. A few brave people began launching avatars in an obvious strategy of aiding Enforcers.

Her pupils flashing slight pulses of green, Terra began following his every step. "I am activating a city-wide, *Stage-1, Emergency Alert*, Regent Manning. The tropopause shield is configuring to Protective-mode as a defense system. The White House *is* under attack. The attacker is circumventing Security. I am countering."

The image of that silver, foot-long centipede flashed

through his mind. "The enemy downloaded what it needed to breach you, Terra, and is trying to use *you* against us." After Terra gave her assessment of the ten percent, data extraction the spyware had managed to copy from the White House Tech and Com grid, he asked her, "Have you determined whether the attack is terrorist related or protester related?" He felt his celebration decay into the taste of stale whiskey on his tongue. "Is General Rand seeing this? With agents here on the ground, Stealth Force must be our defense in the air."

"General Rand was alerted through the Space Station III's Recon grid," Terra replied. "He launched two craft to investigate and counter the attack, and he is waiting for surveillance to stream him the targets. He will fire the appropriate weapon after I analyze the enemy, determine the enemy's arsenal, and calculate the enemy's firepower. In ten minutes, if he does not receive The Regency's order to De-Escalate, as protocol dictates, he will activate the EMP pulse into the White House. As you can hear, I am announcing the impending EMP to the public, ordering people to retreat behind the transparent, blue dome around the White House. 'Only beyond the Blue Sphere will your hardware be protected against the EMP.' I am repeating that directive and streaming it to *all* holosites." She showed him on several wall zones the perimeter of the EMP target area and the crowd's flight responses.

"Good work." He then spotted Jenkens whose chest was heaving in apparent terror. He had to give him something to do, again, to calm him down. "With the exception of Security Screens 2 and 3, I need you to make sure every wall-zone screen system in my office powers down, Steve. A hard shut-down is what we need to do 'cause any other action is useless against a matrix intrusion. Terra, allow the manual overrides." Terra began walking along the wall, and the towering wall zones hummed and droned as all the shows and images from around the world and space extinguished and the zones shut down. Jenkens was alongside her, watching her perform her obvious new ability. Manning said: "Steve, this is *awful*—but also a good thing. We've smoked out the creator of that spyware and now we can nab the criminal…maybe take out the entire Tech-No movement."

"Right…maybe," Jenkens said, double checking Terra's speedy actions. He activated his wrist avatar and streamed a *Request for Location* to The Regency's holosite. The Regents who were in the building during the attack streamed their avatars back to him. Agents had conducted them to the subterranean bunkers. They were safe.

A few more shots pinged through the air, hitting a window, but the protective film absorbed the bullets.

"Gunfire?" Manning gasped. "I thought people had disposed of their firearms long ago."

"We did!" Jenkens confirmed the disposal number for the last seven years since *Global Law II* had been in effect. "Any indication where the shots are coming from?"

"I am searching the perimeter, Regent Jenkens," said Terra. "That burst came from 402.336 meters."

"A sniper!" Manning said.

"No—snipers," Jenkens emphasized. "They're providing cover for the attack…even in this darkness. They're good, whoever they are.

Sirens were blaring. Crowds of screaming people were scurrying through the streets and around the monuments like terrified prey fending off lions. Advertising avatars and promotional zeppelins began a radical liftoff—craft floodlights rounding into the crowd, providing safe illumination. The *Laser Light Spectacular* that holosite networks had scheduled to activate at the forty-minute countdown to Final Transmission stopped. Enforcer craft and the two giant stealth craft from station III began hovering in the air. Stealth Force personnel began rappelling out of the craft into dots-and-dashes of scampering people as megaphones resounded the words: "Move back! Go to designated safe havens! Follow the icons!" Tall military avatars had appeared, directing and guiding people to places of refuge. Clad in virtual helmets and thick vests, Enforcer teams dashed into the White House as the gates clanking shut on Lock Down-mode. Laser trip-systems inside the building activated, sealing the door jams and hinges. Inside the White House, old-fashioned fluorescent lights zapped on. Another round of bullets was approaching the Oval Office, but Enforcers fired laser shots that vaporized them just prior to striking the window.

Flinching, Manning heard Jane Dirk shout an order for agents to guard the long corridor converging from the lobbies to the Press Room, the stairways, the elevators, and the roof. Several agents already had their boots on the roof. With special lenses and scanners, they were searching for snipers and collaborating with Stealth Force craft to scour the monuments surrounding buildings.

Agent Jane Dirk contacted Manning on Security Zone 1 in his office. "Sirs, I have teams all along the foundation, especially under the windows. Two teams are on the roof, locked-n-loaded, prepared to fire. I'm in the Main Lobby, fortifying *all* ten security kiosks at *all* points of entry. That's where Terra can scan and monitor everyone, including all of us, just in case this attack might be part of an inside job, although Terra's told us that statistically speaking, that's highly improbable. I hate doubting one of my own."

After her hologram faded off screen, Manning said, "We gotta get outta here!" He opened the door, stepped through the yellow threshold, and ran into the Press Room. The air was different—the smell ionized with a touch of coolness, the citrus scent obviously extracted, the virtual flowers wilting.

"Thornton—get back!" Jenkens shouted.

Now the seventy-yard, rectangular Press Room was like a deserted zone. Except for rows of high-back red chairs, one long line of nine, glowing, waist-high hologram stages in front of the IMAX transmission screen, and multitudinous robots settling in corners and in designated glow zones; the Press Room was void of all the people who had assembled in preparation for Final Communication. All the noises remaining were like confusing mosaics from surround-sound wall zones blaring static and white noise images and shows.

Agents barking orders and Enforcers locking-and-loading weapons were like muffled countermeasures of a gangster war.

"I got a feeling something terrible's about to happen," Manning said as Terra copied and another hologram of her appeared alongside him. "What's this?" he asked her double.

"My fortification of the matrix, Regent Manning," both Terras replied.

After Jenkens called out that he had a Terra on both sides of him as well, Manning said to the copy, "What are you learning about the breach in Security and the attacker?"

She walked to the largest double door at the center of the room and grew tall. Like a glowing angel, she folded her arms across her chest in obvious Guard-mode.

"This is a *new* capability in her evolution," he shouted to Jenkens. "The attack has to stop now with *this* type of fortification. She must be harnessing special radioactivity the tropopause shield is streaming into all her matrix facilities."

"I show several points of security slippage, Regent Manning," his Terra said. "The signature of the centipedeware and this attack are identical. The creator of the spyware has located you."

"Me? The attacker's after me?" He felt dumbfounded. "Why?"

"Maybe because you won the Executive election," Jenkens replied, "and obviously, someone wants to stop Final Communication. Given the short time left before the IMAX screen activates and the Neltan/Earth wormhole opens, it may be possible for the attacker to succeed."

"Terra, find a way to stop an intrusion into this room!" Manning said.

On the Hologram Stage-4 Left in front of the far right double-door, Terra activated scenes of the hallway, corridors, and lobbies leading to all the security kiosks. Guests were stampeding through the scanning kiosks to leave and Enforcers were dispensing them like shovels out the grand entryways. A few impatient reporters and image technicians who had been setting up robotic media equipment in the Press

Battlefield Matrix

Room were still waiting for elevators, at times pounding and shouting into the Floor Number pad. Those sets of elevators lead to the bunkers below the White House where The Regents, some scientists, and guests were in hiding. He ordered Terra to generate a False Screen at the end of that hallway to give the illusion of a solid wall after the last people entered the elevators. At every archway kiosk leading to the outside, lines of Terra holograms were flashing their green eyes—signals proclaiming the exiting individuals as nonthreatening.

Seeing each person spiking the *Green-Go* under the archways and the Terras clearing them, Manning said to his Terra: "Your evolution to Version III is working, but this place is still under attack. Something's not right. Isn't there someone specific you can detect?"

Terra's eyes glowed bright brown and then she answered: "The Imaging Twister that programmers input is not locating the new intrusion. The attacker is entering in experimental-field matrix territory—hiding in algorithms—thus overriding the archway security kiosks."

"An experiment outwitting *you*?" Manning ran to the wall and peered wildly into a small scene showing on Security Zone 2. "This is it?" Accommodating his visual field, she expanded the show to two screens in length and five in width. "Are we looking for an equation, animal or object? Another matrix virus or virtual engine like that centipede?" He felt restless and helpless.

Terra stepped toward one set of double doors that was vibrating.

"What the hell's that?" cried Jenkens.

"No experiment!" he shouted. "Terra?"

"I am detecting an unknown genetic code at the main security kiosk."

The wood on the set of double doors began expanding and hissing.

"Unknown," she said and repeated.

Jenkens' face shone a twisting look of disbelief. "I don't

get this attack! She's saying, 'Unknown.' It's not matrix, pixel, or outmoded code…and the attacker's not a person—*ha*! But the criminal—criminal!—*is* managing to penetrate our *best* defenses and interface with our all our nano-infrastructures—"

"Thanks to that centipedeware that musta hacked Security and skimmed most of the data—damn!" Manning enlarged Security Zone 1, comprising a fourth of his wall space in the Oval Office. It was the most secure, private, virtual theater system with Live Stream interface with all five space stations—and linking with Agent Jane Dirk's communications grid. He told two scientists on Research Station II: "See if you can make sense of the conundrum Terra's streaming to you. I need your Bio-Cellular experts to corroborate with Nano-Engineers to identify this attacker 'cause Terra's is detecting foreign DNA *and* nano-robotics. Please—work on your end for a solution. Go!"

After he closed the connection, he and Jenkens ran into the Press Room to watch the invasion from a stage-left hologram platform. He was getting tired of racing the fifty-yards back-and-forth between the hologram stages and his office, but he didn't want to interface the two rooms yet. Matrix technology in his Oval Office was the best, and could prove deadly if the attacker had it. He said to Terra, "Create a stable buffer so you can link these places safely." As she complied, all he could was wait and helplessly watch, hoping their forces and the evolving matrix could defeat the attacker. "Damn—we thought the White House impenetrable!"

"We were wrong," Jenkens said, his head bending as he sighed.

Beyond the doors of the Press Room, Enforcers were firing laser shots at the walls down the hallway in a full-frontal assault. Several wall-mount processors were bubbling and hissing, indicating a destructive entity was eating into the building that the Self-Repair materials couldn't counter. The Enforcers retreated. At one large kiosk, guards ran behind a barricade and began defending the grand archway with laser firepower.

Battlefield Matrix

Their yellow-orange strikes reflected off three, transparent, oval, cylinders.

"The attackers are camouflaged!" the guards screamed. "We need a shield wall!" They flanked inward and began another laser-siege on the invisible enemy.

"We need more! Terra, prepare to fire from the kiosk," shouted Agent Jane Dirk. She had received a *Safe to Fire* directive from Terra who streamed her empty biometrics indicating that people had dispersed from that area. "Open fire now!"

The kiosk archway rod began cycling to fire lasers but then revved out of control and exploded in a yellow burst akin to a visual solar prominence. Ceiling extinguishers descended, spraying water that evaporated into pillows of smoke and mist.

As Enforcers and agents began bombarding the air with lines of green and orange laser energy, Jane was inhaling deep bites of oxygen in the downpour. She looked baffled and worn. When more shots fired in her direction, her team threw her a shiny gold shield, and she concealed herself behind it while returning laser strikes at the attackers. "I've got this pistol on Automated Return but I'm not seein' body parts that I *should* be hitting!" As her team lined up alongside her at the T leading to the Press Room corridor, she called out as they fire off more laser strikes: "I can't tell if I'm hitting the attackers or not!" Her team shouted surrender directives at several wavering spots that looked camouflaged to the wall. Their firepower was useless in breaching the enemy's smokescreen. "We know we gotta protect this hallway or the attackers'll access it and head toward the Press Room!" Her gold shield was denting and crimping. She turned to the ceiling hub and shouted: "Regent Manning, the attackers have programmed their bullets with a Modifier that's deflecting *our* firepower back at us! Our shields are—are—"

She fell to the floor. A laser strike hit her shoulder vest that began smoking. "Withdraw!" She waved everyone to the northwest section. "Retreat—but keep firing!"

Manning shouted to the tall angelic Terra standing

preemptively in front of one of his double doors: "Help her!"
She disappeared into the wood. The wood made slurping
sounds, the same sounds he heard coming from the gray,
goopy, bubbling walls at the T in the center lobby.

"She obeyed but wasn't prepared, Thornton," Jenkens said,
showing him red stats blaring on his wrist device.

"Don't tell me we've got a backlash coming!" Manning
gasped. The upper doorframes of the Press Room began
gurgling with a sudden intensity that had obviously eaten up
the angelic Terra alive. She managed to pulse back to them her
white smoking outline. "Whatever energy the matrix is using
to counter the attack, the attacker is harnessing to get to us,"
he added. "I can see that the wall system evolved into a type
of circulatory system. It's pumping matrix power to counter
the attack." He stood staring at the angelic Terra outline that
the wall repaired but left with a white scar of her body. He
told his Terra, "Never get rid of the Terra that tried, ya hear,
Terra? I want everyone to see your improvement, after we win
here today."

Jenkens punched a chair and then kicked it over. "This is
worse than just a physical attack. It took *her* out! She looked
like she had the power of an archangel. This attack is an
attempt to steal our Terra-III. Right?"

"Whatever their purpose is...it's in here...but over my
dead body." He remembered his covert hub weapon. "Terra,
keep by me and away from all the doors." As she appeared in
the center of the room, he said: "Reroute the gamma-burst app
in my office to that corridor to help Agent Dirk. Make damn
sure you protect her!"

"Rerouting—"

The chandelier crystals flashed off as the ceiling processors
cycled a flare of rainbows.

"I am encountering a barrier, Regent Manning." Terra
tapped one of the rainbow-cycling hubs, but the bottom tip
melted and dropped to the floor like honey. The other six
droned loudly, picking up the slack. A meltdown was
impossible, but a gap in the quantum stream was occurring.

Battlefield Matrix

That lapse would surely slow down processing time, Terra-III's evolution, and, ultimately, Final Communication.

When those dark facts entered his mind, he felt sick. "Forget every law that requires a global vote, Terra. Get that gamma burst current down to Jane and disintegrate the attackers!"

After a slight waver in her processing power, again, Terra said: "The foreign nano-robotics are countering the flow of frequency and photonic energy, creating matrix slippage."

"Reverse polarity in that portion of your matrix then, Terra. Or bypass a security grid—*ten* grids if you have to," he shouted.

Jenkens interrupted. "Scientists on Station II are sending us a wall zone message." They dashed to the Oval Office to Zone 1 and retrieved it. Working with General Rand, they had wielded tropopause shield power to launch a special EMP with a cypher antidote for the matrix.

"We're working on ID'ing the attackers, Sirs. In the meantime, this is the only solution we have that might stop them and save Final Communication," said a Project Manager.

At the count of five, he and Jenkens dropped to the floor as the EMP struck the White House, shutting down the electricity. They were in the dark. Until his Terra appeared, glowing yellow in her projection ceiling light.

Far down the hall, he heard Enforcer fire, then staccato moaning sounds. An Enforcer screamed: "I'm hit! We've got casualties!" Then he cried out a piercing death pain. There were the distant sounds of retaliatory boots, more shots fired, and then groaning and thudding—bodies hitting the floor. The camouflaged attackers appeared to be winning, and gaining ground towards the Press Room.

Manning opened his avatar on his wrist device and said to General Rand: "The EMP shut down this grid but the enemy used the down time to strengthen. Nothing hurt 'em!"

General Rand said: "We must shut down communications in the Press Room but remain on Observe-mode with Zone 1 in the Oval Office. I'll get back to you when we can stabilize

J.P. Osterman

an impenetrable buffer and activate a secure verbal-and-visual interface." He was gone.

As the lights flickered on, Manning spotted a residual outline on Hologram Stage-1 Left. "Jenkens—look! Is that a person? A robot of some type?"

Walking slowly to the stage, Jenkens touched the image and a hologram of a tall hunching figure appeared. "It's down the hall! Sleeking right towards us like a Frankenstein. What the hell...it's like deformed—*urgh*! He hailed his tiny Jackie Gleason avatar and had it copy the last flicker of the hunching outline before it completely extinguished off-stage. "Get this to Station II...re-routing it from my grid." He told Manning, "It's after you, not me, so maybe my com grid's not hacked. He said to his avatar, "This might help them and General Rand ID the attackers and help us defeat them." After his avatar nodded in compliance, its image melted. "The damn intruder just got me!" He began an assault to fix it.

Manning could hear Enforcers again pummel the encroaching attacker. When he heard men and women shrieking in pain and Jane Dirk ordering agents to retreat, he realized the attacker was now killing troops like fly spray downing insects. There had to be more than one villainous criminal in the hallway.

"I believe the attackers are using oxygen to cloak, interface with our walls and deflect our laser strikes," Jenkens said, streaming his speculation when his grid activated.

"We have to secure a backup location for Final Communication now, Terra." Manning felt his breath hot in his throat, the heat condensing to water on his forehead. "We must find another secure location to ensure that the event goes off as planned. It's vital...necessary! Nine o'clock is coming up fast, Steve. If the Neltan/Earth wormhole destabilizes in space because the transmission screen in here can't stabilize the current between it and here, the back flow of energy could pass through the shield and harm Earth."

"You're right, Thornton! I forgot about that!"

He had to do something fast. "Terra—link directly with

118

Battlefield Matrix

General Rand and send the last two minutes worth of what I just said to him. Streaming dialogue in bits-and-pieces is the way we can pull off communicating without the attacker realizing what we're doing." As his Terra complied and Jenkens intermittent dialogue with Station II continued, Manning added: "Tell The General to set up a backup screen to accept the wormhole energy from the Decagon system."

"Done, Regent Manning." Terra's hologram was still alongside him, but appeared like white fuzz disrupting a frequency.

A transparent, red web suddenly activated over the ceiling. An alarm blared.

Holding his ringing ears, he called down the volume. "The Press Room is self-arming to fend off the attack," Manning shouted, cowering. He ordered the security net to ascend to its highest level and project on Infrared-mode. The ceiling looked like a red spider web dotted with globules of the rainbow cycling hubs and miniature sparkling chandeliers. "Terra—just make sure that laser doesn't drop down and kill us!" With her alongside him, he ran over to what he believed was an uninfected double door.

"Don't go out there!" Jenkens shouted at him from the Oval Office.

He peeked into the long hallway. At the end, he spotted thin strands of black, glowing, transparent lines springing over the ceiling, eating up the materials. The ceiling looked like that gray bubbling deterioration on the walls that the centipedeware had left in the Press Room. The black strands were diving like dolphins towards them. The devouring network looked smoky evil, consuming each ceiling hub and leaving them processorless and pancake flat. One black strand suddenly whipped off the wall and began slinking toward him faster.

"It looks like the damn thing recognized me! What a heinous force!" He slammed the door and he and Jenkens ordered Terra to seal all the double doors. He knew those actions would be futile, and a whip of that energy from the black photonic invader would be enough to cut a person in half.

Jenkens told him that more craft were launching from Station III and that a biomedical crew on Station II was downstreaming a buffer that might reduce the invader's heat-seekers that were obviously directing them toward the Press Room. He then said: "That black photon monster is gobbling up every link we have to the outside. Soon, it's gonna be in here, and us alone without support. I think we're gonna soon be at its mercy...no, the mercy of its creator."

Manning had Terra unleash two protective curtains out of the transmission screen's special frame. The entire IMAX system was linked to the wall zones on that side of the Press Room, and the two systems interacted, morphing into a giant, towering bass-relief scheme. When the Encantado program recognized Manning's biometrics, it allowed him to touch the silky curtains; and with Jenkens help, they snapped them together. Terra and the Encantado program began displaying a wall-zone illusion, concealing the expansive structure.

"I don't know how well or for how long this illusion will hold up if the attackers detect it," Manning said. Terra said the Encantado algorithm was unhackable and fully able to shape shift to any intrusion and create an antidote or launch a successful attack. He told her to remember her assessment: that the DNA was human, and foreign, a real mutation of some type. When the last bit of material in the screen created a vacuum and burped out the last bit of oxygen, he fell back and nearly toppled over two, waist-high hologram stages.

One stage illuminated and began a counting down of the Black Photon Invader reaching the Press Room: two minutes, fifty seconds.

When he saw that number, he took out the special Sealant stick Jane Dirk gave him, broke it in two, and threw the other half to Jenkens. "Come on, Steve. Help me seal off the entryways." They both raced to each door, pressing the purple nano-putty into each latch. The materials absorbed the sealant that glowed and disappeared as the nano-organics reacted and fortified. "This might buy us time until we, or some genius outside, can find a way to stop that photon entity before it eats up all the walling and lets the attackers in." He felt breathless until the drive to stomp out the Black Photon cloak brought a new energy into his veins. He had to save Final Communication. As of yet, he hadn't heard that General Rand had a backup plan. That meant he might have to stand strong and face that hunching figure he spotted on the hologram stage. Terra had named the attacker, Unknown. Soon, he'd have to fight Unknown, who had some type of profound mangled genetics intermixed with nanobots. He couldn't stop shivering when he realized what Unknown might do to him. All the while, Jenkens kept feeding that fuel-filled fright: "What are they gonna do to us? Whata they want with us! With Terra-III?"

The double-doors resounded in mushing noises as they thickened. The knobs and thresholds increased in size. Gaps in between the door jams and the door frames swooshed shut.

"What's next?" Jenkens sighed in obvious fatigue. "That photon cloak is soon to be behind that door…then, the attackers." Sweat was dripping down his face. He wiped it off, inhaled, and applied the last smidgeon of sealant to a sizzling hinge that glowed golden when it melted into the wood. The metallic finish spread to all the double doors, acting as fortifying agents, thickening and strengthening all interface connections with the matrix.

Manning enlarged the hologram of the Black Photon anomaly on his wrist device. "This cloak looks like spreading poison ivy."

"Damn—some type of attacking Dragon app maybe? *Aaaa!*—another terrorist invention!" Jenkens said.

"No—not terrorists, Steve. We've been disintegrating their hideouts on Earth, thanks to Captain Bartlet's crew discovering them. The terrorists are completely in space." Back in his office, he checked for an update on Security Zone 1. When he saw the Ready display, he knew someone had repaired and reactivity the critical wall zone system programmed to respond to his biometrics. After his Terra informed him that the two rooms could not yet link, he asked Zone 1 to display *The Spider*'s location in space.

The picture divided into two, giving him visuals on two intense battle scenes ensuing around the moon with Captain Bartlet and in several quadrants beyond Mars around the Decagon system. It was apparent that *The Spider* and several other astrofighters were raging heavy skirmishes against a treasure trove of terrorists' craft.

"See this *Galaxy Runner* message that just streamed to The General?" Manning said.

"Yeah?"

"This message means that Captain Bartlet and General Rand determined the terrorists' ultimate mission."

"Yes! A checkmate from those clones you crashed on the moon," Jenkens said.

"Yeah...but obviously not a capture. This *Galaxy Runner* message says they're planning some type of mass exit out of the solar system. It's a fight to the death to stop that."

"These battles could be the last," Jenkens said, glancing back-and-forth at the doors.

"Yep." Then he saw that the flocks of enemy craft were streaking toward the quadrant where the Neltan/Earth wormhole was due to activate. Panicking, he called in his concern to General Rand. "General, as I ordered a while ago, fortify that area before the enemy reaches it! Get a good foothold into that spot and protect that Decagon accelerator."

After the message streamed and then cut off, Jenkens said, "So a Tech-No protester must be orchestrating *this* attack."

When Manning realized the sophistication behind bypassing Terra's fierce firewalls, he groaned. "I believe so...a very intelligent Tech-No group, with a leader who at some time must have had a Black Ops clearance...with state-of-the-art technology and a high-tech facility—"

"That's our Duke University connection that we're still trying to discover," Jenkens said.

The rim around the Stage-4 Left platform began glowing yellow and hummed. Running to it, they saw the stage activate

Battlefield Matrix

a show of the black, photonic network. Several whipping tentacles had tiny sharp claws and were outside the Press Room. They were scraping and piercing the center double door that was countering with hissing energy from the matrix.

"This thing's vicious! Terra, extend the extinguishers and mix the water with nanobot attack agents. Let's see if the water and tech combination stop the attacker's first strike on us."

Terra's eyes flashed green. "Mixing, Regent Manning."

"The Tech-No group must be piggybacking this photonic first-strike on one of the terrorist's abandoned matrix grids before they escaped off-Earth," Manning said.

"Ya think a measly nano-enforced spray is gonna stop that black cloak?" Jenkens asked.

Manning reminded him of *The Tiger of Mysore* virtual invasion as they watched the extinguishers drop from the hallway ceiling, target the black whips of energy, and spray them with thick streams of liquid. The doors crackled and vibrated. "This contains a mixture of what saved Captain Bartlet. Didn't you see what happened?"

"Yes," replied Jenkens, "but do you really believe this Black Photon is a variation of the virtual *Tiger* virus?"

Manning zoomed in on one of the black transparent tentacles that turned one of the extinguishers to mush. After the attack, the black tentacle began striking the doorframe with its morphed talons. The inside of the Press Room door began heating and cracking like old paint.

"*Uh*, it seems to know we're watching it," Jenkens said, backing away from Stage 4, pulling Manning along with him. "The extinguisher failed, or adapted to the cloak that's hiding the attacker. Any more ideas, Thornton?" He opened his arms in a pleading and praying gesture as he gazed at one of the rainbow ceiling processors. "Terra! Help!"

"I am now taking a curative approach, Regent Jenkens." The countdown was at thirty seconds before the first tentacle would penetrate the doorframe.

Feeling frustrated, Manning kicked a chair. "Shouldn't your

cure be working? You're evolving. You should have something new...be receiving biometrics and countering!"

Terra reappeared in front of him and showed him her point on the Turing Scale of Matrix Processing. "My current quantum expansion of the Stellar Map grid application is at .00001, Regent Manning. The open Mysore grid the attacker is utilizing is off-moon, and its morphology, Unknown."

"Off-moon means that *this* open grid the attacker is cloaking with isn't coming from Duke but from outer space!" Manning said.

Terra stopped her Turing Scale status display. "I have initiated a trace on the connection. When I can location that live-streaming communication, I will synchronize with the attacker in the hall. I should procure the attacker's identification. Thus constitutes my half-life curative approach, Sirs. I am using a radioactive isotope with quick decay through the matrix. I will interpose neutrinos into the connection for added tracking and speed." Terra's eyes flashed yellow and red—the sign that the matrix was stretching to its farthest limit to latch on to the attacker's intrusive grid.

A colossal growl echoed through the hallway.

"The cloak sure doesn't like Terra's powerful juice," Jenkens said as they watched the outside scene in the hallway. The air appeared like bad smog, with beams of light like pulsars trying to filter through the murky steam. Those were incoming laser strikes from Enforcers in the center lobby. The Black Photon invader and its camouflaged creator appeared to be intensifying on their firepower. Several, loud electrical sparks rippled across the ceiling. The crackling was arching, lightning streaks.

Terra wavered through the interference. "The attacker bypassed my cure and is diverging. I detect another strategic path."

"Damn—this is like chess!" Jenkens heaved. "This genetic anomaly...Unknown as Terra calls it...is beyond smart."

"Wait—I hear more," Manning said. Watching the hologram of the photonic invader, he noticed black scratches form on the inside of their door. He cringed. "It's like fingernails on a blackboard!" He covered his ears as his stomach sickened. "Terra, decrease the wall tech!" He knew that command would also increase their advantage.

Terra touched the Auditory bar on the Center Stage and the piercing sound faded.

Jenkens was holding his ears. "It's here! Whata we do?" He dashed inside the Oval Office, the place of fortified security. "Where's the escape route? Come on!"

Nodding no, Manning said: "I can't abandon the transmission screen, Steve. I can't."

"You crazy? Get in here! It's camouflaged to the entire wall. When they finally break in, they'll believe we evacuated it. Come on!"

"Terra, activate the partition between here and the Oval Office," he ordered when she appeared next to him.

An Emergency partition seeped down from four ceiling trims, and the wall soaked into the floor and slushed shut. He said to Jenkens and to his avatar that he made appear over his wrist device: "Jane, General Rand, we need help now! Blast through the roof if you must. And send me some type of indication that you have a backup plan for tonight's event in case the attacker destroys *this* transmission screen." As the message sent, he leaned back in fatigue against the center hologram stage. Still, with Terra matrix streaming and slowly evolving, he believed he'd have protection. A brief rush of fresh oxygen streamed in, and he breathed deeply, feeling rejuvenated.

All the lights extinguished. All nine holographic stage lights faded—their ceiling processors whirring and shutting down.

"Get in here, Thornton!" Jenkens shouted. "This is your last chance!" He was about to seal shut the door to the Oval Office. "The security screen in here shows the hunching attacker is right outside the center door. Whatever he, she, or *it* is...it's cloaked...and appears to have hands like it's half-human-half-animal. I can't imagine anyone fighting it and living!"

"No. I'm standing against the attacker...face-to-face," Manning said. "If it's after me, I'm here. Bring it on." He had Terra modify the visual capabilities on all nine the hologram stages to function on his verbal command and biometrics. Only Stage 4 Left he allowed to stream live unobstructed, until he spoke the counter command.

An alarm whirred inside the Oval Office, behind Jenkens. "Oh my God—"

"What!?" Manning began running across the room, calling, "On," into the bases of all nine waist-high hologram stages. Their Smart Bars illuminated, ignited into action and Stage 4 gave him a visual on the attack's location in the hallway. He stood alongside Stage 4, watching the attacker's progress. "Steve—speak up."

"The attacker managed to hack into a wall zone in here, but a gamma burst diverted the intrusion. Still, it disabled the zone that's concealing your emergency exit to the outside. It friggin' fried the entire area! I'm also receiving environmental stats telling us that your roof's heating up too. People are screaming up there!" After Jenkens unclenched the top of a chair, he fell back, his shoulders drooping in obvious defeat. "Now, I'm trapped. My God!"

"Stay in there, Steve! Terra's looking for another way out. But we can't blast it 'cause the attackers'll locate you for sure. Right now, the partition between the rooms is showing an illusion. You're safe." He ran to the window and looked outside. Black ivy was pulsating and extending along the façade of the White House. He dared not tell Jenkens the bad news: the attackers had a team on the outside; their Stealth Force was retreating for fear of accidentally harming civilians; and a forlorn hope was surrounding them.

In the hallway, he could hear a pump of gunfire followed by a man shouting. On Stage 4, he began watching the fight. An Enforcer had managed to eke his way through to the attacker. The man said: "This is your last chance to surrender. Disable your camouflage and surrender."

Feeling relief, Manning called to Jenkens who had the Oval

Battlefield Matrix

Office door opened at a crack: "Jane and her team have broken through and cornered the attackers. Help is here!"

Jane gestured to her troops to form a V-shape pincer maneuver. "Now, fire!" she called. There was a laser barrage, followed by shouts and hysterical cries.

"Fall back!" shrieked Jane.

The hallway floor vibrated with their pounding retreat.

Manning heard wood cracking and splintering on the top frame of the center double doors. Curls of smoke and sharp fumes penetrated the room and localized extinguishers countered the sensory onslaught. Slants of light streamed through the tiny openings.

"The attacker *is* here, Jenkens," he whispered into his wrist device that was showing Jenkens safe inside the Oval Office. "Connect the wall-mount zones by Stage 4 to stream live to General Rand. I can't wait for a sure firewall. Link these rooms now but only on verbal frequency, not visual. It's so low-tech that maybe the attackers won't think we'll use it." He shut off his connection quickly and whispered: "Terra—I need camouflage measures. Ya have any suggestions?"

Chapter 8

Booby Trapped!

A train of bullet fire, followed by zaps of laser firepower, cut through the air.

Capillaries of liquid polymers began pulsing and sloshing through allotropes of carbon tubing in the walls and ceiling. When the liquid tech hit the center double doors, they began self-repairing, attempting to seal all the cracks and deflect the Black Photon—the attacker's first-line of assault.

Manning squatted alongside Hologram Stage-4 Left, but its Smart Bar on the frame was blinding. Terra rotated the platform through its Setting menu, leveling the blaring Smart Bar while concealing the adjustment as a visual glare. Now he could activate a covert verbal connection to Jenkens in the future and he initiated the old code so he could connect Stage 4 with his wrist device. That would take some time. Realizing he only had minutes before the attackers would lose and die or outwit the new Terra and burst into the room, he felt his senses fine tune on high resolution as he took stock of his surroundings. He whispered, "Terra, we're gonna have to modify some of this hardware and generate some snazzy matrix code to hide from the attackers. Let's see what we got." Straight ahead of him were eight other waist-high platforms and their ceiling processors responsible for Live Stream feeds to any connection on Earth or in space. The largest of the nine was Center Stage, positioned yards in front of the transmission screen and capable of sustaining twice as many virtual illuminations. Behind him were two, small deactivated robots with artificial blue eyes on Pause-mode. "Looks like Terra bought me a little more time, Steve. She revved up the Materials Self-Repair and is holding them in the hallway," he said into his wrist device that had Jenkens streaming to him from the office.

"Little is right!" Jenkens had opened up the virtual blueprint of the White House in the center of the Oval Office. He was walking through a transparent world of wood, pipes, wires, and matrix infrastructure. "Before I seal the door, I wanna see if there's a weakness between the two rooms so I can create a hole and sneak you in here when rescuers come."

"I'm glad you're being optimistic," Manning said.

Jenkens was sweeping and enlarging sections of the two rooms that the screen then flashed, *impenetrable*. "The new partition between us appears pretty solid with graphene-ware, ion traps, and silicon. So far, that solution appears bleak, but I'll keep trying."

"You do that!" Manning called, unable to keep his eyes off the vibrating door.

"In the meantime," Jenkens began, "Terra and I are working to locate a place in the partition where she can create an imager so people can see you, gather data and help us. I'm streaming code into the nano-walling. That'll give me the capability to generate a better scene and include an imager."

The electricity in the Press Room flared.

Manning heard people in hallway crying in agony. Covering his ears, he said, "I'm sure those are guards that the attackers, or their Black Photon weapon, are killing. I can't stand this! I have to see what's happening." He had Terra connect Stage 4 to a distant hallway hub. The visual was static-filled but discernible. He began watching the Live Streaming event.

Enforcers were belting the Black Photon entity with laser strikes from a defensive line far down the hallway. The black wall of ivy was whipping smoky stands of energy back at them.

"Get this black crap off me!" a woman screamed. "*Ahhh*! It's—*ahhh!*—my skin!"

Loud sizzling and crackling noises echoed into the Press Room. Then silence.

Intense laser fire erupted between three camouflaged bodies and two lines of Enforcers and guards. The photon beast bellowed out a monstrous squawk then a piercing shriek.

"I think we hit it!" a guard shouted.

Another said, "This thing's a virtual Kraken!"

The Photon entity suddenly scuttled to the ceiling hub as if detecting his presence.

"Off!" Manning said, extinguishing the show. Gasping in fright because the photon-based creature was now directly outside, he spotted Jenkens' shocked, whitewashed face in the doorway of the Oval Office.

He said: "That photon monster killed that poor woman! Ate her alive! *That* voice sounded like Agent Dirk's!"

"No! Can't be!" Manning shouted. He wanted to open up a connection to her to disprove Jenkens' suspicion but dared not. That would jeopardize his location. "Damn-and-*damn*-again!" He felt helpless, as when he learned of Lynn's death. Then hate-induced revenge began seething through him—fortifying his determination for retaliation and retribution. "Terra, is Agent Dirk *really* dead?" He fell sideways—his hipbone burning when he hit the edge of Stage 4. He saw his reflection in the yellow projection light. The ashen look might be the last thing he'd ever see.

Terra's eyes flashed green. "Agent Jane Dirk's body is lying six feet, two inches from the far-east Press Room door. I am not receiving her biometrics."

Manning felt his heart rate skip. "Can you move her out of harm's way? Please!"

Battlefield Matrix

"The floor is conveying her body toward the center lobby," Terra replied.

"At least her team can grab her before the attackers shoot more ceiling-ware into black rain of dying nano-organics," Jenkens shouted. "General Rand's streamed me twenty-five images of decaying corpses as a body count."

Manning kept repeating: "I can't believe this. Dead...Jane! She became an agent right after I took office as Regent. She helped renovate this place."

Terra said, "I am assessing the shot that Agent Dirk used to wound the attacker."

"The attacker's wounded! That's good news but at a horrible price." Steve Jenkens began watching a hazy scene on Zone 1 in the office.

Manning said, "Get the info to Jane's team so they can modify their weapons and take down the criminals." He saw more capillaries flow through the walls' infrastructure. "Can you create a linear conduit with the infrastructure in here and generate a plasma flow to the double doors? How 'bout that type of defense? We have to protect the transmission screen, Terra. The backup might not be ready in time." He began rubbing his side, his hipbone still sore from its hit against Stage 4. "I know that'll take a few minutes, but your new quantum system should have the capability to activate a plasma conduit. I can see that from the metallic capillary transfers you've been initiating. If not that, then one of your matrix upgrades *must* contain a solution." He was struggling to conjure up more answers, but with the escalating sounds of terror rising in the hallway and outside the building, he felt trapped, his mind fogging.

Terra's brown eyes appeared watery. They had a glow of exuding sadness. "Jane Dirk...Jane Bethany Dirk is dead. I will stream her death to The World."

"That's it, Terra?" Jenkens snapped. "That's *all* you're gonna do? That's *all* ya got?"

"Wait, Steve." He looked intently into Terra's tearing eyes and saw a spot of green heterochromia as was once apparent in

Lynn's left eye. No, Terra wasn't Lynn, but gradually, *his* Standard Terra was becoming more entangled in an obvious attempt to identify or copy every bit of Lynn. He wondered: for me?

"No time to wait!" Jenkens shut the Oval Office door.

Kneeling alongside Stage 4, Manning hailed Jenkens whose image began hovering over his wrist device. "Steve, I see something in Terra...a burst of sudden energy."

"I could sure use energy in here!" He still had the virtual blueprint of the White House blaring in the center of the office. With a baffled but determined expression on his face, he was perusing architectural markings and Neltan symbols. "I'm trying to figure out how to connect our two rooms on a shadow grid so the attackers—Unknown, as Terra called one of them—can't glean the connection with you and the space stations. It involves wires, Thornton...plain old-fashioned hardware...the brains for this entire wall scheme that's interlacing with polymers, organics and Terra. I can't cut *any* wires or touch any graphene ware 'cause that will ruin everything. Ouch! Just cut my thumb! I'll be helping the attackers if I cut something else 'cause that will disable the partition, and *us*!" He gestured in helplessness. "But this move is the only way to get us some help and—" He checked his watch. "Save Final Communication."

Manning watched Terra begin to interact with the transmission screen that was radiating a light-blue burn and fizzing static. "Steve, this new Terra-III is advancing to a real intelligence with the Neltan Encantado screen dynamics. I see electron magic happening right in front of me." He jiggled his wrist device so its nano-projectors could image the transformation for Jenkens. "And some type of mysterious impenetrable force..."

After he stopped sawing the wall, Jenkens said: "Looks like Terra's absorbed, from somewhere, a Higgs boson shot from The Matter Stream. Wow! That kinda power can't exist outside a vacuum. You're right, Thornton. Terra is evidencing a new power and it has to be streaming into her matrix from space! There's definitely a new charge in that room. Your Smart Bar is receiving a blue Doppler frequency. Something big is happening with Terra." He pulled a small box out of the wall that sealed like a zipper. "I'm fixing this, but still keep our visual."

Suddenly, a copy of Terra appeared and began stretching toward the ceiling.

Backing away in awe, Manning said, "Go Terra…fight this damn photon energy that killed Jane!" He covered his eyes through the heat. An extinguisher popped out of the ceiling, sprayed water, and then reset. He captured the leftover drops into his cupped hands and splashed his face—sucking the dregs to his dry tongue. "Terminate the assassin, Terra! Eliminate even the ashes." He said to Jenkens, "I hope people on the space stations are seeing this."

"*Whoa*—spaghettification," Jenkens said. "Terra's ceiling processors are generating energy like a singularity in a black hole, transforming space and time into a totally new processor." Then, with a look of terror on his face, he pointed at the center double door. "Take cover! Look—they're hot and smoking! That photon first-wave is breaching the doors!"

As his Terra stood statue-like in Process-mode in front of the gray oozing door, Terra's thin copy continued to stretch and brighten. The beehive ceiling-hubs *thwoooshed*—their rainbow-light processing power filling the room. The ceiling began waving and swooshing like a thin sheet of rubber flapping in a strong wind.

Manning ducked to the floor and dropped his call to Jenkens.

The room rumbled. A small section of the ceiling's infrastructure began radiating an orange light. Nudging between two rigid robots, he peered at the changing ceiling. It was thickening in that spot—bulging into a ten-headed, ferocious, fan-chomping, red-tongue, slithering black snake.

"Terra, Terra!" he whispered, wildly tapping his wrist device as an all-out cry for help. Another set of double doors was on his right, but the photonic creature altering into bodily form by way of the ceiling's nano-organics would surely detect *that* escape maneuver. Then there was Unknown...the snake's creator. He, she, *or* it was somewhere close by and in the hallway. All Manning could hope for was help from Jenkens, his Terra, or agents still firing on the attackers. Obviously, this hideous snake was the morphology of the centipede invader...and Unknown's eyes and ears, scouting the Press Room.

The virtual snake's black and orange body completely solidified into a ten-headed monster. It began rattling and sidewinding on the ceiling—its hisses and slithering undulations echoing through the room. Then, the venomous entity coiled around a rainbow ceiling hub, tightly snuggling it. Its eyes were pulsing red, obvious probes, scanning for biometrics.

He realized that *he* was the snake's prey. It was deadly, most likely akin to what infiltrated *The Spider* and nearly killing Robert Bartlet. Then he remembered that Terra uncovered a rogue, terrorist communications grid. That meant that even though the attack wasn't terrorist related, it had something to do with the Tech-No movement.

"My God! A damn virtual serpent!" It was Jenkens' voice coming from his wrist device. Covertly, he activated the system.

He imagined Jenkens curled up on the floor with his face buried in his arms. He couldn't calm him down as usual. Jenkens was on his own, but at least he had the partition protecting him from the heat-seeking, hissing leviathan. The new partition was functioning as an illusion that Terra had interfaced with the Encantado program in the transmission screen. After recognizing the threat, the partition assessed it and generated the most plausible illusion capable of warding off the threat. Now the wall between the Press Room and Oval Office was displaying a virtual jungle: the location Terra-III assessed as the location the serpent would feel at home in and therefore not attack. Realizing he was crunched down between cold motionless robots and afraid that one hair on his head might fly up and divulge his location, he wished he had taken Jenkens' advice to retreat when he had the opportunity. Face Unknown? What was I thinking? Then he spotted the giant transmission screen blending with the wall. It was interfacing with the Neltan Encantado program and activating a veil of protection. Images of Nelta flashed through his mind. More than anything, he wanted to step on that world. For that to happen, people needed Final Communication. That was just minutes away! He had to defend the screen the moment the snake might detect it. He began imagining how he could kill the snake—a virtual entity. That fight would prove useless because the snake was radiation-based, would go straight through him and disintegrate any part of his body touching it. He needed quantum help.

He felt a cold chill strike his cheeks. The ceiling vents began pumping snow into the room, dusting objects with white settling down. The ten-headed snake whipped off the ceiling processor, its fangs striking the air. Like an angry cobra, the black and orange monster began sidewinding on the ceiling, obviously hunting for the person responsible for the change.

The divide between a set of windows across from him bulged and turned blue. A long body began forming in the wall that looked like a caterpillar. He wiped away the frost on his eyelashes, but he could barely see the creature that appeared icy and shiny. Then he recognized his Terra. She was counter striking with her rendition of the ten-headed snake. The second she formed, she began oscillating across the ceiling toward the orange and black cobra monster.

The scene reminded him of the old *Boa* movie; but these two snakes were virtual-mutant, filled with fanged lethal radioactivity. Seeing his breath escape in the chill while pulling on a coat he had retrieved from under a chair with his feet, he called Jenkens to appear on his wrist device. "The photon invader is in for a fight now. Ya getting all this?"

Terra's venomous form began striking the ten-headed cobra. The room echoed their violent hissing, thumping and thudding sounds. One of Terra's sharp tails slashed the enemy's orange flesh. White blood splashed through the air that the snow attracted. Terra's caterpillar body enlarged. Like a sponge, her shiny body absorbed the white granules, strengthening. Her new capability was now copying the enemy's assault maneuvers and matching its speed.

Chandelier crystals crashed to the floor. Two hologram stages on the opposite side of the room began rattling—their yellow projection lights like beacons that were reinforcing Terra's virtual blue snake while tracking the orange and black cobra. The windows were in a wild state of fogging, crystalizing, and melting—the cycle repeating through the ferocious battle between Terra and the vicious ten-headed cobra.

Then, Terra spiked off the ceiling and dove into the new partition that changed into the scene of a deep arctic freeze.

Lashing out in anger, the ten-headed cobra suddenly paused in front of the new scenery—its red eyes flaring, its fangs dripping white ooze.

Surging from a crack in the glacial ice, Terra struck her foe with her ten razor-sharp tails, slicing off two of the cobra's heads at their necks. Fangs detached from its mouth into virtual javelins that struck the floor. The sections began boiling and bubbling in poisonous pools—the Self-Repair activating.

Ten wall zones flared on in a long line above him—their volumes blaring on high until the Auto Adjust decreased the volumes. It was Jenkens, who was had established a connection to the Press Room and created that blaring noise to mask the matrix Live Stream. That meant that scientists and General Rand were watching the battle, and contriving a solution.

The two snakes tossing and tumbling in a bitter brawl suddenly slurped through the double doors into the hallway.

Spurts of animal screeches reverberated, followed by whipping sounds, like bullwhips slashing the air. The snakes were now striking each other with their tails. Terra had the

Battlefield Matrix

advantage: all ten of her snake's heads had their fangs.

Manning heard an unfamiliar voice that sounded half-human and half-computer next to the center double door. "Terra—reinforce this room! The transmission screen!" he called as his Terra materialized next to him.

"What's happening? I see you, Thornton, but we can't get a visual of the hallway," Jenkens said, his image hovering over Manning's wrist tablet. Screwdriver in hand, he was inserting an imager into the partition. His hair was unkempt, his collar wrinkled, and a few navy-blue carpet fibers were staining his white shirt. Definitely, he had dropped to the floor in fear of the photon beast eating him alive as it had devoured Jane Dirk through her skin. Now, Jenkens appeared to have bounced back to his old self.

As more shrieks and whips resounded from the snake fight—their slashing sounds fading—Manning said: "Is the photon entity dying? Sounds that way."

Jenkens showed him the hologram of General Rand on Zone 1 and then replied: "That's what an Enforcer is streaming to Station III. Terra modified one of their weapons based on that successful strike that wounded one of the attackers. We have *one* prototype. We need time for additive manufacturing to process more and then a distributer willing to bring them here."

The ceiling vents suddenly flapped shut and sealed. The cold air stopped flowing. The snow dust began suspending in midair.

"Terra is manipulating and using gravity now!" Manning noticed the transmission screen glow in its bas-relief suspension. "She's interfacing with the Encantado program in the screen to wield more power."

The shrill, snake shrieks halted.

Terra said, "The Black Photonic weapon is gone."

"Yes!—she defeated the beast!" Jenkens shouted.

Exhaling in relief, he quickly set the robots back to interface with the wall, grabbed a chair, set it up straight, and was about to plop down. "Thank God it's over."

Jenkens said: "Not so fast! You don't have time to even breathe. The photon beast is gone but the attacker's at the door. We're getting a few good images right now. Ya see?"

Manning saw the hunching, hooded figure on Zone 1 next to Jenkens. The other two attackers were still camouflaged and exchanging fire with agents down the hall.

Jenkens said: "Where's Terra? She did an awesome job defeating that snake!"

On Hologram Stage Center materialized an image of the virtual Terra snake from the Research Station II. Terra said: "Matrix Techs wrote and downstreamed the bio-morphological creation. When the Terra snake eliminated the photon invader, the invader snatched it to its death. Both are gone."

Manning felt his eyes sting and felt transfixed on the center double doors. "So there's nothing I can do...and nothing that's going to stop Unknown from coming right in here and getting the transmission screen." He began glancing around for other places to hide.

"Well, neither you nor the screen can walk through walls," Jenkens said, "although I'd give anything to make that happen. Right now, General Rand and researchers are working on activating a back-up screen. I'll stay on Silent-mode and setting up an illusion of complete decay to make Unknown believe his photon weapon destroyed the Oval Office."

The thirty-foot-tall partition turned into a cascading landscape of oozing shiny liquid—a real, 3D contaminated sewage site from the pipes having burst in the adjacent restrooms.

"*Ugh*—smells like puss," coughed Manning.

"Good, huh? It looks like nothing's behind it...that the ten-headed snake decimated the office and slaughtered people," Jenkens said. "I'm activating that Stage 4 next to you so you and the rest of us can at least see when Unknown will be breaking in. It's on automatic, so when that double door gives and opens, the show will extinguish and the stage shut off. We'll have to communicate via your wrist tablet for now, but I'm working on a better way. Just know we're all watching you, through the matrix, and doing our best to ID and defeat Unknown and his, her or its accomplices in crime."

Ten feet to the right of Stage 4 that was showing the attackers in the hallway and obviously contriving the best approach to breach the doors' tech, Manning spotted the countdown to Final Communication on the Smart Bar in the Encantado frame of the IMAX transmission screen. The front of the screen contained layers of superconductivity. The back of the screen housed delicate, beehive quantum processors. In thirty minutes, people around the globe would holosite into the Press Room to stream live with the event. He realized that the phenomenal global experience was in jeopardy on Earth and on Nelta.

"We have only thirty minutes until the Neltan/Earth wormhole opens, Steve," he said. "Time's critical!" After Jenkens reassured him that they were doing everything to activate the backup, Manning waved for Terra to sit down beside him on the carpet. Opening his wrist device, he had Terra copy into his tablet the image of Unknown's weapon. "Terra, this is old-world rifle technology with added laser infrastructure and high-tech polymers." He threw the image at one of her rainbow processors. "Analyze the weapon! Get the results to The General."

The rainbow processor flared over the beehive mound in acceptance and then stabilized. All twenty-five of them were functioning again, but still in rampant Repair-mode. Every so often, Terra would waver out of existence.

Jenkens still had an expression of fear pasted on his gray tired face as he glanced around the Press Room through Manning's wrist device. Sheltered safely inside the Oval Office, he appeared impervious to any attack as he walked with strength between holograms of General Rand on Station III and scientists on Station II. He said: "Terra, you beat that photon snake—the worst possible virtual weapon outside of a virtual zombie! But you can't take down *three* people? I don't understand! Do you understand, Thornton?" He barked out expletives against the new Version III and then added, "Darn matrix is experiencing kinks in evolution all right."

On Stage 4, Manning noticed the exchange of fire in the long smoky hallway escalate. Unknown was fortifying a small area in front of the center double doors—a virtual barrier. Manning showed Jenkens the hooded attacker deflecting a laser-burst fire from two agents who dropped dead after they launched a counterattack. Seeing the scene as overwhelming even for the most gifted alien race in the universe, the Neltans, he said: "When Unknown gets in here and discovers the screen, I don't think the Neltan Encantado program can fend off such firepower."

Jenkens said: "Good news! General Rand has secured a screen in the Rotunda. He's keeping the new site a secret, but it's going to take around twenty minutes to create another grid to align the Decagon accelerator system with the Rotunda screen. I can't give you a visual in the Rotunda 'cause the Tech-Nos could have spyware in there. The incoming attackers could be Tech-Nos...maybe not. The General's working to ID Unknown."

"I believe these attacks are Tech-No protesters, Steve." He explained the reasoning: They were using a rogue terrorist grid, an altered version of *The Tiger* virus, and experimental weapons and matrix programs developed at Duke University.

Then General Rand's face appeared on Stage 4. The Neltan Encantado program was camouflaging the screen to the air and wall. Except for a slight gleam of oasis reflective heat, the screen was projecting the look of vapor coming out of a ceiling vent. Manning told The General that the incoming attacker had to be a genius in order to have synthesized answers to complicated problems, puzzles and enigmas. Unknown—with an unknown face, unknown DNA, unknown identity and unknown accomplices—had gleaned much intelligence from the first physical assault—the Black Photon Cobra—and the preceding matrix invasion, the centipedeware. Unknown could work magic through the manipulation of Neltan technology and the four forces. The Black Photon cobra was evidence of that. "But what Unknown might do next, General? Heaven forbid! Unknown could destroy Earth if he, she or it doesn't give a damn. We don't know the workings of his, her or its mind!"

After he showed General Rand the camouflaged screen on his wrist device that streamed more data to Station III, he asked The General to assess the ceiling hubs and walling, and give him the status of their functioning. "At least they have capillary action...and act as distractors."

Algorithmic code scrolled over Manning's wrist device. Some code had severe gaps.

The General said, "When the attackers breach that room— "

It was certain: Unknown was incoming. The double doors were red hot.

General Rand continued: "There's no guarantee we can protect that room while Terra is continuing to evolve up here to version III."

Beneath the transmission screen flashed the countdown to Final Communication: *25 minutes*; then suddenly, *24*.

"What are we going to do?" Again, he squatted next to Stage 4, using the hologram platform for cover. He breathed in a citrus smell, the sensory mood booster he had ordered for the Press Room earlier, but his brain felt no uplift. "Less than twenty-five minutes...that's it, Steve." He glanced at the rainbow-cycling processors and said, "Twenty-four minutes, General. This last discussion with the Neltans *has* to happen. Everyone!—snap to it! We're running out of time. Go work to create that new connection between the Decagon and the Rotunda, now!"

Chapter 9

Identity: Unknown

Manning tried remaining calm while his heart beat in his throat. "How am I gonna stay alive? Unknown is gonna be in here—in here!—any second!"

His shocked face still hovering over Manning's wrist tablet, Jenkens said: "I see a small, white light flashing in your ceiling hub. What is it?"

"The processor activated that experimental gamma app I showed you earlier," Manning answered. "Terra is expanding Security."

"What?" he cried, recoiling.

"Stand beneath it, look up, and say, *Lynnalt823*," Manning ordered, repeating his password. "Terra's Firewall read you before. After you do that, the grid in there will obey you."

After Jenkens complied, the app light extinguished. "*Whew*—now what? What good is the gamma weapon in here?"

The center double door was glowing white-hot, the nanomaterials disintegrating in the attacker's firepower.

Battlefield Matrix

Manning pointed at a small line of tiny processor mounds forming inside the new partition. Jenkens insertion of the imager had worked to initiate an expansion of a Reporter-Recorder app. The partition was still projecting the illusion of a destroyed Oval Office; but over the ragged doorframe, he could see concave niches where the matrix was creating new imagers and processors. Unless Unknown had intimate blueprints of the two rooms, Unknown would never be able to detect the new matrixware. He told Jenkens, "Whoever steps under that door leading into the office, besides you or me, *will* fry. The gamma app will reach that spot."

An expression of hope wafted over Jenkens' face, and he said: "Hey—after Unknown and his cohorts enter the Press Room, I'll figure out a way to draw their attention to the Oval Office. At some point, I'll change the scenery on the partition to make a slight opening appear. When they investigate, I'll open the gamma app and disintegrate them." He pointed past Manning. "You don't have much time. They're almost inside. Hide!"

Manning breathed deeply and then gulped down some cold water from a bottle he had hidden by one of the paused robots. Then he began a frantic search for more objects to set around him so he could hunker down. "These few robots aren't enough," he said to Jenkens.

The interior of the center double door was vibrating and bleeding orange-white metal. The carpet in front of inferno was flaming and bellowing smoke. The alert was on low volume, but still the pitch hurt his ears. Extinguishers began showering the flames with a long line of concentrated waterpower. The air smelled pungent, ionized. As Terra guided him to the best furniture to use for his fortification, he broke out in a sweat. The wall vents were flushing cold air on full-blast to maintain a cool seventy-five degrees. It wasn't working. He grabbed two chairs and arranged them alongside two decorative saplings that grew tall, sprouted leaves, and unfurled flowers when a ray of full-spectrum light touched their branches. With those as sufficient cover beside Stage-4, he crouched down and hid.

"This should be a good hiding place," he told Terra. "It's a plausible display...one I hope will fool Unknown. If I can pounce on the criminal, I might be able to grab a gun."

He called on Stage-4 and linked it with his wrist device when Jenkens gave him the signal. When the stage glowed yellow, he adjusted hologram reception to low-image frequency. It had to match the other eight in line to the left of him—except Center Stage which was larger and sticking out farther to accommodate the camouflaged transmission screen. Now the platform was synchronizing with the Oval Office— the right side of the virtual Smart Bar right up next to his forehead reading his biometrics.

Outside the White House, he heard a sudden commotion. People were screaming in fright, anger and panic, demanding answers to the violence that had managed to invade the White House. Enforcer hovercrafts were firing countermeasures of EMPs to squelch an inflow of Tech-No visuals on the sides of monuments. Obviously, Unknown was using White House Security to hack into holosites and instill fear. Spotlights were sweeping through the crowds, markets and eateries. The Regency and General Rand were communicating through their avatars and military icons that White House Security was counterattacking Unknown with elite Stealth Force personnel in the air. General Rand was assuring everyone—via a massive Emergency Send—that they would soon be apprehending the Tech-No attackers, securing the White House, and continuing the scheduled events for Final Communication at nine o'clock as planned.

Then he spotted a countdown on the side of Washington's Monument that appeared to be coinciding with Unknown's pending infiltration of Press Room: one minute. That's all he had left before Unknown would be inside. "Less than a minute!" Jenkens continued to holler.

Manning ran out from his hiding spot and kicked down a few chairs to appear as if he had escaped earlier. He shouted to Jenkens: "If Unknown doesn't have a biometric detector, I might be able to avoid capture if I can just remain hidden. And if I'm lucky, Terra might enable some type of new weapon—or the gamma app in the partition as you said." He dashed back to his hideout. "Terra, play some type of soft music and stay by me. Camouflage to something."

Terra faded into the foreground of an artificial tree.

As Jenkens' image began to fade over Manning's wrist device, he whispered: "Thornton, I just received a veiled message from General Rand. One of our Elite Units is here. They're positioning to fire once The General gives the signal, but first, they're scanning for powerful EMPs that Unknown says he has arranged in several secret locations. The attacker is threatening to unleash the deadly EMP explosives that have laser-wave capability and can kill everyone within a two-mile radius."

"We don't want *that*!" Manning cried.

"We know!" said Jenkens. "General Rand tells me he can only spare two elite teams. All our forces are battling terrorists in space who're fighting to solidify their stronghold, pool their resources, merge, and escape the solar system. Definitely, the terrorists are spacefolding toward the Decagon accelerator system."

"No!"

Jenkens whispered: "Hold on...we just secured that quadrant, at least for now. The enemy has to activate spacefold technology to leave. They don't have that capability unless they seize the Decagon."

"So that's why they've been stealing shield panels, modifying them, and altering old Terra-ware," Manning said. "They want to link and generate a rip in space when they leave."

"Yep," Jenkens replied, "and that's why we have three-fourths of all our forces in that quadrant fighting them. At least the Neltan/Earth wormhole will activate on time in that quadrant past Mars. In the meantime, we have to concentrate on getting *one* transmission screen up and running so we can connect it with the Decagon."

He suddenly noticed that *his* safe-time was depleting. "Terra, I have an idea." When she uncloaked, he said: "Line up all the robotic imagers and server bots. But do it gently, slowly. Sync them to *this* Stage 4 hologram platform. I'm hiding under it, so I can whisper directions and maneuver the roboticware. You can receive the waves of my voice and help me that way."

After Terra's eyes flashed green in compliance, Jenkens said: "What're ya thinking?!" Doing *that* will give away your location if Unknown detects the connection!"

"I don't know how, but maybe I can use them to get us out of this bad situation," he replied. "The interface could prove to be my saving grace as Terra continues her evolution."

Terra then camouflaged to the tree, leaving behind a phantom outline that quickly faded.

Before Jenkens' image completely extinguished, he covered his mouth and let out a gasp of despondency. He had obviously heard the commotion outside and was panicking because of what the Tech-No protesters were threatening in the Mall and all the streets. "My God, *this* attack *could* stop Final Communication even if we're successful in preventing the terrorists from interfering with it. I wish we could get an emergency signal or distress message to Nelta to tell them we're experiencing trouble, and not to worry, and that we *will* comply with our part of *The Pact* just in case we can't formally sign it as planned."

Manning plastered his body against the floor. The attackers would be piercing their way through a white-hot circle in seconds. "Get General Rand to activate that back up screen now!"

"But it's—"

"Ready or not, have him recalibrate the Decagon with the interferometer system and intensify solar power to the backup screen. I want us ready to receive Ambassador Shaesar's image in case my counterattack to secure this screen fails." He breathed hard. "We have to remain focused, Steve...and calm." He realized he was encouraging himself.

Battlefield Matrix

"What counterattack?" Jenkens asked.

"Discovering what Unknown is after *is* my strategy," he whispered after he fine-tuned the interface between him and Jenkens on Stage 4. With the objects and Stage 4 surrounding him, he felt encapsulated inside a secure tent, but this was no childhood game. "Through this open connection and the processors in the partition; you, General Rand, and researchers on Station II can contrive a strike that'll kill these attackers. Unknown's DNA is different. We need to know how, and Unknown's purpose. Are there more? Track their com grids. Locate others. I'm off my wrist device now. Stage 4's now our only way to communicate."

"Will do," snapped Jenkens. "Out!"

At that moment, the center exploded out of the double doors. White, smoldering, crackling particles and cinders began dancing across the carpet. When the fiery bits hit the chairs and hologram stages, the extinguishers engaged and snuffed out the flames.

Manning felt heat ripple over his body. He could hear shouts and screams. One voice he recognized. "Dr. Holton!" He whispered into Stage-4's Smart Bar through which Jenkens was receiving his every word: "Steve—the attackers *have* Elisa Holton! You seeing this?"

"Yes! I see her!" Jenkens whispered back. "The individual covered in a white blanket has her by the arm."

"How'd *that* happen?!"

"I'm hearing that Unknown's guards grabbed her in the corridor when Security left her unmonitored to retrieve Jane Dirk's body. They musta realized they needed her...maybe to get to you, I don't know. That's why Enforcers and guards stopped firing Unknown. He was using *her* as a human shield."

"Damn! Dirty and sick!" Manning said. "*That's* who we're dealing with...someone bent on killing thousands to make a statement...a psychopath!" He noticed spectral colors appear inside the virtual Smart Bar, indicating clear reception to Stations II and III.

A panel of molten-white silicon hit the carpet.

J.P. Osterman

Jenkens whispered into their own private connection: "I'm streaming everything that's happening to The World. People will sympathize with you and when you make it outta there alive and well, they'll surely nullify some of the privacy intrusions you've been keeping covert."

Manning gave out a slight facetious laugh. "Never would I have thought that *this* would be the way to sway public opinion!" His hot breaths reflecting back to him off the carpet, he felt suddenly isolated and powerless. Peeking up through a crack, he saw two men enter the Press Room and then seal up the door with silicon-mending sludge. He couldn't see the leader, yet.

"Set up stages so I can stream live to The World," a man ordered the two men. The voice was definitely male...husky and guttural.

The two men were middle aged, tall, buff and weather worn, like mercenaries or survivalists who were once in the military but chose not to transition to Global Enforcement after 2057. The agency most likely refused them. Immediately, they ran to distant places in the Press Room, obviously obeying Unknown's orders.

Unknown connected to Security in the Center Lobby and said: "I have a hostage. Don't retaliate or she's dead."

Manning wanted to shout out in retaliation, but then ducked and trembled when he saw the crusty scabby skin on Unknown's knuckles.

Then he heard Dr. Holton say: "You'll never get away with this, Dr. Coflin. One of our quantum physicists *will* stop you! You'll *never* be able to infect the matrix. There's more power in this evolving Terra-III, that I worked on myself, that you can't *begin* to circumvent and infiltrate. Never!" Her tone of voice was stern and penetrating.

Dr. Darrel Coflin? Unknown *is* Dr. Coflin?! He remembered the previous matrix attacks harboring *Sender*'s signatures. Unknown had to be Sender as well, the mastermind of the nano-robotic Locust attack on all the Stealth Force craft heading toward the Decagon, the Skolkovo attack, *and* the blackout. That would make Dr. Coflin's intelligence beyond that of any human genius ever recorded. But how?! A memory flashed through his mind.

The day prior to First Communication, Lynn left him an urgent message telling him about her new boss, Dr. Darrel Coflin, the new Director of Biochemistry at Duke. Lynn said that Coflin had innovative ideas but believed in conducting experiments and studies in the most sterile, isolated and controllable settings. He remembered Lynn's exact words as she laughed out a bust of hot air: "Thornton, this guy's OCD. A clean freak. God, I just know I'm gonna *hate* working for him. He's gonna have us—your old team—clear out our labs, scrub the floors five times, and then install monitors in every corner. Thornton—this man's gonna make life hell!" She was almost in tears and completely expressing dread. "Any positions in your Regency? Any way you can create a job for me if there isn't, Thornton? For old times' sake?" She had tears in her eyes and folded her arms across her chest like straps on a straightjacket, implying that she was terrified for her future.

He sent her only his automated response: "Regent Thornton Manning is Out of Area. In the event of an emergency, contact The Regency's One-World Media Site. Good day." He never conferenced with her that day because he was scheduled to be at Duke the following day. On that day, chaos broke out due to First Contact with the Neltans. They forgot the problem.

Self-loathing circled through his gut. He thought: Damn! I hate myself! Maybe if I had answered her cry-for-help and met her that day, we might not have been in the lab, and she might not have volunteered to be part of *Greeter*'s mission and die in the explosion. That reminded him of the suspects he had been informally investigating. It's him! The same Dr. Coflin accused of sabotaging *The Greeter*!

Standing up, he kicked away the chairs and pushed aside Stage 4. "Coflin—*you*. *You* downed *Greeter*! *You* killed those people." He lunged at him with his clenched fists.

J.P. Osterman

Coflin flung off his gray ski mask and white cloak. "I'd think twice before taking another step," he threatened, pointing a new type of gun in Manning's face.

Seeing his face apparently for the first time, Dr. Holton cried out and dropped to the floor in terror as Coflin's red-blond hair spilled out across the collar of his black leather jacket. He looked lion like, his yellowish teeth pointy, his eyes bulging out of his sockets, and glowing.

"What the hell are you!" Manning gagged. "Dr. Holton, stay down, don't move."

Her brown hair flowing around her face, she began a slow crawl toward Manning. She kept repeating: "What the hell! What did you do to yourself?"

Coflin's face was manifesting only a few human characteristics. His nose and the shape of his face, eyes and ears were human, but his yellowish skin, long thin nose, deep-set eye sockets, and bulging eyes were Neltan, but even they appeared ghastly foreign. Every now and then, he would stop everything. His body would shake, his skin alter in hue. He was still changing; and, from the appearance of his blotchy skin tone, he was reverting to some type of pre-historic Neltan.

Gesturing at several changed features, Manning said: "Terra's been referring to you as Unknown. She can't identify your DNA. Is *this* why?"

"But why?" interjected Elisa Holton. "Altering your genetics is insane!" She sat up but kept her head turned away from him. "To do that? To yourself?" Heaving breaths of disbelief, she added: "What you've done to yourself must have taken *months* of experimentation...shots every hour or so to achieve such a bio-cellular alteration in anatomy—"

"And physiology," Manning exclaimed, stepping away from the Stage 4 but covertly ensuring that its Smart Bar was partly in direct view of Coflin. He knew others were seeing everything. "Can you be specific on biometrics, Coflin? Specific as to your morphology?"

"Shut up!" Coflin rasped. "Stay where you are and I won't kill you, Manning...Regent Thornton Seth Manning. Just the

Battlefield Matrix

Executive I wanted to see." He called ordered to his two followers who were trying to manipulate the large center stage in front of the transmission screen. The screen suddenly uncloaked. The frame revved and emitted blinding light. Then the Counterattack program subsided.

Manning whispered as loudly as he could to Elisa: "That shouldn't happen! The screen should be launching an all-out attack on them."

The curtains unraveled as if welcoming a gentle breeze and an unexpected friend.

"Hurry," Coflin called to his two assistants, "we don't have much time!"

"Why did the screen do that, Regent Manning?" Elisa asked. "It's supposed to defend against *all* intrusions." She was scooting closer to him at a tortoise pace.

When Coflin grimaced at them, Manning motioned for her to stop moving. "He's half Neltan. The Encantado program recognizes its own."

Chapter 10

Eye Glow

"Whataya want, Coflin," Manning asked, trying to avoid looking at the transmission screen. Coflin was counting down seconds as well. If he could keep the crazed scientist distracted, maybe he could interfere with his sense of time, discover his purpose, and protect the screen. And if he could find a weakness from his past, maybe he could use the flaw to his advantage.

Dr. Daryl Coflin definitely looked different from when he appeared before the Investigative Committee to give his most recent report on *The Greeter*'s explosion. Manning was the Lead Officiate at that hearing six months ago and Center Chair on the bench. When asked to step forward and stop looking down, Coflin shook his head no. For over seven years since *Greeter*'s sabotage, no one could produce any evidence against Coflin, or motive, although he had the means and opportunity to destroy *The Greeter*. He kept repeating: "Prove it. You can't. I'm innocent. And why...*why* would I blow up *Greeter*—huh? You think I'm stupid? I'd get the death penalty, or neurologically re-arranged. *Who'd* want Station V? Not me!" He shrugged in an air of defiance, turned a slow three-hundred-and-sixty-degree circle of imperviousness, and huffed into the air with exaggerated arrogance and spiteful dismissiveness. He had a week's worth of stubble that looked like prickly cactus. He obviously hadn't combed his shoulder-length, slicked-back red hair in days. When he walked, his steel-toed military boots vibrated the floor. Finally agreeing to approach the bench, he sneered at the committee and mumbled cuss words until Manning demanded that he stop or go to jail. That cured his badass attitude fast! He wanted to leave ASAP. He said: "I have people to see, places to go, tech to invent. I'm outta here after this...off-Earth...and ya can't stop me." Dressed in shabby blue jeans and wearing a tattered pale-yellow shirt, he simply stared over the heads of the committee when they asked him questions—the same old questions regarding where he was, what he saw, who he was with, and what exactly he was doing prior to, during, and after *Greeter* exploded. For two hearings prior to that, he repeated the same answer several times: "I was in the lab." He always provided convincing scenes with time stamps. No one could find a glitch in his testimony. Now, Manning realized that Dr. Daryl Coflin had been a lying chameleon the entire time, buying precious time to transform himself into a monster.

Six months ago, Coflin looked normal—not like the mutated monster standing yards in front of him. The new species he was morphing into resembled the redheaded Wolverine character from the comic books. Lynn had described him as obsessive compulsive, but not as profoundly antisocial as post-*Greeter* explosion. Some horrible trigger had changed Dr. Coflin's entire worldview in a matter of hours after First Communication. Some intense stressor had obviously changed the man's personality to make him want to him morph himself half-human, half-Neltan. Neither Manning nor the Investigative Committee ever delved into Coflin's life because Coflin always managed to block any type of inquiry of the archives or physicians' notes. Coflin said hackers sabotaged all his records. No one believed that, but again couldn't prove it. The Investigative Committee finally concluded that until Coflin would submit to a lie detector test and comply with all their demands for a month's worth of surveillance, they would continue to order him to return at six-month intervals before them for questioning. That's when Daryl Coflin disappeared, and obviously began a cunning covert hunt for Neltan technology and a plot to attack.

Manning noticed the time: 8:50 p.m., ten minutes to *the* most important dialogue since First Communication. He had to act quickly, do something, to stop Coflin. He called to him: "Coflin! Tell me what you want. To kill me? To dismantle Terra? That's what it looks like." He and his men were probing the walls, and inspecting and scanning the ceiling hubs. But when he saw Coflin's contorting face develop another scaly layer, he knew that a simple deceleration in technology wasn't what the deranged scientist wanted. "You know what this means...not opening the Neltan/Earth wormhole, right?"

Dr. Holton slid closer to Manning, her breath fear laden. "Sir, he's here to change people on both worlds."

In quick bursts, Coflin fired his laser pistol that melted rows of wall mounts on the opposite side of the room. Towering wall-zone screens began melting, the materials hissing as the Repair app activated. That would take a long time. He had to be fearful of a counterattack and spyware; but as of yet, no one had fired on the partition.

"She's right," he snapped. "That wormhole is going to change *everything* after *my* system links with the evolving Terra-III."

Terra materialized with flashing red eyes, outstretched arms, and sparking fingers to launch a directed energy counterattack.

Coflin shot her main ceiling hub. The rainbow processor flamed, extinguished, and curled with smoke.

Working frantically and using his fingers as enumerators, he said: "First, I have to disconnect the new Terra matrix from this room. Second, I will configure my system that I developed on *The Heed* to the central hub. Third, then I connect into the matrix. *Then* everyone will know me, my movement and how we are saving humanity." His wrinkly face and bulging blue-green eyes shone a scary wild excitement.

Manning connected that comment to *The Greeter*. "So you exploded that shuttle and killed all those valuable people so The World can know you. Pretty narcissistic!" He clenched his fists at him and felt his teeth grind to a gritty taste on his tongue. "Damn you...Damn you, Coflin. I'm gonna kill you when I get my hands on ya!"

"And I'll help him!" shouted Elisa. "One of those scientists was my best friend." Her eyes filled with tears.

The ten ceiling hubs in the room hissed as Terra's hologram completely faded.

"Yes, Regent Manning," he said, lisping. "I exploded *Greeter*. That's what you've been wanting me to admit for quite some time, isn't it? Isn't it!" He appeared to like the pain he could inflict. "No regrets, Regent Manning. I don't regret exploding *Greeter* at all."

If he could, Manning would order an instant disintegration of Coflin's flesh. But Terra was gone, the partition too far away, and eight of her twenty-five hubs, not including her main ceiling processor were melting down. The other hubs were rainbow dysfunctional as if struck by lightning. They were helplessly at Coflin's mercy until Jenkens, General Rand, Enforcers, or Matrix Techs on Station II could find a way to stop Coflin from modifying Terra-III. While Coflin's two guards continued their matrix interface, the main ceiling hub droned in Wait-mode. All nine hologram stages were flashing the message: *Rebooting*. In a short time, Final Communication would permanently change.

"No! Stop!" Manning shouted.

"Shut up, stay back, and I'll let you live," Coflin said gruffly. His blotchy arms had a fine growth of new hair. His teeth were pink-tinged, his gums outlined with blood. "Move again, just one more time, and you and Holton *die*."

Vents burst opened and fans whirred on. Extinguishers sprouted from the ceiling and doused a few tiny flames. Streams of ant-bot armies bubbled out of the baseboards, a new Self-Repair system. Like a torrent, they flooded all the damaged areas on the wall zones and began repairing the microscopic Terra projectors. The walls looked like translucent wax ligaments and metallic organs.

Elisa pushed back her brown bangs; and through blushing sweat-stained cheeks, she whispered into Manning's ear: "No way can Coflin interface with all the hardware in here and change the new Terra-III. He'd have to renovate the entire White House!"

Then Manning spotted a glowing virtual string hovering over Stage 4 behind them. Gradually, the glow string was gliding toward the Smart Bar. Jenkens had found a new method of communicating with him.

Manning stepped next to the red virtual Smart Bar and pulled Elisa along with him to answer the call. "We might have help," he whispered to her. "I have eyes and ears in this room. Just stay by me." Keeping his arm hidden, he tapped his wrist device, swept the glow string over it, and Jenkens appeared as a tiny Jackie Gleason avatar over his wrist tablet.

"I hope Regent Jenkens has something that we can use against Coflin and fast," Elisa whispered. She slipped down into a red chair and scooted in front of the little avatar.

"Just stay right there and keep covering for me as I talk to him," Manning said.

When Coflin stopped his sporadic gunfire and glanced their way, she coughed—a purposeful move to hide the low hum that Jenkens' avatar made as it began streaming information to Manning.

Speaking in a whisper, Jenkens' avatar said: "I have information about Coflin that might help you talk him down. A hacker at Duke retrieved a medical file indicating that he experienced a psychotic episode right after First Communication."

"What happened?" Elisa whispered over her shoulder.

Battlefield Matrix

"His wife was moving to Duke to join him on the job when the wormhole opened up in the stratosphere that day. On the Pennsylvania turnpike, her car was one of those that uplifted in the electromagnetic and gravitational fluctuation. She and their unborn child died."

"Sounds like he never recovered from the tragedy," Holton said, softly.

"So revenge must be part of what ignited his anti-Neltan passion," Manning said.

"That's what researchers on Station II are ascertaining now that they input everything the hacker sent them into their Profiling program," said Jenkens through his little avatar. "Coflin is delusional and paranoid but a genius. He uses an umbrella of caring to seduce vulnerable people to follow him. He and a band of Tech-Nos have been living off-Earth for some time. His holosites keep eluding even our best Matrix Security by using camouflaged addresses. That's why we can't locate any of them...except that small cell in the desert that you and I discovered earlier." He coughed. "For years they've been pilfering and altering technology. Obviously, everything they've been working on has been leading up to tonight's attack."

"He's definitely the Leader of the Tech-Nos," Manning said.

"But why do they want to alter matrixes?" asked Elisa. "What Coflin and his followers are attempting seems beyond making a simple statement to us and the Neltans."

"Good questions," Jenkens answered. "A genetic reading of his DNA indicates that Dr. Coflin is *not* human. And he must have expert team helping him with the morphology and infiltrating this place."

"Who and where?" Manning asked.

"Moles in our Secret Service probably helped him breach the White House, and disillusioned scientists helped him change his body and contrive this mysterious plot of theirs."

"Where are they hiding and how're they getting in and out undetected?" Manning asked. "Did you see more people in the corridor, Dr. Holton?"

Gently, Elisa shook her head no. She was busy concealing Jenkens' avatar with body movements, yawns and coughs. She whispered over her shoulder: "Check all floors. I remember hearing about one tunnel leading to an old sewer system and an attic passageway leading to an outside exit…both from the Civil War era."

"We'll begin a deep biometric scan to hunt for them," Jenkens said. "General Rand is close to homing in on their craft in space. A Stealth Force team is tracking several signatures of Coflin's cosmic trails leading from the moon and past Mars."

Manning remembered *The Spider* and other Stealth Force craft present in that area and battling terrorists. "My God! I hope Bartlet and his crew don't run into an entire convoy of Tech-Nos as well as terrorists! Warn them!"

"We know and that's done," Jenkens' avatar whispered. The avatar's face was turning from side-to-side. Jenkens was transmitting everything to General Rand and Station II.

"What's Coflin's background?" Manning asked. "Is there information from his past that we might be able to use to persuade him to change his mind? Soon he's going to realize that linking with the new Terra is going to be problematic. The evolved hubs won't interface with any outmoded hubs. He's gonna get *really* pissed off." Manning watched as Coflin accessed his avatar over his wrist device. He appeared suddenly angry and began barking orders to his crew as he kicked over three chairs.

Jenkens said: "Dr. Coflin is part Swedish, Argentinian and German."

"So—like most people, he's part of the global melting pot," Elisa said.

"Yes, but there's more to his story." Jenkens tiny avatar opened a file and began reading its contents. "Dr. Coflin's great-grandfather was Milburn Wilhelm Kauflin, a Nazi who fled to Argentina during World War II where he married, began a new life, and had a large family. He remained undetected and died in 1967. Then his grandson, Dr. Coflin's grandfather, immigrated to America where Dr. Coflin's parents tried to do everything possible to obliterate their Nazi heritage. They were extremely embarrassed and ashamed of their ancestor, *Milburn Kauflin*, who was part of the Nazi research aimed at manipulating DNA. They committed horrendous crimes against the Jews in Dachau."

"Hence the name change, Kauflin to Coflin," Manning said.

Elisa said: "His parents must have brought him up to abhor genetic manipulation."

"That doesn't make sense," Manning countered. "Look what he's done to himself."

"Makes perfect sense if his whole intention is to shut down all Neltan-based advancements," she replied.

"We need to stop that goal because it could involve infecting the Neltan/Earth wormhole with something deadly for people on both planets," Jenkens said.

Then Manning heard the pitter-patter of feet on the roof. Security officers were racing back and forth to gain entrance into the Press Room. "They're here!"

"Wait, I—" Jenkens little avatar fizzled off Manning's wrist device.

Interference had turned the quantum-based com grid to static.

Gunfire broke out. People were getting shot and dying.

"Damn!" Manning said, cringing through the death moans. "Damn and—"

"*Shh*," whispered Elisa. "Sorry for such strong language, Sir, but your continued connection with Regent Jenkens is in jeopardy. Coflin keeps giving me hateful glances. He knows we're doing something covert, Sir."

Enforcers not only had surrounded the White House, but they were also rappelling off the roof. Black clad bodies were positioning themselves around the windows as torches ignited on the window frames. The thudding and grunting sounds of people dying were sure signs that Coflin had a small army of Tech-No followers attacking from the outside. They had dashed out of the crowd to begin what looked like an ensuing war on the steps of the White House.

Elisa covered her ears. "Coflin's followers are killing a lot of us! Terra!"

The space in front of them crackled and sparked in a beam of yellow light. She had evolved to electro-laser defense in the holographic stage projector, but that image dwindled when her virtual body attempted to solidify.

Manning whispered to Jenkens: "Terra's matrix has to assess a different way to counter strike 'cause Coflin's defeating her."

Coflin's red hair was progressively graying by the minute. His skin was discoloring from blotchy to yellow, and the bones in his fingers were thickening.

Manning saw the deteriorating condition as an opportunity. "Coflin, if you agree to surrender, I can activate a world-wide Emergency Holosite grid. I'll give you a chance to make a statement." When Coflin didn't answer but continued to sweat hard under a ceiling hub, Manning said, softly: "You know we have scientists who can reverse what you've done to yourself. Just give up. There's still time to repair the genetic damage."

"No—ha-ha," he wheezed. "I must wait here for the wormhole to open. I—I can't surrender!" His lips were cracked and white, his face anemic and ashen. He was obviously beginning to buckle under the intermittent excruciating pain of his transformation.

Elisa said in a gentle tone of voice: "I can help you, Dr. Coflin. You know my skill set."

He sighed and paused from applying silicon to the hubs.

"See? She can reverse what you've done if you just give up," Manning added.

Vehemently, Coflin shook his head no and resumed tossing nano-organic putty to his followers who were busily helping him alter the ceiling Terraware.

"Is this revenge, Dr. Coflin? For what happened to your wife and child?" She kept talking to him, soothingly, obviously trying to reach his heart and change his mind.

Battlefield Matrix

As Coflin raised his gun to fire, Manning backed up slowly. He remembered the information Jenkens had given them. Now was the time to use it. "Is this attack really an attempt to save your family name? If so, we can do that easily. We'll construe this entire episode as a sympathetic broadcast in the archives, not a mass murder contrived by a Nazi descendant who snapped and started killing people…like his Nazi racist forefathers."

"Stop it!" Coflin said. His cheeks were sinking inward—a Neltan feature. The slow change was making him shake and grimace in pain. Something terrible with his self-morphology was striking the cells of his body.

"You don't want to go down in history as the wacko who killed people in a maniacal fit, do you Dr. Coflin?" He waited…but no answer.

His followers in the background were inserting organics into the main ceiling hub that flashed on and began swirling blue light. Exhaling in pain, Coflin grabbed the frame of the glowing transmission screen, nearly collapsing on it. A small robot veered under the screen, saving it from toppling sideways. Coflin raised his sleeve. Someone was hailing him on his wrist device. He told his men to hurry with the matrixware modifications and then he answered the call coming to him from space.

Manning spotted the glow string on the edge of Stage 4. It was Jenkens again.

"Give, give me your, your wrist de—devices," Coflin said, reaching for them. He staggered toward Manning and Elisa, his steps hard across the floor like the words that were stuttering over his lips. His fingers looked half-scaly-half-skin, and his arms were now hairless, white, bumpy, and crusty in spots. The fine hair that was full over his arms and neck had all fallen out, exposing thick welts that looked like crocodile skin. His blue-green pupils were beige rimmed, not white. He began squinting, the light obviously paining him. "Come on— I know you have wrist tablets. You're trying to communicate with the outside. Hand 'em over, now." He raised the gun into Manning's face.

Unfastening his wrist device, Manning stared into the small red-glowing barrel.

"I *will* shoot…so hand over your wrist devices, now."

"I don't have one…see?" Elisa said, extending her bare arms for him to inspect.

Coflin glanced at the long line of hologram stages in front of the towering transmission screen as if searching for the correct stage into which to insert Manning's wrist-device.

"Tell us why, Coflin…why you altered yourself to look like—a freak!" Manning said. "You say you don't want to stop Final Communication but you want to change the future. Why? Come on, give back my wrist tablet and we can discuss other means of presenting your cause—"

"Shut up!" Coflin threw his wrist device to the door after one of his followers told him the processor was useless in linking with the IMAX screen. After he dismantled Manning's thin round processor from its main wrist-frame, he inserted the device into the center of the long shiny metallic-looking bar at the base of the IMAX transmission screen. The Encantado program flared with yellow intensity around the thick frame of the screen. Now it looked half the size of an old outdoor movie screen. Neltan symbols and yellow mathematical code began cycling around the frame as the Encantado shape-shifter bar glowed green. That meant the screen was preparing to receive the quantum signal from the Decagon.

Coflin screamed in anger; and he hit the wall. White nanobots bubbled around his flesh but then dropped off as if the taste had deactivated them.

"Manning whispered to Elisa, "He's discovering that linking to Terra isn't easy compared to linking with the screen."

Elisa said, "Dr. Coflin, from your symptoms, I think you only have minutes to live. Let me help you…please!"

Manning pulled her back to his side. "Listen to her, Coflin. Death can't be worth changing a future that's already set. We made a deal with the Neltans. They healed our ozone. We owe them; and tonight, we are signing *The Pact*…and in a little over a year, a crew will launch to Nelta. That's the future. We're inextricably tied to the Neltans. First Communication happened! You *can't* reverse our two species interacting in the future."

Coflin pounded a table and appeared ready to punch it to pulp. He was increasing in power, and strengthening. "Is this what you want? Something like me?! A half-breed?! Look at me…take a *looong* hard look." He was hideous—half human, Neltan, and something else. He had hunching shoulders like a bear, shiny gray-white skin, and blotches of scaly yellow scabs on his arms and face. "I could be the future of humanity!" He voice sounded as if he had the vocal cords of an animal. "Stop it…stop this—me!—from happening, Regent Manning."

Manning heard shouts, screams, and the crowd outside the White House still reacting to the attack. He said: "Tech-No Leader or not, Coflin, you'll be doing worse than destroying the ozone if you stop us from signing *The Pact*. You know how billions of years more advanced the Neltans are than us. You know what's inside the *Attack Clause*. They've been completely peaceful in spite of all our fears that they might rain down terror on us. We must seem like ants to them. Who *knows* what they'll do if we simple don't answer their wormhole call. They need our DNA. They bargained with us to get it."

Coflin gestured in defiance. "I won't *stop* the transmission, Regent Manning. I'm going to use it as an opportunity to show everyone on both worlds that the possibility of interspecies breeding will create a monstrous new species…like me."

Elisa said, "This isn't good…not good at all…*terrible!*"

A hologram suddenly illuminated the time: 9:00 p.m.

"Coflin! We need to activate the transmission screen! Those symbols on the frame are cycling like they're going to send out a destructive EMP. It must begin receiving the Neltan's quantum-communication from the Decagon," Manning cried. Then he realized that the screen's large frame hadn't illuminated its typical, white halo. It was in Reboot-mode. "I wonder if the backup screen in the Rotunda is activating to take the place of this one," he whispered to Elisa.

"I didn't realize we had one operational there," she replied.

Then the large center hologram stage illuminated its Smart Bar. The Automated voice resounded: "Neltan/Earth Wormhole activity in a new synchronicity: 9:10 p.m., Eastern Standard Time. Reboot unsuccessful."

The crowd outside received the new, pre-Final Transmission preparation time through the loudspeakers, and the matrix was holositing the information around the globe.

Manning sighed in relief with his hand over his heart. "That gives us a half-an-hour extension with twenty testing minutes. An event horizon musta interfered—what great luck!"

"You say, *luck*. I say *divine* intervention, Sir." Elisa pushed back her sweaty brown bangs and then gulped down some water. "I wonder which event horizon between here and Nelta altered. Whichever one it was, wow did we catch a great break."

He added: "Or maybe General Rand managed to get a message to Ambassador Shaesar in the wormhole. I don't know. Whatever good thing happened, this means we have an extra ten minutes to stop Coflin, and five minutes before the transmission screen glows white-yellow and all the symbols begin re-cycling. That's the prep-signal indicating that the Decagon is positioning. Fifteen minutes after that, the Neltan/Earth wormhole should activate and Shaesar's hologram appear in this room, if the backup isn't up and functioning. Nine thirty...9:30."

Elisa whispered, "Coflin just activated a string of linking wrist devices on the Smart Bar frames of all nine hologram stages. You think he might have discovered a way to circumvent Terra-III and superimpose *his* program?" She began breathing long hard breaths of frustration. "We just had a miracle happen, Sir, but I don't see another striking twice. All he needs to do is synchronize with the Neltan Encantado bar at the base of the screen and all chaos could break out.

Battlefield Matrix

What's next, Sir? If you have any ideas…including something that might jeopardize our own safety, please, just tell me and I'll do it. I don't wanna die, but, hell…stem-cell treatments will fix me…even though missing a limb in a laser-light battle will be painful…that is, if I survive until I can reach the medical center around the corner. I'll do—"

"Nonsense, Dr. Holton," he chastised. "In no way would I sanction such a thing." Although, he believed she had a good idea and began conjuring ways to attack Coflin without sustaining loss of life or limb. In spite of the man's deteriorating condition, he realized he couldn't survive a fight with Coflin. When Coflin doffed his denim jacket and pitched it to the floor, he noticed his thick powerful chest—twice the size of a normal man. He was six-foot-five—a towering gargantuan! He had to be on some type of potent steroid regimen.

"I think he's been injecting some type of nano-cellular regeneration serum," Elisa whispered after Coflin gestured at them with his gun to sit down next to the Stage 4. "He's progressed beyond my help."

Coflin began calling commands into the long line of hologram stages. "Which stage should I use? Which one! Damn—I don't know…can't remember…having trouble calibrating my system with this matrix!" He flicked on his miniature wrist avatar, which materialized as an image of his old normal self. It began streaming with the far-Right Stage 4 at the opposite side of the room. He continued to move down the line of hologram stages right toward Manning—his avatar bandying from stage-to-stage, interfacing with the stage and all his followers holding up in various locations around Earth and in space.

"He's getting progressively irrational," Manning whispered to Elisa. Then he had another terrible thought. "No telling what he'll do when he realizes that the screen won't activate without my voice command *from* my wrist device."

Elisa's hands were shaking. He saw her like that before, on First Communication Day, the last time he'd seen her after

J.P. Osterman

Lynn died. Now, she appeared jolted, but calm and strong under pressure. She drew out her arm slowly from her side and secretly raised her sleeve. She had on a bracelet device—a more feminine and expensive version of the regular wrist devices but just as sophisticated. The silver rim was glowing green in Ready-mode. "It's a prototype several researchers have been testing."

Seeing her open connection and feeling a bolt of hope, Manning told her about Jenkens' Glow string. "If you can capture it, we'll have communication with the outside."

She covertly slid her device into the Glow string hovering inside the Stage 4's Smart Bar, and Jenkens' small avatar appeared.

"*Great* break for us," Manning whispered, "but get the avatar to process on your device not the stage. Coflin's coming."

After she switched hardware sites, Jenkens' Jackie Gleason avatar said: "We've learned that just prior to Coflin attacking the White House, he disembarked off *The Heed*. He's syncing with *that* astrofreighter and attempting to join, piggyback on, or subvert the Neltan/Earth wormhole when it activates in seven minutes at the Decagon. That gives you a twenty minute prep and translation time for images to coalesce through the screen."

"That must be the base of the Tech-No group—on the *Heed*," said Manning.

Just then, Coflin insert Manning's confiscated wrist tablet into the Encantado frame.

The Press Room filled with floodlights as Coflin's modified ceiling processors emitted yellow projection rays to their respective hologram stages.

The transmission screen glowed golden, and a deep hum resonated. The center of the screen began pulsing like a pool of rippling water. Coflin jumped back, obviously to avoid the quantum connection from sucking him inside. Manning pulled Elisa away from Stage 4, and all nine hologram stages began shining puzzle pieces into the droning transmission screen.

Battlefield Matrix

"Those shapes are signatures of the Event Horizon map from Nelta to Earth. Coflin's trying to alter them," Manning said.

Jenkens' tiny avatar interrupted him. "Coflin's group in space is uniting in echelon formation. They're starting to fire energy *at* the Decagon. They're positioning themselves to intercept energy as the wormhole quantum accelerates into the accelerator!"

Manning whispered: "Tell Rand to deter Stealth Force craft from the skirmish with terrorists. Attack *The Heed*. Block their attempt to penetrate the Neltan/Earth wormhole.

On the large transmission screen, outer space materialized.

A light breeze began sweeping through the Press Room—cosmic static filtering through Earth's atmosphere that the ventilation system began countering with flushing sounds.

On the screen appeared a gauntlet of terrorist craft in another quadrant in space. They were aligning and firing white lasers into a singular point inside one of the ten-mile-wide accelerators intertwined with tiny interferometers inside the Decagon.

Speakers in the Press Room activated a countdown to the incoming wormhole from Nelta: four minutes.

"From two different quadrants in space...the Tech-Nos and the terrorists are preparing to intercept the wormhole," Manning gasped. "*This* kind of battle is *completely* out of our control!"

Elisa said. "I have an idea, Sir."

"What?"

She pulled over a server robot and began rotating its body. "There should be an organic mound into which I can slip a connection." The serverbot's eyes flashed green after she ejected a pin-sized processor from her wrist device and inserted it into the serverbot's back hub.

"I asked Terra to line them up and synchronize them," Manning said. "I was hoping for a weapon, although that strategy now seems totally useless."

The interior of the transmission screen suddenly cascaded

outward. Coflin hurled his avatar at it to stop an influx of radioactivity.

She began sweeping apps from her wrist device into the serverbot's modified processor. "I believe I have a solution. Just a few more seconds…"

"Dr. Holton, I sure hope the Neltans are smart enough to think that something *like this* could happen to us who are so far behind their high-level of social consciousness. If the worst-case scenario *does* happen, I hope the Neltan Advancement Committee will have predicted it, hold off on their stasis, and try again to reach us somehow. In other words, I hope *they* have a backup plan." He felt numbness creeping through his body and static on his skin. He smelled burning oil. "The air in this room is changing…like it's taking on the Neltan atmosphere." He rotated Stage 4's now difficult Smart Bar to show stats of the room. The oxygen level was climbing, the nitrogen level decreasing. He coughed—the air stinging his nasal passages.

After she gasped for air, she whispered, "Don't give up hope, Sir, 'cause I'm *not*!"

"What're ya doing?" He had a peripheral eye on Coflin, still occupied with the screen.

"I'm linking *my* avatar and all its apps to this serverbot. A simple program insert won't suffice to generate a new power conduit. I'm working to increase energy." Squinting as she struggled to stream in more apps, she sat still when Coflin stopped his activities and grimaced at her. "I just hope the hum of the activation apps inside the serverbot doesn't give me away."

"What type of energy conduit?" Manning asked when Coflin resumed his hacking tasks.

"Regent Jenkens showed me a gamma conduit in your office. I can interface *this* robot with that conduit and generate a weapon."

"Yes…that could be done. Good thinking," he said, noticing that Jenkens had streamed to her the Confidential blueprint. He couldn't feel angry. They needed it.

Battlefield Matrix

"And with the apps I'm about to stream into the serverbot, all developed from research several of us have been conducting on Station II, my device can interface with the other animalbots and serverbots you aligned. If I can get them all to lock on to the main ceiling hub, we can target Coflin and take him down," she said. Slowly, she slipped another wafer-thin processor into the serverbot's silicon belly.

"Talk to Dr. Coflin now, Sir. Make it appear as if we're engrossed with his each-and-every action. He craves for people to hear him. If we can appear as if we agree with him on everything, we will be redirecting his focus and use *his* technology against *him*."

In a calm voice, Manning pointed out to Coflin a flaw in the center stage that could affect its connection to the screen. He continued to pump him for more information as Elisa swept the gamma app into the serverbot's eyes that glowed green with activity and acceptance. After the serverbot turned toward Coflin, the other robotics began aligning in the same direction.

"Regent Jenkens," Elisa began, "download your weapon program into my avatar that's positioned in front of Regent Manning. It's programmed to generate an energy conduit through all the robotics into the main ceiling hub over Coflin. When my avatar appears in the main hub above him, activate the energy boost on your end. I don't know how much time it'll take because we're streaming through a few sources and we might encounter some parallax distortion, but after we generate a good buildup, the avatar should induce an explosion and stop Coflin."

"I hope the explosion'll be controlled," Manning said.

"Don't know, Sir," replied Elisa. "We'll have to hope the upsurge takes quickly."

When Coflin turned away to monitor the puzzle pieces forming on the huge screen, Manning whispered, "Disabling *The Heed* first must be your priority, Steve. It's Coflin's connection to this room and the place through which he's planning to make his big statement."

J.P. Osterman

Elisa reached down and double-tapped the serverbot with the top of her shoe when she saw the mechanical creature shine a red beam into the heads of the other robotics. Her tiny avatar appeared on the serverbot's back where only she and Manning could see it.

"Link with the other twenty-two robots and create that energy conduit," she whispered. "Keep constant that Corridor of Strength with Regent Jenkens as I programmed."

The interface is working," Manning said. "Your avatar's jumping from robot to robot."

She nodded yes at the main rainbow processor, now cycling wildly over Coflin. "When it cements there in place, it will begin to amass power and swell." She suddenly gasped as she peered up at Coflin.

"What!?" he asked.

She shuddered. "Either his body is undergoing some type of automatic modification, or he's injected himself with nanobots that are acting like genetic triggers. His skin is pitting and peeling. The bones in his fingers are about to break through his skin. His fingernails are black. They're about to fall off!" She trembled and gagged. "What the hell *is* he changing into 'cause he sure isn't Neltan *or* human!"

Manning pulled her toward him in a comforting gesture. "I don't know...never saw anything like this."

"Definitely, he's gone completely insane, Sir...poor guy," she said.

"Poor guy—huh!" he countered. "He's holding us hostage and could be responsible for the destruction of Earth if we can't stop this attack, Dr. Holton."

Elisa huffed out a sigh of contrition. "I'm sorry, Sir, how thoughtless...especially now that we know that *he* downed *Greeter* and killed my best friend." She tapped a bulge under her blouse that was under her top button.

Manning recognized the outline—Lynn's gold locket. "You have it...on you."

"Yes, Sir," she replied, her eyes appearing sorrowful.

"Well, Dr. Holton, if we get to the point where we realize

we might not make it outta here, I'll ask you to open that up so I can see her...see Lynn's face." He closed his eyes, imagining her next to him. When he opened them, he believed he might see Terra. Nowhere.

After a second's pause, Elisa said: "The guy was once a famous Biochemical Engineer with a meteoric rise in reputation. At one time, he solved the puzzle of the terrorists' hideouts."

"Well, you can plead that cause for him then after we apprehend him and I demand they give 'im the death penalty," Manning said. "I think that was sheer pretext though for contacting the enemy so he could elicit their help! That's how I'm going to portray him in a trial."

Suddenly, a hologram of the giant astrofreighter, *The Heed* lit up on a hologram stage in the Press Room as Coflin's avatar enlarged.

Terra appeared.

"She's back!" Manning shouted, lunging out of his chair.

Elisa tugged him back. "No, Sir, she's not. It's Terra, but this program is working for Dr. Coflin. I can see by the Eye Glow. This Terra's Standard Form is shorter, and her hair and face shinier like it's a character in a decade's old, Sky Rim game."

"Activate the wormhole now," Coflin ordered. He stepped up onto the large hologram stage in front of the transmission screen. A large beam of bright light from the main ceiling hub engulfed him. The image of his body was about to stream around the globe for all of humanity to see, *and* the Neltans.

As Coflin zoomed in on *The Heed* and activated a conference call, his Tech-No guards threw him a flash pin that he inserted into the stage. Faces of engineers on *The Heed* appeared in virtual form in front of him. They began a series of actions to summon the Neltans. A bright, white ray of light swept over Coflin's body.

Elisa flicked her avatar at the shadow side of the ceiling processor where her red avatar was expanding and surging with energy. From the center of the new partition between the

Press Room and the Oval Office—still displaying an illusion of smoking rubble—was a thin, red, laser beam striking her avatar. "I can't get a precise time, but my avatar will overload in approximately three minutes, Sir."

"That's the destruct sequence *we* have," Jenkens avatar whispered through Stage 4's Smart Bar.

Standing in his white aura, Coflin straightened his shirt and patted down his frizzy, thin, red and gray hair.

"He looks like he's positioning himself to make a speech," Manning said.

A vibration began cascading through the White House.

"*That* feels like the entire planet is cracking up!" Manning said. Coflin tipped over a bit, appearing to almost fall but then stood back up. "It's time—9:10!" Manning said. "The preemptive opening of the Neltan/Earth wormhole at the Decagon!"

"*The Heed* isn't adjusting quantum frequencies between the Decagon and us," Jenkens barked, "and the terrorists attacking the Decagon don't know that's happening! General Rand says that every atomic structure emits a frequency. If these two groups don't calculate for that frequency adjustment, we could die as the Neltans direct energy into the Decagon to open the Neltan/Earth wormhole."

"Damn—can't Stealth Force in both quadrants in space compensate for the maladjustment? We're fighting off two enemies in two locations, and only we know it." Manning felt a crippling panic almost drop him to the floor along with the quaking ground until Elisa lifted him up. As she gave the two-minute countdown to her avatar's overload, Manning added: "Jenkens, can't we re-align the tropopause shield to deflect *The Heed*'s interference? Or maybe engineers on Station II can send a laser pulse into the terrorists' line of battle and disintegrate *that* channel to the wormhole." After Jenkens' avatar whispered that The Military, engineers, and researchers were doing everything to stop Coflin, Manning shouted: "Jenkens! All our astrofighters will disintegrate...that's the *complete* annihilation of our forces—*thousands* of people—if this gravitational fluctuation continues!"

Dr. Coflin's body began glowing. Each hologram stage began projecting onto him its interfacing, processor ceiling light. A quantum-transporter was now operational.

The puzzle pieces on the IMAX screen began solidifying into faces.

"It's exactly fifteen minutes after nine, and I have established contact with the Neltans inside the wormhole," Coflin said excitedly to his two followers who had just finished re-enforcing the double doors in the Press Room. His voice raspy and wavering in the quantum current, he ordered his men: "Activate Regent Manning's processor inside the Encantado frame. I am streaming his words to interface with the Decagon so people around the globe and the Neltans will see and hear me."

"I have about one minute until my avatar explodes and takes him out," Elisa said through piercing angry eyes.

Coflin began to speak. "Everyone...on Earth and on Nelta—" He paused and inhaled an expression of pain.

As he spoke, Elisa said, "Can the Neltans *really* hear this, Sir?" She checked the avatar that was accumulating energy and power by the second.

Manning thought a quick prayer, asking for an immediate explosion. "Yes, the Neltans can see *and* hear him."

Ambassador Shaesar appeared next to Coflin with a shocked expression on his face. He had some features in common with Dr. Coflin: enlarged frontal brow, tall physique, bulging chest with disproportional thin limbs, thin and sunken-in cheeks, thin and very long eyebrows, and the Neltan large brown eyes. Nothing more. In contrast, Coflin's wild red hair, warty and scaly skin, and two-toned flesh were gruesome mutations. Shaesar began walking around Dr. Coflin. Extending a round palm device that was obviously medical, biometric, and genetic in orientation, he began scanning Coflin with the flashing-edged tool.

"Yes!" said Coflin, "this is what I want you to do, Ambassador...to see a real interspecies creation. Me."

J.P. Osterman

Shaesar waved forward a few of his colleagues who had been standing in the background inside a Neltan cavern. When they appeared virtually in the Press Room alongside Shaesar, they began scanning Coflin as well.

"*True* quantum teleportation," Elisa said. "Coflin is harnessing and perpetuating power from all the holosite feeds of his Tech-No groups on Earth and his astrofreighter, *The Heed.* Then he's reversing the magnetic field and gravity, and dislocating himself in space/time."

The nine hologram stages began vibrating.

Shaesar disappeared from the room as the crowds outside the White House began screaming and shouting in panic and confusion. They had been watching the teleportation via large airships and virtual shows on the sides of buildings. They had shut off.

Jenkens said: "Somewhere along the fifty-million, light-year, wormhole network, there is...what we can best discern...a type of wormhole conflagration that's occurring."

"What! No," she and Manning gasped.

"Unfortunately, yes," Jenkens' avatar said. "Using the backup screen in the Rotunda that's functioning on half-power, I was able to quantum-transmit an image of what's happening to you through the wormhole. I asked the Neltans for help and patience as we work to resolve the problem, hopefully, before the event horizons misalign and sever the connection between our two planets for good at midnight."

Elisa held her stomach in gesture of anguish. "If you don't stop the conflagration, the incoming energy could explode and radiate planets everywhere between Nelta and Earth!"

"Yes, Dr. Holton," Jenkens said through his tiny avatar hovering over Stage 4. "Space Station II's astrophysics section is back-tracking to discover the problem as General Rand directs two battles from Station III. They're using all our high-tech capability to stop the Tech-Nos and the terrorists from interfering with the wormhole and to reconnect us to Ambassador Shaesar."

On the modified Center Stage in front of the giant screen,

Battlefield Matrix

Coflin's body began fading in and out of existence. He was present inside the Press Room, but at the same time, somewhere else. He said into the screen, "I am half-human, half-Neltan."

Shouts and screams outside the White House quickly stopped. The World was listening. That meant the Neltans were hearing his every word as well.

Coflin continued: "This is what—*who*—you might see in the future if you sign *The Pact*, if *Sagan* journeys to Nelta, and if, at some point in the future, our two species comingle, that is *if Sagan* returns to Earth. From DNA maps we intercepted from Nelta, I genetically modified myself to help you make that decision. Have you thought about the future? Two or three thousand years *into* the future? *If* the *Sagan* crew votes to return to Earth with Neltan visitors, as people around the globe have been envisioning, what will humanity become if we procreate with the Neltans? Think of marriage! Children! As you can see, my body is completely unnatural and contrary to God's law. A person like me will never be accepted into the family of humanity. I believe that most of you will agree that my current form is deeply offensive to social norms. If you allow *this* to happen—" He pointed at his body. "You will destroy humanity."

As he continued to speak, Elisa was staring at her avatar in Overload Mode inside the beehive hub processor above Coflin. The intensifying power was now draining energy away from Coflin, making his body and voice waver and echo. The wormhole disturbance in space was also exacerbating his deteriorating condition.

Coflin said: "Ha—have you, everyone, *everyone*, on both worlds, re—*really* considered what you are, *you are*—" His voice was de-materializing from reality. "Approving by allowing The Regency to sign tonight's—*night's*—Pact?" He glanced down at his body with a shocked expression on his glowing face. He was obviously aware that something had gone terribly wrong with his quantum teleportation to Nelta. His two followers began shouting commands into all nine hologram stages in an attempt to stabilize their leader's image. The stages were showing places around the globe where people had gathered to hear Final Communication. Many of those locations were those where Coflin's Tech-No groups were waiting in obvious eager anticipation of their leader's success in stopping The Regency from signing *The Pact*.

As Coflin faded in and out of existence, Manning said, "Everything about him that makes human is gone. Dr. Coflin is dead."

Elisa said: "The Neltan DNA is the dominant species, but because he altered *his* DNA, he's completely deformed...*ooo*," she grimaced. "Notice that his eyes have completely altered, his nasal bone is thin and straight, and its cartilage is convex." She gasped in an expression of awareness and added, "Oh—I get why this genetic deterioration is occurring so fast!"

"Why?" he asked.

"Over the millennia, at some point or points in their history, the Neltans must have participated in a massive eugenics experiment," she began. "As someone researching that growing area of nano-cellular biology, I believe that's why we've been seeing all the drastic changes in Dr. Coflin that appear to be set to automatic in his DNA."

"I see," he exhaled. "Eugenics, nano-technology, organic biology and morphology is at work simultaneously within the Neltan's DNA."

"Maybe, in part, because of the effects of The Matter Stream on their planet?" she asked, seeming to pose the question for future inquiry. Her eyes widened in enthusiasm as they reflected Coflin's changing body. "*We* can't really know what's going on though, nor do we have the time to ask the Neltans, considering that we're supposed to be signing a pact with them yet tonight. And we really won't know the full details until people from Earth arrive on Nelta and encounter the Neltans face-to-face."

"From what we're seeing right now, Sir," began Elisa, "and I'd bet my savings on it, that the Neltans' altered genetics is most likely *why* they need us to transport *perfect* human DNA to them. Without us, their species will surely die."

Manning felt his anxiety intensify. As the quantum stream from Terra's hub continued to hold Coflin's body precariously in two locations, he said: "Coflin, *The Pact*! We *have* to stabilize the wormhole. Cut off this connection to your *Heed* now!" He felt a drag in his voice as if he were trying to speak through thick air. "We're running out of time before all hell breaks loose and destroys the Earth! What use will your statement be if we're all dead?"

"Then the two species surely won't mix!" he cried in reply. Coflin's body began wavering rapidly inside the teleportation light—his guards responding by manipulating the Center Stage to stabilize the quantum-communication stream from the Decagon.

At that moment, Shaesar's image appeared in front of the transmission screen. Wearing form fitting black pants and an ivory shirt, he appeared taller than before. His yellowish skin was glowing with vibrancy. Surrounded by The Halo Effect, he had the brightness of ionizing photons quantum processing through intergalactic electromagnetism, gravity and dark matter.

"Ambassador, we have a problem but we're working to fix it," Manning called.

"We know," Shaesar said, waving his hand over Stage 3 right, which was directly right of Center Stage on which Coflin's body was teleporting. Shaesar had an expression of fright on his smooth shiny face. "We are working on our end to stop an impending destruction near your Decagon. I'm activating a link with the new Terra to help us. But we might not succeed. Too many of our scientists have entered stasis chambers. We cannot revive them so quickly without killing them." On Stage 3 appeared a full-blown cosmic tornado: the Neltan/Earth wormhole. "This is what we now have to contain," he said.

A small team of Manning's Enforcers finally burst into the Press Room.

Coflin's two bodyguards managing to keep them at bay as

Coflin yelled: "Before you sign that Pact, ask yourselves: What *kind* of specie-soup are you permitting?"

At that, the beehive hub above Coflin began popping and blaring rapid pulses of rainbow light. Elisa's avatar had just slid past the tipping point, triggering an overload. The matrix processor emitted a ball of white light. Coflin's body began stretching—the top of his head disintegrating into particles.

Through a horrified expression, Coflin cried: "What's— what happened! Stop!" His mouth evaporated into quantum-teleporting particles that streamed into the hub and disappeared.

Manning pulled Elisa back when she wanted to help him. "No matter how well Coflin altered the new Terra to his specifications, the hub alone can't teleport his body while holding Shaesar's image constant here. The evolved matrix alone cannot process this type intense quantum flow without more energy streaming from Nelta."

Jenkens' body in virtual form materialized on Stage 4. The matrix Firewall was working to stabilize security in the Oval Office now that Enforcers had captured Coflin's henchmen.

"What do we do? Can we help him?" Elisa asked. "But we dare not get within the teleportation ring of that processing zone or we'll get sucked in like that too!" She scooted to where her back hit the wall and looked as if she might soak into it.

The quantum beam sparked as the hyperspectral transporter light flickered. Whenever the light flashed off, it revealed Coflin's peeled skin, red flesh and patches of bone. Outside the White House, people were shouting words of shock and terror. Holograms of him were blaring everywhere, showing him gradually lifting into the hub and disintegrating.

"Terminate the live stream through the Firewall to the outside, Steve!" Manning ordered. As Jenkens complied, the show extinguished to the public. The tropopause shield was on Reflect-mode, its repelling forces pointing toward space.

Jenkens said: "General Rand is expanding the shield twenty miles and ordering all five space stations to descent to protect them from the wormhole conflagration that could unleash radioactivity on Earth. Our Stealth Force craft have contained the Decagon—"

"Thank God!" sighed Manning.

"But because of this powerful fluctuation in magnetism and gravity, and the matrix being unstable, communications are out. I can't give you more info until this Neltan/Earth wormhole settles. I'll keep ya posted," Jenkens said, and then he faded.

Elisa's energized avatar then vaporized. Tiny rainbows struck the teleportation beam surrounding the remainder of Daryl Coflin's body. The lights began cycling like a high-energy laser-light show. Still the teleportation conduit wouldn't extinguish.

Manning called Jenkens who re-appeared on the stage. "Coflin musta input a stolen fraction of The Matter Stream somewhere that's holding open this conduit. Steve, you've got to help me find the source and extinguish it!" He grabbed a small, incoming Enforcer drone and threw it into the quantum-transporter. It broke into pieces and left the room in a lightning strike.

As Coflin's followers began struggling against the Enforcers who captured them, Manning shouted, "If you help us, you won't do time. Where'd he put that stolen Matter Stream sample? We need it to keep this place from completely blowing up!"

Dr. Coflin's body began stretched like taffy into the ceiling hub. Everyone covered their eyes, peeking through slat in their fingers, to watch the spectacular anomaly. A Doppler blue rainbow burst into a final flash of light. Coflin's was gone. Center Stage glowed green, with a sparkling outline of his body. Droning like thousands of angry bees, Terra's rainbow cycling processor sucked up the outline.

The Press Room quickly turned silent, the air still lightly smoking.

Chapter 11

Encantado

"That residual flash was blinding!" Elisa Holton cried, rubbing her eyes.

"Keep 'em closed, Dr. Holton! The flash blindness should subside soon," Manning said, blinking through the stinging sensations. "Something treacherous must be occurring inside the Neltan/Earth wormhole. I hope people outside weren't exposed to the flash."

"This sure hurts," she said.

"Jenkens...General Rand," he called. "I need updates." He felt as if he had just stepped out of the Space Simulation Laboratory where they had tested satellites with the equivalent of "1.5 sun" brightness.

On the walls of the Press Room, twenty main Terra mounts expanded like small red, balloons ready to pop; but instead of exploding, they imploded to gray goop.

He felt the static of their electromagnetic discharge pricking his scalp and pinching his skin like nettles. Jenkens was hailing him, but his words sounded like stretching vowels.

Battlefield Matrix

Elisa grabbed her tattered jacket and flung it around her neck. "I feel a pull to the center, Sir." Her voice to was being distorted by the air. "The gravity in here is unstable!"

Feeling the magnetic tug as objects in the room appeared to slightly wave, he pressed against the edge of Hologram Stage 4 Left for support, grabbed the edge, and gently pulled her to him. "I remember this feeling. The air has that same tang as on First Communication Day."

"Then we better find cover 'cause something wild's about to happen!" she called.

The IMAX transmission screen droned. The center liquefied. The oscillating, resonating deep hum weakened his knees and he fell to the floor. "The screen! It's trying to activate to bring back the Neltans, but the Four Forces are vying for supremacy like matter and antimatter colliding!" He saw a red pool of color in the screen "Is that...blood?" he shouted to her. As she pushed back her brown bangs and nodded in agreement, he said: "The matrix hasn't reported any accident or death toll. And we haven't heard about any deadly accident inside the wormhole..."

As he was about to call out an order for Jenkens to perform a death scan and locate a death site, Shaesar appeared with five Neltan scientists from the Advancement Committee. Their images were quantum streaming through the Neltan cyclotron and the Decagon system, but there was drag time from the circuitous connection they had established via the backup screen in the Rotunda. Jenkens' image appeared on a small wall-zone in the partition between the Oval Office and the Press Room. He had altered the Illusion of Destruction, returning the partition back to its original state thus rendering the door to the Oval Office visible once more. He told Manning and Elisa that General Rand and scientists on Station II were working to deactivate the backup screen so the Press Room screen could process more particles and increase in resolution.

Shocked at the sudden appearance of the Neltans but happy to see them in spite of the wild atmospheric conditions,

Manning tried to focus on what he needed to say to them. This was it—Final Communication. No telling how long they really had left to sort out the details of *Sagan*'s future mission and the precise instructions on what they were supposed to do after disembarking on Nelta. Many times, Shaesar had said they needed to input an algorithmic world into *Sagan*'s navigation. Did builders fix Navigation from the earlier terrorist attack? Obviously, the Decagon was functioning because the Neltans were linking with it through the wormhole network. But what happened to the terrorists and Tech-Nos who had been trying to interfere with the Decagon? And no one had heard anything regarding *The Spider* and other astrofighters that had been battling their enemies. Interference was rendering that section in space, *Null and Void*, nonexistent! Impossible since the Neltans were standing in the Press Room vis-à-vis all the quantum technology. He had to make the best and most of their precarious and fragile time to seal their bargain and sign *The Pact*. From the wide-eyed and blank stares on their faces, the Neltans appeared frightened.

"Something's wrong. I see your concerned expressions," Manning said.

"That malfunctioning processor in your Press Room opened a hot continuum on your end, Regent Manning," Shaesar began in a foreboding tone. "We are working to strengthen *our* communications wormhole, but somewhere, on your end, after our spacefold conduit interfaced with the Decagon, some catastrophe has occurred in the translation imagers that are obscuring our view of one another."

"There was a wormhole conflagration at a fork-in-the-network beyond Mars," Jenkens interrupted, "and General Rand is trying to reestablish contact with our astrocraft that were battling terrorists in that area. In another section of that same quadrant, we had astrofighters in a skirmish with those protesters we told you about. We thought they were an insignificant opposition, but we were wrong, as you can see by what just occurred inside here...this messy Press Room, with Dr. Coflin, their leader. Given what we know, but that we can't analyze fully due to wild interference from the conflagration, that quadrant you're referring to is unstable—"

The floor vibrated and a low rumble flowed through the Press Room.

Feeling static waft over his skin as he lost his footing, Manning grabbed the edge of the Stage 4 that almost dislodged off its base and would have struck Elisa Holton. He pulled himself back to safety alongside her as the ground stabilized. "What can we do to stop this hot continuum, Ambassador?" he asked, and then he called for General Rand to send launch craft to assist astrofighters in that quadrant. "And don't bring people back in here just yet. Keep them in the bunkers for safety."

The red lava mixture at the center of the transmission screen began extending into the Press Room like a branching tree.

Shaesar shouted to his scientists who were manipulating the wormhole's flow through a facility inside Nelta: "Stop emitting the magnetic/electrostatic pulse to the Decagon!" When a small vibration cascaded through the room, he gestured in overwhelming relief. "The space/time dislocation rippled through the spacefold network between us, terminating at the fork-in-the-network inside that unstable quadrant," he explained.

The Smart Bar flashed the time as it cocked back into place: 9:35 p.m. After another slight rumple, Elisa stepped back and had a lost and forlorn expression on her face. "I hope we can fix the disorientation because this air in here is getting more ionized by the moment." She wrapped the jacket around her neck and shoulders. Her teeth were clattering. "I don't like this," she added, glancing around as if spotting ghosts and doubting her senses. "Terra just activated briefly and showed me the stats on the environment. She's still fizzled out and her matrix repairing, but the emergency must have forced her into a brief stasis. Some molecules in here appear to be altering. That's why we're seeing distortions in all the objects."

"A dark matter and magnetic convergence...that's what this

feels like to me," Manning said, and then he ordered Jenkens to search the entire solar system to see if the Wilkinson probe could detect the exact alteration in space/time. He told General Rand to counteract all anomalous dark energy pulses with solar emissions through the Decagon.

The red center of the transmission screen abruptly swooshed as a bright ball of white energy whipped out of the screen and struck the area where the green outline of Coflin's body once stood. When the energy slushed back into place, it left a small, crystal green entity that began hovering over the white, glowing Center Stage. The rainbow processor above the sharp-edged being was cycling wildly—shining light brightly on to the creature.

"Is that a crystal or a rock?" Manning asked. Shaesar and his Advancement Committee retreated to the far side of the room and began their assessment using various types of devices on Nelta. Their images were still present, but barely, like a mirage. If the screen were to warp further, they'd be gone. Manning realized he had to protect that screen at all cost.

Elisa peeked out of her hiding spot between the two artificial trees that were now dead branches in the tingly air. She slowly retrieved her bracelet device off the serverbot, activated it, and began scanning the entity. "Whatever the formation is, Sir, it's feeding on the atmosphere."

The hovering green crystal was crackling and snapping as it began branching out and slowly expanding.

Enforcers and Secret Service agents dashed into the Press Room. Their weapons whined as they lined up in three rows and targeted the sharp green entity.

The glowing shiny entity retaliated, crackling like shattering glass as it whipped gaseous extensions at the officers.

"No laser fire!" called Manning. "If the entity *is* energy oriented, a laser strike could fuel its expansion."

As the troops retreated, the entity unleashed two wisps of green gas at two Enforcers. One streak sliced off the top of an Enforcer's head. The second whip impaled the other Enforcer whose gun accidentally detonated, deflected off the entity and nearly skewered Elisa.

"Back down," Manning shouted through shrieks and moans. "And retrieve those bodies!"

From inside the sanctuary of the Oval Office, Jenkens ordered another line of incoming troops: "Use a bullet defense!"

After throwing down their laser weapons and catching an arsenal of guns, Enforcers fired on the green entity with semi-automatic rounds. Line-after-line they bombarded the green shiny entity with bullets. Their firepower continued to bounce off an invisible circle of warped air as the Press Room filled with smoke and sparks from rainbow cycling processor hubs still in a state of serious repair. Sprays of extinguishing rain unleashed from the ceilings and then reset.

"It should be on the ground by now and not still floating," Elisa said, her scanner still analyzing the entity. "Its structure is not of this world, Regent Manning…nothing the terrorists or Tech-Nos could have created. This Particle-app I'm using to analyze it indicates an increase in fermions." She flicked her wrist device, and Jenkens acknowledged receiving the information through his previous connection to Stage 4's active Smart Bar. As he holosited the data to the others, she added: "All matter around the entity is undergoing superconductivity."

"That's why the thing is absorbing laser strikes and expanding," Jenkens said. "But what concerns us is the creature's circle of protection. That space convection around it is like an event horizon with the entity at its singularity!"

"After all this bullet fire, the crystal formation should be dust," Manning said, gently guiding Elisa alongside him as he slowly sidled along the wall, his goal the Oval Office. They had a long way to go: in front of five giant sets of double doors and seventy feet of wall zones. Shaesar and the Neltans were still appearing there. Maybe they'd have more suggestions if he could talk to them face-to-face.

She had a firm grip on the artificial trees, gliding them in front of her as shields. Officers and their firepower were protecting the double doors, and the Encantado program on the base of the transmission screen was glowing orange in Analysis-mode of the creature. The next stage of the program's activation would be the red Counterattack-mode.

Manning said, "That shape-shift program should soon launch a defense...I hope."

"It feels like we're in the middle of one of those old horror flicks from the 1950s," Elisa scoffed. "Nothing we're doing is capable of stopping it!"

When the entity swelled and pulsed as if it might again expand, Enforcers retreated to the double doors, shielding Manning and Elisa as they began slowly to maneuver behind them.

"Where the hell's this thing from and how the hell do we stop it?" Manning cried.

Jenkens appeared in a small wavering hologram over Elisa's wrist device when she reiterated that question to him. "With Terra's matrix mending, I'm able to redirect the Gamma app on the doorframe to align with the growing creature. "A gamma fire might evaporate it. Move back. I'll try."

Shaesar's streaming image solidified on obvious emergency power. "No—not a gamma strike! This being is from another dimension!" With the same palm device he had used to analyze Dr. Coflin, he displayed the results of the creature over a small hologram stage that had lifted next to him on Nelta. "Dr. Holton is correct in assessing the fermion reading and the entity's surrounding superconductivity. If you attack with a gamma frequency, you could explode another multiverse into this reality, or implode this universe into another multiverse. *Nothing* you are currently using will affect the entity, send it back to its own dimension, and terminate its dimension."

Meanwhile, officers began falling back to the double doors, waiting for further orders.

"This is the onset of a matter/anti-matter extinction event!" gasped Elisa.

"We don't want that," Jenkens shouted, "but if you're right, then we gotta stop it!"

"No further countermeasures, Steve, just wait for further instructions from the Neltans," Manning called, "and keep General Rand's connection open, and that of Station II, so we can prepare for whatever information and countermeasures Shaesar gives us."

The creature had obviously detected Shaesar's presence. It began whipping green, thin tentacles of glowing gas into his image. Snaps and crackling noises resounded like glass continuously breaking.

"It must possess an intelligence we can't understand," Elisa said, calling up her tiny white-coated avatar over her wrist device. "I'm linking to my lab on Station II to assess the creature's anatomy and cellular composition. That facility has the most advanced medical grid and is synched with the facility on *Sagan* so I could prepare for the interview with you, Sir, but for a deeper connection to that special matrix, I have no access." She whispered, "Analysis, please," and her avatar's eyes turned green in Scan-mode.

"Wait—I'll get you that access to *Sagan*'s entire matrix, temporarily, of course," he replied. "Since Terra has selected you for The List and to be one of the Regeneration Specialists, you'll have access to most of those areas anyway."

Glancing at the area of looming disaster, she appeared surprised. "Wow—yes, *yes*, Regent Manning! Thanks!" She exhaled a breath of tense relief. "Now, after I link to those specs, I should be able to run a molecular and genetic program, decode the creature's composition, and find its vulnerabilities—"

"Finally—a gold lining in a black cloud," he said.

All the while, the green, shiny crystal entity was continuing to wreak havoc: toppling chairs, frothing the ceiling, and staining the carpet that was bubbling as the Auto-Repair app kept activating. The crackling and snapping entity kept its locus-of-directional expansion on Shaesar—whipping its gaseous tentacles into his spacefolding image and teleportation beam.

J.P. Osterman

"I wonder why the creature wants him?" asked Elisa. "It looks pissed at all of them, like it's retaliating against them. Did the Neltans do something to the species in that dimension?"

After uttering his code to Elisa's tiny avatar, Manning said: "Go…find something we can use to send back this entity into its own dimension. Whatever is occurring between their two species, we can't concern ourselves. We've got our own deal to seal with the Neltans."

"Yes, Sir." She began her diligent search-and-retrieval through *Sagan*'s matrix.

Shaesar and his colleagues stepped back—their holograms filling with static—when General Rand ordered two special scientists into the room. They positioned themselves behind nano-infused tungsten barricades. One scientist inserted Skyrmion wall instruments into the carpet to analyze composite particles at work throughout the room. Her colleague had wheeled in robotic probes and then began a deep scan of the entity's slow-branching shiny ivy.

Shaesar said to Regent Jenkens: "What you need to do is to align the hologram stages to emit a red-shifted signal at the entity. That act should inhibit the creature from spreading beyond this room. We have used neutrino bursts to manipulate dimensional windows in the past. We'll try this mixture of neutrinos and rift-shifted light to shove the entity back into its dimension and seal the space/time rip that allowed it to enter here."

Jenkens linked with the center stage. "Hologram stage alignment complete. We're on standby for further orders."

Manning felt discombobulated in the wild whiplash of wind and ions. "What happened, Ambassador? What brought that thing here?"

Shaesar's posture straightened in an expression of certainty. "The fluctuation of polarity inside Dr. Coflin's conduit opened up the dimension, Regent Manning. This dimension is polymorphic, and the entity will eventually adapt to Earth if you don't send it back."

Battlefield Matrix

"It could *stay* here?" Jenkens grimaced. "No!" His image and the background of the Oval Office were now appearing on a Security wall zone next to the office door.

More moaning scientists entered the room. One shouted, "Sounds like we're in for trouble!"

"Yes," Shaesar added, "and until we can determine *this* creature's composition and how it's interacting with Earth's atmosphere, continue bombarding it with red light, low frequency sounds, and magnetic-electric neutrino currents. Through the screen, we're quantum streaming an ion mix into the room. Working together, they *should* counter the fermion-charged space with an approximate light-speed spin of atomic strings around the creature. Blasts of Strong Forces at the creature's point of entry should render that location hostile to others of its kind and stop them from permeating *this* reality."

The bluntness of Shaesar's answer shocked Manning. "What if we can't stop the entity, Ambassador? You said it could...adapt?"

Shaesar's yellow-tinged, glowing face took on a sad expression. "The entity will become a problem for Earth."

"It could suck us into *its* world ya mean!" Jenkens cried. He began barking orders to scientists on Station II. "Find a solution with Dr. Holton, people...now!"

With shields in hand, scientists clad in protective wear dashed into the room, interfaced with detectors alongside the steel barriers, and then raced to strategic locations around the entity. When their hardware vibrated to capacity in high-pitched drones and electrical Tesla flashes, they set their targets to the green branching creature with energy as per Shaesar's instructions.

Manning ordered, "Fire!"

They attacked the entity with red, laser-light power, a low cascade of musical notes, and bursts of neutrinos.

Manning felt the drone churn through his intestines as static crawled across his scalp. He held his chest in the moments when the pulsing forces stopped. "It looks like your containment plan won't last long, Ambassador," he said, noticing a green crystal climb like glow-ivy creep toward the ceiling. "The entity seems to be converting oxygen into water and growing."

Shaesar replied, "Yes, but without your countermeasures, the creature would be all through this room—"

"Like bindweeds devouring a garden!" Jenkens interjected.

The dimensional entity continued to crackle as its sharp round body slowly inched across the ceiling. The creature looked like a glowing mound of green coral with the whipping tentacles of an octopus hovering in the center of the room.

The sight triggered a memory. "This may sound simplistic, but when I was a kid, I saw something like this."

"What, Sir?" Elisa asked.

"We called them Living Rocks. It was a store-bought science experiment," he replied. "We put the crystal starter kit in water and they'd immediately start to spread and grow...their growth directly correlated to their supply of water. This dimensional alien appears the same."

She quickly looked up from her research. "This *entity* could have the same construct."

Jenkens said, "Makes sense...and this could show that matter in other dimensions might have matter in common with ours...or that other dimensions sprout from one another."

She brought up the image of the crystal kit over her wrist device and her avatar began a comparative scan. "I'll have results in seconds, but my guess is that the creature is using our air much like the living crystals use water to grow...salt, water and air."

When Shaesar concurred, Manning waved to the scientists and said: "Quick! Bring in sprayers filled with various concentrations of salt water and commence spraying the entity." Then he ordered Jenkens who was streaming with matrix techs: "At the same time they're spraying, you deprive the entity of oxygen by blasting it with that magnetic-electrostatic string current. That will show us if Dr. Holton is as correct as her calculations indicate."

As they complied, Elisa said, "This alien entity...holding its dimensional space…seems like it's analyzing its new environment and purposefully maneuvering around us—*whoa*!"

Suddenly, the ceiling buckled. Dust fell in a scattering, nano-robotic rain. When the robotic particles rippled toward the entity, its gyring current swept them up, wherein they self-organized, morphed into sharp shards and struck the floor like knives. Another vibration ensued, the rolling sound echoing reverberating to the outside atmosphere.

"What was *that*?" Manning shouted, looking to Shaesar for answers.

The green creature bounced, its gaseous tentacles imploded like a fired rubber band. Enforcers began a concentrated spray of a saline solution.

"Shaesar's hologram is still here," Jenkens began, "so that meant the disturbance wasn't related to the Neltan/Earth wormhole." His body shook in a fearful expression when he announced that the earthquake was felt globally but had not resulted from any geological activity. The time was 9:45 p.m. Manning said, "The catastrophe must be atmospheric." He ordered all live streaming scientists watching the Press Room to assess the tropopause shield.

Shaesar shouted, "The encroaching dimension and this creature are not responsible!"

"It's like the poles are about to shift. Hear that wind?" Manning asked, remembering First Communication. "Check beyond our orbit."

"My connection to the Research Facility is weak," Elisa began, "but I'm receiving an A-Okay signal. Station II is structurally sound, and everyone's safe. Oh wait—now we have a tidal wave in the Pacific heading toward Tokyo."

Manning turned her wrist device toward him, linked to the International Seismic Facility, and began watching the wave until a geomagnetic interference disrupted the connection. He said to General Rand's wobbly image that had materialized next to Jenkens in the Oval Office: "Consolidate all data. We need the cause of these disturbances. It's not this in here, so what cosmic event occurred beyond our atmosphere?"

General Rand replied: "We've been trying to hail Captain Bartlet on *The Spider*. He's in a good position to analyze the quadrants around the moon. We believe he just completed a heated but successful battle on the lunar surface. We can't know for certain, however, 'cause of all this damn interference and space/time distortions due to that wormhole conflagration. We're receiving no clarity from anywhere in space."

"Damn!" Manning said. "All this mayhem started with Coflin and his crude accelerator *The Heed* disrupting the Neltan/Earth wormhole."

"We're doing everything militarily possible, Regent Manning, to assess and repair everything that went wrong at the Decagon site so we can maintain the Neltans' images in the Press Room," began General Rand. "But we're limited in troops and stretched out thin between protecting the Decagon accelerator and fighting terrorists and Tech-Nos."

Noticing the green entity strengthening as its sharp tentacles expanded, Manning felt a sudden impending doom. "Keep calling Captain Bartlet, General." He inhaled deeply and huffed, "Damn—everything's so chaotic!" He felt numb—a deep sickening intuition. "I'm contacting all solar stations through Dr. Holton's holosite and ordering them to intensify power to the tropopause shield. If anything's coming from space, that shield should protect us."

When Enforcers fired another intense stream of saline on the crystalline entity, the creature froze and turned shades of shiny sea green.

Elisa paused. "I think we stopped it...yes!" She and Manning were now only ten yards away from Shaesar and the Neltans, but they had to pause and wait.

As an Enforcer was about to touch the entity, its crystal shell began vibrating and shedding its saline-based mold.

"Try hitting it with acids *and* bases!" Manning shouted.

Along the creature's path appeared streams of nanobots that began repairing the damage. As a few of the nanobots met the edge of the green crystal entity, the nanobots melted, creating black stalagmites on the floor and dripping stalactites on the ceiling. When the mess united with human blood from the entity's attack on several Enforcers, the red-and-black globs blended. The DNA began replicating.

"What's that rotten smell?" Breathing and gagging, Elisa put her hands over face. "Look over there, Sir...next to the entity."

Manning pointed to the ground. "Jenkens...you see that? Redirect the Repair grid to stop mending the materials in here."

"What a mess!" he replied.

Those are human parts...fingers!" cried Elisa. "There...toes!" She vomited.

Shaesar shouted and waved for Manning and Elisa to retreat to the wall. Through a connection on one of the small wall zones, he said to them. "The unstable teleportation of that scientist created a quadrilateral singularity, Regent Manning. That is how the entity slipped into our dimension. The concentration of quantum-nonlocality released what we have determined is Dimension Eight." Shaesar showed them the results that were gyring over his hologram stage on Nelta. The frequency readings were unrecognizable, 3D algorithms and musical notes. "You have Dimension Eight and one of its inhabitants in *your* presence."

"Dimension Eight?" Manning repeated. A lash of sickness stabbed his stomach. The glare of the green glowing entity stung his eyes, its pungent zone making his sinuses water. "You said String Theory is fact; but until now, I never woulda believed it!" He blew his nose and shoved the Kleenex in his pocket. "What do we do to get rid of it, Ambassador?"

"There are many composites of that Dimension Eight world, and we're in the process of determining which pattern is manifesting," Shaesar said as the numbers 8A through 8F appeared in holographic spheres around him. On Nelta in the background, three scientists were busily analyzing Gravitational Lensing Mirrors—doors into other dimensions. They were quantum-imaging all their results to Shaesar, who upon receiving the 8A through 8F dimensional windows from them added, "When we know the dimension's precise structural equation, we can advise you how to send it back and seal off the space."

Jenkens said: "Every time that thing crackles toward the double doors and windows, we're blasting it with red-shift waves and spraying it with hydrogen chloride. That combination seems to be inhibiting the entity from spreading, thus far. Engineers are working to get the ceiling processors back on-stream inside and activate Terra. They're also sending in new nano-robotics to stop the spread of human tissue growth—"

"Thank God, 'cause this sight's horrible!" Elisa interrupted.

"And make sure that every scientist you can get ahold of is working on a solution to evacuate this entity and get Terra's savvy matrix up and streaming in here fast," Manning said.

Elisa wiped her eyes. She had been crying. "I received another assessment of the creature, Sir. The software adds an IQ app to its Body Imaging Scan hardware." The results appeared over her wrist device as a molecular reading, genetic design, and atomic structure. "The entity's polymorphic fractals are functioning as human fingers. That's why we're seeing human body parts where ever the entity comes in contact with our DNA. It's exploring."

"The entity *does* have intelligence," Manning said. "Stream that to Station II."

"Unfortunately," she began, "if its fractals continue their rate of expansion, this room's going to look like a square of solid green glass. See the trails it's leaving behind?"

In spite of the intense strategies to stop the entity, everywhere it managed to touch down, green crystals began spreading.

"But glass and crystal can be broken," Manning said, "right Shaesar?"

Regent Jenkens opened the door to the Oval Office and peeked outside his spot of safety. "Thornton, String Theorists are in the hallway. They brought a portable cyclotron to diffuse the encroaching dimension, *if* that's what Shaesar says we need to do. We're prepared to bring it inside. It's on low power and they can energize it on command."

"Do it," Manning said, "and be prepared to send down an EMP from the tropopause shield. The small cycloramic emission might stop the creature."

Elisa lifted her wrist device and showed them a picture of an augmented molecule that exploded. "Blowing it up isn't the answer." Her face was red, her eyes shining a terrified pool of greenish hazel. She definitely had acquired a new type of understanding of the entity.

"Then what *is* the answer?" Manning asked. She was breaking out in blotches on her face. "Are you all right? I hope the same thing's not happening to me—to *everyone* who's been in this room with that thing!" He looked at his reflection on her bracelet device. Nothing yet. "Jenkens—we're experiencing some type of weird reaction—"

"I'm calling the docs!" he shouted, and he shut the door and began a manual tight seal.

Through watery eyes, she replied, "I'm alright. Having trouble focusing, but I'm okay." She called on her tiny avatar, stopping its interface with Station II. "Sir, if I can get your wrist-tablet that Coflin stole from you, I believe I saw one of the apps on it that could help us."

After Shaesar gave his consent because the device had embedded into the Neltan Encantado program, Manning ordered two Enforcers to charge the transmission stage and yank out his red, glowing, round wrist device from out of the long bar on the frame of the screen. As they finally extracted the processor, the interior of the screen flashed a past image of Dr. Coflin. Manning waved for the Enforcer to toss it to him and then get out of the room. A green gaseous tentacle was approaching. On her way out of the double doors, the entity whipped her with a green tentacle. The Enforcer fell to the floor, shattering into green, red, and brown globs of crystals. The new nano-robotics in the room swarmed her, devouring her remains.

J.P. Osterman

After the gruesome scene, Jenkens said: "The singularity is expanding. Closing that singularity *must* be the answer to stopping the dimensional intrusion and the entity."

Agreeing, Manning asked Elisa, "What are going to do with my wrist device?" As he held it, the device began extending limbs like twitching spider's legs. He began volleying the squirming processor between his hands. "As you can see—"

The glowing red disc was twice the size of an old dollar coin and beginning to bubble with multicolored silicon welts. "The Neltan Encantado program has altered this thing. No telling what it can do, Dr. Holton. It's definitely Black-Ops hardware in the state it's in, and no telling the effect it'll have on one of us humans."

"Sir, I have an app we've been experimenting with...part anti-terrorist weaponry and part camouflage ware. Interfacing my wrist device to this new one—" Struggling, she altered her device to Hover-mode and positioned it over his morphing Encantado device. "Could prove highly useful...even save us all!" A powerful determination spread over her face. "Yes...this experiment is dangerous, but we have no other alternative. We must try something new or continuing to watch *that* dimensional explorer make mincemeat of our officers while it gradually conquers Earth, Sir. I don't know about you...but I can't stand by idly, or wait for Shaesar's analysis 'cause he doesn't have experiential atmospheric conditions on Earth."

"*Huuh*..." gasped Manning. "Then by all means...do it."

She set his matrix processor gently on the inside of her wrist, opposite of her wrist device. Like opposites attracting, the devices linked—their silicon processors combining and the nano-organics replicating and spreading—to form a thick glowing band that began creeping over her entire forearm. "Ouch! This feels like pins!" She began shaking her arm.

Manning tried grabbing it and finally managed to steady the morphing processors. "This seems like...like it's...it's got ahold of ya good, Dr. Holton...I can't...*urrr*...rip it off—"

"No—stop! Removing it hurts worse than its morphology.

Battlefield Matrix

It's like clamped into my skin…like it's becoming part of me."
She kept inhaling, struggling for breath. Around her, Terra
began appearing and disappearing. Stage 4, now on the
opposite side of the room, began emitting light into it via the
transmission screen.

Shaesar finally had a clear line of visibility to inspect the
new device. "It has a Gem program—a matrix software also
processing in our Neltan archway that orbits our planet in
anticipation of alien visitors. The device is interactive with its
host."

"What?!" she screamed—her eyes appearing shell shocked.

"You are not in danger, Dr. Holton," Shaesar said in a
reassuring tone of voice.

The long forearm device solidified and began developing
bumpy, glowing mounds of matrix connectivity that appeared
to contain the qualities of rare Earth gems.

Jenkens said: "Whatever is happening in that device, Dr.
Holton, it's also working to repair Terra's matrix. This is a
good thing! It's what you want…what we all need!"

Shaesar ordered, "Drink something." As she gulped down
water, he added: "The Encantado program works as an agent
of its host. As our program interfaced with and protected the
transmission screen, so it is now melding with everything about
you, will process your situations, and help you." Putting down
her water, she cleared her quenched throat and the armband
jiggled. She laughed, "What an awesome energized feeling!"

"You, Dr. Holton, are now linked with a Neltan shape-
shifter," Manning said, turning her hand palm-side down. "See
if you can generate a verbal connection."

She put her lips close to a shiny, blue mound that was
reflecting her image back at her. "I'm calling this, *Gem*. You're
Gem," she said in a beauteous innocent voice.

A tiny, light blue bump on the device, between her wrist
bone and her hand, glowed.

"It heard that!" she marveled.

"Say something else," Manning whispered, watching it
closely while keeping his peripheral vision on the flailing green

entity.

She couldn't move her wrist, but instead lifted her arm to her lips and said, "Gem, re-establish my connection to Station II."

A small stripe in bas-relief on the back Gem glowed green. The entire armband looked like a bronze beehive Terra hub, void of a rainbow processor. Some edges were gilded, but the entire shape-shifter entity was dotted with various shimmering, shining mounds and prisms.

"It works!" she said. "Thank God—*haah*...Shaesar was right...it's safe."

The Lead Researcher from Station II appeared over the small emerald stripe. "Elisa, we are down-streaming two molecular structures you can sweep into any Terraware to help you."

After Elisa ended the call, she began scrolling through the files that Gem activated as holograms. "Gosh—this is giving us just what we need and fast."

Shaesar called: "I'm streaming to the Gem device what one of our scientists is receiving of the entity's dimensional world. The data inside the processor should postulate a solution."

The glowing gems and their vibrant light rays began processing the incoming data. Squinting as she watched the results materialize over Gem, she said: "From the info I'm receiving, if we strengthen the two Weak Forces in this room while simultaneously weakening the Strong Forces around the entity...that will generate an immense pressure on the contained creature *and* force it back into its."

After Jenkens copied the information through a Terra hub that came back on-matrix, he said, "Scientists should soon have a mix for Enforcers to use on the entity. Great!"

Shaesar expanded Elisa's solution on Nelta's stage processor. "This viable solution looks promising, Dr. Holton...Weak Forces vying with Strong Forces in one, well defined, concentrated spot...enough to close the singularity. Yes!—your solution *should* work."

Looking up, Manning gasped in fright. A green crystal was

scouring the ceiling above him. The sparkling center appeared to have eyes. "Where'd it get those?" he gasped. "Off one of our officers!? My God!"

After a pause, Jenkens said, "Those are DNA readings of Agent Tina Hopper."

"Gem!" Elisa barked into her processor. "This is inhuman, Gem. Can you please—*pleeeze*—get rid of those eyes!"

As her device began firing rays of pink light into the center of the tentacle, Manning craned his neck toward it and said, "The entity is trying to communicate with me!" He felt compelled to touch it. "It's so intricate…delicate…rainbow beautiful…perfect.   Wow—I   see   brilliant diamonds…spectacular!   Each   facet   has   millions   of reflections…so easy to jump into—"

"No, Regent Manning!" Dr. Holton shouted. She pointed Gem at the creature, and it shot a blue, 3D equation into the center of the tentacle that was about to impale Manning's eyes.

Shrieking, the tentacle whipped the air and retreated into the entity.

Shaesar said, "That worked to drive back the entity."

Jenkens ordered Enforcers to fire on it using the same augmented blue-light code.

"That thing's *really* dangerous, Sir," Elisa exhaled.

Sitting against the wall, Manning was catching his breath and rubbing his eyes. "What—*what* the hell happened? I feel as if I briefly disappeared from this place."

Giving him water, Elisa whispered: "Maybe you did, Sir, or a part of you. I believe the entity is capable of translating the electrical impulses in our brains responsible for generating images. It can *read* us, Sir. That's what my new Gem device—*ahem*…sorry, I mean *your* Gem device—showed me."

A tiny, yellow light inside one of the sparkling prisms on Gem was shining on the green creature. The two were exchanging data.

Shaesar had received information from one of his colleagues because he waved a gesture of gratitude to someone in the background on Nelta. "You *are* battling a Halite Being,"

J.P. Osterman

he said. "Thanks to information we received from the Gem processor, we know the entity's composition." When Elisa's image of the entity joined with his scan of the creature on his Neltan hologram stage, he added, "We can definitely send back the being to Dimension 8."

Manning shouted, "Yes!" He felt a rush of victory—clenching his fist at the green expanding creature that was raging its gaseous tentacles at everyone. Then he ordered those who were linking with the Press Room: "Everyone, let's get those Terra hubs and wall processors back on-matrix so we can send this Halite critter back to its Dimension 8 reality."

The ceiling shook. A tentacle on the green crystalline creature crackled as it whipped close to the Oval Office. Through the main Security wall-zone next to the door, Jenkens shouted, "Get back!" A large shard of crystal on the entity's multifaceted body crested like an ocean wave toward the screen as if responding to Jenkens' defiance. Meanwhile, Elisa had been setting up a barricade of artificial trees and two sparking robots in the throw of self-repair.

"Soon, chairs and techware won't help us, Dr. Holton," Manning said, splashing cool water over his eyes. "Finally—I can see!"

Elisa ducked as a green crystal tentacle whipped toward her. "The Halite Being appears about ready to divide, Sir. It's pulsating and cracking open in parts. From simulations Gem is generating and I'm receiving from Station II, soon we'll be fighting off *two* entities."

Manning streamed the info to Enforcers while dabbing sweat off his brow. "Come on, people...develop and mix those counteracting Four Forces. We're running out of time!"

Elisa began directing the small robots to surround the Halite Being covertly. Several imaging zones on the walls flashed with green power and activated. Manning ordered the military to target the creature as soon as scientists mixed the proper Weak Forces and the matrix could contain the entity with the proper mixture of Strong Forces.

Elisa said: "Maybe, Sir...maybe we could find a way to

preserve a little of the Halite Being...to study it. I want to save—"

"No way, Dr. Holton!" he countered. "I don't want to take any chance that this thing could exhale outta here and inhale into every ceiling processor and wall imager on Earth." Noticing her disappointment, he said, "I know you value life, all life—"

"Yes," she said.

"But *this* life can't exist here, Dr. Holton. Maybe, one day after we disembark on Nelta, Shaesar and his Committee will allow us to study Dimension 8...but from a safe distance."

Her face brightened. "Yes—I do hope we get that chance, Sir, 'cause obviously they've experienced Dimension 8 at some point. They know so much about it."

"Or maybe they experienced the place through those safe Gravitational Lensing Windows," he speculated.

A blast of green crystal shot out from the creature and hit the wall behind them. The Halite Being had divided in two like mitochondria. At the point of impact in the wall, the green shard penetrated the nanomaterial with its tentacles. Like ivy spikes, the tiny crystal entity began grinding into the nano-technology as mortar fusing bricks.

She shouted, "Regent Manning—watch out!"

"Duck!" shouted an Enforcer as she blasted the entity with an electromagnetic current.

Gem glowed bright bronze in color. Whenever it had new information, Elisa had commanded Gem to get her attention. "Yes, Gem. You have something?" she asked. Over one of Gem's radiating mounds, blueprints of various types of emitters appeared. "Yes!" she said excitedly, showing the images to Manning and Shaesar and then streaming them to scientists and the military. When she swept those images into a deactivated robot that began vibrating for attention, the images permeated the robot. Like a rock skimming over water, the new software spread to the other roboticware around the entity. They began reconfiguring and morphing into equipment, instruments and emitters.

Shaesar said, "I am down-streaming a formula for a special radioactive isotope from Nelta into the Gem processor."

As Elisa received the formula, she replied, "When someone gives me the go ahead, I'll direct this fortress of roboticware to shower the Halite Beings with Weak Forces as you continue to spray them with the hydrogen chloride solution."

Manning ordered the tropopause shield engineers to generate two EMPs around the entities. The EMPs began buffering the entities' event horizons. When he saw two transparent bubbles form around the squirming creatures, he ordered General Rand on Station III: "As the detector in here pounds the entities with pulses of Weak Forces, you begin extracting the Strong Forces from their containment fields. He counted down from five. "Now!"

Jenkens showed them a simulation of the result. "One solid minute of that intensive drive in current should eliminate the Halite Beings and their Dimension 8 reality."

The tiny crystal on the wall jumped, its faceted shards crackling wildly.

Regent Jenkens shouted: "They definitely understand what we're saying and doing!"

Shaesar traced the course of the entities in the room and said, "They realize they can't go out or up, so they're drilling down."

As Jenkens set the duration of the assault to one minute, Elisa said after a mathematical calculation appeared over the armband, "We need General Rand to intensify the EM Pulses now because his earlier power output didn't take into account the presence of the second creature."

The ground began vibrating. Static broke out through the room. The robots were shaking and jumping as their new designs continued to remold and expand to handle the overload. They were at their nuts-and-bolts limits, but dangling together while emitting focused currents into the entities. Dry wind and a cold chill filled the room. Outside the White House, crowds were groaning, gasping, and cheering...obviously reactions to what was happening inside

Battlefield Matrix

the Press Room. That meant that The World was watching the entire event. Manning looked to Shaesar for progress on their "viable solution."

Shaesar was maintaining a calm stance—a reassuring expression. "That's the Strong Forces leaving their locus of existence, Regent Manning," he said. "As levels of gravity and magnetism intensify inside the creatures' containment fields, these weak particles will drive straight into Dimension 8's singularity."

With her Gem glowing like sparkling rocks and prisms in the sunshine, Elisa directed the robotics to increase fermion emissions when a monitor detected expanding green radioluminescence. "We don't want to be sucked into that dimension, Sir!" she shouted. "I think it's encroaching...or pulsing in and out of existence all around us—*ahhh*!"

Manning told her to drop to the floor when he felt his cheeks pinch with static. Pressing into the carpet, he felt a Cushion effect as the nanomaterials reacted to his carbon dioxide, creating oxygen. He could breathe again, in spite of his drowning feeling. "You're right, Dr. Holton. The Four Forces colliding are powerful." He felt a sudden sharp coldness bristle across his back. "I—*ha*—my God!—I feel the other world right over us! Freezing stings all over me!" When he opened his eyes to search for a familiar face, he saw only rainbows. "This world's bright...like I'm *in* a prism!"

"No, Regent Manning," shouted Shaesar, "you can see Dimension 8, but that sensation you are experiencing is the containment field protecting you from the Halite Beings. Hold on! Deterioration in their faceted structures is occurring. Thirty more seconds!"

Manning wanted to give them a signal that he was okay, but he couldn't move. He could only see fields of rainbows in a vacuum. He had to keep his nose to the carpet for air.

Droning sounds from the interacting robots pulsed through the room. The Halite Beings began flattening out like radiator fluid on a desert pavement. The lights flickered off and on.

Seeing frost appear, he sat up and helped Elisa. He

remembered experiencing that same feeling before. "How much longer, Jenkens?" he shouted, "'cause I think we might have a wormhole activate in here if we keep up this intense manipulation of the four forces...just like what happening during First Communication."

Elisa was sitting up and gripping the carpet. She appeared frazzled and overwhelming with fear but directed Gem to record everything. "You're right, Sir. This is the same type of atmospheric condition that occurred that day inside the lab at Duke." Her voice wavered in a redolence of sad memories. "I remember that day."

He knew she was referring to Lynn. More than anything, he wished Lynn were alongside him. Then another thought occurred to him. Maybe Elisa Holton had a part in Lynn's death. She was part of the Assembly Team that in that short time knit together *The Greeter*. She worked closely with Coflin and should have been more astute. She should have detected Coflin's dark plan and exposed him. Maybe then, none of *this* would have happened.

"Sir...are you all right," she asked with a puzzled expression.

"Fine—yes," he rebuffed.

After gasping through several messages that appeared over the Gem, she said: "I hope so, Sir, 'cause we've got a *real* wormhole initializing in here and I might need you to help me direct Gem in case I need to focus more energy on the entities. It's getting heavier, Sir. I'm not used to such weight on my arm even though this looks light."

Acknowledging her, Manning watched the creatures fade in and out of existence. "These things seemed to be cracking up in our counterattack and about to explode into shards. We really don't need a wormhole in here blasting 'em through the windows."

Manning couldn't see Shaesar but he could hear him. "The inter-dimensional portal is now open," Shaesar began. "With the energies flooding them, they *must* escape into it!"

"I gotta sync with the ceiling hub that's sustaining the

portal and fast," Elisa shouted. "Regent Jenkens is giving us a new countdown. Forty-five seconds. I have to keep that current running between the robotic servers. I could sure use the new Terra in the room now." Her brown hair was blowing over her face. Her eyes were shock wide, the pupils dilated. She was breathing hard through all her words. "But I can't find an app that'll connect with the evolved Terra…the right grid to direct the new Terra-III to the Press Room. Damn it Gem…*you* try." The bronze armband lit up in tiny, colorful nano-organic bubbles and patches. It was now a complete, artificial, living entity.

Manning felt frost stinging his skin. "Wait! Maybe I can help. If we don't' do something, we could freeze like statues." Seeing that the Stage-4 Left still had its red Smart Bar activated; he dashed through Enforcer lines; and with their help, unclasped the stage from its base and rotated it back to Elisa who was coaching him on the best place to establish a matrix connection. Tipping the edge of Stage 4 so that the Smart Bar aligned with Terra's beehive ceiling hub, he said, "Try bringing Terra in here now using Gem."

She said into the armband, "Direct Interface."

His Terra-III appeared next to the hologram stage.

"Terra—you're, back!" he shouted, laying his hand on her shoulder. It passed right through her. He noticed that his Terra was still manifesting as Lynn—with her tall hourglass figure, beautiful oval face, and athletic demeanor—the way she looked on that last day. An empowering force rushed through his veins, igniting him with strength and hope.

"Sir, stay down!" cried Elisa.

The Halite Being whipped one last tentacle at him. The sliver struck his arm.

"Ouch!" When he saw the gash that instantly cauterized, he said, huffing in pain: "Terra, now send back these creatures…please!"

Elisa extended Gem in Terra's direction; and Terra began an interface with the armband, the robots, and the tropopause-shield energy distributor. When the rainbow cycling processor beams touched the hologram stages, their Auto Positioners activated. They tilted and concaved, morphing into refractive lenses until they steadied and aligned in perfect synchronicity to fire on the Halite entities.

"The evolved matrix is now channeling Weak Forces into Dimension 8's singularity," Shaesar said. "In moments, The Halite Beings should cease to exist in this reality."

Manning realized that meant death. "I hope that means they disappear!"

The Halite Beings began crackling, crunching, and splitting under the intense pressure of the conflicting Four Forces. Elisa said: "They're in pain! I wish we could do something and help them. After all, this mess isn't their fault."

Manning exhaled a depressing groan. "But if we don't send them back, *we* die."

Regent Jenkens shouted out in panic: "I see a problem! The hologram stages aren't capturing the entire ionization pattern streaming from Neltan. That's what's preventing them from entering the Dimension 8 portal!"

Shaesar swept together several algorithms and atomic numbers inside his hologram stage and then said, "I am sending a more intense mixture of the radioactive isotope." Two of his colleagues' images appeared in the Press Room. With their palm devices glowing bright red, they began throwing a more intensive hit of radioactivity at the writhing entities.

"I can increase one of the Weak Forces to delete energy bonds," Elisa said, extending her armband toward a beehive ceiling hub.

Gem brightened—its shimmering crystals and prisms glowing pure colors.

As Gem burrowed slowly into the silicon, nano-organic hardware, Elisa shut her eyes and said, "Terra, connect with the Neltan Encantado program in the armband. Increase the fermion current when Gem's energy reaches maximum."

A bright white light emitted out of the center of the beehive hub.

Battlefield Matrix

Manning said: "Dr. Holton—look away! The radiance will blind you!" He dashed through pools of black ooze and shoved a thick piece of torn curtain into her right hand. "Cover your eyes with this shielding material!" He ducked under Stage-4 Left. "Dimension 8, leave, leave now...*leeeave*," he prayed.

Terra appeared behind the Halite Beings. She inserted their mirror image into the singularity that loomed like a black circle behind them. The Strong Forces suddenly punctured. A forty mile-an-hour wind swept through the room.

Elisa fell to the floor. The processor mounds on Gem were gleaming, sparkling and brightly shining. When the armband stuck the carpet, their radiance subsided.

The giant beehive ceiling hub stopped oscillating wildly. "Done," Terra called. Then she reappeared on the floor under the hologram stage next to Manning. In seconds, the room filled with millions of reflections of the two Halite Beings.

"We must be in both worlds...wow, beautiful!" Elisa exclaimed, breathless.

Shaesar said, "Yes, but Dimension 8 cannot exist here for a second longer or it will supersede here...reacting like anti-matter winning the war with matter and then—"

"Kaboom!" cried Elisa.

When he and his scientists turned their instruments on to the walls and began emitting pulses of radioactivity, the bright-green world of Dimension 8 disappeared, leaving chunks of our reality mixed with blotches of its world. The center of the room appeared as one giant puzzle with black holes where pieces were missing.

Manning felt something stab his ankle. "Ouch!" Glancing down, he saw a sliver of the green Halite Being around his sock. A swarm of tiny repair bots had begun streaming out of the floor, attacking the green shiny tentacle. "The small one's got me!" When he felt the entity yanking him towards it, towards the windy black zone of Dimension 8, he grabbed the artificial tree that instantly branched out, bloomed, and began dropping flowers on the entity's tentacle.

J.P. Osterman

When dead blooms touched it, the tentacle crackled, unleashed him, and whipped back into the creature's scattering body.

"Sir," Elisa called. "I think that attack was the Halite Being holding on to *our* reality. Who knows what life is like in Dimension 8. I saw solids everywhere...no air...and I got this feeling that it's light there *all* the time."

"I saw overwhelming rainbows too everywhere," Manning said, dabbing his ankle.

"I think it got a taste of our atmosphere and was cleaving so as to *not* leave," she said.

"Or, the aliens tasted human flesh, liked it, and want more," Jenkens countered, gesturing with disgust. "Blast the damn green puzzle pieces with more fermions and let's end this dimensional tug o' war now!"

Since the teleportation beam from the transmission screen stabilized and the Encantado program established maximum resolution, Shaesar was able to step closer to the entities with his two comrades alongside him. They linked with the ceiling hub and began emitting a radioactive current into the disassembling creatures. Elisa grabbed an animal-bot, severed its leg, and struck another green glowing tentacle.

In loud cracks, the appendage broke into slivers that disintegrated in the air.

"Thanks, Shaesar!" Manning exhaled in relief. "I don't know why...but I think that one entity liked me a lot or hated me."

"Did the creature attach?" Shaesar asked in a concerned voice. All the green Halite pieces were popping out of existence, the small black singularity now a dot with warbling air cycling around it.

Manning raised his sock and inspected the tiny gash. "I don't feel anything like glass."

Terra walked up to him and ran her virtual hand over the wound like a Double Body Imager. "Nothing, Ambassador. I show a complete cauterization."

"Then you're fine," Shaesar sighed.

Battlefield Matrix

Jenkens said facetiously, "I'm not at all gonna ask what woulda happened if you *had* discovered a shard lodged in him."

Manning coughed and Elisa began wheezing.

"Something's still wrong with the air," Manning said.

Through the lime-hued, glowing haze and viridian colored beams of the fading Halite Beings, the windows suddenly unsealed, *pfffff*, and opened wide.

Manning inhaled deeply the fresh air. "What's the smell?" He coughed from nearly choking and drank gulps of water along with Elisa Holton.

The windows shut when fumes began permeating the laser-yellow shielding to the outside world.

"Oxidation is occurring," Shaesar said. "A copper gas is reacting with *this* reality."

Terra opened all the vents and began flushing the room with cold air. Feathery dew lighted on the carpet. She said, "I am countering that copper emission with a flow of protons."

"This room's becoming a nursery for new elements like a nebula on the smallest of scales," Jenkens said, his face still On-screen beside the Oval Office.

"That's not good," said Manning, coughing some more.

"Give the concentrated oxygen five more seconds and the reactions should subside," Jenkens said.

The dew on the furniture disappeared as the last hovering piece of the Halite Beings and their Dimension 8 reality dwindled. Only their bright glowing reflections remained on the walls.

"We're done, Sir...it's over," Elisa said, and then she exhaled a huge breath of relief as her back hit the wall in an expression of utter fatigue. "But I'm not sitting down yet."

"Yes," Manning said, pushing away the two dead artificial trees. "I think we have a few more minutes to go before the dimensional portal completely seals."

"And you managed to send them back without killing them," Shaesar added.

Elisa peeked up over Stage 4. "*That* means they're alive in Dimension 8, but probably hurting 'cause we sure taught 'em a

J.P. Osterman

good lesson." She appeared pleased as if she had accomplished a great feat. "At least they're alive...if just being alive is good enough."

"That Gem armband worked successfully, Dr. Holton," Manning said excitedly. He grabbed her shoulder in a congratulatory expression. "I believe your idea of hitting the entities with opposing Four Forces saved us."

"Thanks Sir," she said, waving off the complement.

"No—you did it...*your* idea," he said firmly. "I thought for sure we were dead."

As the double doors opened, Enforcers entered the Press Room and began securing the area for Final Communication. Manning heard the crowd outside cheer. People seemed happy—extraordinarily happy—as they began linking their holosite worlds to the Press Room, wherein a few Regents began streaming an A-Okay broadcast around the globe. Regents, guests, dignitaries and the Media were flooding the elevators on their way back up to the Press Room. When he peered outside, he noticed the dark sky, and the shiny tropopause shield array. The Matter Stream sample had healed the ozone. For once, he could see a constellation...this time of year Leo. Then he spotted a space station. It looked all right—its orbit stable—yet he remembered General Rand's last comment of foreboding devastation. He sounded disturbed about a cosmic anomaly. Thus far, Jenkens hadn't told him anything dire, so he believed that he didn't have anything to worry about except preparing to sign *The Pact* with the Neltans.

Regent Jenkens dashed up to him and said, "Thornton, ya rested up yet 'cause Shaesar and I need your help reconfiguring the transmission screen. Astrophysicists just powered down the backup screen in the Rotunda. I have so much information to tell you. Midnight's closing in. That's the time the Neltan/Earth wormhole extinguishes. And—"

Manning stopped him from talking. "Look at that," he nodded at the moon, noticing a large shadow under a bright-white area on the surface. "That entire area is different...you see?"

Battlefield Matrix

Jenkens squinted at the sight. "Yeah...I see an atypical brightness, but that's probably because Bartlet and our other forcers took out the terrorists."

Then he heard a great cheer coming in a splendid wave from the huge crowd. All around the White House and extending as far as light could reveal their presence, people began shining victory icons into the air and shouting words of celebration.

"What's going on, Steve?" he asked. "Sounds like another alien contact out there!"

Jenkens patted him on the back. He had the widest smile on his face. "You've been fighting for life in here so long that you haven't heard the good news. That's one of the things I wanted to tell you."

"What?"

"We won."

"Won?"

"Simple. We won!" Jenkens' droopy eyes were fire-wide with excitement. "World War Three is over. We defeated the terrorists. I don't quite know all the details because of that damn wormhole conflagration, but somewhere in between the moon and Mars, our forces took out all the terrorists. That's why everyone's so damn happy." He grabbed a bottle of Champagne.

Manning fell back a bit when he felt the irritation in his throat turn into a happy tickle. "Won...we *really* won?" The word felt so foreign, rolling over his tongue.

"Yeah...General Rand just announced the end of World War III! Isn't it great?" He pointed to the Capital. "Someone's plastering the VJ-Day picture from *Life* magazine on the dome, and people are copying The Kiss. Victory—it's everywhere! Alleluia!"

Manning waved to a group of people who flashed his name in lights with his new title of Executive Regent. A small crowd began cheering his name.

"See? They say you saved Earth, Thornton. You and Dr. Holton—"

"And I bet you didn't leave you name out of the mix either, right?" he joked.

In an expression of feigned shyness, Jenkens tipped his head and said, "Well, yeah, but we're all heroes, everyone who battled Dr. Coflin, his Tech-Nos, *and* the terrorists."

"What won us the war?" Manning asked.

"As the Tech-Nos were imaging Coflin's body to Nelta in a wormhole generated by *The Heed*'s accelerators, little did they realize that the terrorists were inside another wormhole spacefolding out of the Milky Way. The two wormholes collided—"

"That conflagration we experienced before the Halite Being appeared!" Manning said.

"Well, that tidal wave was, in part, the effect of that conflagration...but not totally...and we don't quite yet know the cause of the conflagration, but are still looking into it—"

"Go on—about winning the war," Manning pressed him.

"Well, basically, the terrorists escape route—that wormhole—collapsed and crushed them," Jenkens said.

"All? All gone? Their troops all dead? Their craft *all* destroyed?"

"Every single one of 'em, as far as General Rand knows 'cause he's been tracking them," Jenkens said proudly. "Their entire convoy, although we still may find a few cells now and then. But still, we have them beat." He shimmied in a funny dance as he happily decreed: "We, took, them, down!" He jumped in victory as the crowd outside cheered. "Hear that? I think people'll be celebrating for weeks!"

"Whew! This is so unexpected," Manning said, the heat in the room settling in a ring of sweat around his neck. Even Shaesar and the Neltan Advancement Committee looked stunned. "A wormhole collapse...a simple collapse won the war. It reminds me a bit of that Trojan Horse that fooled the enemy. Amazing!"

"General Rand also believes that the 9:15 Neltan/Earth wormhole had something to do with starting the whole conflagration," Jenkens began. "*The Heed*'s accelerators malfunctioned as the transmission screen in the Press Room activated."

"Oh—a space/time conflict," Manning said.

"Right, Thornton, the wobbly singularity that materialized the Halite Being into our reality."

"What about the Tech-No movement? You think *it's* completely dead?" Manning asked.

Jenkens shook his head. "You kidding? No way! Our hackers are still tracking 'em. Remember what we learned just a few hours ago. When the terrorists left covertly for space, the Tech-Nos began moving into their evacuated hideouts. They're still there...all around us like sharks in water."

When a crowd began cheering Regents' names in the victory celebration, Manning said, "Well...we'll continue hunting them down. But for now, this is all so unbelievable...and such an overwhelming surprise." He felt dizzy with astonishment. "All terrorist craft...gone. Crushed. Wow." He reached for a glass of champagne a robot server lifted to him on a tray.

Jenkens drank a toast to a Regent who shook his hand. "We're all celebrating, Thornton, but us especially."

"Why?"

"Our promotions...remember?"

"Yes—right!" He yawned but perked up when he spotted Shaesar. He still had so many hours to wade through before he could quit for the day. "Sorry...I'm so tired...could fall asleep right here on the carpet."

"Don't do that," Jenkens chided, patting him on the back and slipping an energy drink into his pocket. "We both have pinning ceremonies...this day." He called on his Jackie Gleason avatar that displayed the date in the month in starbursts. "February 27, 2068, 9:57 p.m. I programmed my avatar so it'll blast me with the anniversary every year." He took another long sip of champagne. "Grab a glass and celebrate. The Regency is preparing to sign *The Pact* with Shaesar and the Neltan Advancement Council as soon as we clean up a bit more and intensify the spacefolding images to this room from the Decagon."

Feeling like something was still way off kilter but trying to divert his thoughts to the good news, Manning swept up a glass of champagne, toasted the success, and said, "Fine, you're right. Everything's working out just fine." All the while, he felt his intuition rev with quite the opposite. "As soon as we sign *The Pact* with the Neltans—" He set down his half-empty glass. "*That's* when I'll celebrate, Steve...when *The Pact* is signed, the bargain finally sealed between our two species, this entire evening over and done, and us on our way to *Sagan* for our brief tour.

Chapter 12

Red Star World

Terra's ceiling hubs suddenly illuminated white as an electromagnetic current swept through the room. Two copper/silicon hologram stages broke off their platforms and whirled to the floor like a tornado tossing metal. The hubs were repairing too quickly, energizing the stages too fast. Manning ordered a manual shut down of the White House matrix grid until they could resolve the cold-flowing fluctuation. Fifteen matrix techs dashed into the room, tossing nano-organics into the twenty-five ceiling hubs. When they synchronized, the processors reset to their normal rainbow intensity.

Shaesar's image resolved in the quantum communication beam, and the room calmed.

In his effort to relieve the tension in the air, Manning exclaimed, "This place makes me think of California. Everything is amazing except the earthquakes." After a few Regents laughed at the joke, he ordered the windows to close, muffling the outside celebration. "Well, Steve, it looks like our new Terra-III matrix has stabilized and our hubs interfacing at one hundred percent. But *when*—" He plopped into a chair. "This room's in complete disarray, like a hundred children made a mess and left without cleaning up."

Maintenance and their roboticware cleaning crew rushed into the room. They'd soon have the place ready for the meeting with Shaesar who was busy directing matrix techs and astrophysicists with last-minute preparations and algorithmic files for *Sagan*. There were so many questions and so little time to resolve all their issues. He opened up his Neltan File avatar over his wrist device and sent it to the techs who immediately replied. They would present his concerns about *Sagan*'s Friendship Mission to the Neltans, along with possible emergency scenarios—the ones Jenkens discussed with him earlier—that could affect the astrocity's arrival time on Nelta. Then he walked over to where the Halite Beings had just existed and cautiously touched the place where they had vaporized. "Gone." There was nothing between his fingers and the invisible reality of Dimension 8.

"They're not *really* gone though, Thornton," Jenkens said, straightening his tie and donning his extra-large jacket. "They're in another space/time. Thank goodness—huh?"

"Yep." He felt he had lost something. "Too bad we couldn't have kept a little of one of them, as Dr. Holton suggested, or encased a smidgen of Dimension 8 to watch and study, at least onboard *Sagan*." When he felt the hot spot on his ankle where the Halite Being had tried to rope him, he realized that keeping even a nano-portion of alien crystal was a bad idea.

"And have that thing accidentally break out?" Jenkens scoffed, "We'd all be crystals!"

As they laughed, Elisa approached them with Gem still snug around her arm as a glowing, knobby parasitic intelligence. She had a bouncy vibrancy about her now. She was living her research, not conducting it in a sequestered sterile lab on Station II. "Regent Manning, is there anything you need me to do right now?" she asked, and then she shook

Battlefield Matrix

Jenkens' hand, thanking him for being so quick in his disaster response.

Manning noticed her cradling Gem against her ribcage, but he didn't want the Neltan Encantado device back yet. He still had a cautious line of sight on the spots where Dr. Coflin once stood and Dimension 8 existed even though Shaesar had insisted that the danger was over, the emitters had evacuated them. Taking a sip of water, he said to her, as Jenkens left to join a crowd of scientists, Regents, and guests flowing into the Press Room: "If you wouldn't mind, I could sure use you to be part of the team that's trying to explain to The World what happened in here. Who else could do a better job other than us who survived it?" They laughed.

"Sure, I'd be glad to help," she said, following him over to the transmission screen. Shaesar and the Neltan Advancement Committee were busily opening up and exchanging files with scientists from *Sagan*.

After Manning pointed her in direction of several Regents meeting with the media, he walked up to Ambassador Shaesar and the Neltan scientists and said: "We only have a few more hours before this Final Transmission ends. Please, let's work fast to begin the signing ceremony. Let's get rollin'!"

"Rollin'?" Shaesar glanced quizzically at his colleagues.

In spite of the forty or so meetings he had with them in the past, Manning still felt nervous. He could see a bit of his reflection in the quantum-communication light streaming their images from Nelta to the Decagon, to the IMAX screen and the ceilings hubs. He looked awful. His hair was disheveled, his collar crooked. The campaign nickname The World slapped him with flashed through his mind: Beethoven. Yep, he thought, now definitely I resemble that whacky musician…although he's still remembered and he sure was creative! Then he realized that he didn't have a creative bone in him. Smiling at the Ambassador after Shaesar finally interpreted, "rolling," as, "getting started," he saw in his reflection specks of brown energy bar between his teeth. He sipped more water and straightened himself up quickly,

217

thinking: gosh what a horrible impression I'm making. I feel like an idiot standing next to these aliens who have immeasurable IQs. I bet they think I have the intelligence of arthropods compared to their advanced cognition of twelve billions of years of existence!

He finally said: "At exactly 12 o'clock midnight, on *that* clock, our communications conduit will close. It's 10:05. That gives us about two hours to sign *The Pact* and iron out all the technical problems our engineers are encountering on *Sagan* and some unfinished business with our *Friendship Mission*." He really wanted to discuss *The Attack Clause* in *The Pact*. Is ten minutes alright to exchange more files with our people?" He watched them whispered among themselves. As what just occurred with the word, "rollin'," people were still often encountering communication problems, which resulted in lag time as they resolved misunderstandings

"Yes, Regent Manning," Shaesar began, "when signed, *The Pact* will resolve all your questions. We only need to gather ourselves and commence with its signing. Thereafter, we have a final presentation for humanity as an expression of our gratitude. It is intended as a taste of technology to come for your future."

Manning said: "Okaaay…but the difficulties Navigation are experiencing on *Sagan* are *big* concerns. We'll be *living* on the astrocity for a hundred years. Some people on The List are panicking because the wormhole network to Nelta is so complicated…the ship's becoming so big…each of the nine levels so deep and intricate with plasma propulsion hardware…and their living accommodations are separated by matrix hardware that if stretched out would wrap around Jupiter! The more we follow *your* blueprints that you *say* you used to build *your* fleet, *Sagan* is beginning to take on an identity of its own…*real* self-building, Ambassador." He showed him an image of a section on the Regeneration Corridor. The gurneys were glowing with Body-Double scanners. "No one turned these on, Ambassador." Closing that display, he brought up an image of a section of living cubes—their walls, ceilings and floors configuring as if intelligently accommodating the person soon to be living inside them. "I can understand the matrix directing construction, but I've had to make a personal modification to one of *Sagan*'s turrets to create some privacy for The Regency."

"Yes, the astrocity is interfacing with its matrix as specified in the multi-view designs," Shaesar said.

"Yes...but *I* made a modification...me, myself...that's *my* concern," Manning said, feeling numb with all his secrets stirring in his mind...feeling exposed and fearful of discovering. "Will anything drastic?—horrible, I mean, occur if someone needs to add or edit something—anything technical—on or to *Sagan*?"

Shaesar's deep-set eyes had a glow of understanding that appeared capable of reading a person's soul. His torso rose and fell as the peaks of his thin lips spread into his cheeks. He had a guttural laugh. "No harm done, Regent Manning," he said as his colleagues stopped their gentle chuckling. "As we speak, there is an exchange occurring between two of our scientists and the engineers managing *Sagan*'s construction. Isometric details are quantum streaming to *Sagan*. The modifications you just discussed are inserting into *Sagan*. When we sign *The Pact*, you will see the modifications you *can* make and those you must avoid."

"Good—just what I need to hear. *Whew*—I'm relieved," Manning said, feeling puzzled.

As people moved to their seats when Terra announced the start of the ceremony, Shaesar began walking in a circle around Manning. In an analytical bearing, he said, "You are a human who always needs answers."

"Huh?" Manning asked, stepping with Shaesar's eyes. He felt engaged in an alien dance.

"You are uncomfortable with loose ends, loopholes and uncontrollable situations."

"Everyone human being is that way though, Ambassador," he said, folding his arms and feeling red-faced embarrassment.

"I have noticed, in a few instances, when people try to

work with you, that you do not say anything encouraging but instead maintain a serious angry expression…as you did when we could not help you defeat your War against Terror."

"Now, Ambassador—"

"Remember, Regent Manning, that the most difficult "why" and "what if" answers only occur because one is always *choosing* from among a realm of possibilities," Shaesar said.

Manning felt confused. He saw Jenkens' gaping mouth and squinting eyes as Jenkens walked up, patted him on the shoulder and said, "Deeeep…that's interesting about you, Thornton." He stepped back, obviously fearful of receiving the same type of profound assessment. "I'll never mention it, *ahem*."

Shaesar finished his circular reading and leaned down into Manning's eyes.

Feeling struck down, Manning put his hands in his pockets and said: "Yes, thanks for that. I get it. Sometimes things get out of control and I hate that. So do most humans, Ambassador. I thought you had figured that out about us by now." More of Shaesar's colleagues had gathered around Shaesar and listening in. "In spite of that weakness, you and your people seem to like us. Friendship is in our DNA…and the need to form attachments and bonds with others even though we know relationships sometimes incur damage and need special mending. You'll be receiving that too when you combine your DNA with ours in the future." He realized he had struck a delicate note of misunderstanding when they bent down closer to him in intensive perusal. "No matter how ya slice it, edit it, reconfigure it to adapt our genetic codes to your Neltan code, *human* is who we are…strengths and weakness. We can't readily see our own frailties. One day, you may know that *reality* as well…and have to *choose* it."

After a long pause, through which Terra called for people to take their seats, Shaesar's lower lip disappeared under the shadow of his lowering eyes. The expression was foreboding.

"Is there another problem, Ambassador?" He felt dislodged some more.

Battlefield Matrix

Shaesar said: "General Rand has not personally contacted us yet to receive details concerning our update of plasma weapon rods for *Sagan*."

Confused, Manning told Jenkens to call him on Stage-1 Left next to the Center Stage in front of the screen. "This is not like The General to take so long to update us on battles either. He's always acting near the point of obsession to ensure we've met all your requests for info and data. Still, no one's received *any* word of *any* catastrophe concerning the troops or any of our astrocraft or astrofighters. Don't worry, Ambassador. I'm going to fix this lack of communication now. I do know there's been static...and interference...some unusual cosmic disruption, but that should have been resolved by now. I don't get it." A line of Regents walked into the room. He asked them if they had received word from The General. They hadn't.

With Terra showing a few global disturbances in conjunction with victory celebrations, he felt as if a grand turbulence was brewing somewhere. He felt jumpy and jittery whenever he glanced at a happy scene on one of the hologram stages and wall zones. Again, he ordered Terra to send an *Urgent* request to Rand's personal holosite and Station III's military holosite, demanding that The General immediately appear in the Press Room on Center Stage. "Tell him this: 'General, get in here *now*. The Neltans are asking for you, now! Is this insubordination or what, 'cause when you don't respond to *umpteen* hails, that's what your lack of respect is telling us. *Call* us now!'" He felt enamel from his tooth on his tongue, and he spit it into a napkin and then shoved the wad into a serverbot's small trash bag.

Meanwhile, the Regents who had been assembling in the front rows were busily greeting Shaesar and the Neltan Advancement Team. Ten additional Terra holograms materialized at the double doors to help manage the huge influx of guests and the media. After processing their Ticket-icons over their wrist devices or necklace-cone processors, the Terra hosts continued admitting the audience as Maintenance picked up the remainder of the trash. Rubbing shoulder-to-arm, people were sitting down quickly, eager to be a part of the historic *Signing of The Pact* ceremony. The media were in lines in the side aisle under the towering wall zones. Their Holosite Projectionists began barking orders—directing roboticware to configure their imagers to capture the ceremony for holositing around the world. Now-and-then, one or two Projectionists began arguing with a few maintenance workers over seating. Locked to a time constraint, the workers were hurriedly polishing hologram stages, replacing fried wall sections, and vigorously vacuuming up crusty specks of nano-silicon death and deterioration. As their Tilt-n-Roll vacuums suctioned the dregs of Dimension 8's aftermath, lines of nanorepairbots slipped under the baseboards. More vents opened, flushing out the dregs of ions from Coflin's disintegration and the Halite Beings' manipulation of human flesh.

Two large wall zones activated in the partition between the office and the Press Room, prompting Elisa Holton and other scientists to address the public's concerns about Dr. Coflin and any adverse effects that his abnormal teleportation might have had on Earth because the conduit conflagration had crushed all the terrorists' craft. The weather was still reading abnormal on the Smart Bars. A few coastal cities were on alert. Several families of services members were inquiring about their loved ones because they hadn't heard from them since the onset of that final battle. Military Station III was transmitting a Black Zone code, signifying a temporary lapse in matrix connectivity. That was the site with all the answers, but currently dead.

After listening to the families' pleas and determining that Elisa Holton and the scientists couldn't provide answers, Manning asked Shaesar: "Can you tell us what happened to Dr. Coflin? Maybe he has something to do with all this. We know he had managed to glean a bit of The Matter Stream sample to teleport out of here, but we can't locate him—or what's left of him...you know atoms...or *anything* that will enable us to ID his body."

"Space/time has Dr. Coflin, Regent Manning," Shaesar

began. "He is a compilation of particles spacefolding through a wormhole. He created a spectacular technology…a wonderful containment field to teleport a carbon-based life form. Scientists from both our worlds will one day be able to examine the energy field and possibly replicate it for short-distance cosmic travel." From Nelta, he showed Manning and Jenkens a sample teleportation conduit that appeared over a small hologram stage that he and his scientists we using to solve complicated problems for scientists on Earth. "However, Dr. Coflin was not bodily prepared for this type of particle teleportation. He did not have The Mix in his system that would have translated him into a safe, stasis state for such a complicated teleportation of molecules. No telling really if he'll even make it here in half-a-piece so we can gather him up completely, capture and contain his mind, or clone him after we coalesce his elements."

"*Ooo*," Manning grimaced. "How did he even get through Earth's magnetic field?"

Shaesar answered, "Prior to his teleporting from that room, Terra captured his genetic code, used your Mandelbrot Zoom Sequence program to analyze and translated his DNA, and then the Decagon accelerator system sent his particles on a course to Nelta." He quickly turned away to answer a question concerning *Sagan*'s Navigation Center.

Shaesar always spoke in a matter-of-fact tone of voice but he was *not* expressionless. The Neltan's most famous scientist appeared in-tune with human emotions and well versed—whether from practice, intense observation, or prolonged research—in reading people: our verbal intonations and our ever changing, countless repertoire of body language.

Elisa approached Manning with Gem glowing next to her chest. Cradling the armband processor delicately, she had obviously listened in on their conversation. "Is Dr. Coflin *really* heading *to* Nelta? Wow! I thought you said no one could do that. I thought—"

Shaesar stopped her. "No one can *physically* teleport, Dr. Holton, except that *the* wormhole that Dr. Coflin activated that created a molecular container specific to his biology. The discovery of such a molecular invention is phenomenal."

Elisa showed Shaesar her avatar's recording of the event. "Yes...phenomenal indeed! When'll Dr. Coflin arrive on Nelta? What'll happen to him if he reaches Nelta before we arrive there because everyone on Nelta be in subterranean stasis chambers? Or, will he just materialize as a pool of organic soup?"

Shaesar answered: "We are running simulations based on our wormhole configurations. In five minutes, we will attempt to answer those questions."

Manning felt startled by her gregariousness. He didn't know what to say when he saw her look of confusion and Shaesar's puzzled glance at her. "I need some answers too, but of a different nature...concerning the end of our *Friendship Mission*. I'm worried about our arrival in the Neltan solar system. Our current wormhole has us entering your solar system close to one of your suns, and I certainly don't want to burn up after our long journey."

"We are crunching the future time stamp to determine *Sagan*'s path to the nanosecond," Shaesar said.

"Don't worry about *Sagan* burning up upon entry," she said jokingly. "We'll be arriving at night."

After Shaesar laughed—the first time Manning had ever heard his high-pitched chuckle—he said to Shaesar: "Coflin *killed* our friends, Ambassador." He remembered Lynn again. "He has to pay for his crimes." Trying to extinguish Lynn's face from his thoughts, he reset a hologram stage and an imaged flashed on of the Tech-No protester's quadrant in space. All their craft that had activated *The Heed* were gone. The show abruptly fizzled off. He no longer had reception of outer space. After asking Jenkens, again, to check into General Rand's persistent state of silence, he thought of Elisa's questions and asked: "Is that stolen Matter Stream sample Dr. Coflin took keeping him stable as he teleports through the wormhole?" He thought: Humanity could use The Matter Stream to travel throughout the universe someday. From what

Battlefield Matrix

Shaesar had just divulged, he had learned that The Matter Stream must contain some sort of "special mix" to stabilize carbon-based molecules and an inter-dimensional component.

Shaesar tapped his lower lip and exhaled. When he breathed, his chest remained unmovable. Neltan air had a slightly higher degree of oxygen concentration than Earth, and their lungs were situated toward their backs and four times as large as human kidneys. Taking a great pause in the conversation, he was obviously thinking of an appropriate reply. Either he was unsure of what to say or he was being cautious so as not to offend someone or divulge too much.

Meanwhile, news of the end of World War III continued to stream around the globe. Through their holosite worlds, people were entering The Regency's special *Victory* Holosite that a few Regents had begun hosting in Manning's Oval Office. On another screen at the back of the Press Room was a live-feed of surveillance images streaming in from Station V's Prison Facility. Enforcers and troops who had been raiding hideouts and capturing Tech-Nos and terrorists on Earth were marching the POWs into processing lines, prison cells, and high-tech labs on Station V. A debate began to ensue on the same *Victory* Holosite: Imprison them for life or cognitively modifying them "in some way," and, "to someone's standard of behavior?" Several Regents contacted the Voting Site in China, calling for behaviorists, the military, and the public to make suggestions. The new Terra-III would process the responses and post them for a global vote in two weeks. Enforcers had thus far captured over five hundred Tech-Nos and fifty terrorists. Now they were waiting for word from off-Earth.

Definitely, and finally, the War on Terror—World War III—was over. Using the Emergency Broadcast Channel meant for global catastrophes only, The Regents made an exception and sent the great news into *every* individual's holosite world.

Jenkens said that he still hadn't heard from General Rand.

Manning asked: "Any word or signal though from Captain

Bartlet? Did *he* destroy those terrorists on the moon? There might be some survivors, you know. Have you received any signal from any other astrofighters who might have assisted Captain Bartlet? I'm mighty worried!"

With his head low, Jenkens whispered: "No—and I'm worried too."

Manning dashed to the Oval Office, excused himself to a few Regents for interfering with their broadcast, asked them to leave, had Terra darken the room, and then he activated a Full Augmented connection to *The Spider*. Nothing…only a black-and-white grid in a dark room. He heard General Rand's automated message: *Please leave a copy of your avatar, voicing your concern, or contact your Regency representative.*

"Damn!" He hit his desk, sent out another fiery retort to The General and stomped out of the Oval Office. When he reached Jenkens, he said, "Not a word from *one* astrofighter, Steve."

Jenkens confirmed that fact in his own holosite. "Nothing here either."

Manning moaned and said: "Something's wrong…horribly wrong. This cosmic disturbance seems to be hanging around and Terra unable to stream beyond the tropopause shield. I'm getting its readings showing a hardy ozone level but nothing else."

"While you were gone, I asked the Neltans for help, but they couldn't connect with The General either," Jenkens said. "He confirmed a wide-spread victory in space but no details then nothing. *Uhhh*—this silence isn't like him! We'd better hear from him before the media starts *demanding* answers. They eat up conspiracy theories. Reporters tend to graph images and generate shows when they don't get immediate answers to their questions. They can—"

"No they can't, Steve," Manning countered, tapping his collar. "I don't have stars here yet, but no one can vote you *or me* out of office, ever, no matter *what* show *or* image *or* out-of-context quote he or she revamps and holosites to The World. I'm Executive Regent. You're Second Regulate. We're permanent.   Besides...*ahem*...we're heroes."   He felt untouchable.

Outside the White House, people were continuing to cheer and applaud in waves.   One large crowd kept repeating through loud speakers, "On to Nelta!"

A group of spectators was projecting icons of *Sagan* into the dark sky when suddenly, a long beam of light blasted Dr. Coflin's face on the top of Washington's monument.   Under his half-Neltan, half-human figure appeared the words: *Dr. Coflin, Pioneer.*

Enforcers immediately jetted their craft to the site in search of the dissidents.

Manning felt an ache strike behind his eyes.   "Looks like we have people who believed in the mad doctor's cause and are trying to make sure it lives on after him.   I wonder what *this* coalition is going to call themselves?"

"God—I hope they don't infiltrate *Sagan*!" said Jenkens. "You said you've got ways to detect dissidents, but ya never know..."

After the small astrovessel dodged a burst of Enforcer firepower, it disappeared into a patch of clouds.   The dissidents left their glowing statement in a tombstone icon on the Rotunda: *RIP Doc, Until Nelta. Daryl Coflin forever!*

"Oh no," moaned Jenkens.

Manning waved off the 3D mega-tombstone before an Enforcer hacked into the grid and expunged the projection. "*Na*—they're irrelevant. Remember our cognitive weapon on *Sagan*."

"But people might find ways to fool or slip through Terra's matrix," Jenkens countered.

Standing in front of the Ambassador and his long line of tall scientific colleagues, Manning noticed that Elisa Holton had the glowing, Gem-Encantado armband cradled to her body.   She seemed infused with confidence and exuding affability.   So unlike her, he thought, but the change in her personality is probably the result of Gem—which is Neltan in origin. He wondered how else Gem might have affected her.

Around Earth, and now among the Neltan Advancement Committee, she had created a name for herself and a favorable impression.

"People here on Earth like everything Neltan," she said, addressing them with respect and solemnity. "So please, don't let what just happened upset you. We want to have a future relationship with your species. *The Pact* is important—as you can see from all these people requesting holosite connection to the signing ceremony." The popularity bar in a wall zone was ninety-percent full, and continuing to receive results of various opinion polls that the matrix was gleaning from the public. "Everyone's celebrating our new ozone...and winning the War and—"

"You can add Neltan technology to that victory equation," Manning added. Then he gently moved her aside to make room for him and Jenkens.

Shaesar stepped back and cleared the way for a full view of the transmission screen. A landscape scene of Nelta was solidifying. That mean they were close to beginning the signing ceremony. He said to Manning: "Years ago, after you streamed your genetic code to us, we were curious as to how our two species would mix biologically. Asking for a volunteer...who we could clone to normal after the experiment if he or she so desired...we conducted the same inter-species experiment as did Dr. Coflin."

An image of a woman appeared next to Shaesar. She had an oval face, short nose, small earlobes, blue eyes, and thin fingers. The rest of her traits were Neltan.

People in the room stopped what they were doing and began watching the show.

"I assume this is your half-human, half-Neltan, *um*, person?" Manning asked, sweeping his hand through her image. The silence in the room turned pin dropping.

Nodding yes, Shaesar answered, "Several of you have asked about Dr. Coflin...what will happen to him after he arrives on Nelta."

Manning copied her image to Stage-1 Right of the Center

Stage. Terra now had it in the matrix. Other Regents and a geneticist stepped forward and began inspecting her with hand-held Body Double Imagers. Shaesar included a file with the woman's IQ scores, personality profiles, strengths and weaknesses on a bar below her name: *Mercy.*

"She's beautiful," Elisa marveled. "I wish we would have known this sooner. Maybe Dr. Coflin might not have conducted his experiment and endangered Earth."

Jenkens streamed the results via a Top Secret grid to *Sagan.* "I still don't think that would have prevented the event. Coflin used his own body as a variable to deliver *that* outcome."

"Yes," Manning began, "Dr. Coflin was bent on making a *physical* statement, apparently hoping he'd ignite fear and cause a revolt against us having any further contact with Nelta."

"*Hmm,*" Shaesar said after one of his colleagues began displaying a hologram. "Odd."

"What?" Manning asked. When he saw Mercy's image stamped with an earlier date and time, he exclaimed, "I never saw this!"

"We quantum streamed the file to Earth." He called up a date that appeared under Mercy's name: *September 25, 2065.*

You sent this file *where*, Ambassador?" Elisa asked. "I never saw it. And being that I'm cleared to open up medical plans and blueprints from Nelta, I should have seen it and sent it to The Military or a Research grid."

As people in the room began whispering and conjecturing, Manning said, "Oh—Station II has the image I'm sure. It's probably misplaced in an archive with one of our dialogues."

Knowing otherwise, he remembered a special black-and-white augmented grid inside *Sagan.* It contained a medical bin in the covert section of the astrocity that he had altered. Any Black-Ops labeled blueprints would have automatically diverted there and stored. It was around that time that he asked Shaesar to stamp all messages containing sensitive plans with a special Neltan cypher: *Regency Only.* He was so busy securing his office and appeasing the public daily that he must have skimmed over that file and surmised it was misplaced because it contained someone's name. *He* had mismanaged the file. *He* was the one who might have been able to stop Coflin's catastrophe if *he* had just opened the Mercy File and made it public. *He* could have put a positive spin on the experiment and generated a flow of intelligent discussions between people on Earth and Nelta. Feeling a negative flood self-recrimination, he poured more champagne and slugged it down.

Jenkens asked him, "Are you all right, because you look pale...like you saw that Halite Being and you're about to choke for air." He chuckled.

"Why, why!?" Manning rubbed his hurting eyes until he remembered Shaesar sharp diagnosis. "Forget it. The situation is what it is. We've gotta move on."

Jenkens appeared confused, his droopy eyelids twitching. "Yeah—*uh*—for sure. No one's blaming you for a thing, Thornton, if that's what—"

"I said...move on," he repeated.

In the interim, Elisa was commenting on the half-human experiment teleporting from Nelta. "You say that Mercy is now in stasis with the remainder of your population, so she's okay." Her apparent concern allayed when the Ambassador showed Mercy in her body chamber and hibernating. Elisa signed in relief and added: "She appears to be a perfect, biological composite of our two species. Her skin looks clear, and I can see from her genetic code the strands that constitute her humanness." She pulled out a pinch of Mercy's virtual DNA that was scrolling on the bar under her hologram. "These replications are advancements in human intelligence, cerebral codes, and ATP molecular Neltan structures."

"We can see that you have a keen knowledge of cellular genetics and cellular dynamics, Dr. Holton," Shaesar said. "We created Mercy in one of our stem-cell projection chambers before we created the artificial sun that is now containing our Matter Stream. The chamber is a special one of the type we used to transport beings to Nelta to study them long ago."

"You what!?" said Manning.

Battlefield Matrix

"Long ago...we experimented with alien life from other planets, but not for millennia," Shaesar replied. "We stopped transporting alien life to Nelta billions of years ago."

"*Whew*—I'm glad 'cause you never mentioned *that* in any of our discussions...the experimenting part," he said. "The exploration of planets—worlds throughout the cosmos—yes...but not the experimenting part. Exactly, *ahem*, what do you mean, 'experiment'?"

"We don't," Shaesar said.

"Don't what? Ambassador?" asked Jenkens, gesturing innocently.

"Experiment any longer," Shaesar said firmly. "*That* is in our past."

"We learned from that Experimentation Era and that is why we stopped," another Neltan added. "If you check the grid we streamed to you when we sent you the blueprints for your quantum system, you'll find the details."

"Didn't you activate that grid?" Shaesar asked as Elisa and a few others began researching that outdated Terra-IA version.

After moments of wild searching ensued that yielded nothing on the historic subject, Manning noticed people in a state of shock. He said to everyone after he noticed the time—a new constraint: "Look! We're waste precious time. Later, when we have extra time, that is if we can sign *The Pact* right now, we can ask the Ambassador and the Committee to explain this part of their history. I'm sure we'll get answers to the questions we have."

A member of the Neltan Advancement Committee stepped into the transport light. She appeared to be the model behind the Mercy Experiment because the two looked alike. She said: "Mercy will greet Dr. Coflin when he arrives on Nelta. We have a place assigned for them both. They will have immediate passage to another planet."

Lynn's face popped into his mind and Manning felt betrayed. "What!? You're saving that mad scientist's life!? Jenkens, open up the file and show them *The Greeter* exploding." After the explosion extinguished off Center Stage, he added: "Coflin killed *them*. He killed *ten* valuable people."

Elisa said softly, "One of those scientists was my best friend….and a special friend of Regent Manning's."

Manning realized that the Neltans had perceived him as being callous when he saw their disappointed expressions. He felt compelled to set them straight as to the procedures of justice and punishment under *Global Law II*, Article 2. He stepped forward and said: "Respectfully, Ambassador, I hope that after watching those deaths that Dr. Coflin caused…and the lives he took right here in this room—" He pointed to the spot where the mad scientists once wreaked havoc. "That when Dr. Coflin materializing on Nelta, you will incarcerate him until we arrive so we can punish him ourselves. You see, here on Earth, Ambassador, if someone is a traitor or a killer, we apprehend the criminal and send him or her to our prison station for trial and punishment. Please, reconsider your plan and put into place some type of punishment for Dr. Coflin…not a beautiful existence with a soul mate." He *wanted* to say, "That's ludicrous!"

As he waited for Shaesar to consult with his Judicial Board on Dr. Coflin's fate, the Neltan Advancement Committee linked with *Sagan*. When engineers at the virtual helm of the astrocity quantum streamed *Sagan*'s coordinates, the Committee streamed the Navigation Course into the helm. Due to their limited time to iron-out the final details of the voyage to Nelta, Shaesar told The Regency that the unexplained download was a necessary short cut in preparation for a quick *Signing of The Pact* ceremony.

Specifically, the Advancement Committee streamed the fixed intricate map containing the network of intergalactic wormholes for *Sagan*'s one-hundred year, Real Time spacefolding voyage to Nelta.

While the map and network streamed into *Sagan*'s Navigation, Shaesar directed Terra to open Nelta's holosite grid on Earth and prepare it for a surprise expansion.

People often downstreamed updated information from the Neltans into their holosite world so they could virtually enter the bright-white Neltan doorway, chose an experience, and then participate in the oldest or most recent virtual scenery, events, or day-to-day life experiences of individuals on Nelta.

When the Neltan doorframe appeared on Center Stage, Shaesar stamped it with a red-star. That red star meant he was about to leave humanity with a vital experience that individuals on both planets should imprint in their minds and hearts like a holiday.

Then a glowing white scroll materialized under his arm. It had the appearance of originating from a place of divinity, not of this universe.

When everyone in the room saw the splendor, delicacy, and shining magnificence of the glowing scroll, they gasped and briefly covered their faces. The light was that blinding beauteous. Regents in the front rows began dabbing their tear-filled eyes. They were standing up close and personal to the shining scroll that had tiny threads moving around the edges. Shaesar explained that the gold strings were all the visual exchanges between Earth and Nelta—discussions, images, events and interactions from First Communication to the exact moment in the present, February 27, 2068. On the other side of the scroll in orange dancing threads was the language in English and Neltan of the bargain they made on October 4, 2061.

In the seal of the scroll, Shaesar said they had embedded every scenario from the time the last Regent signed *The Pact* to the time they had programed *Sagan* to establish orbit around Nelta and assist them: February 28, 3070. That seal represented several possibilities for the future. However, they had already named the future day, *The Meet*, in a moving icon in the center of the seal that showed Shaesar shaking hands with a representative of *Sagan* whose face was blank, whose figure indiscernible.

"Who is that person, who it seems, is the first person to set foot on Nelta?" Jenkens asked. He had his tiny avatar active over his wrist device. The avatar was flashing a Facial Recognition app at the illusive individual in an attempt to

J.P. Osterman

identify him or her.

"I don't know," Manning replied, "but we have over a hundred years to find out. Obviously, something profound is going to happen on *Sagan* that'll make us choose who will first step on Nelta, help their Lead scientists wake up, and present him or her with our DNA."

"From this display, it doesn't look like we're all there," another Regent said.

"This is a *possible* simulation," Shaesar declared, "not fact. That is why the individual is unrecognizable and the event not fully loaded into the Archival Archway that will be the landing site for one of your craft. This is only one possible window into the future."

People continued questioning one another concerning the future identity of the person greeting the Ambassador until Shaesar unraveled the scroll and a glittering gold virtual pen appeared. He said: "Our signatures represent our promise to uphold our agreement. Your atmosphere is repaired." Earth's ozone readings appeared inside the yellow hologram light and then streaked like lightning into the golden glowing scroll. "Our agreement to exchange a sample of our Matter Stream for your DNA is now irreversibly set in *this* reality."

Manning could hear Elisa exclaim from two rows behind him: "Wow—both species are indelibly connected for eternity!"

Shaesar tapped open the red-stamped holosite world for humanity to stream to their private systems. Inside the holosite world, the Neltan terrain appeared as a lapping savanna redolent of Earthly-appearing species of gargantuan oaks, ferns, and redwoods interspersed with small Yuccas and various shrubs in full bloom. The air was balmy, but the soil gritty, sandy and dry. That was Nelta's Mid Quadrant, a ten-thousand mile preserve. Stepping on the simulated ground felt like sinking one inch. The atmosphere smelled ionized, sweet, as if the air was in a constant state of fresh mist from soft morning rains. The flowing rusty and blue sedimentary terrain in the southern part of the holosite world was teeming with the

234

sounds of soft and shrill birdcalls. In the distance on the northern landscape rose a giant monolith almost touching the blue, orange-tinged sunlit sky. Billions of years ago, they had constructed one of many such religious buildings as part of the identity of their land. They had many such worship centers: Holy grounds to The Divine.

Stretching out his arms to humanity in a gentle loving gesture, he said the following: "The ciphers, codes and symbols we are streaming to *Sagan* are event horizon coordinates— instructions for the *Sagan* crew upon arriving on Nelta, and our Matter Stream release programs. We are embedding these…engraining each detail into the identity of the astrocity. *Sagan*. Under any circumstance, *do not* deviate from this course. The intergalactic roadmap to Nelta, *I* now set forth inside *The Pact*. I now include *our Pact* with this red-stamped, update holosite of Nelta."

An Algorithmic ball appeared over the doorframe of the red holosite world. As the energized force expanded to a white glowing gas, the ball generated a wind in the Press Room.

Manning felt prickly static waft over his skin. "Is this another dimension—like 8?" he shouted. "Terra! What is this high-energy force?"

Terra put her virtual hand over his. "This is *The Pact* ceremony uniting Nelta and Earth, Regent Manning. This force is *The Breath* quantum manifesting in both worlds, moving among individuals on both planets to seal your covenant. Everyone is receiving *The Breath*, and *The Breath* is receiving each individual. I am holositing the message of interplanetary unity so people will understand, not be frightened of the unifying spirit, and remember their agreement."

The windows *swooshed* open. The powerful wind left the Press Room.

The lights outside—even the tropopause shield—began flashing.

People everywhere were gasping as the wind began circumnavigating the Earth. Some people were trying to clasp the powerful breeze, others were inhaling it, and most people were capturing the experience with their avatars to stream to their holosites.

Someone said through a bullhorn, "Quick—grab a jar and get some!"

But the energizing spirit was gone, like lightning.

Jenkens waved for all the guests in the Press Room to remain seated. Then he said as he gestured at the popularity bar streaming responses from people around the globe: "This energy—*The Breath*—touched people indoors *and* outdoors!" He pointed outside to a zeppelin and several craft that had ridden *The Breath* like sailboats on a turbulent sea. "And those trees are vibrating like a tornado just pummeled them, but they're fine. Amazing! Terra's right. This *Breath* entity...spirit, wind, whatever...is harmless, but I'm sure potentially deadly. I guess I'm thinking about that Plague of Darkness that God unleashed during the time of Moses." He gasped breaths of air but then wheezed. "This definitely makes me consider connecting to my Jewish heritage!"

The wind finally returned and entered the white Algorithmic ball.

The windows slashed shut.

"Some *Pact* signing...and we haven't written our signatures in it yet," Manning said, rubbing sense back into his cheeks. He hadn't remembered ever feeling such fear...except for a few seconds during First Communication. He remembered Lynn's words because she believed they were going to die: "I love you." He felt his eyes sting with hot tears of loss.

The white gyring ball suddenly melted into small 3D pools of colorful ink containing the purest type of clarity as on medieval manuscripts.

Dashing to the front row and bending down to talk to Manning and Jenkens, Elisa appeared breathless and said: "I'm receiving millions of complex codes through the algorithmic world. That ink *is* us *and* the Neltans...*each* individual on both planets. They *know* us. *They* care about *each* person! They're quantum-imaging everything about us to Nelta and including us in their eternal plan!" Her every movement exuded a pensive seriousness and overwhelming gratitude for the Neltans' deep acceptance. Gem was glowing. Obviously, the device was showing her privileged information of a deep interpersonal, spiritual, intimate nature.

Feeling envious, Manning patted her shoulder. Others around her were absorbed in describing that same level of intimacy, but he wasn't feeling The Breath's warm fuzziness. "Keep the armband connected to the matrix so we have everything it's experiencing to study later."

"I'll try, Sir," she began, sniffling through her tears of obvious overwhelming joy, "but I don't think Terra's powerful enough to process The Breath or even analyze the entity's composition or origin. We'd have to discern the beginning of Multiverse Time—the space/time that's existed since before this, our universe. That's why this is so overwhelming. I caught a glimpse of the expanse of The Multiverse through The Divine's inter-dimensional eyes!" She wiped away her tears. Gem showered a light-blue glow over her face. A surge of calmness appeared in her rosy cheeks.

"Dr. Holton, seems like you experienced something way beyond the rest of us," Jenkens said, peeking askance at Manning.

Terra appeared next to Elisa. "*The Breath* is the Neltan way of leaving aliens, whom they visit, with a lasting experience so that those species remember the Neltans in the future."

Another Regent leaned over and whispered, "Beautiful experience, but deadly I'm sure if we don't follow through with *The Pact*." She pointed her finger in a chastising gesture at Manning and added: "Thornton, as our Executive leader, it's up to you to ensure we do just *that*." Regent Itonovich was snappy, firm and demanding. She reminded him of a buxom, blond, Russian KGB agent he had seen in an archival show—always watchful and suspicious.

Elisa gestured for her to join their circle quickly. "From the research I watched on Neltans ancient religious ceremonies, Shaesar is embedding this spiritual reaping that just occurred into *The Pact*. We all *are* the final detail. Each of us is important to the Neltans." She began crying and breathed deeply to contain herself. The spiritual experience and Gem was changing her.

"Are you alright? If not, I need to get you to somewhere you can debrief," Manning said.

Finally composing herself, she said: "Excuse me, but wow—*ha uh ha*—I can hardly believe that I'm right here and actually a part of this ceremony, watching history-in-the-making in person! I feel—" She put her right hand over her heart as Regent Itonovich handed her a Kleenex. "I feel like I just saw God! At the speed of inter-dimensional Planck Time, *Breath physically* touched *each* soul. If you noticed the Enforcer statistics of those moments, they're showing zero crime around the globe. Everyone was so engrossed in basking in *The Breath* that all fighting ceased. Amazing!"

Realizing that probably most of humanity was feeling the same way, Manning tried to read the details streaking around the scroll. When he recognized several items that The World had approved, he said, "You're right, Dr. Holton. *The Breath* is transcribing images of each person on Earth, from this direct contact with them, and sealing them into *The Pact*. Everyone is in the Neltans living archival database. At least now we can feel secure in the knowledge that Shaesar programmed *Sagan*'s Navigation."

When the golden image of *Sagan* materialized on the doorframe of the Neltan's inviting holosite world, Jenkens asked Manning: "Thornton, do you think those threads could be dangerous? From what Shaesar said, if we veer off course, those threads could...well, come alive. Could they kill us? A string...hurt us?" He shivered a bit in obvious fear.

Manning waved off his terror. "They need us, Steve. They'd never do that because then they'd never receive our DNA." He felt uneasy as he watched more images permeate their archival doorframe. This was a significant ceremony—a serious sacred exchange of oaths and covenants for the Neltans. If an exchange of blood could unite two people as

Battlefield Matrix

brothers, this occasion was just that—a holy signing ceremony to seal, connect, and inextricably bind two species over fifty-five thousand light-years apart in the cosmos.

As he watched everyone celebrating, another fearful thought occurred to him. He had studied human dynamics and realized some aspects of human nature. People around the globe were happy. World War III had just ended. Terrorism appeared to have become instantly extinct. Most importantly—like acquiring a second chance at life after recovering from a debilitating disease—people had a new ozone layer. We were okay…safe, the Earth healed, although some people were fretting over possible harmful ramifications of The Matter Stream sample. He worried: Would people follow through with *The Pact* once the Neltans were in stasis and no longer communicating with humanity? As time would pass, people would change. After Final Communication, after *this* day, people wouldn't hear a word from Nelta. People could change their minds, minimize *The Pact* with its newly updated, red-stamped Neltan world and vote to stop *Sagan*'s construction.

Jenkens was now in front of him signing the holographic, bright-white sacred scroll with the virtual, golden shimmering pen he had dipped into a glowing pool of ink. He had chosen the color yellow from among hundreds of small rainbow hues that the algorithmic ball poured out over the Central Stage. His hand was shaking, his signature jagged. All the while, he was looking Shaesar in the eye. Up close, the Ambassador's pure holographic face in the teleportation light appeared with the resolution of a bright full moon against the blackness of Nelta's subterranean stasis facility.

After Jenkens let go of the virtual pen, Manning stepped up in front of the white scroll, took the pen as best he could between his fingers, and quickly signed his name. "There, Ambassador Shaesar. It's done. The great exchange between our two species. I look forward to meeting you one day on Nelta." Then he recalled the image on the scroll's seal and realized that the person greeting the Neltans might not be him.

He stepped back—a wave of foreboding shock rippling through him. Glanced at his signature on the white scroll, it was dazzling and red like fresh blood on snow. Will I make it there?! he wondered.

Shaesar's holographic hand touched Manning's hand. "Farewell, Thornton Seth Manning. Until we meet on Nelta."

He felt an instant jolt of optimism. "Great! I was wrong then—*whew*. I thought—I imagined...oh well." He felt dizzy with excitement. All the fatigue that had been building up inside him throughout the day evaporated as he looked over The Regents' signatures in *The Pact*. Each stroke was quivering and pulsating...almost breathing. It seemed that each name could pop out of the scroll, expand and begin dancing. "Finished...*haaa*—finished...yes!" He stepped back and lightly bowed to Shaesar and the Neltan Committee.

Shaesar rolled up the bright white scroll and placed it into the teleportation light. The scroll appeared on Nelta, where another member of the Advancement Committee grabbed it and clutched the document under his arm. Shaesar proclaimed: "We will infuse this scroll within our Archival Archway. When *Sagan* arrives in orbit, it will update *Sagan* with vital information that will have been processing throughout our thousand-year stasis. Meanwhile, for your journey, the scroll has been entrenched in *Sagan*'s Navigation Center. The astrocity is intertwined with Navigation, where the quantum computer is processing *The Pact's* identity."

"*The Pact* has an identity? I never heard of such a thing, Ambassador. It's in *Sagan*? An advanced intelligence infused in *Sagan*?"

He remembered some of the untranslatable files that Matrix Techs and Plasma Engineers had been streaming to him lately, showing parts of the astrocity shifting as if automatically accommodating "an environment." There was a statistical significance between added construction and an increase in self-organization. He had examined the newest models and noticed a correlation. The more nano-organics, materials and fabrics that workers added, the more the ship increased in its

Battlefield Matrix

self-guided/self-directed "behavior." No wonder its infrastructure was advancing and completing so quickly...at times erecting barriers so workers couldn't enter or inspect niches and complicated extensions.

The other Regents were whispering the same questions and concerns among themselves.

Jenkens activated his avatar that streamed to *Sagan's* Navigation section to confirm Shaesar's statement. "It's there. *The Pact* is there, and it's gradually lighting up the entire astrocity even though it's only seventy-five percent complete!" He had the grandest expression of wonderment on his face. "Navigation is powering up...every terminal, tech station, ceiling hub, wall zone and cubicle. We have a viable virtual Navigation Helm and Navigation Center right now!" He appeared dizzy in the incomprehensibility. "Personnel up there are streaming to The Regency that they're hearing sounds...energetic rumbles and vibrations. I received a message that a Plasma Tech in Propulsion felt like someone tapped her on the shoulder. She's scared the place is haunted with the ghosts from people who died in that bad accident a while ago. A Helm Tech said she was in a conduit linking organics to connect to the matrix when she got stuck and almost crushed by a silicon tumbleweed until a giant wind ripped open the wires and freed her."

Elisa said, "I guess it means we'll have guardian angels while we're on our voyage!"

His eyes moving from Regent, to guest, to reporter; Shaesar appeared to be soaking up every word. "*The Pact* is a virtual palindrome, an intelligence-in-a-sequence...a directional guide—no, compass—for any astrocraft venturing through the cosmos. The palindrome is permeating *Sagan*."

"That *still* didn't answer my question," Manning whispered to Jenkens.

Jenkens said: "It's gonna take us some time to figure out what this living *Pact* is capable of doing. No circumventing this I believe...as you thought you might be able to, Thornton."

Shaesar stepped toward Manning—a shining yellow vision

teleporting from Nelta. "Regent Manning, I have an answer from our Judicial Panel concerning Dr. Coflin."

Manning felt his irritation change. "Yes—but wait, I want *everyone* on Earth to hear the decision too." Again, he thought of Lynn and her vacant tomb beneath her statue at Duke. "People need to know that he will pay for what he's done." He called open a hologram of *The Greeter* memorial. "Okay, we're ready." A blinding light from a projector briefly hit his eyes, fueling his need for revenge.

Ambassador Shaesar appeared impervious to any sort of verbal retaliation should anyone oppose the Judicial Panel's decision. Exuding the standard Neltan characteristics, he was tall and lean. He had long slender arms, no fingernails, a thin nose, deep-set, iris-less black eyes and glowing skin, the later due to the Quantum-Communication Effect. A row of Neltan judges clad in royal-red, velvet robes lined up behind him. Shaesar said: "Dr. Coflin believed that we all should consider the ripple effects of our actions. I will show you."

Dr. Coflin's body appeared in a hologram so that humanity and the Neltans could get a good view of the scientist. It was an image of him from 2058, after the terrorists unleashed their ozone bombs. Below his image scrolled all his background information from the time when the scientist began his career to the time he began experiencing delusions and psychotic breaks. Shaesar's straightforward stare indicated he was about to proclaim something powerful. "After analyzing Dr. Coflin's unique genetic sequence, our Judicial Panel has determined that Dr. Coflin assimilated Neltan DNA and generated a new genetic code. This sequence binds Dr. Coflin to Neltan Law. That means *we* will hold Dr. Coflin accountable for his actions."

"How?" Manning asked, feeling completely dissatisfied.

Guests in the Press Room briefly mumbled tones of dissatisfaction as a few Regents shouted derisive comments.

Shaesar delivered more of their consensus. "Dr. Coflin disobeyed Neltan Law by stealing and misappropriating The Matter Stream to create an alien being. Dr. Coflin misused and

Battlefield Matrix

misdirected energy in Earth's quantum-system Matrix you call Terra-III."

Terra stepped forward and opened two holograms showing Matrix Techs and Engineers working hurriedly inside two matrix facilities containing low-fusion reactors and particle colliders. Obviously having a status report, she said: "Disaster Recovery in progress. Scalability and Elasticity into the Cloud-III Facilities in Africa and at the South Pole are under repair and will initiate a full-grid interface with patrons in those vicinities in two hours."

"Yes, Terra, that's a good update, but you don't take into account the death toll in the White House," Manning said angrily. "He killed Agent Dirk. Those Halite Beings he brought in here turned our people into sashimi! And we haven't heard a word or even an archaic signal from The General yet, so who knows how many others out in space he's affected. But I'm sure we more have casualties because of…of, Dr. Daryl Coflin!" He tasted dry dirt on his tongue.

The room stilled until the teleportation beam crackled out an echo. Shaesar said: "Dr. Coflin endangered lives on Nelta as well when he interfered with the *Pact* signing ceremony. Thus, the Neltan Judicial Panel sentences Dr. Coflin to one Neltan solar-system year of In-Matrix Suspension."

He opened a hologram showing a fission cloud gyring around a tiny holographic body. It looked like the bright-white Algorithmic ball containing *The Breath*, but this cloud cycling around Coflin's image appeared razor sharp and ice cold—a simulation in the future.

"I didn't know a matrix could evolve to such an interactive reality," Manning said.

Shaesar closed the projection. "There is more. Because of Dr. Coflin's experimental action, inquisitive nature, and the new species he created, our Judicial Panel ruled that after his punishment, Dr. Coflin deserves a haven somewhere in the universe, with restrictions."

When Manning saw The Panel leave Shaesar's side, he realized he couldn't argue any further. He coughed down the memory of Lynn. He felt his fists needing to meet a face as he turned away from the teleportation light and met the eyes of his colleagues who were motioning for him "to cut" this part of their valuable communication so they could move on with the final portion of ceremony. A few Regents showed him messages from individuals who were positing important questions. He gestured abruptly for them to give him a few more seconds.

"We are genetically calibrating an old teleporter to accept Dr. Coflin once he materializes in a portal beneath the surface of Nelta," Shaesar said. "Mercy will meet him, explain his sentence, and escort him to a chamber where he will begin his one-year Matrix Suspension."

Manning noticed a comforting expression appear on Shaesar's face as he stepped forward and set his holographic hand on his back.

Shaesar said, "I see how upset you are." His words were sympathetic, soft, and genuine. "You perceived there has been a great injustice."

"Yes—yes you're right!" he replied, ignoring Regent Sylvia Itonovich who whispered in his ear that he needed to move on with the ceremony, fast.

"There is one thing you do not know but that you need to consider about corporeal teleportation," Shaesar said. His deep-black, deep-set round eyes were transfixing up close.

"What, Ambassador?"

"Dr. Coflin is now *living* a controlled quantum state-of-existence," Shaesar said. "His body and mind are experiencing the pain of being in multiple places simultaneously. Someday, you will face Dr. Coflin. When you do, I know you will ask us stop punishing him...to nullify the one-year confinement. We would."

"That's if anything's left of Coflin from the sound of what the Ambassador just said," Jenkens interrupted. He had finished readjusting a tower of robotic equipment. "Maybe tele- porting is enough punishment for the guy, Thornton. *Uugh*—I shudder to think of what he's experiencing right now from what the Ambassador just said."

The quantum-communication light suddenly crackled with a loud white-noise static that sounded like five-times the normal deep-field frequency interference. The Neltans disappeared. White and yellow ribbons appeared around the ceiling hubs. The rainbow processors were Off-Quantum Visual mode.

Shaesar called, "Terra, strengthen the energy stream through the orbiting accelerator!"

Terra appeared in the center of the room, and many other Terras materialized in an obvious response to unsuccessful interventions.

Shaesar said, "I'm here...but for how long...I cannot discern." He was panting, a claustrophobia expression on his face. "Terra is maintaining our connectivity in a circuitous path that is bypassing the bad connection."

General Rand materialized on the Center Stage but then his image fizzled.

"Get 'im back in here! What the hell happened!?" Manning shouted.

Jenkens calmed two Regents and ordered robot servers to hold open the exit doors. He called to Manning: "We knew something was wrong somewhere but nothing like this! People *everywhere* must be *totally* panicking. I'm streaming a protocol to Enforcers to maintain order."

"From what's been happening anyway lately, I'm about to order a permanent, Stage-1 Alert and send people to shelters until this night's over," he replied, running to the transmission screen. "Terra, intensity connectivity and, at least, fortify Shaesar's voice."

Jenkens called out: "It's 10:15. There's nothing scheduled that could be causing this!"

Manning said, "Yes—the time...I have an idea." As guests began pouring out of the Press Room, he said to Terra: "Let's keep track of every nanosecond. No telling what's happening that's causing all this and we need a trail."

The twenty-five beehive hubs suddenly connected, their

rainbow processors activating to a new bright intensity.

"The last evolutionary feat in Terra-III just occurred," he sighed. "But let's hope General Rand has reinforced the Decagon. If that Neltan/Earth wormhole isn't held constant during a quantum communication, a whiplash could occur and stir up the Oort cloud."

Jenkens was analyzing the transmission screen with another Terra at his side. He continued to assess connections until he stopped abruptly and declared, "Thornton, this is an outer space issue. Sustaining our quantum communication will require help from Nelta."

Manning shouted into the wavering image of the Ambassador: "Shaesar—we need help from you...*you*! Terra is tracing the connection through the matrix as far out into space as the system can reach, but I need *your* Committee to extend energy into the Decagon accelerator. From what you've told us, Matter Stream energy would work, if you have more to spare." He felt as if he was talking through layers of plasticized air to get Shaesar to hear him even though he was in front of him.

When Shaesar finally replied, all anyone could understand were low-sounding intonations. "We, are, *are*, streaming...unison *wi*—with Earth...locating *prooblemms*."

Manning ordered Terra to double-stream the event to General Rand. "Tell him that if he doesn't do something to fix this bad interference, that *his* neglect...neglect!...could disconnect us from Nelta for good before they can answer all our concerns...some of them being *your* questions!...about *Sagan* and our mission. Rand—I'm about to take, your, stars—damn it!"

"Continuous message streaming in Double Force-mode to *all* Stealth Force craft and space stations, Regent Manning," Terra said. "Everyone in space and residing in interplanetary colonies will receive the message."

The flooding sounds of *Stage-1 Emergency Alerts* stopped.

Battlefield Matrix

Chapter 13

Spider's Descent

The Security wall zone next to the Oval Office suddenly extended with a flashing yellow alert. The bar at the bottom lit up: *Station III.*

"General Rand!" Manning said, dashing toward the incoming show. Regents were returning to the Press Room, but Enforcers and Security had the media and guests barricaded behind the double doors.

General Rand's image was fuzzy.

"Switch to 2D, strengthen the live-stream on Station III, and fix the image-in-an-image so we can get a good view of the Decagon and see what's happened there," Manning ordered.

As more solar energy fed the tropopause shield array—sending power through the matrix—a cloudy section of space between Mars and Jupiter resolved to crystal clarity.

"The time stamp shows two minutes ago, but this view is much older according than what Terra told us." Jenkens leaned into a blurry section and squinted. "*Whoa*—what the hell is that giant debris field?"

Manning directed the show to Stage-1 Right next to Center Stage where techs were working to activate General Rand on Station III. "*Definitely* this quadrant is craft debris. Zoom in, Terra...I see letters." He read slowly, "D...half an O and this is an S...T, R."

"That's *The Droidster!*" Jenkens cried. "The Droidster and—and several other of our craft!" In an expression of dismay, he plopped down in a chair while Regents in the room began gasping in shock—their lamentations surging to the media in the long hallway where reporters began a massive rush of *Request for Information* to the Regency's holosite. Waiting for permission to admit them, Enforcers were barricading them at the long line of double doors.

Manning had Terra replay the order he had given The General hours ago, then he said, "That's one of the five astrofighters I ordered to that quadrant to support Captain Bartlet." He felt a sting in his eyes as he strained to locate *The Spider* in the black vacuous ocean of debris. He called for more Regents to help him. "I don't see it!" When they couldn't spot the astrofighter either, he asked Terra, "Can your matrix detect anything of *The Spider?*"

After a minute, Terra said, "The probes around Jupiter detect no evidence of *The Spider.*"

"Keep looking, Terra, and give me an exact time when all this happened. That bout of interference was pretty intense." He gestured at the Center Stage around which Matrix Techs were attempting to solidify The General's hologram. "And please help *them* bring *him* in here."

Several Regents broke out in tears as the view of the debris field intensified. Clumps of matrixware, serrated metals, and jagged pieces of Stealth Force astrocraft and astrofighters appeared. They were dispersing outward, propelled by expanding gases even though the sites of the explosions remained unclear.

Terra stepped forward. "9:30 p.m., Eastern Standard Time this event occurred according to a weak message from Space

Battlefield Matrix

Station II. Matrix Techs and Projectionists on Level 3 of Station II are compiling images from ten probes in order to generate a show of what occurred."

As Jenkens began communicating with those workers, Manning said: "That time stamp makes sense. I know the Neltan/Earth wormhole was open then and Shaesar in this room."

"Station III communications are still severed," Terra continued. "However, I congealed one presentation through the disturbance through that same weak message."

Manning dashed to the window when he saw another flash of light. "What the hell's going on up there!"

"Incoming Radioactive Interference, Regent Manning," Terra answered as a Radioactive Alert resounded. "Solar energy is increasing in the array to fend off the influx of radiation."

Energy surging through the shield array was turning the tropopause into a yellow net. Spectators who had remained in the streets and throughout the city were marveling at the anomaly. Small security icons were still illuminated everywhere through the streets, the Standard Alert to persuade those people to seek immediate sanctuary.

"We're getting bombarded with radioactivity?" Manning asked. "From what? That's probably why we haven't been able to receive a decent visual."

Regents and scientists rushed into an intensive quest for answers. He began worrying about the space stations. Straining through the fine lines of the shield array to see them, he finally spotted Station I—*Sagan*'s construction site. It was okay. The huge saucer-like station was appearing white in in its geosynchronous orbit. Next in line, albeit in the southwest, appeared Station IV, the construction warehouse; and next, albeit beyond the horizon, was Station V, the Prison Facility, which was probably on a High-Alert/Lock-Down. No word from *anyone* onboard any stations, only a few Matrix Techs and researchers on Station II, thanks to Dr. Elisa Holton and her new Gem. He called Terra to request a report on the welfare of people onboard all the stations and then he assisted a Matrix Tech in hoisting up and attaching another ceiling processor to increase holographic downstream and upstream capability. Elisa was using Gem to interface with the transmission screen and reconnect it with the Neltans. She stomped in frustrated when two of Gem's illumination mounts showed holograms of dead space.

After he finished his job, Manning asked her: "Can you discover a way to use Gem to cut through radioactive interference and communicate with General Rand? If we can contact him, he has craft at the Decagon capable of reeling in images of the Neltans. Then Gem can interact with the screen to re-solidify that reception in here."

Patting the glowing armband that extended an inch up her arm like a long sleeve of comfort, she said: "I'll stop what I'm doing and work with Gem on that then, Sir."

He then returned to study the debris field, fine-tuning frequencies. As he panned sections of the debris field, he and the others believed they could hear Doppler screams coming from the men and women who had lost their lives during the explosions. Feeling the weighty death toll, he told them: "It appears like a gauntlet of enemy craft surrounded our astrofighters and firing full-streams of plasma-bursts at them." Then he spotted more debris that looked like grave markers floating through space—an ebbing and eddying cemetery. "Gone? All our craft in that quadrant gone!?" Pacing around a few crying Regents, he tried to count the loss of craft with his fingers. He ordered Terra to compile a true body count.

Then, another burst of unexplainable radioactivity collided with the tropopause shield, rendering Terra useless for her matrix to connect to Station III. He said: "This radioactivity has to be a byproduct of dark energy 'cause Terra can't detect it. Only General Rand has the answer. Only Station III has those delicate detectors that can assess the energy so that we can discover what's generating the radioactivity and stop it."

Manning hailed several CEOs of private corporations— pleading with them to launch craft to Stations III. After they

Battlefield Matrix

agreed to dock with the station, but under the stipulation that they'd have to return if the dark energy became too overwhelming, he shouted so that everyone in the Press Room stopped to listen: *"All* our astrofighters in that quadrant gone? No way! I can't accept this!" He inhaled oxygen that made denial rush right out of him. "Okay, okay…but how many are destroyed? Really?"

Jenkens answered: "Terra can't calculate yet. But if we can return Shaesar and the Neltans, they might be able to track the damage through the Neltan/Earth wormhole."

"Where is that wormhole's event horizon, Terra?" Manning asked.

Terra replied, "The Ambassador's image is somewhere between Earth and Nelta."

As Manning directed to her to open more probe connections past Jupiter and scan those quadrants, another Regent shouted: *"How many* crew members were onboard *each* of those astrocraft? And those astrofighters? God—that had to have been three-fourths of our Stealth Force that was out there! All gone!? No way!" Others shouted her same sentiments, absorbed in speculating on the losses in the field of debris.

Regents were moaning in sorrow, crying, and shouting words of shock and horror. Outside in the long hallway, the media were preparing to re-enter the Press Room. As Regents began feeding them the tragic information without all the details, reporters established a holosite grid to broadcast the cosmic destruction of the military to The World. All the dignitaries and guests began lamenting over the deaths of the courageous astropilots, their exploded craft, and their brave crews. Several Terras appeared and consolingly put their virtual arms around several grief-stricken individuals. Escorted by a trove of Enforcers, a medical team dashed into the Press Room and began rendering assistance.

"Regent Manning," Terra began, "after a circuitous connection established with Station III, I received a cypher message.

J.P. Osterman

"Finally a bit of hope!" Manning breathed. "What?" Everyone stopped to hear her.

"Sensors and particle detectors inside the tropopause array are detecting high-yield, radioactive particle emissions...and a continued bombardment of dark energy."

As Jenkens hailed a few scientists to investigate space from telescopes on Earth, Manning said, "Those yields only occur when wormholes collide, Terra."

"One wormhole *did* activate during the course of another wormhole," she said. "I received the occurrences to the nanosecond when radioactivity from that wormhole struck the tropopause shield. I rounded up the time as per your instructions earlier: 9:15 p.m., Eastern Standard Time. "The wormhole that collapsed on the terrorists occurred at 9:30 p.m. Eastern Standard Time."

Inside a beam of holographic light, General Rand's image from Station III suddenly materialized on Center Stage in front of the IMAX transmission screen that was still humming and droning—the Encantado program configuring to re-establish Shaesar's image. Rand's projection was static-filled and pulsing—both indications that the processor was skipping.

General Rand's image strengthened as the Encantado frame extinguished. Manning told two techs who were adding another ceiling processor above the screen: "Keep that flow of organic repair correlating! We need the Neltans back. We can't lose that quantum connection." He sensed heat from the screen scorching his eyebrows—flowing into an intense rage for General Rand. Accidentally flipping over a serverbot on the way to The General's image, he said: "What the hell happened? Where've ya been?"

General Rand's figure grew to twice its size. He appeared like a wobbly reflection in a carnival mirror.

Jenkens barked, "Why haven't you answered our calls?"

"Damn it!" Manning gulped down air. "We're about to get radiated down here. And between the Mars and Jupiter we see an ocean-of-debris that's all our troops! Explain."

Jenkens' face almost hit The General's stabilizing image

inside the virtual projection beam. "I'm calling for your resignation—"

"Back off, Steve!" Manning said. Jenkens and other Regents retreated, and he added, "We get details now or I order you Off Helm and I take your stars...*your* stars."

With a stoic presence, The General appeared surrounded by a bluish-white aura. That type of energy inside a holographic projection was abnormal. Something beyond their understanding had occurred...a cataclysm that had produced an energy dispersal way beyond The General's capability to handle. Perhaps no one could have prevented the interference that had kept The General from replying to their hails...except for the person, or people, who had started the event in the first place.

Gaining his breath and some semblance of understanding, Manning stepped back. "What happened?" he asked again, slowly, calmly, pointing to the view of the cloudy quadrant filled with expanding metal in the black vacuum of space. "God man—what, *what* happened."

General Rand swallowed hard. His thin face was gaunt, his cheeks sallow as if he had been wandering in a desert. "Let me show you." He coughed and drank water. "I apologize again that I couldn't reply promptly to your hails. We are gradually compiling and decoding these events as several satellites are synchronizing with probes and sending us data. They experienced such interference—went haywire!—but the satellites are now interfacing and sending us info. That's why I didn't answer your initial holositing requests. I was waiting to receive all the information before we could generate answers to *all our* questions. You like facts and solutions, Sir, and hate it when people constantly whine about the problem—"

"Speed it up, General," Manning ordered.

Elisa Holton ran up to him, showing him a Message-Avatar hovering over Gem. "This is for you, Sir, from a lab on Station II." She swept the assessment into Manning's wrist avatar.

The General leaned toward her small display showing

wavelengths colliding with Earth. "Yes, that's what's happening where you are. That's intense dark-energy unifying with gamma radiation striking the shield array. From out viewpoint, the array is lighting it up like a constant display of fireworks. The same thing's happening to *all* the stations with their shields powered on high. We increased the output of our electromagnetic hardware to protect us. The downside is the inability to communicate through the matrix."

Elisa then showed them a visual that Station II had sent her. "This disturbance is rippling through the universe and on a continuum, Sirs. The Lead Researcher on Station II said it's coming from the debris field. Unlike us, she's receiving the image clearly now."

After he ordered her to stream the info to General Rand, he said, "There must have been a *huge* interaction in order for us to still be feeling profound ripple-effect hits."

"Those deadly waves sound like they'll go on for an eternity," Jenkens huffed. "I hope they stop soon, or—or— God I hate to even *think* of worst-case scenarios for Earth! We're looking at intensive tropopause shield monitoring. *One* panel failing could mean—*huh*—"

"Breathe, Steve." Manning had to calm him down. "You're *not* getting the facts." He turned to Elisa. "Keep the connection with scientists on Station II open and stream *everything* you receive to The General and The Regency's holosites. Tell your boss and her team to add another protective layer to the tropopause shield to squelch the ripple effects hitting us. We'll discuss what to tell people later on after we receive some designs."

As she left to comply, General Rand said: "Here's the show we've been able to re-construct so far in spite of the interference."

One of General Rand's officers interrupted him. "This is what occurred, Sir. The entire, *ahem*—" He wiped his eyes. "*Ahem*, battle. It's all in-coming right now."

A quadrant in space appeared. Stealth Force astrofighters had surrounded Dr. Coflin's astrofreighter, *The Heed*, its cyclotron station, and several of the Tech-No Protesters' smaller spacecraft. In the distance, two, long, white wormholes that looked like glowing lines in the void were about to collide. Their origins were indiscernible and untraceable in the spacefolding conduits of the cosmos.

"One wormhole is Coflin's that's running parallel with the Earth/Neltan wormhole," The General said.

General Rand opened up another quadrant in space and continued his narration. "While *these* troops were trying to capture the Tech-No Protesters in *this* area, our Stealth Force astrofighters finally caught up to the terrorists in *another* quadrant in space. We had them right where we wanted them and were about to take them down—"

"What the hell went wrong then?" Regent Sylvia Itonovich demanded.

Pausing the battle, General Rand bowed his head but then resumed his stoic stance. "Ma'am, unknown to us, the terrorists had wormhole capability. Most likely they assembled a cyclotron with the panel they stole a while back and coupled it with their modified quantum-computer system, Demon Terra we named it. Remember?"

"Yes, we know," Manning said, gesturing for Regent Itonovich to back down. "Captain Bartlet had located that panel's reading on the moon. He tracked it to the site where those terrorists had managed to escape between the time they fired on and hit *The Spider*, and the time when *The Spider* returned to engage them again later. Since he didn't have time to give support to the destroyed craft in the debris field, he must still be somewhere around the moon." He wondered about The Captain's current location. "By the way, where is *The Spider*? We haven't received a word from Captain Bartlet. He's supposed to be destroying subterranean hideouts with that Gamma Globule weapon his team invented." General Rand put out a cosmic call to The Captain as more Matrix Techs entered the room to reinstate Shaesar's image.

"I'm sure *The Spider*'s and its crew are fine, Thornton," Jenkens said. "Bartlet's survived some pretty big skirmishes.

J.P. Osterman

He's the best."

General Rand along with several of his personnel showed everyone a holosite doorframe on one of Station III's giant hologram stages in the background. The General said: "This is Captain Bartlet's zone of attack and where he's been since after he left us after making repairs on *The Spider*. As a precaution, we're using an archaic internet back-up channel. We've been signaling *The Spider*, but this damn blue-energy interference has us stymied. Our last communication was at 21:27:17 when he was in a skirmish with a terrorist cell on the moon."

"That was just prior to that battle that destroyed our astrocraft," Manning gasped. "I hope he's all right!"

"Terra hasn't detected any *Spider* debris in that area," Regent Itonovich exclaimed.

During a slight pause in The General's display while more holograms down-streamed from Station III, Manning realized that The Regency had allowed the media back into the Press Room. All eyes were on him. Several reporters and holosite hosts were recording *the entire* dialogue between him and General Rand. The World would soon be able to experience virtually *entire* battle scenes and see debilitating losses first-hand: astrocraft exploding, the last moments of their heroes' lives…maybe final goodbye messages. Nothing repressed! He thought about implementing a Secure Zone and ordering them to a distant area in the Press Room. Then he realized that if people knew *right away* all the facts behind that cosmic battle and what had happened, perhaps people might grieve faster and be able to resume their lives sooner without a long-and-drawn-out inquiry or the standard Investigative Committee procedures.

General Rand resumed the hologram show of the battle now playing out on several stages. Terrorist craft were firing laser bursts at Stealth Force astrofighters in a heated skirmish.

Reading new stats of the event from interfacing satellites on *his* screens and hologram stages, The General said: "When our *Sneaker* and *Droidster* finally surrounded the terrorist craft, their leaders tricked us into believing they were surrendering. We gave them five minutes to surrender. From the time I see here, that was at 9:14 p.m. They took one minute and then activated a wormhole into which to escape." He showed them the time, 9:15, and the image of the terrorists positioned around a giant accelerator and opening up a wormhole in spacer. What looked like a giant hive of enemy craft began entering the wormhole's event horizon where their craft immediately disappeared from view. "Behind the terrorist's wormhole, way in the background, another problem is brewing."

He expanded the field-of-visibility to include two more wormholes streaming parallel in the distant cosmos. The appeared as white whips of lightning ripping through space.

"The terrorist's wormhole needed a boost because its point-of-termination was in a far-away galaxy," The General continued. "As I said, we had them surrounded. We fired on them as they surprised us with more counter fire. We took down *three* large craft of theirs! That loss cut into their cyclotron power. As most of their craft escaped into the wormhole, the rest took cover in the rim of the wormhole's event horizon. The flow of energy around the rim acted as a mirror, camouflaging them. While *Droidster* and *Sneaker* worked to outwit them, we now know that the terrorists had begun feeding the wormhole with a consistent infusion of elemental particles to enlarge it so it could accommodate *all* their craft to that distant galaxy. That's when our huge *Recon* ship picked up the following reading that demonstrates that there is nothing we could have done to stop the reaction. Here's the Recon recording."

The final moments of life onboard *Recon* appeared. On the helm's huge navigation stage appeared the analytic detector readings: "W-boson particle, 80.4 $GeV/c^2[N_{Edd}]$<Gauge-bosons, UNSTABLE."

Manning said: "That's an instantaneous build-up of elementary particles!"

Jenkens swept up the Gauge-boson calculation into his tiny wrist avatar. "That's unachievable, beyond physics."

"Obviously not," countered Manning.

J.P. Osterman

As she paused from an urgent communication with a scientist, Elisa called: "Sir, the center of a black hole is in that area now. That's what is responsible for the dark energy and gamma problem we're experiencing."

"Then get those labs on Station II to find a solution to close that wormhole!" he said.

As she established a hologram connection for Manning to speak to the Director of Station II, General Rand said, "Three places in space/time warped and converged faster than opposites on magnets." He had a hopeless look on his face. "From this view, you can see what finally lead to us losing so many astrocraft and—"

"Not just craft but people!" Jenkens shouted.

"We lost *so many* people!" said Manning, cradling his face in the palms of his hands.

General Rand continued to describe the battle scene: "Every time we swept around to down a terrorist craft, we took more plasma blasts from 'em. They were gleaning so much energy from the event horizon! We compensated by discovering their mode of energy extraction and using that method ourselves. But there's never time to learn in the heat of battle—never. They took their new technology to the heights...impaling our craft with explosive plasma shots before we could even see 'em coming. They had twice—twice!—our firepower from that energy absorption...*and* they had camouflage. Camouflage! That damn Demon Terra they stole and modified—most likely using Neltan technology that they intercepted and developed— helped 'em with their camouflage capabilities. *This* point of view shows that three of our pilots believed they had shot down their craft or disabled them. But before our craft could escape the powerful tug of their wormhole, they maneuvered in front of them, fired on them, and—"

"Wait!" Manning interrupted, feeling pressure because he knew The World was observing everything. "I still can't understand how the two skirmishes—one with the Tech-Nos and this one—took out three-fourths of our troops. Three-fourths!"

In-Progress materialized in yellow in the center of the hologram light.

"We should know that soon, Sir," General Rand said.

Stage-1 Right re-illuminated, displaying a huge vortex into which the last terrorist craft escaped. The time-stamp was on the bar below the show: 9:30 p.m.

In the distance, in another quadrant, the Tech-No Protester's wormhole was streaking through space like a whipping piece of lightning toward the terrorist's wormhole. He spotted the time when Dr. Coflin's body quantum-transported out of the Press Room: 9:30 p.m. Next to those wormholes, the Earth/Neltan wormhole was streaming through its last spacefold conduit to the Decagon, responsible for translating the quantum communication to the IMAX-transmission processing screen. A spike in energy occurred fifteen minutes after their visuals materialized in the Press Room: 9:30 p.m.

Manning sighed as he realized what had happened. "All three wormholes merged at the precise same time...disrupting space/time...creating an unstable vortex. It crushed the enemy, after *they* kill our troops...damn...and the disruption left a small black hole."

In the meantime, several Terra forms had appeared as the matrix gradually stabilized. The Terras were sweeping all three events into an Assessment grid, copying them and crunching the mathematics and algorithmic realities behind the anomalies on Stage-3 Right next to the holograms of the battle scenes.

"Bottom line, Sir," General Rand began, retracing with his forefinger the wormhole conflagration, "that vortex was three-miles in diameter. Our readings confirm the interior of a black hole but without the event horizons or ergosphere. It was a distorted conduit. It imploded. That implosion crushed *all* enemy's craft. No survivors." The show then displayed the vortex clamping shut and an explosion ensuing. The detectors went off-chart. When The General added an oxygenated model to the imagers, the hologram stage itself almost ignited as an photonic eruption occurred within the vortex's singularity.

With a team of tired scientists by her side, Elisa Holton said: "Ladies and Gentlemen of The Regency." After they stopped to listen to her, she said: "The black hole in space *is* closed." She showed them proof from Station II, even though the view was out of focus.

"What a distortion it left though!" Manning cried. "The collision of energies generated a terrible whiplash. That's the effect we're *still* feeling on Earth. But from what we can see now in those quadrants…from instruments on Station II and craft that survived the battle…the imploding vortex *did* crush all the terrorist craft. The whiplash thrashed *The Heed* and the other Tech-No Protesters' astrocraft in that area."

His Terra enlarged like an archangel in the center of the room. "Two astrofighters survived but are disabled. Two thousand troops are accounted for and returning to Station III."

All the Terra forms suddenly disappeared.

"What's she doing?" He glanced around, feeling vulnerable.

"The transmission screen isn't fixed…the Neltans aren't back!" he said. "Terra—what's going on?"

"The matrix!" Jenkens and everyone in the room began repeating.

"Terra is functioning," Regent Itonovich said. "All thirty hubs are processing. No deterioration at any facilities either."

Terra rematerialized and began reproducing exponentially, but taller than before, and surrounded by a more intense hologram presence. Manning ran up to one of her forms as her holograms began spreading in waves out the door and windows.

"What's happening? This is like that *Breath* entity!" several Regents shouted, hailing their avatars over their wrist devices for answers.

"What's the matrix doing?!" Jenkens gasped.

Manning remembered the drill they had relegated to the

archives long ago. "Steve. I think I know." Laughing and feeling foolish, he shouted, "Everyone—stop...listened!"

"Enlighten us finally, will ya?" Jenkens said, rubbing his fingers over his face in a gesture of confusion.

Terra forms began rippling around the world like a rumble circumnavigating Earth.

Manning laughed as he remembered what *he* had helped write. "We programmed Terra to broadcast this show when she determined the formal end of World War III, Steve. *That's* what's happening." After his Terra rematerialized next to him, he had her stream that calm message to The World, along with the 2060 attachment of *The End of Terror* that everyone approved by ninety percent, but mostly likely forgot. Everyone in the Press Room and Oval Office joined him in his laughter of relief, after which they stood speechless in awe and tears.

Streaming the message to everyone as a holosite world, Terra proclaimed, "Americans, Africans, Europeans, Australians, Asians, and Indians...World War Three is over."

As Terra's *End of Terror* program continued, Jenkens was wringing his hands in worry. He said to The General: "We're forgetting about Ambassador Shaesar. Where is he? Time's running out to finish Final Communication."

The General directed his one functioning probe beyond Neptune to activate a quantum stream and zoom in on a tiny circle of white-thread energy. There, the last spacefold photon accumulator was holding constant the quantum communication from Nelta. The interaction looked like two stars gyring. Electromagnetic energy and dark energy—the later a product of moving celestial bodies—were fueling the thread-sized conduit.

When the instruments on the probe returned with a status update, he said: "Luckily, the Neltans have an algorithmic palindrome conduit—a back-up that's holding steady a temporary wormhole until we can fix, or generate, a stable quantum connection." He then showed them the termination site of the wormhole whiplash. "The tail of the whiplash missed Mars, but struck its moon, Deimos. Fortunately, it didn't leave Mars' orbit. Thank goodness! The people there have taken refuge in subterranean cities and are fortifying them." He showed them a display of three abandoned domes on Mars, historic sites tourists visit to see the rover displays.

Meanwhile, Terra's *Ending* show had extinguished, and Terra had normalized to her Standard Holographic Projection intensity inside the room. Jenkens waved off a glass of water from a serverbot as some Regents remained glued to the tragic battle scenes that were on Replay-mode. Other Regents and a few reporters were conversing through their wrist avatars and holosite projectors to give the latest news of casualties and survivors to people around the globe. Vents in the room swooshed open, flushing out stuffy air and the building stench.

Jenkens said: "This is God awful...our losses terrible...and we *still* can't re-establish contact with the Ambassador." He sighed and plopped down in a chair. "Things couldn't get any worse. World War III is over, but I never believed it would end like this." He rubbed his hands over his red face that looked swollen, and old. The droopy skin under his eyes appeared to have sunk a centimeter, and his balding scalp was dull from layers of built-up sweat. "I feel like hell is crawling through my bones. And now, we have to worry about countering a never-ending ripple effect. Whata we do, Thornton?"

Waiting, Manning shook his head, closed his eyes, and listened.

Emanating from a few shows on wall zones at the opposite end of the room was a Niagara of laughing and cheering—celebrations of World War III ending. Experiencing the sadness and joy, he then felt a bold of fear like that lightning rip. He remembered that strange blue-white aura he had just seen manifest around The General. It reminded him of a full moon. That reminded him of Captain Bartlet.

Manning noticed The General's anxious demeanor. "Something's wrong. What?" He asked him again, each time louder.

Battlefield Matrix

Regents in the room, reporters and guests stopped dead in their tracks to attend to The General who looked more nervous—tenser than before when he had broken the terrible news of all the exploded Stealth Force craft and dead astrofighters.

The General's officers stepped forward and took his side in protocol—the military response of accepting responsibility for failure.

"What's wrong?!" Manning asked as Jenkens gave The General an evil eye.

"We just received a brief, re-routed signal from *The Spider*'s navigation stage," General Rand said. "The red, *Emergency* time stamp shows the outset of a great battle occurring at 9:15 p.m., Eastern Standard Time."

"The time *almost* coincides with all those wild wormholes converging," Manning said.

"That archaic signal had an abrupt start and end...which means the crew experienced a total blackout of the entire battle." He coughed. "That was an hour and forty-five minutes ago."

"It's eleven o'clock now," Jenkens said.

"This doesn't look good," Manning said. "I don't' like this at all!"

A Regent said in a deep vibrating tone: "That means Captain Bartlet must be dead...all his crew. And *The Spider* destroyed."

Silence mixed with shock spread quickly through the room.

Feeling shock trickle through him, Manning saw that destructive time stamp as a bright red devil. "No!" He fell into a seat, and Jenkens began a stream of muffled cuss words.

Ladies and Gentlemen of The Regency," General Rand interrupted, "due to the communications black out that occurred because of that black hole disturbance, I have no other detailed images of what happened after 9:15 p.m. to *The Spider*. All we currently know is that it went down and everyone onboard appears dead. We have a search-and-rescue team there now, approaching the wreckage."

J.P. Osterman

"What happened?" Manning felt out-of-body. He picked up a glass and threw it into show. The projection beam hissed; the stage became a hot plate as The General's image wavered. "What the hell happened, Rand? You were supposed to send astrofighters to support 'im!" Robert Bartlet's face and those of his crew flashed through his mind: Gone, dead, immeasurable talent stolen by useless war and the ultimately enemy—death.

Jenkens whispered: "I know he was your favorite, Thornton. This is truly—"

"Shut up!" He shoved Jenkens' hand off his shoulder and raced toward The General, needing to strangle him, but his hands moved right through his hologram. "You were supposed to have astrofighters supporting him!" He felt more hands on his arms and back—obviously Regents trying to pull him off-stage and comfort him. He sloughed them off and felt the cold air vent through his nostrils.

General Rand's chest rose and fell rapidly. "Sir, we had to divert *two* astrofighters that *were* supporting The Captain to the skirmishes with the Tech-Nos at *The Heed*. We only have ten, *ten* astrofighters. The rest are mini-vessels...not powerful enough to defeat the army of terrorists we had at our cosmic doorstep around the Decagon. We had sixty-seven mini—"

"Had!" Manning shouted. "The word is, 'had'. We *had* troops. We *had* ten astrofighters. We *had* sixty-seven mini-vessels!"

After a pause, General Rand continued: "You can see for yourselves, Ladies and Gentlemen of The Regency, that three battles—three!—were raging at once: One with terrorists, another with the Tech-Nos, and that dangerous cell on the moon that Captain Bartlet was attempting to destroy." After a short break, he said slowly: "We were outnumbered. We—"

"Yes, yes, now go on with why you didn't provide support," Manning ordered.

General Rand began a slow pace around the rim of one of Station III's grand navigation stages. "The *Recon*, our giant astrofreighter, was trying to stabilize the Earth/Neltan

Battlefield Matrix

communications wormhole. We were doing *everything* we could to contain the fluctuation in gravity and magnetism that *The Heed* was instigating. We were focusing the flow of fission-fusion power in all twenty engines of that *Recon* to maintain the integrity of that Neltan/Earth wormhole we needed for Final Communication." He took a slight pause, breathed, and then continued softly: "We offered Captain Bartlet all the mini-vessels we could spare. He told me he could handle the assault on the moon, Sir. I'm streaming his *exact* words to you for view later. That's what he said. We believed him. Then the brief show you just saw occurred...then the blackout...then nothing. We can't know more unless we actually find a way to time travel, Ladies and Gentlemen."

"His pride...Bartlet's inflated ego!" He knocked down a chair. Struggling to shake off the fog in his mind, Manning noticed an uplifting force on the moon. He was about to point it out until General Rand announced that they had replicated the new Gamma Globule weapon that *The Spider* crew had used to penetrate layers of moon rock and wipe out that terrorist cell in a succession of light-speed accuracy.

Rand said: "It's because of *this* weapon they sent us yesterday that those terrorists-in-hiding are dead. The Captain and his crew *are* heroes. They annihilated the last stronghold. If not, they'd be reinforcing, and we wouldn't be celebrating the end of World War III."

"No, the heroes aren't just Captain Bartlet and his crew, General...but all the brave men and women who fought in all three battles," Manning corrected. After asking Terra to order Metals of Bravery in recognition of their services, he added: "We need to inform all the families of our profound losses right now, with our condolences before The World sees the widespread destruction and death on every holosite network. That's just not right...not respectful." He was thinking about demoting General Rand to disassembly duty at the Area-51 base when he noticed another abnormal bulge in the lunar surface along the terrorist route of deception. He called his Terra over to the holographic show that The General had On

Hold. "Is that a fissure beneath the lunar debris field? It appears to be widening. Analyze that area after the interference subsides and alert me to the results."

Another Terra translated *The Fall of Captain Robert Bartlet* battle to an archival grid. Along with other battle shows, the media and Regents began swiping segments of the show into their wrist devices for eulogies and ceremonial preparations.

Manning joined Jenkens in front of Center Stage and asked The General, "Are you sure there are no survivors on *The Spider*?"

General Rand told them that scanners in orbit and sensors on probes could not detect any biometric readings on the lunar surface. "But a recovery team is at the crash site, Sir," he said. "It's murky waters, so to speak out there right now, but we ordered them to conduct an intense search-and-rescue mission. Still, the scientists on Station II say they're pretty sure we won't find any signs of life...any survivors."

"It's still necessary to follow protocol," Jenkens said adamantly.

Manning felt water pool in his eyes. Leaving Rand's image and walking over to Stage-1 Right, he reached into the hologram beam and touched images of bits-and-pieces of *The Spider* peppering the lunar surface. He said to Jenkens: "Just hours ago, it was so grand...The Captain and his crew *right there* in front of me in an augmented world I activated *right there* at the center of my office and then all around me." He pointed at the spot lost in time but still burning brightly in his memory. "I can't—just can't believe...they're—gone. God I hate death!" An image of The Matter Stream jetted through mind. With it, he believed he could conquer life's ultimate enemy.

He intensified the colors of the magnificent astrofighter to confirm its identity. Dust and large pebbles were settling in a circle around the moon. He cleared his throat, wiped his eyes, and ordered several Regents who were with him, also viewing and discussing the zone of devastation: "Now it's time we broadcast all three events of death-and-destruction in their entirety to The World. But intersperse the disasters with images of the military personnel and the crewmembers' lives. They're all heroes. Let's make sure we portray them in that light."

Meanwhile, robotic crawlers, thickly clad technicians, and a medical team were scouring the lunar debris zone for survivors.

"Steve!" Manning called, waving for him to join him in a quiet corner. He whispered, "Remember I told you about those clones I ordered to infiltrate the terrorists on the moon in that *Galaxy Runner* command?" Jenkens nodded. "Well, that's their craft right there!" With his back to the crowd of Regents who were busy transmitting segments of the end of the war to The World, Manning enlarged a shadow section along the rim of a small crater. "The clones never got the opportunity to escape in the heat of battle. But that's their craft, see?"

"What should we do?" Jenkens asked.

Manning had an idea. "Get to the Oval Office. Kick out Regent Itonovich and Regent Pervis. They're just busy creating a holosite presentations for the ceremonies. They can do that in another area."

"Then what?"

"Using my password again, link to the Clone-Tech facility on *Sagan*. Technicians will be there. Tell them what happened with Captain Bartlet and his crew. Tell them to intercept General Rand's search-and-rescue team. Discretely have them recover some remains of the crew and take them to *Sagan*." He reached into his pocket and pulled out a pen-matrix drive. "Insert this into my Security wall-zone through which we communicate when Coflin held me captive."

Jenkens slipped it in his shirt pocket. "Got it."

"This software holds the missing part of the mission for the Clones. When those techs on *Sagan* acquire the information on this matrix drive, they'll be able to redirect the remains of Captain Bartlet and his crew to their biological storage sites on *Sagan*."

Jenkens tapped his pocket. "But General Rand's team will

question the authority of *Sagan* techs and docs."

"I'm taking care of that now." He walked over to The General's hologram on the Center Stage and told him to accept the small *Sagan* craft. "Please, have your team work with the *Sagan* specialists. I'm directing them to assist you, as you respectfully process the remains of Captain Bartlet and his crew." General Rand gave him a puzzled expression, and he countered: "Work with my team." When The General turned away to carry out the new order, Manning whispered to Jenkens: "Sometime in the future, we can clone Captain Bartlet or his crew...use their knowledge and skills to help us in whatever endeavor we might need assistance. I just hope we find cerebral material that's not too damaged. I hope we can do this!"

Jenkens said with an eager expression, "We'll have so many innovations, advancements, and potential. I can't wait until we can actually board the astrocity and launch."

Manning knew what he needed but didn't have enough. "We need more Matter Stream samples, Steve. I need more of that creation force than just some left over remnants we're sweeping up from the sample that healed the ozone. Our capabilities could advance exponentially if we could only get our hands on that creation force." He thought of the stasis cell pods that he might be able to reconfigure to experiment with life-extension technology. "Damn that the Neltans refuse to give us more! Damn their *Universal Law*!" The words of their law flashed through his mind—the English version he helped translate during Forth Communication:

Beings on Other Worlds, we absolve ourselves from any types of retribution, retaliation, acts of hate, vengeance, or persuasion for refusing The Matter Stream to species throughout this universe, The Multiverse, or other dimensions.

Jenkens shrugged and said: "Well, Thornton, we just took part in that grand show and signed away our lives, vowing that we'd adhere to their laws and follow through with our part of the bargain. And contrary to how people in the past have always portrayed advanced extraterrestrials, the Neltans have never *once* implied they want Earth, except for that *Attack Clause* in *The Pact*."

Manning felt his blood pressure rise in his neck. "Yeah, that's got me worried. That's why we need Shaesar back in here before midnight to have him elaborate on that *Attack Clause*."

Jenkens said: "*Hm*, why? *The Pact*'s signed. They're gonna be gone and in stasis."

"World War III is over, Steve."

"And Earth's ozone's fixed, I know."

"Yeah? And?" Jenkens said.

Manning felt his breath rough in his throat. "*Uh*—if The World starts to believe that the *Attack Clause* is simply a threat, what will make us adhere to the agreement we made with the Neltans?" Jenkens was deep in thought. He continued "Imagine another scenario. In a thousand years, they'll revive and we won't be there. In that time, people will dismantle all the wormhole technology and probably figure out a way to block quantum spacefold energy. If the Neltans call us, they won't get an answer. A few generations after that, they'll be extinct because they won't have *our* DNA. There...that's it Neltans gone."

"*I see*," Jenkens began, "people will think we're off the hook because so much is going right. The Earth is healthy again, especially after we stop this dark energy/gamma problem the tropopause shield is fending off." He perked up as if enlightened. "Wow—what a betrayal that would be! *Ooo*...I don't know. Ya think we'll just revert to basking in the technology they've given us without giving anything to them in return? Turn our backs on the Neltans who saved us? Ya think The World could just renege on their word? Ignore the Neltan's conviction that The Divine united our two species? I don't know, Thornton. *Many* people believe that The Divine was the driving force behind First Communication...and *your* inspiration to erect the massive deep-field array that reached the Neltan who were calling us for help. That *Breath* experience was sure convincing!" Jenkens shook his head in an expression of caution.

Manning yanked him to his side and whispered: "Don't say those things so loud so the Press picks them up. We've have a ship that's close to completion. You want massive fights on our hands now that we no longer have to worry about daily elections? I don't know about you...but I want to leave here. There's more than a pact—a bargain—that's motivating *me* to finish *Sagan*."

"For me and others on The List, it's exploration and gratitude that's motivating us to keep *The Pact*," Jenkens said.

"Well, other people who didn't make The List might feel differently 'cause their tax dollars are funding the astrocity," Manning said. "That's the bottom line...what *will* motivate people to keep *The Pact*?"

"*That's* a good question that, regardless of the answer, we'll have to work hard to enforce if reneging becomes a global issue. But I have to go...take this matrix drive to the office and contact those techs on *Sagan*." Jenkens left.

Manning began to imagine some headlines already circulating in holosites that might snowball into rebellious movements around the globe:

Our DNA to Nelta? What the hell are we thinking?

And,

Spend billions on an astrocity to send DNA and explorers to a species who might want to exterminate us in the future?

And,

As Darrel Coflin showed us—do we really approve of interspecies breeding? Could you marry a Neltan? What will Earth look if some of them decide to come here and settle down?"

And finally,

It would have been better for the ozone to kill us rather than the Neltans rule over us!

He felt dread start its slow flow through his body. How would he ever convince people to keep *The Pact*?

Chapter 14

Maureen Strickler

Elisa Holton sprinted to the front of the transmission stage. She had been collaborating with a few scientists on Station II who had upstreamed a special zirconium mix to the Decagon. They had managed to repair the quantum-communication conduit and re-establish Shaesar's image inside the Press Room. Showering Elisa and her colleagues with words of gratitude, Shaesar was brimming with happiness that the interference hadn't severed their communication before the midnight deadline after which they wouldn't dialogue again until the *Sagan* crew would meet them in person. In just a few hours, Earth time, their entire species would be in deep hibernation in underground stasis chambers.

The Neltan Advancement Council appeared behind Shaesar in one of those subterranean zones that looked like darkness slowly eclipsing an extensive city. Shaesar kept glancing askance at a long row of illuminated body pods into which techs were inserting Gem programs. From the outstretched cavernous background, it was obvious that most of their population was already in hibernation. Wearing red ceremonial robes but without their usual white collars, he and the Council comprised of female and male representatives looked eager to make their final statements to humanity before they too entered stasis pods. Ambassador Shaesar had the original glowing white scroll under his arm: *The Pact*. Next to him and in front of the first row in the Press Room he called forth the red-stamped holosite world that he had created for humanity before his quantum communication beam ceased. On the doorframe of the world appeared the words: *Our Gift to You from the People of Nelta.*

In visuals on wall-zones around the Press Room, Manning saw what seemed to be the entire Earth's population brimming with overwhelming emotion. As First Communication Day had given Earth a new awareness of advanced alien life in the universe, Final Communication Day was illuminating another new perspective. We had become a single global government comprised of interconnecting beehive communities, like a neural network fueled by a new quantum matrix system. Our new civilization was functioning—really working! The Beehive-Matrix Age of Terra-III might go down in Earth's archives as the greatest of all ages, thanks to the Neltans. An alien race millions of light years away had created an extraordinary ripple effect and awakened humanity's consciousness. In future millennia, perhaps humanity would reach out in the same way and have a profound positive effect on other species on other worlds.

Noticing the scroll's bright intensity, Manning remembered Shaesar had told him that they had implanted a Living Duplicate of the scroll inside *Sagan*'s Navigation Center. He remembered Shaesar's words: "Do not deviate from the plotted course once *Sagan* launches. The spacefold wormholes are now set in a specific, structured, intergalactic travel map." That meant that meddling with Navigation would be tampering with the Sacred Scroll they had all signed. *The Pact* was now a living entity inside *Sagan*.

Battlefield Matrix

What *that* meant, he didn't know. Later, he'd order his techs to scan the astrocity's burgeoning matrix. Terra's matrix Flow Field was only now beginning to process on Level 7. Hopefully, before the field finished permeating through the astrocity, they could insert an algorithmic program so they could locate the Living Scroll and monitor its presence. As he was about to ask Shaesar about an emergency navigation plan, he noticed that Shaesar had a look of awareness that seemed to anticipate his worry.

He said: "Regent Manning, our explorers have traveled galaxies for millennia on millions of astrocities the likes of *Sagan*. Any questions you have while on the astrocity, simply speak your question, concern, or worry to The Helm. It will guide you through the long voyage and run interference in case of any emergencies. It is a fail-safe astrocity in every respect."

Regent Itonovich stepped up and moved between them. Breathless, she said, "Ambassador—the *Attack Clause*. We have questions—"

"Again, ask The Helm when Navigation finishes expanding on *Sagan*," he answered, appearing weary of people doubting him, and for once appearing to lose a bit of his adamantine patience. Then again, he also seemed overly zealous to enter his stasis chamber, which lay open for him in the background. It was larger and at the forefront from the other stasis chambers harboring Neltan scientists. "Navigation's Helm will address all your concerns, run simulations, and generate unique responses to all the difficulties you might experience on the voyage here to Nelta." As Sylvia Itonovich backed away obviously perplexed, he said: "Now, our time with you is at a final end, at least for the next thousand years." He pointed at the clock bar on the transmission screen. Its bright green light was at the end of its illumination indicator. Earth time, it read 11:28 p.m., EST.

Manning quickly holosited the time to all the Regents who were occupied with giving interviews, setting archival projectors, and finishing their participation worlds so people could experience the event. "Come back. We have to conclude the ceremony before the quantum communication conduit closes…now!"

Seconds thereafter, Jenkens returned with Regents swarming into the room behind him. Shaesar was about to unravel the Living Scroll for final viewing when a mild earthquake rumbled the room. The IMAX transmission screen vibrated, and the miniature decorative chandeliers jingled. Everyone began checking their wrist devices, investigating the location of the epicenter, the quake's cause and effects.

On Nelta, Shaesar and the Advancement Council remained unshaken. "Regent Manning, the problem is occurring on or around Earth. We detect no anomaly in the intergalactic wormhole array emanating from Nelta," Shaesar said.

"That was a magnitude 3.1 quake and was felt world-wide, Ladies and Gentlemen," a scientist said after appearing via a hologram from Space Station II's Research Facility.

Manning told Jenkens: "That means there's no epicenter…that the quake's global. Has this ever happened anywhere before?"

Jenkens searched for the answer and quickly replied, "Nope, never a global-wide quake, except for the last flood basalt eruption around 250 million years ago."

Manning looked at the seismic reading that was back to normal. "That 3.1 was no precursor to a flood eruption though."

Speculating that the cause could be matrix related, Regents began searching Terra-III's eight processing facilities. They fired back information that Terra was streaming one-hundred-percent quantum connectivity with wrist devices, small discware, portable tablets, and wall-zones around the globe. Inside the Press Room, her many Terra forms were unwavering as they assisted Regents and guests—addressing and researching all their concerns and questions. Those facts meant that the quake and its subsequent fluctuation in tidal currents were not the fault of any disturbance in the matrix or Terra-III's evolutionary expansion. Ending the Global Matrix Scan, Terra's Standard Form appeared in the center of the room and announced: "I cannot detect any photon obstruction or magnetic globule capable stalling data flow and instant access."

When the Terra Scan faded, Manning said, "This 3.1 global disturbance is a total mystery...completely unexplainable." He hailed his tiny Beethoven avatar and said into the yellow projection: "Stream to Woods Hole, NOAA, the Bedford Institute, and the Caryl Johnson International Seismic Facility. Tell them The Regency and space stations II and III need all anomalous readings and any global abnormality that could be the cause of what we just experienced." Then he sent the message as a *Top Secret* bullet icon that would stream all responses from any sender directly back to him with their identities—a deeply entrenched security filter. Under *Global Law* V's Article of Transparency, those facilities were required to stream any seismic activity to The World automatically, but he wanted to learn the results first-hand before anyone in a position of scientific power could demand that The Regency stream another global Emergency Alert. He noticed from several shows playing around the Press Room that community leaders in safe havens and beehives were overworked and their supplies dwindling. They needed a break...not another stampede of panicking people in case the quake was insignificant, as only scientists could determine. Meanwhile, the Earth's crust was stable.

Around the globe, crowds of people were streaming into the Regency's holosite world, demanding information about the quake while virtually experiencing the Neltans last appearance inside the Press Room. Throughout D.C., people were returning to the streets, congregating in entertainment sites, watching the end of *The Pact Signing* event on hologram stages, IMAX screens in neighborhood centers, and on the surface of low hovering Zeppelin craft.

While Manning and Jenkens were standing alongside Shaesar's image, Elisa rushed to the front rows where all forty-eight Regents were beginning to calm down and take their seats. Manning sent a Flash-message to her on her Gem armband, asking her to keep all information from Station II confidential and for *Regents Eyes Only*. She began whispering to scientists who were messaging her for updates: "That was no ordinary earthquake." Over Gem, she activated a small spectroradiometric view of the Earth's blue-and-brown terrain from outer space and showed them the view. "We have a change in ocean current. You should be receiving the app so you can get this same image from Station II. I'll send you more info when I receive your verbal biometrics as a security precaution. After Manning approved her request to consult with other scientists in the room and researchers on Station II, she told her colleagues: "Under orders, you cannot divulge *any* data to *anyone* except Regent Manning or me...I mean *Executive* Regent Manning. Stream anything you find to him and me. We need your help in locating the problem so we all can put our heads together and solve it. I repeat: Do not spread any data!"

Manning glanced at the time on the Smart Bar of his wrist device: 11:35 p.m. He quickly took center stage next to Shaesar. "Ambassador...Advancement Council!" He pointed at the time. "Twenty-five minutes. That's all we have remaining until we see you in a thousand years. A thousand years!" That timespan equaled one-hundred Space-Fold years for the *Sagan* crew, but he didn't want to deal with semantics. "Please, I want to make sure all our signatures are inside *The Pact* and that scientists on The List have received all the answers to their questions." He called out the order for everyone missing to return immediately to the Press Room. "Guests and Ladies and Gentlemen of The Regency, we don't have seismic data and we can't stop this important event to wait for it. Let's finish what we've been preparing for since October 4, 2061 when we approved *The Pact* with our Neltan friends." Then he ordered the double doors sealed after more guests entered and robot ushers, avatars, and icons seated them.

Dressed in sophisticated formal wear, newcomers were congregating in the back with late global delegates. They had

Battlefield Matrix

been waiting for the *Executive Pinning* ceremony, but the time was late and they were growing restless in the hallway. Jenkens ordered their early admission. Now, the Press Room was standing room only. When the Lead Delegate finally quieted his section, Manning spotted the platinum box in her hands. Inside set the gold stars that would soon be on his collar. Then he would officially be Executive Regent, *permanently*.

He thought: If my father could see me now...if Lynn could see *all* this happening right now. Then, a sinking feeling of dread struck him as he felt their loss. The reality of the fragility-and-finality of people, places, and things was an anxiety like a dioxide that made him tremble. Death...no stopping that. When he saw that Shaesar was still alive although he had once told him he was eons old, Manning wondered how The Matter Stream could be that life enhancing, that regenerating, that restorative...a subatomic, multiverse creation energy. It didn't make sense; but then again, everything their scientists had given them or divulged, people had once labeled as "defying physics." Even Terra. But there she was in pure holographic form and standing beside him: a quantum-photonic-magnetic processor that had self-organized out of Earth's cloud computer facilities, data storage centers, phone towers, live-stream security systems, electromagnetic frequency stations, imaging hardware/software, and cellular-spectrum traffic to form a matrix...with help from Nelta. He wanted more. He hated that the Neltans had The Matter Stream and humanity didn't. The one question kept invading his thoughts like the whereabouts of his jacket: What if we did? When Shaesar spoke again, his deep voice snapped him out of his wandering thoughts.

"People of Earth," the Ambassador began, gently unraveled the Living Scroll. "We leave you with one last gift."

The room stilled. The temperature slightly chilled. As if on Autopilot, Terra touched the scroll with her left hand and extended her right hand toward the world.

In waves, people outside began ooing-and-ahing and

clapping.

"What's happening?" Manning smelled ionized air as static lifted hair on his body. All sorts of low frequencies were playing on his skin.

Jenkens ran to his side. "I think atoms are shedding electrons! Which compounds they're affecting, I don't know."

Low in the dark sky materialized a network of soft yellow light that looked like a giant spider's web outstretching. Inside the Press Room appeared miniscule particle beams streaming through the ceiling hubs and crystal chandeliers. The spectacular show appeared as colorful lights in a state fair.

Gasping in obvious awe, Elisa ran her finger through a stream of light that duplicated her finger in 3D. She cried out: "The matrix is making a visual presentation! The Encantado frame around the screen is the catalyst, straight from Nelta!"

"It's like the sun is rising and it's daylight everywhere," Regent Sylvia Itonovich marveled, activating her tiny avatar. "Everyone…record this for posterity!"

In obvious solemnity, Shaesar stepped forward and his Advancement Council moved back. People and crowds around the globe turned silent as they began experiencing the Neltan matrix show. Shaesar said softly: "Humanity, until we can communicate with you again, we give you this final show—an expansion of the matrix." Again, on Center Stage, he opened the Neltan holosite world, now containing the new Red Stamp on the virtual doorframe, *The Breath*.

The other hologram stages and wall-zones flashed on, showing places around the globe as well as awe-struck individuals, their marveling expressions and surprised gestures. People everywhere began activating their portable tablets, discware, and wrist devices to record the Neltan matrix gift. Manning noticed the Live-Stream Intensity of the matrix processing—evidence that people were acting quickly to experience the final message from the Neltans.

The bright crescent window in the center of the virtual doorframe contained a small moving picture of a black, lifeless, cosmic body absorbing a long streak of blinding white energy

Battlefield Matrix

like the birth of a star. It was an artificial sun beyond Nelta that scientists had built to protect and The Matter Stream for a thousand years. At the end the time, the Neltans programmed it to unleash and begin healing Nelta months prior to *Sagan's* scheduled arrival.

Next to the crescent window appeared a green thread. It represented the bright future the Neltans were expecting after *Sagan's* arrival. Opening up this green section would activate a simulation of the astrocity arriving in orbit around Nelta.

On the other side of the virtual Neltan doorframe was an image of a small grassy Neltan landscape. At its center, the Neltans had built a colossal sparkling archway under which was a winding path leading into Nelta's main subterranean stasis chamber. On the archway appeared the words, *Human DNA*, written in English and Neltan. The grand Welcome Archway had on its façade colorful, glistening string programs. They were stories from Nelta's ancient past to its present. Any advanced beings that might happen to land on Nelta could touch-activate or voice-activate the Experience Strings and virtually meet the Neltans. In a small section on the side of the colossal archway, appeared Earth and its solar system in the brightest gold infused with a dose of life-enhancing substance from The Matter Stream. As an inextinguishable and inexhaustible energy-and-force—matter, particles, and effervescence from an ancient black hole from an ancient multiverse—The Matter Stream comprised all the ideas, substances, and formulae of String Theory, Particle Physics, Astrophysics, Wormhole Theory, and Multiverse Theory intertwined. Writing humanity into this section of the Welcome Archway, the Neltans were branding humanity in their *Recording Of Times*—the words at the very top of the archway. They had explained to humanity years ago that this archway was one of several they had positioned throughout places they had explored in the cosmos. Whenever they added a new species to their list of encounters, the archways would all update. This one main Welcome Archway on Nelta was a grand beacon for the entire universe; and on it, one entire section appeared to be expressing their gratitude to humanity.

Besides being a cosmic welcome sign meant to attract alien life, assist intergalactic explorers, and educate alien species; the sixty-foot Welcome Archway was now the Neltan white-flare for the *Sagan* crew who would someday step on a renewed Nelta and present human DNA to Ambassador Shaesar. Human presence on Nelta, in the future—after a thousand-year stasis—would mean unprecedented celebration for the Neltans. The Neltans were expecting the crew, counting on human beings to be "Our Saviors for Our Race." Those words, written by their scribes, they branded in the gold lines of Earth's solar system on their Welcome Archway.

Manning saw something else embedded in the section on Earth: harsh consequences that the Neltans could unleash upon humanity—or other alien civilizations unleash upon humanity in their stead—should humans not fulfill their part of *The Pact* that The Regents sealed in sacred, representative, "blood signatures."

After the Neltan virtual doorframe updated, streaming to every processor on Earth as Terra confirmed, Shaesar said: "Remember us, until we greet you on Nelta."

The night sky looked like yellow dawn as particle clouds inside the atmospheric matrix-web exhibit increased in brightness. The globules inside the matrix exhibit began showing events of the various times when Regents and select individuals communicated with the Neltans.

At the zenith began a historical show—from the vantage point of an old digital camera at Duke University—of First Communication when the wormhole from Nelta finally activated.

Following that display, another globule appeared, showing *The Greeter* shuttle shattering in golden shimmering pieces as it exploded. The pronounced outline of this globule display was obviously an intense gesture of sympathy for all those who lost their lives in the attempt to stabilize the quantum communication conduit between worlds.

Another image appeared on the Capitol dome: Shaesar,

Battlefield Matrix

waving goodbye to humanity.

People around the globe cheered. Some cried, lamenting the end of Earth's communication with the Neltans for the next millennium. Worship centers were filled with people singing prayers to The Divine as an image of the Welcome Archway appeared in the east. People began activating their personal icons and avatars that were waving farewell. Those gestures were quantum-stream to Nelta, appearing around Shaesar and the Neltan Advancement Committee. It was a beautiful exchange of instantaneous messaging through spacefolding technology, never thought possible prior to Terra-III. When someone from Earth flashed a sign of thanks or a personal symbol of gratitude for The Matter Stream sample, the Neltans would see the messages and respond. The chime of a grand clock rang out on both planets. It was 11:50 p.m. EST. Midnight and Termination Point were approaching.

Inside the Press Room below the ceiling, the matrix exhibit continued to illuminate more historical shows. The media, guests, and Regents were gazing in amazement and recording the quantum laser-light displays that were appearing as a slow-moving slide show. Teary-eyed scientists were wildly scanning and analyzing the magnificent splendor of the Neltan's advanced matrix capability.

One scientist fell back as if she might faint, crying, "Expressionism and impressionism interweaved with quantum physics!"…

Elisa caught her friend, Dr. Maureen Strickler, by her scrawny shoulders and steadied her. "I guess the Neltans put on *this* show in *here* for The Regents. Now, for sure, *no one* can forget the Neltans," Elisa said.

As more events swept over their heads like boxcars progressing behind a train, Maureen said: "But not you, Elisa. You're one of those High Priority people, as everyone's calling people VIPs like you. I'm still on the Wait List for Terra to select me. But hopefully, if more people back out, I'll receive an automatic, '*You're In*,' message and contract."

"What do you mean important person?" asked Elisa. "I'm

no V, I, P!"

Maureen looked at her as if she was joking. "Ya sure are! After that wacky Coflin disassembled outta here, people began streaming that you're a hero. They saw the final moments of that hostage situation then how you saved everyone from that Dimension 8 expansion event. Wow...that Gem armband is fantastic. And *you* were able to get it operational!"

Elisa shrugged off the compliment with a bashful expression. "I didn't do anything really. The device just molded—"

"People have been commemorating you in a special holosite. See?" She showed Elisa an app that she could receive and participate in the entire heroic event. "I think you're one of the last people Terra is adding to *Sagan*'s list of passengers. I know thousands who'd do anything to be in your shoes. Like I said...I'm in Wait-mode."

Elisa patted her on the shoulder. "There's plenty to do on Earth, especially rebuilding out in the open since the ozone's healed. Things are *really* going to improve as scientists continue to implement climate control. No more dust haboobs or polar tornados—"

"Yeah, thank God," Maureen waved, exasperatedly.

"Hey—cheer up. Who knows?" Elisa bumped her in a spritely gesture. Then her "hero" label gave her an idea. "I tell ya what..." She called opened The Regency's holosite on Gem. After Maureen complimented the armband, Elisa said: "I'm calling in your name. If what you say is right—that I'm VIP—maybe they'll peruse your resume again and include you. Just copy me your ID grid and it's done."

As she swept her Living Resume into Elisa's holosite, Maureen thanked her and exhaled a restless sigh. "Now I wait." She coughed—a horrible congestion. "The matrix *Declined* me twice though."

"Maybe this time, the matrix, or The Regents, or the new Terra version won't," Elisa said cheerfully. When Maureen coughed again, Elisa noticed she looked thinner and paler than last month. Something was definitely wrong. She's probably getting over that bad norovirus, she thought. She whispered, "I can direct you to a new nano-cellular treatment for that bad cough in case you secure an interview."

After Maureen accepted the medical referral, she said, "At least you have an adventurous life ahead of you...living longer than the rest of us, and being one of the first people to meet real advanced aliens face-to-face."

"Yeah, but don't forget the challenge it'll be getting there...living on a spacefolding ship...not touching solid ground except in some artificial park...and being engulfed in augmented surroundings. I hope I can make it," Elisa said, touching one of the last historical strings of the Neltan matrix exhibit. The end was approaching. Peeking out a window, she could see the sky clearing of its unnatural dawn to its true midnight pitch.

Maureen's cheeks filled with a burst of rose. "No—you've got to make it, Elisa! Just think—the entire experience is gonna be mind-blowing! Every day you'll wake up and have in your sights that goal of reaching a habitable planet. I'd give anything—" Sniffling as if she might break out crying, she appeared bored with Earth.

Elisa said, "You look tired. You've been working on Station II too long. Go grab a swing and take a break in a subway park. Do something fun."

Maureen dabbed her forefingers under her lids, gently drying her eyes. "Well, I guess it'll be goodbye for you and me soon, just as Shaesar is saying farewell to everyone right now. But there's something different about the two situations."

"What?"

Maureen moved her arm out of a show that was displaying the March 20, 2067 event of Beth Tufter regaining consciousness after her mind quantum teleported to Nelta. Elisa was standing in a long line of professionals behind her, preparing to give her medical assistance. The Neltans had her name below her image, in her own signature. After Maureen brought the scene to Elisa's attention and they marveled at it, she said, "There'll come a day when *I* won't ever see you again." She gave her a quick hug. "Never."

The outside atmosphere dimmed, and the crowds began cheering and applauding. Some grand display was about to occur, obviously the final show-burst before the program's end.

"Oh—I never thought about saying goodbye to people I know," Elisa said through watery eyes. "I better start doing that even though I have over a year until *Sagan* launches. Saying goodbye, mending fences, and having closure are so psychological important for people. It's those little things about being human that I think even a quantum computer matrix like Terra-III will never evolve to extrapolate from data into experience."

"Yeah...so it's good that we've had this time as pals 'cause we *might* not *see* each other a*gain*," Maureen said firmly. "Glad to have known ya, pal." She shook Elisa's hand—a humorous gesture.

"People on The List *need* to make sure we attend to these little things before we launch." She said to her little, white-coated avatar before she streamed the concern: "People who will be leaving Earth should meet with those we'll be leaving behind. Furthermore, it's important to make the best of the remainder of our time together before departing...even recording the experiences so that while onboard the astrocity, we can remember our attachments to our friends and families. Bonding with people in relationships is in our DNA. Thank you." She closed the app and her avatar faded. "There—message streamed. I hope The Regency doesn't get offended or think I'm trying to be a know-it-all."

Laughing, Maureen said: "No...that's sound advice. And you sent it as a consideration. If they don't implement it, they're the ones who might be sorry one day."

"We'll see. If I get a reply, I'll let ya know. I'll definitely feel better about being on *Sagan* then 'cause I'll know that the future leaders are responding to our concerns."

Maureen activated her Calendar app and a small date book appeared. "So, let's go celebrate your new job tomorrow." She swept the book over Elisa's and secured an open time slot. "Oh, one more thing."

"Yeah?"

Interrupting them, a colleague called Elisa's attention to a historic show projecting in a cloud globule in the southern part of the sky.

Elisa felt infused with surprise and joy. "Another one? I can't believe it!"

"That's Second Communication," Maureen said.

"Yeah...I consulted with Regent Manning on the Neltan genetic code. That's me giving the results before The Regency and the Neltan Advancement Committee."

Maureen exclaimed: "You sure *are* written in their Welcome Archway—wow!"

Elisa wiped her eyes. "I think this is the most important moment of my life...right now."

Maureen drew closer to her as they watched the show disintegrate in the golden glow of the radiating sky. "Yes...we're like little dots and dashes in the span of time...but *they* keep portraying us as being so vital and lasting. The experience is so...so—*ha huh*—overwhelming."

Tenderly, Elisa said to Maureen: "I hope Terra includes you. I'm praying she will...then we can start making plans *together*...to leave Earth *together*...start deciding what to pack up and what to leave."

"Sounds great! *I'm* in." A robot server presented them with small beverages and they drank a toast to their dreams.

"Now that'd be exiting," Elisa exclaimed. "I'll have a friend onboard!"

Maureen suddenly turned, looked down and whispered, "Watch him."

"Watch who?" She glanced around. "What are you talking about?"

Maureen lowered her face some more. "Regent Manning...now Executive Regent Manning. He's now a powerful leader...unfettered from the Global Vote."

"You look scared. What's wrong? Did something happen?

J.P. Osterman

Maureen...tell me!"

"*Shhh*. There's a clandestine subculture holositing through the matrix. I think it's an off-shoot of the captured Tech-Nos who spread a last-minute campaign against him."

"What!? But why?"

"*Shh*," she snapped. "I have to tell you this. We don't have much time before this exhibits stops and—" She glanced at a few points on the ceiling. "Before all eyes and ears start turning back into the Press Room."

"Okaaay...go on," Elisa coached.

"A researcher I know—we both know from years of working together—told me that Manning might be manipulating technology without global approval." She gave the thumbs up toward the sky, towards *Sagan*, and Elisa gestured in astonishment. She continued: "Parts of the astrocity are filling up with some sophisticated experimental hardware. I had a project pulled from me immediately after some *Sagan* techs approved my proposal, and Regent Manning ordered a medical team to surrender their data to a top-level matrix engineer."

"That's illegal—against the Transparency Clause even on *Sagan*!" Elisa shook her head. "I don't believe it. Not him. Regent Manning?"

"*Shhh*," Maureen whispered. "We've been friends for what now...over five years?"

"Yeaah—"

"I wouldn't lie to you." The green in Maureen's eyes shimmered around her thick black pupils. She didn't look well, again. "I'd only tell you facts. You and I are both alike in that way. We seek the truth and substantiate claims and accusations with data. Hell girl—that's how we voted several Regents in and out of office several times, remember?"

"Sure." Elisa rubbed her arms and shivered. "Okay, now ya got me curious...go on."

Her friend continued in a low whisper: "I'm hoping that no Terra processor or roboticware is picking up what I'm saying to you, but I guess I'll have to take that chance. I had to corner you though…warn you. You're my friend. I guess I *do* hope I'm chosen, 'cause then you have someone onboard *Sagan* with you in case anything goes wrong."

She leaned close to Maureen's lips. "Go on…about the group."

"The small group is trying to monitor Manning and several other Regents covertly."

"How? Security's tight wherever Regents work and make appearances," Elisa said.

"From what I learned through the research link that Station II made with *Sagan*, this subculture's trying to expose what Manning's doing, especially before *Sagan* launches. Just be careful around *him*…here and if you should find yourself suddenly on that astrocity. You might have to spend time with him and the other Regents when they give you a tour of your working area, show you your Living Cube, or invite you to attend seminars. Remember, once you're gone from here, and out there—" She gestured toward space. "You're beyond anyone's help from here. Anyone." She dragged that word like a rock carving limestone.

Elisa folded her arms across her chest. "Gosh…Regent Manning doesn't seem that way, and I've never detected anything sinister or criminal about him as long as I've known him, and I've known him since First Communication! But I'll do as you say for sure, Maureen. I'll be respectful, and avoid him. Those words coming from you *definitely* mean that I need to pay attention to everything he says…make sure I record all orders and have my wrist device on Visual as a backup measure in case I ever need to defend myself. Thanks, Maureen and—"

…

Suddenly, the laser-light sky show from Nelta ended. The Advancement Council faded from the background, leaving a gold shimmering outline of Shaesar's dancing-particle body, front and center of the transmission screen. Rolled up, *The Pact* glistened as a phantom impression in the place where Shaesar once stood. It was a final signet: the last object to extinguish, like old royalty used beeswax to stamp and seal their special messages. Obviously, the Advancement Committee designed the sparkling visual as a reminder for humanity to keep its promise to delivery DNA to Nelta. As the Living Scroll hissed and sealed, every Regent's signature materialized in red and gold and then disappeared.

At the end of the long list, Manning spotted his name. He felt the colors indelibly burn his eyes.

"Goodbye," Shaesar called.

Everyone in the Press Room started the reply that reverberated around the globe: "Goodbye."

Shaesar and the Neltans were gone.

Battlefield Matrix

Chapter 15

Lunar Turmoil

An hour later, after the *Pinning Ceremony* and all the ticketed guests had left the Press Room; most Regents, dignitaries, and reporters surrounded Manning, congratulating him on his Executive position. Many others were mingling in the Press Room or still consulting with their personal Terras.

Noticing an annoying reflection from the gold stars on his collar, Manning kept pressed them down. Through all the celebration, the reflection was stinging his burning eyes. Later on, when he'd disembark on *Sagan* with Jenkens for their tour, he could reposition the stars. He didn't want to live with a nagging glare in his eyes that was reminding him of the years of stress—and the toll on his body—he had endured to hold on to his Regency job. Even *that* should reverse tomorrow, he thought. Tomorrow, he had a rescheduled Body Regeneration. He was a bit afraid of the side effects, as Jenkens had voiced. No telling the photon effect on his eyes! All side effects of a full Body Regeneration were individual based; but with stem cell therapies and nano-biological repairs available, easily corrective. Still, the emblem reflection was grating on his nerves. If not for one bad thing, annoying person or obnoxious group getting under his skin, it was another obstacle. Life's just one giant fight after another, he thought...one damn hurricane followed by a tornado! Then, he spotted Jenkens. In one afternoon, he had befriended him, made him his ally, something he never thought he could do. If he could accomplish that, surely, at some point, he could divulge all the covert technology on *Sagan* to the rest of The Regency once they launched for Nelta.

"Steve, over here!" As Jenkens approached, he said, "Or should I say Second Regulate, my *Second* in Command." Feeling revitalized, he shook his hand; but Jenkens wasn't saying a word, and he had a worrisome frown on his face. Manning wondered why because everything *finally* seemed calm. Around the high-tech Press Room with wall zones and hologram stages showing celestial views and last night's news, a few virtual Terra were still assisting and directing people. *His* Standard Terra was just a few feet away from him, but moving along with him, on Stand By. Terra's Version-III matrix had evolved to generate as many quantum computer-assisted virtual forms as needed, but he wasn't sure when the evolution would stop or what more capabilities the evolving matrix could elicit around Earth. Two more Terra holograms popped up...a little unusual, but nothing that could cause anybody to worry over, he believed. There was no alarm...no blaring alert.

Thinking that Jenkens was just tired and in need of sleep, he pulled him over to the side. "Steve, we need to plan the trip we discussed earlier," he whispered. "The trip...to look at those places I told you about on *Sagan*." He launched the Calendar app over his new wrist processor, and the date and time appeared, February 28, 2068, 1:10 a.m. The app was on Management setting, with the capability to process rates and distances, compensate for uncontrollable delays via news from the matrix, and adjust accordingly to a host's needs—with a biometric analyzer. "We can sleep on the astrocraft on our way there…this says by 1:45 if we leave now." He continued to schedule detailed plans. "I want to show you the new Terra-III advancements in clone technology." He also wanted Jenkens to assist him with the incoming spy clones from the moon. "They need stasis chambers, but repair crews are still fixing that damaged area." He also needed help with managing the engineers he had ordered to collect the human remains of Bartlet and his crew. He had ordered them to sift through and scan viable body parts in search of DNA they could preserve in order to clone The Captain and his crew later if The Regency needed them on the way to Nelta. "But we must be secretive about the paths we take. We don't want our colleagues aware of all the technology until after *Sagan* launches from Station I."

Obviously disturbed about something, Jenkens began waving his hands like stop icons. "Thornton—something's wrong."

People stopped in their tracks, statue-like.

More Terras streamed down from the ceiling hubs like gently falling leaves through the Press Room and Oval Office. They began directing people to holosites where they could begin to access information and safety concerns.

"Everyone—look at all the displays of Earth's vitals," Jenkens yelled. He then ordered Terra to recall the scientists and engineers who had left for home.

As people activated their wrist processor apps, Manning ran to the left side of the room, to hologram stages 1 through 4. "Steve—*what's* wrong?!" Then he noticed the *Normal* tropopause-shield reading that had a rippling, red, ocean level reading: *Above Normal.*

"*That's* what's wrong," Jenkens began, "worldwide disturbances!"

Manning ordered *his* Terra: "Activate that spectroradiometric image on Stage 4 Left that we're receiving from the USGS at the Caryl Johnson Global Earthquake Facility on Oahu."

"Yes, Regent Manning," she replied. Inside the yellow

projection beam appeared an image of a large wave that suddenly settled to ocean water where an arctic island once existed.

"Two minutes ago, this area was inundated with extreme tides, just like that," Jenkens said, snapping his fingers. "Then there are the earthquakes we've been experiencing." He showed him the last seismic reading that surfaced over his wrist processor. "This one occurred around the entire southern hemisphere...a 3.3 on the Richter scale."

People began hailing various scientific centers and facilities to confirm and gain more data on the abnormal readings.

Manning said, "I have one *real* sighting, but I'd like to see as many afflicted areas as we can from the tropopause satellites."

Wall zones began imaging ocean swells lapping inland in several crowded coastal areas.

"Instruments show that the sea level *should* stabilize at this level," he continued. "For how long? We can't determine. Our tides are off-kilter. This *could* get much worse—"

"No—downright ugly," Regent Sylvia Itonovich yelled.

Terra's eyes glowed green in an obvious interface of information. "Regent Manning, there was a small tidal fluctuation during Dr. Coflin's interference with the Neltan/Earth conduit at 9:10 p.m., Eastern Standard Time."

"And that atmospheric disturbance," Regent Jenkens interrupted. "That was right after 9:30, the time of the wormhole conflagration...when that small black hole ignited and we lost our quantum connection with Nelta prior to finalizing *The Pact*."

"Yes...but the Open Science Facility at Cal Tech streamed to us that Station II had reinforced the tropopause shield and Rand said he stopped that radioactive whiplash from frying Earth's ozone," Manning said.

"At 9:55 p.m., Earth experienced a one inch rise in sea-level worldwide," Terra added.

"A global quake then too! But how? *How* can *all this* be happening on a *global* scale?" he asked. He knew his Oval Office ceiling processor had more advanced capabilities that

Battlefield Matrix

were linking with covert technology on *Sagan*. Jenkens had linked that processor with the Security wall-zone next to the Oval Office door when Coflin had held him hostage. But there was only one way to use the new system while at the same time maintaining a smoke screen of secrecy. "Terra, open the partition between these rooms." Terra had infused the partition with a destructive illusion when Coflin had invaded the Press Room. "Transfer all partition imagers to the Security wall-zone system next to my desk. I want *you only* interfacing with processors. We *now* need all the apps in my office *in here* now." As Terra activated The Room Enhancement program, he asked: "Was that earthquake the result of some other type of wormhole interaction? Or something else…like a deep space energy backlash? The times of all these disturbances on Earth are so close together." He felt dread enter his lungs at his next breath.

The wall dividing the Press Room and Oval Office vibrated and hummed as it cracked open in four places. The doorframe and threshold crunched together like an accordion and then glided into place with the other folding sections. The top half of one wall retracted into the ceiling while the bottom glided like a rolling carpet into the floor. Meanwhile, maintenance workers had dashed over to his desk and furniture, guiding them across the moving carpet and positioning them under the long windows. Terra's two main beehive hubs bubbled like amoeba and divided—forming four new hubs. Glowing with their bright rainbow processors, they slushed across the ceiling like cascading jellyfish toward their new locations. When they reached their equilateral ceiling positions, they sprouted nano-organic roots, clamped down, and interfaced with Terra's matrix. Regents were talking frantically on their portable devices, pacifying inquisitive reporters and family members who had received the abnormal measurements from the Caryl Johnson Facility.

Dr. Elisa Holton and more scientists and engineers entered the room. Taking orders from The Regency, they began assisting them with research and interpreting results on the

Earth's vital statistics and incoming data surfacing from the oceans' depths. Elite officers clad in business suits were rushing in, activating advanced q-pads capable of direct interface with Terra's evolved new matrix. The flashing devices were Black Ops Division and Global Intelligence oriented from McLean. As they activated their apps, more wall-screen zones and hologram stages began displaying translations of every available reading on Earth's biometrics. Frequencies from space were also incoming...but not blending with current instrumentation. When they finished, they briefly huddled—obviously puzzled while conferring among themselves. Then more data from space appeared on several stages. They had scanned for Dr. Coflin's biometrics and a possible alien intrusion. Then one of the scientists announced: "We did not discover any biological or quantum incursions that might be responsible for the abnormal tidal activity or current earthquake activity, Ladies and Gentlemen."

Manning said: "Thanks, but continue your monitoring and recon. Some types of data are sure to bubble up from the oceans' depths that'll indicate what's happening."

Over Gem, Elisa opened up a Lunar Field app and zoomed in on a topographical area that appeared like milk-white expanding suds. Wiggling her way through to Manning and Jenkens, she pointed at two, red zone lines and said: "A few of us researchers have been using this experimental app to detect enemy contrails." She showed them the red-dotted, flaring, valence spikes. "Sirs, these aren't enemy craft...and I'm not sure of their origin, but two craft *did* leave the moon a-half-an-hour ago for *Sagan*. I wonder, well, why *we're* not receiving *this* information 'cause it could be vital in explaining any type of anomalous lunar activity." She coughed—a dry uncomfortable expression. "Interference? Again maybe?"

Sweeping her image on to Stage-1 Left next to Center Stage and enlarging it, Manning rubbed his eyes when he saw dust spraying from a rugged lunar fissure. The crack seemed to stretch on endlessly through the far-sided darkness. "What's this?" He called over two astro-geologists. "What the *hell* is

Battlefield Matrix

this!? Where'd it come from? How come we didn't detect it?" Despair and a feeling of loss hit him. The place was close to Captain Bartlet's deathbed.

As astro-geologists scampered together to discuss the particulate matter spewing into lunar orbit that was beginning to form a tiny ringlet, Elisa said to Manning and several gasping Regents: "Some type of activity on the moon caused the disturbance in Earth's tidal currents. *That* disturbance, whatever it is, has to be the source of what's happening to us here. But I'm not an expert in planetary geology. Maybe those two craft that were on the moon a bit ago had something to do with this lunar crack. A mining accident maybe?"

"We'll send out a frequency signal to check," a scientist called back to her, "but we're still encountering a high level of interference from the tropopause shield."

"The shield's still gleaning solar power, and also powering down from its heavy fight against that radiation bombardment," a Regent called. "The Decagon system is repairing from sustaining battle hits. *All* its imagers and its matrix are off line. Our remaining troops are way Out of Quadrant—space folding back to station III."

Jenkens said, "The space stations' imagers can see a pencil on the moon!"

"The space stations are experiencing the same types of radioactivity issues as the tropopause shield," a scientist countered, activating energy readings from the tropopause array that showed its entire intake and output at *High*. "That's why we're having so much trouble connecting with everyone on the stations and sustaining their visuals in here and around Earth."

"Well then find a way to connect to 'em *through* the high readings," Manning ordered. "Whatever activity occurred on that far side of the moon must have been profound to affect us so soon and in anomalous tidal ways." Again, he tried hailing scientists on Station II.

Jenkens linked Center Stage to a matrix grid connection that a *Sagan* engineer had downstreamed into the room's new burgeoning processor. A close up image of the moon on Center Stage illuminated.

"This shows a roughhewed section…but why?" Manning asked.

As Terra entered the arena of analysis but continued to complain of radioactive interference, Jenkens said: "I'm generating simulations based on data we've already got. Damn disturbances from gravity fluctuations and our shield are like groping through an unfamiliar building in the dark! This lunar dust gully *could* be an issue with the moon's orbit." "I'm more concerned at what I am *seeing* rather than relying on the data we're receiving. That fissure on the surface appears massive. I don't like the looks of it at all."

Manning blew into his icy cold, cupped hands. "What the hell's going on up there?" He began barking orders and other Regents followed suit. "We need all this interference gone. Come on people! Get with it!" He clapped them to motivation so hard his palms burned. "Now that we have a modified link, tell those scientists on Station II that I want some type of counteragent to nullify the interference that's inhibiting our view of the moon. We're supposed to have twenty satellites monitoring that far side area. Where the hell are they?" He remembered that *Sagan* had utilized those small lab-based satellites earlier to help locate the crashed *Spider* astrofighter. The search-and-rescue craft had used them. But the new processor in his office and *Sagan*'s matrix weren't transmitting any lunar orbiting data. Something was horribly awry if *Sagan*'s Neltan infused Navigation Center wasn't able to pick up or relay lunar information. A Matrix Tech on *Sagan* told him the bad news: Navigation was concentrating power on construction and self-organization, particularly, The Helm, Shaesar's most recent downstream of complicated, vital, and delicate programs. Until the boost completed, *Sagan*'s resources were contained at one-hundred percent to the giant ship.

Elisa said: "Some of the interference is negative matter, Sir, that's why all our visuals and space instruments are failing.

Battlefield Matrix

This is bad…but the miniature annihilations could be occurring on Earth. It could be worse, Sir, even though what we're going through is pretty bad." She had an app streaming over Gem that was showing a small cyclotron they had been testing as a counter agent. Then on Stage-1 Right, Station II's Lead Researcher appeared with a much larger display of a cyclotron probe. Elisa continued: "This is in the experimental stage. We've been using the probe to counter extreme levels of radioactive isotope and neutrino poisoning. Thus far, in controlled settings around Station II, the probe's been successful in neutralizing negative matter emissions from particle accelerators."

"That's success to me, Dr. Holton! How many such probes do you have up there?" he asked the Manager.

She replied, "Two, Sir."

After several scientists gave him coordinates, Manning said: "Launch them ASAP to the locations I'm streaming to you now. Hopefully, they'll render the interference null so we can see what's happening on and around the moon." She complied, and then he ordered her to stream a message for him to all craft off-Earth. "Please, direct your optics or sonar on that lunar site. We need your help to investigate that lunar crack and its surrounding locations." Then he asked Terra to call General Rand. "I need him Center Stage…and put all visuals from Research Station II on the Stage-1 Right, next to him. Tell Rand and the scientific community that I want them to put aside all their differences and work together."

Elisa whispered in his ear, "Good thinking, Sir, 'cause I do believe the military and the scientists would sooner see the Earth explode than to shake hands."

Chuckling with her, he said, "Yep—you're right about *that* long-standing feud. But it's gonna stop now."

When The Manager of Station II told him that she had launched the probes beyond Earth's orbit and that they were successfully countering the matter and anti-matter disturbances between the space station, he told her: "We need to launch more probes to the moon *immediately*. I know you told me yesterday that you were short on lab-based probes, but launch what you have." Her image on Stage-1 Right was resolving to crystal clarity. The two experimental probes were working. Behind the Manager, various shapes and sizes of available probes appeared. Ten of them began rolling toward an escalator that would set them on a wide launch pad. "Program the probes to send us back the following information, specifically what we're requesting, but confidentially to me...for Regency Eyes Only, *for now*." He said the later so everyone could hear. He didn't want to create another problem with the media examining every image, complaining about his every word, and generating the wrong spin. Scientists around him were sweeping apps and data into the Manager's holographic image where her wrist processor caught them on Station II and swept them into the research grid. He continued: "With what they're requesting, we also need the extent of that fracture—everything from length, width, depth and movement. We're doing crafty detective work now...and we must also scan for anything biological that mighta contributed to that rip, crevice, crack...whatever it is."

"Yes," Jenkens intervened, "*who* know *what* those terrorists had fomenting in their hideouts."

Manning added: "I know this might be a stretch...a wild speculation...but let's also consider an alien biological agent or entity." As people in the room gasped, he said, "You're the researchers up there. Use everything ya got to tell us what's happening on the moon!"

"Yes, Executive Regent Manning," replied the Manager, and she began directing her teams in programming the probes as Elisa assisted her with data streaming into the Press Room.

When an image of General Rand and a fellow officer appeared on Center Stage, Terra said: "Here are the military probes Station III has ready for launch. They are weapons infused with asteroid fracturing and particle diversion capability.

General Rand said, "We heard your order to work with the docs on Station II."

Battlefield Matrix

"That's right, General," Manning snapped.

Exhaling an obvious distasteful acquiesce, Rand then said: "As we speak, our grids are adding data to Station II and linking to the Caryl Johnson Facilities on Earth. All three of us can now receive, disseminate, and interpret all incoming information. Any facts our military probes receive will stream to you and Station II automatically. If you wish to stream data to other facilities on Earth and in space that are *not* scientific in nature, that's beyond my prevue, Sir."

"Terra can do that," Jenkens said, and Terra complied.

Manning felt only a seconds worth of relief. Several Regents had surrounded him. He interfaced Terra's projection of him to higher wall zones where everyone could get a good view of him and hear their discussions. The whole area—all twenty-six thousand square feet now—was bustling with people, holograms, data flow and virtual views. He enlarged one important data interpretation and stepped away from Stage-1 Right so *everyone* could view the spectrographic results. He said: "There are lunar particles that dislodged when *The Spider* weeded out those terrorists. But I can't tell the extent. I also see debris from that far-side coming into the sunlight right now." A field of matter was lifting off the moon like flowers doffing colorful petals.

Elisa was obviously representing a group of scientists who had completed a thorough inspection of the tropopause shield when she broke apart from them and announced: "The tropopause shield *will* protect Earth from any of those objects, Regent Manning, should they reach us. As the shield's globules have targeted and disintegrated large objects since its inception in 2062, it *will hold* up against average strikes of matter from the moon. For larger objects, we can still use the space stations to destroy or disintegrate them."

"We'll need more orbiting gamma hardware then," a Regent shouted, and the Manager and General Rand began collaborating on a solution.

"But this lunar debris and activity looks different than any ordinary asteroid matter or meteoroid stream," Jenkens said.

J.P. Osterman

"General, what's *your* analysis of potential damage to Earth?"

Another scientist from Station II interrupted them. "Several NOAA buoys are detecting a global-wide, hadalpelagic zone rise in current. The oceans' depths are abnormally churning."

Manning ordered, "Add that information to this puzzle."

When images of Station III launch sites materialized inside General Rand's huge navigation center, he said, "Our probes should arrive around the moon in thirty minutes, taking into account the ten minutes to activate and deactivate their spacefolding cyclotron turrets. That'll put the probes a mile above the lunar surface." He then ordered his officers to send the new *Alvin* submersibles to several oceanic positions and interface them with the lunar probes.

"The data they process together *should* yield a cause, Sir," General Rand said.

"If we get bombarded with debris, *no way* can the shield stop all that. We could incur hundreds of meteor strikes per second!" cried a Regent.

"God knows *that* would be an extinction event of the highest order!" a reporter shouted.

A journalist dropped a robotic tripod in a gesture that implied she was surrendering to an unseen force. "And the Neltans are gone—gone for good!"

"All help's gone," a Regent cried, dropping to her knees.

Chaos ensued in a frenzy of chatter as Regents and scientists argued over the intensity of the potential cosmic pummeling, cures for it, and informing the public. Black Ops and Global Intelligence began packing up. Manning received a *Confidential Emergency* message that they were heading to several Top Secret secure locations to prepare for the absolute worse type of extinction-level event. Those included the following: all major science and medical facilities and universities, Terra's eight matrix centers, *The Mountain*, the Greenbrier secluded resort, USAG in Germany, *Chongqing and Shanghai* in China, the *Norway* bunker in Norway, *Nizhny Tagil* in Russia, the *Jerusalem* in Israel; and, the largest, the St. *James Railway Station* facility in

Battlefield Matrix

Sydney, Australia. After learning from the aftermath of the 2057 nuclear and biological strikes in the ozone layer, The Regency set up new Emergency Protocols, one being to have those facilities ready to accommodate the public. Global Intelligence had already ordered Terra to determine who should be included in the ultimate List of Survivors. As soon as the group of Regents in charge of that G.I. organization would give the order, agents around the globe would direct those people to those locations. All Enforcers, Secret Security, university leaders, high-tech CEOs, and the old National Guard had automatic inclusion on Earth's List of Survivors.

When he overheard ten Regents about to stream an image of a lunar fissure to The World, he cried: "No—don't send that yet! We have a thirty minute wait until we begin to receive concrete results." He smashed a scientist's wrist device right off his arm while he was in the middle of downstreaming a hologram. "I said no...*no* to divulging *anything* that's going on in this room!" As the tearful and shaking scientist slowly picked up the pieces, Manning shouted to everyone: "Let's get facts first. Let's consolidate all data into solid findings before we jump to conclusions and begin a worldwide panic. God knows we had enough of those yesterday." He sipped water that a robot server lifted to him.

"Could the crack be something that *The Spider* or the terrorists accidentally unleashed during the battle?" Jenkens asked over all the chatter. When everyone stilled, he continued: "Maybe we're only discovering now, something that's always been there but that's now being unleashed. You, Thornton, speculated on an alien biological...and astronomers have seen transient lunar lights and unexplained phenomena. Perhaps those sightings *could* be metallic geysers containing unknown properties, minerals, or ancient amino acids?"

"The crack *could* be matter from an earlier universe," someone speculated.

Another person said, "Perhaps Dimension 8 misdirected from in here and into the moon."

Someone else conjectured that perhaps the Neltans covertly

infused the moon with some type of highly advanced particle detonation meant to explode in case humanity didn't follow through with *The Pact*. She said, "Perhaps their detonator prematurely malfunctioned, igniting an explosive chain reaction...a possible payback for abandoning them."

Through more incoming speculations, Manning ordered Terra to search her matrix for the truth and verbalize solid facts.

"No evidence. That cannot occur," Terra kept repeating.

"The fissure could just be a tiny seismic fault," Regent Sylvia Itonovich said, "a bothersome but innocuous consequence caused by the terrorists holding up under the lunar surface for so long. Or...when they abandoned their stronghold, their craft unleashed dark-matter rod material that caused a slight change in lunar orbit. That change, in turn, is affecting Earth's hadalpelagic zones. Maybe *that's* all that's gonna happen...a slight rise in ocean water. Hell, if we survived an ozone depletion we can live through something simple like that."

"Yeah," cried another Regent, "who knows *what* the enemy did to the moon while they were there...damn 'em! They're getting the best-and-last revenge on us for sure."

Again, the room reverberated with shouts of confusion and bantering of possible answers.

Manning had enough. "Stop! All this is useless."

Everyone paused as his voice reverberated over all the sounds of the incoming abnormal readings that continued to scroll inside wall zones and holographic projection beams. "We have about twenty minutes until the probes begin streaming us solid facts. Everyone...stop this senseless panicking and waste of time." Feeling drained and numb, he stepped away from one frightening simulation of the moon that showed it breaking apart at the fissure site. Someone had generated it, surreptitiously. Another image blossomed on a wall-zone, depicting a shock wave hitting all coastal areas. Another simulation had a massive meteor assaulting Earth that was leaving the sky encased in darkness. They were

Battlefield Matrix

apocalyptic graphs *someone* from inside the room had illegally gleaned, holosite-shopped, and was streaming to The World.

He raced to his desk beneath the long line of picture windows. He had the gun buried in the bottom drawer. He remembered when Elisa Holton had given him the weapon meant to protect him on that Communication Day of August 23, 2060. He'd never touched it, until now. He believed he'd never have to use it. Until now. Pulling out the pistol, he unlocked the mechanism and fired it. "Everyone! Stop!"

The acoustics cushioned the ear-ringing *bang* and the ceiling slurped up the bullet.

Two Regents fainted. Most people dropped to the ground. Several scientists dashed to the double doors as a reporter yelled, "Lemme outta here!"

"Lock down, Terra!" he called.

She echoed his command, and armed Enforcers entered the room, after which the double doors clamped shut.

He was about to fire a bullet to stop the reporter from attacking an Enforcer, until Terra shut down all screens and the room went completely dark. He had forgotten that the cover of total darkness was her last resort, her Firewall protocol against matrix intrusions occurring inside the Press Room. One by one, the hologram projector beams began re-illuminating. "Everyone," he began, "we've got a hacker! A hacker's in this room *right now*."

Someone had linked with one hologram stage and was rendering it as a virtual hostage. The hijacked Stage-4 Right was showing massive impacts from chunks of the moon slamming the Earth. The voice of a metallic-sounding narrator bellowed: "Whatever remaining, that is alive, will most likely drown, freeze, incinerate or starve to death. Subterranean facilities, fortified fortresses, or military strongholds won't ensure survival. This is what you get when people of power determine who lives, who dies, and who suffers. The Regency is our enemy!"

More Terra holograms appeared and stepped inside the holoshopped show to block the illegal hack. Finally, Terra discovered the sabotaged grid and re-routed it. All power fizzled out on the Stage 4, except the energy powering Terra's beehive rainbow processors. They were changing colors as evolving securityware activated. In the morphing lights and flashing colors, everyone grew quiet. Fear mixed with self-preservation filtered through the air.

Manning ordered Terra to project his face high on a central wall-zone so everyone could view him. "See," he said, trying to breathe calmly. "It was *all* a hoax." Meanwhile, the lights had re-illuminated. One-by-One, Terra reactivated all the hologram stages and wall zones.

When he saw images of General Rand's and the Manager of Research Station II appear, he continued: "I've ordered Enforcers to hunt down the spy, hacker, or *whoever* you are. We *will* find you." He slid the small gun into his pocket as Enforcers dressed in gray and black began walking among The Regents, reporters, dignitaries, robot servers and maintenance crews. "We're scanning for you now!"

Then he spotted the one person he had never seen panic, even after *Greeter*'s explosion. Yes, Dr. Elisa Holton had cried; and yes, she had been angry, but she had *never* lost her cool. He had an idea: the Neltan-infused armband technology she was still wearing contained special properties. Interfacing with Terra's matrix, it could deactivate a quantum connection and fix a dimensional intrusion. Several times, he observed that she had tried forcing the device off her arm, but it hadn't detached; and she seemed to have adjusted to the inconvenience until, as she said, she could, "find a way to force Gem off." Maybe they could use the Neltan-based technology to help them.

"Dr. Holton?" he called.

"Yes, Sir," she replied, stepping out of a crowd of scientists and walking up to him.

With her brown hair pulled back into a ponytail and two strings of bangs crisscrossing on her shinny forehead, she appeared worn and weary. If not for the color of her hair, her brown eyes and slightly shorter height, she could pass as Lynn

Battlefield Matrix

Altmin's twin. That energized him.

"Dr. Holton, it appears that you have a calm handle on the incoming facts and seem to be keeping order where there's bedlam," he said. "Is that due to information you've been receiving from the armband device, Gem?"

"I have as much control over information as I can receive and store on this thing, Sir," she sighed and chuckled as she lifted her left arm.

The glowing gilded armband was still attaching to her like a thick bronze tourniquet. Winding around her entire arm from the base her of fingers almost to her shoulder, Gem moved along her skin as an interactive processor—breathing with her and radiating her emotions as well as its own biometrics. The multifaceted jewel processors that had popped out hours ago had morphed into shiny, colorful processors with the capability to function as multi-level hologram projectors. They were linked to Terra's matrix and shape-shifter Encantado entities from the giant transmission screen now functioning as a giant wall zone ready to activate images from Earth or outer space.

Obviously frustrated with Gem's inability to provide answers to their complicated questions, she said: "Gem is processing all the data along with Terra. But like us, it needs more information. Or maybe, more expansion. I guess we could do that...if we knew how."

He ran over to the bottom frame of the transmission screen. Hours ago, the Neltans had used the screen—and the beehive processors behind it—to quantum-appear in the room. With a protective tool in hand, he searched for the most intensive area measuring the highest levels of photons, ions, and valences. He scooped up the new fabric the Neltans had infused with a new energy to strengthen the screen for their final matrix gift. Not knowing fully the new light-blue glow around the bubbling patch, he applied the jiggling organic material to Gem that began emitting a low frequency hum. This time, the screen didn't resume its usual Repair-mode green glow. The quantum connection to Nelta was gone.

"This feels like ticklish...*wow*, the power feels like opposites attracting!" she marveled.

The multi-faceted connectivity mounds solidified into beautiful, sparkling multi-colored diamonds and rare gems. "These are *really* processors," she said as Terra's eyes glowed green. Other Terras throughout the room briefly stopped their interactions with their hosts, their eyes flashing green as well, and then they resumed their interactions. "This new application is advancing to uncontained photon and electromagnetic frequency processing, and meant for matrix connectivity. Maybe even *more* than that 'cause of this blue glow I see."

"It's Doppler shifting," Jenkens said, recording Gem's morphology.

"With that new concentrated blue material," Manning said, "Gem bloomed instantly like a field of flowers on time-lapse."

The entire armband device began shimmering with nano-technology that looked like fiber-optic lights imbibing capillary energy into a body. The radiance of color was light powering up to perform and self-organizing into one whole artificial intelligence.

She closed her eyes. "I feel a flow of energy here!"

A scientist next to her received a shock from the armband when she tried to grab Elisa's arm in a helping gesture. "Are you in pain, Elisa? That thing just stung me."

She shook her head no. "The increase in energy doesn't hurt. Honestly! The device must be synchronizing with the air...molecules in the room...and light as particles and waves, and electromagnetism most assuredly."

"And gravity I bet," Jenkens said, reaching to touch it, but then pulling back. He called for more people to scan the device from a safe distance.

When Manning approached her and then stopped, Elisa said, "I'm—I'm, well, just afraid a bit...that's all." She was breathing as if surfacing for air. "Gem looks different than before, Sir, but feels the same...metal but silk soft, and flexible."

"Is the device interfacing one hundred percent with Terra?"

he asked.

She replied, "Don't ask me how I know, but I believe this small line of green glowing facets on the back side indicates that the device is fully linked with Terra's matrix."

Terra's eyes flaring a new stronger hue of green, she stepped up and nodded an affirmative. "My matrix *is* in synchronicity with the Neltan armband device, Executive Regent Manning. However, only Dr. Elisa Holton can order the device to perform a function."

"What's the device capable of now, I wonder?" he asked Elisa.

She reiterated his question into the three-inch green glowing cavity over where her pulse point set. A small show of Terra's entire matrix, streaming around the globe, began hovering over the back of the armband.

"It looks like the armband can generate *fifty* grids *right* into this room and open up additional hologram projections," he said.

"Yes Sir," Elisa agreed as more spectators gathered around her to watch the spectacular matrix show. She pulled Gem close to her chest, obviously uncomfortable with their attention.

"We need to interface with all the craft and space colonies in order to put the pieces together of this God-awful puzzle happening on the moon, Dr. Holton," he said, guiding her by the right elbow toward Center Stage and the giant IMAX screen behind it. "It's *you* that the device bonded to, attached to. It's obviously in tune with you and perhaps your consciousness."

Other scientists continued to marvel at her bronze armband device. The gold edging was continuing to self-stitch around the patch Manning had added to her wrist area. Whenever she held it away from her chest, the device glowed in waves, and the tiny rows of colorful connectivity gems on its surface warbled.

"When I listen up close to it," she began, lifting the device up to her left ear, "I hear this slight humming sound," she told inquisitive people. "It's like a purring animal…but *I* believe the sound frequencies are really subatomic strings resonating and sifting through everything in the room. *I* believe Gem is also experiencing *everything* in Terra's matrix…soaking up information like a sponge…an artificial intelligence processing reality and growing. People experience reality in various ways: through perception, the environment, and relationships. Gem is experiencing another component of reality…a matrix perspective."

"Maybe space/time perspective as well!" another scientists shouted.

"These gems appear to be quantum connectivity entities," Manning said, pushing away a few engineers with envious eyes. "They're attracting and harnessing confocal frequencies. They're optics, fractal, self-replicating, and electrostatically receiving their power from energy and forces all around us. *You*, Dr. Holton, are the intermediary between Gem, Terra, and the transmission screen."

The device shocked a reporter who slipped his hand under her arm and tried to touch it. Apologizing, Elisa said up close to Gem: "You can't do that! You can kill someone. Didn'tcha hear Executive Regent Manning tell ya what you're made of?"

Five brilliant facets on one, half-inch blue gem blasted out a ray of bright orange light.

Several scientists jumped back.

"I don't think Gem liked ya touching it," Elisa said. "You better stay back. I can't control it yet. As you can see, I'm only just beginning to communicate with it."

"Looks like you have a complicated task ahead of you, but a relationship we need proficient for Gem to help us with our lunar problem," Manning said, squinting at the blue crystal stone that was settling down, obviously satisfied that no stranger was intruding on its private space. "Gem is definitely protecting you."

"So it'll probably help us with our moon puzzle soon because Dr. Holton's life could be in danger," Jenkens said.

She groaned as she tried pushing Gem down her arm. "The

device has definitely been evolving, Sir," she said. She poked it. "And it's tingly, like it's eating up electricity and might electrocute me—*ahhh*!"

"It won't," Manning said, steadying her fingers, being careful not to touch the device.

She began shaking it a bit. "*Ahhh*—this feels like it's never gonna leave me!"

A small gem began glowing in soft, red luminescence.

As she sighed in its apparent instant comfort, Manning grabbed her by her right shoulder and looked her in the eye. "Dr. Holton, the last quantum communication with the Neltans must have infused the Encantado organics with special particle energies to stream that last matrix show of theirs from Nelta. The communications conduit might have even picked up an unknown resonance, or sub-atomic activity from the cosmos. Who knows! At least the device is a helping agent...not a destructive agent. It's working with Terra, so it's not poisonous or murderous."

"But getting it off o' me, Sir?" she asked.

Several strings on the bronze device glowed in a beauteous gold.

"Wow...so calming."

"See?" he began. "It'll just be a matter of time before you two learn how to relate to each other...and you learn how to doff it and reapply it. But for now, I believe the device can assist us in seeing things our limited technology can't detect and see."

Two Regents approached him with images of the lunar fissure hovering over their wrist devices.

"Sweep them into Gem," Manning directed, and then said so that everyone could hear: "Any info or data *any* of you receives from *any*where, whether you deem it important or not, stream into the matrix, directing it to...to *where* in your matrix, Terra?"

She gave them the science grid location and said: "I have expanded ten holosite grids to accommodate the influx of statistical data, measurements, and images. I am prepared to receive, process, direct, or stream everything incoming upon either Dr. Holton's command or your command. However, Dr. Elisa Holton *must* direct the Encantado armband processor, Gem."

"And here I go," Elisa exclaimed. When she extended her arm, the device copied the holographic images displaying throughout the room. Then she directed the device towards the IMAX screen. "You said that the device is an intermediary. I guess, I'm in the middle of everything." She inhaled deeply, twice, appearing a bit dizzy and overwhelmed but resolute. "Let's see what Gem can do." When a few connectivity gems glowed, the screen illuminated in a burst of white light, and two tiny 3D puzzle pieces appeared onscreen.

Regents and scientists began bantering expletives of shock and amazement. They were also receiving incoming probe images, data, and Earth's vital statistics.

Manning ordered them to add all information they were receiving into the 3D twirling soup mix of puzzle pieces. "Dr. Holton, sweep *everything* into the IMAX screen!"

Nodding in agreement—with a pensive expression on her face—she began talking into the device: "There appears to be a bad disturbance on the moon, Gem. We need to know its cause-and-effects. We need *you*, Gem, to compose a picture and tell us what happened and when it happened. Use the information streaming in from the probes, Gem. Process who, why, and how from *everything* you have available, Gem."

Gem blasted a date and time on to the screen: 9:30 p.m., February 27, 2068.

Battlefield Matrix

Chapter 16

Unseasoned Past

"Gem's picking up an image *live* from the past," she gasped.
Several people exclaimed, "That's when wormholes went rogue, and we kept losing Terra's matrix connectivity!"

"Tell Gem to roll back the clock, Dr. Holton," Manning ordered.

Nodding yes, she said, "Gem, I need *you* to bring us a show, or continuous slide show, or at least several pictures of what happened that caused *that* fissure on the far side of the moon, please." She swept into Gem another picture of the moon with a dust ring forming around its surface. "Who was there? Who did this? What did this? Was it an accident? An invasion? *You* have all the data, so help us."

"That's a dive into the past," Jenkens said, and others agreed. "Not possible."

Elisa's face turned bitingly stern. "Sure is possible with Gem. From those puzzle pieces materializing on the screen, Gem is receiving the shreds as if the past is still in existence."

As Manning gently coached her and swept more shows into Gem, he said: "It fits the Neltans' belief that time is inseparable from space. It's just the hard technical task of accessing *past* space that's the problem."

"Time travel," Jenkens scoffed.

After Elisa repeated, "Yep, time travel," she said: "*You're* gonna have to dive into The Past to get what we need, Gem. But be careful. We don't want to open up another dimension or bring an alien presence into *this* reality."

A tiny crystal facet on Gem glowed green.

Elisa smiled and her eyes widened as she said, "Gem acknowledged that."

"So the device *is* processing with Terra...*and* with a protective buffer thank goodness," said Jenkens as grins of relief brightened the gray bags under his eyes.

"Dr. Holton's face looks like it's reflecting an aurora borealis," called the concerned Manager from Station II. "Keep monitoring her. We want to make sure she isn't absorbing radiation. And Elisa, if you experience any ill side effects, tell us if immediately." After Elisa agreed, The Manager began directing the setup of equipment.

A connectivity gem glowed red—the shift denoting a reversal in time and space.

"Yes, good, keep going, Gem," Elisa said, touching her temple. "I feel like it's reading me...touching me, on a deep—" Tears formed in her eyes. When her friend, Maureen, ran up into her face and asked what was happening to her, she replied: "Love. That's all I can say, Maureen. It's like Gem cares about me on a level that no one ever could."

"Like God's warming yer soul, huh?" Maureen said.

Immediately, images materialized on the towering screen, expanding to a quarter of the size of the Wailing Wall.

Manning ordered several Matrix Techs and Projectionists, "Expand that entire wall-zone section!"

"Parts of a show are solidifying," she called out in excitement. She appeared to be adjusting to Gem's capability to quantum-synthesize data that was beaming like God rays from its multi-faceted mounds to the IMAX screen.

A scientist picked off an image from *his* wrist device, reached up tall in front of the IMAX screen and set his image in between two puzzle pieces he said needed the information he had just received. Several people warned him—told him, "Watch out!"

Elisa said: "Please—step back! I can't redirect 4D stream after the time retrieval!"

Through the humming and droning sounds resonating from the screen, he called, "I have to manipulate just this tiny picture for size and intensity." His shoulder-length hair was whipping from the screen's powerful output of magnetic current. "The position of the image is negatively impacting the live show!"

Elisa ordered Gem to compensate for the scientist's unpredictable presence, but the man appeared suddenly trapped in an invisible tug of war. She ordered him: "Push off the frame! Now! You could get sucked into the past! I won't be able to bring you back!" Enforcers ran up to the screen, but a static flow of force catapulted them back. Pointing the illuminating Gem at the flailing scientist, Elisa said, "I'm able to run interference with the anisotropic magnetic components...but not for long!" She appeared to have Gem processing at its peak.

The trapped scientist looked like a floating stick figure in front of the giant screen that was whipping images around him with gravitational intensity. The man's hand disappeared, and he fell to the floor.

"He's free!" shouted Elisa.

Wild eyed, he noticed his missing hand. "My God!" he shrieked, touching the dry stump. "It's gone! Where?!" He stood up—raging in panic, the screen almost capturing him again.

His severed hand was floating in black space inside the screen.

With a medicinal wand, a doctor rushed him, trying to pin down the terrified scientist who kept crying that he couldn't

J.P. Osterman

feel a thing. His arm was neither bloody nor jagged. The physician examined it for complications as another physician called in an order for a stem-cell therapy.

Regent Manning said, "Like a knife, the screen just severed it."

"No," Jenkens said when Terra showed him her results. "The nothingness between The Past and *our* space/time took his arm." The man screamed in terror until a sedative rendered him unconscious.

"Maybe we can save it." Elisa had Gem isolate, and hold constant, the severed part of his arm so it couldn't float into space any farther. "If we don't act fast, that arm'll be lost. He needs it 'cause the process is starting to eat away at the rest of his arm. Soon, he'll be gone."

Grabbing the unconscious scientist by the shoulders, Jenkens and some Enforcers set the man on top of robotic tripods. "Dr. Holton, keep the polarity stable so we can't whip around," Jenkens said. "I believe I can retrieve the arm." Jumping onboard the tripod platform, Jenkens directed the roboticware to lift him and the unconscious scientist toward the screen.

"Steve, that's the location! Stop!" called Manning.

Jenkens maneuvered the man so his right side was facing The Past. When the tripods stopped, he thrust the man half way into the screen until his torso disappeared.

Elisa said: "Gem—reverse! Now!"

After seconds elapsed in which Jenkens was engaged in a tug of war between the screen, puzzle pieces of The Past, and the twirling scientist, Jenkens yanked him back to the vibrating tripod platform where he fell down alongside him in relieve. The man's arm looked normal.

When they reached the floor to slide off the platform, the scientist awakened. He began telling everyone that he was just inside *The Spider*, and watching the crew, like a fly-on-the-wall. Jenkens said he recalled that the man might have struck one of the 3D puzzle pieces but not an entire reality! Still, the man kept repeating: "I'm telling you, I was there. I'm not

Battlefield Matrix

crazy...and I *wasn't* in some delusional state. *I, was, there* on *The Spider!*" Sweat began beading on his forehead. He had his healed arm extended for scientists and doctors who were astonishingly inspecting it. Through his white weak state of consciousness, he said: "When I began seeing them, the entire crew of *The Spider* was in a state of panic. There was smoke...*ha-huh*, and fire...*ha-huh*...and terrible flames. People were choking...like the inside of the craft was suddenly exposed to the lunar atmosphere and at any moment the crew would soon *kaboom*, explode!" He was gasping as if he had been trapped with them. "The Navigation Stage was cracking up and caving in. Terra's beehive hub was dripping. The nano-organics musta been *highly* overheating! And the wall-zone screens were melting like butter!" He appeared on the verge of collapsing from exhaustion. "Believe me!"

Pacing the floor and realizing that some of the man's details concerning the astrofighter fit the description, Manning doubted that someone could teleport through space and arrive at his or her destination in one piece. They had tried teleportation once with special approval from the Neltan Advancement Committee. The animal decayed. That's why they had to transport human DNA personally to Nelta. However, during that small timeframe, the scientist was in The Past while in The Present! Jenkens disagreed, but Manning interrupted him. "Terra, store what the scientist just said. If we see where his story might fit in with the big picture, we'll believe him; but for now, I take what he said as being a simple story." When he glanced at Gem, he noticed the right side of the device glowing rainbows. In one facet, he thought he saw a little slice of time he had never seen before. It was of Lynn, suited up in white space wear before *Greeter* launched. He wished he had been in that very spot in which Gem was now viewing Lynn in The Past...to say something to her. He then realized that the armband truly was dipping into another space and time. "What the guy told us *could* be true," he said.

"Why do you say that, Sir?" Elisa questioned.

"I just saw someone who is dead," he replied, stepping

toward that particular gem that was showing him the past. "Lynn." He felt heart-piercing pain.

She quickly turned the device to look as a medical team wheeled out the weary scientist who had fainted again. "Gone? Darn! Maybe I could have told her not to board *Greeter*! Darn!"

Meanwhile, the expanded IMAX screen was continuing to interface with Gem, Terra's matrix, and the new probes— receiving their information as 3D moving puzzle. Whenever pieces connected onscreen, people began speculating about the entire picture. One small section locked permanently, revealing several enemy craft launching from a covert portal on the moon. A second section locked after a scientist added a message she had received from a Plasma Engineer she was dating on *The Spider*. Being that he was in charge of weapons' assembly under Marty Hernandez, his background hologram stage showed Captain Bartlet at Navigation, ordering his First-Chair team to fire on escaping enemy craft. The barrage of laser power blew up several craft but missed two others that had decoys and escaped.

A bar displayed the date and time: February 27, 2068 9:05 p.m.

"That's when Dr. Coflin was in here but before the terrorists reached their rendezvous point where they activated their wormhole." As Elisa spoke, more moving puzzle pieces clasped and illuminated. She added: "I believe now, Terra can add what the scientist said *he* saw occurring inside *The Spider*." Terra acknowledged and included the scene.

Positioned inside a sanctioned safety zone, Manning told some Matrix Techs to slough off their fears of getting fried or suctioned up into the screen. "Move up so we can sweep in your data. We're up close...we're okay...nothing'll happen to you." Many people had backed up as far as the door. "The Cause-and-Effect command *is* reconstructing The Past. Good job, Dr. Holton. You and Gem are succeeding!"

Shadowing her face behind Gem, she gestured that *it* and Terra were holding all the power. "Thanks, Sir...and from what happened to Dr. Stafford's arm, it appears that if we wanted to, and I'm not advising this, I could pause the show, and we *could* step in and actually *be* in The Past to see what occurred on *The Spider* ourselves. Except this time, we could experience the reality safely, if Terra activated a protective barrier."

Terra said she could instigate one in five minutes and Elisa input the time into Gem.

Suddenly, a small, round circle appeared inside the middle of the screen. The current shifted. A drone resonated. The transparent circle looked like swirling glass.

"What's that?" Jenkens gasped, and then directed Terra to counter the singularity.

"Uh-oh—the Four Forces misappropriated when Gem and Terra interfaced to construct the protective barrier." Elisa touched a light-blue connectivity gem that glowed when the window began expanding. "Sorry! Just wait…I can fix this! Gem can fix this…" Her touch activated a flow of images that began streaming into the air over her armband.

Terra said, "The quantum information processing from my matrix into Gem is overlapping space/time."

"It's like a double-pane window!" exclaimed Jenkens.

"Maybe the entire screen could divide into two!" Manning added. "That cycling window appears to be an expanding membrane between *two* realities."

"Perhaps a cipher emoticon jumped into the mix and triggered this dual-pane problem," Regent Ruth Stein interjected. "We had so many Firewalls and Security precautions streaming all the time between Station III and *The Spider*. On a much smaller scale, I've seen such a window as this in my holosite world when someone lodged a complaint."

"Can't be that something so small as a cipher-mite could cause this!" Jenkens said.

Manning glanced around and felt as if he bit into a bitter pill. "That spy…*that* spy!"

As he ordered Enforcers to intensify their search of the spy, Elisa said, "Then the second window activated via a hacker if it

J.P. Osterman

truly is cipher oriented." Gem was streaming images so quickly on to the screen that the tips of her fingers were turning purple. "I'm trying to cut the cipher off at its point of origin inside the matrix...but—ouch!—I can't stop—"

"I am slowing processing speed," Terra said.

"Trace the cipher emoticon to the spy in this room, Terra," Manning ordered, opening the terrorist's old *Tiger of Mysore* doorframe and sweeping the virtual entryway into Hologram Stage-3 Left. The modified Tiger absorbed the wild energy flow.

Terra's ceiling processors decreased in intensity, the cycling window closed, and the coalescing puzzle pieces of The Past rematerialized on screen.

As people applauded, Elisa sighed in relief and said, "I'm amazed at how Gem and Terra stopped a time rip so quickly!" She drank some water and sat down on a stool that a Regent shoved under her when she appeared fatigued. "What energy they are harnessing—and can manipulate...from everywhere around us, wow!"

Jenkens slipped next to Manning and whispered: "Gem, Terra, or *her*? I wonder."

Manning lowered his head toward Jenkens' ear. "She's harmless, Steve. Lynn Altmin once told me that Elisa Holton is the loyal type. And I must say, from what *I've* noticed about her these last two days, she's also the subordinate type, in *no way* a trouble maker."

Jenkens backed away. "We'll see. Time will tell."

Meanwhile, more images from The Past had connected onscreen. As more puzzle pieces streamed in from several wall-zones and hologram stages, Elisa said, "Gem seems like it's going to continue to evolve until I take it off."

A gold thread suddenly refracted a soft orange light into her face.

"I think it likes me!" she replied, smiling.

Her friend and colleague, Maureen, walked up to her with some refreshments. As Elisa ate, Maureen said: "What's happening on the screen reminds me of the quantum exhibit the Neltans put on for us before they severed their connection."

Elisa unwrapped an oatmeal bar, bit half of it off, and chomped it down. "I've famished. I could eat ten more of these!"

Giving Elisa a vitamin brew that a physician had handed to her, Maureen said: "This ordeal appears to be exhausting you, Elisa, even though the Body Double Imagers indicates you're fine. Still, who knows how much more energy Gem will zap out of you...or how much more time all this quantum type of work will take."

"Yeah...I feel like a boxer regaining strength in between bells," she said, jokingly.

"You need to keep up your strength 'cause your A.I. pal is definitely depleting you." Maureen positioned a robot server next to Elisa, and it began vacuuming wrappers and dust from the screen's exhaust.

"Yeah—right! Thanks, Maureen."

As Elisa gulped down her quick meal, more images swept from the Gem to the screen. Layering, webbing, and circling on the screen, an entire show had almost completely coalesced from frequencies, musical notes, 3D QR codes, and outmoded pixels. Terra's matrix was quantum sifting through *every* stored piece of data ever entered in computer history.

"Some of this data isn't making sense," several people interject now and then.

"The device can't possible snatch The Past and superimpose, with precision, lost moments into The Present," a few scientists said as they inserted their holosites and old images into the screen after Manning approved them.

Elisa replied: "If some images aren't fitting together right, it's probably because the quantum recovery task is so difficult that it's overwhelming Gem and Terra. I just hope we'll receive one cohesive show."

Manning said: "I believe we're beginning to see the show from several possible vantage points—from multiple angles. So tell Gem we need an interior viewpoint...right from *The*

Spider's navigation helm. That's the lens out of which we need to see."

After she spoke the vantage point to Gem, she said: "Sir, I'd also like to suggest that we insert some type of Purge or Delete command after this is all over. We do have a spy—"

"Or spies," he said, checking on Terra's tracking of the criminal.

"Yes, and terrible things could happen if anyone acquires this time slicing capability," she said, and several eavesdropping Regents and scientists agreed.

Terra abruptly interrupted everyone's conversations. "Subatomic fractals of dark energy are interfacing with the properties of light and Earth's gravity and magnetism. Together, they are interacting with space, functioning as matter and antimatter springboards. This process is allowing Gem, Terra, and the screen to manipulate Time and manifest The Past, again, in a repeat state of existence."

"Uh-huh...right, Terra," Elisa said. "I've had research and science enough to where I thought my brain would explode and I *still* didn't understand that."

Several Regents laughed, until Jenkens finally said, "Basically, the technologies are acting as interspatial time magnets."

A soft breeze, droning and humming sounds, and a static resonance were ebbing and eddying gently through the room— the product of several interacting forces and currents—as final moving images continued to stream from the matrix to Gem and on to the screen.

Elisa's lips suddenly parted in an expression of fright. "Could the process you just described harm me? I thought it had a protective program!" She touched Gem in several places.

A shining facet on a mound sparkled and then emitted a hologram of red lips and a laughing sound.

Maureen leaned into Gem a bit and said, "I believe Gem just said, 'Are you joking'?" She chuckled and handed Elisa a cup of steaming peppermint tea. "Drink this. It'll calm ya."

Battlefield Matrix

Inhaling a breath of air, Elisa replied, "But from what Terra just said, maybe some type of nano-virtual virus from the future could infiltrate my body." As Manning began countering her concerns, she buried her eyes in the bend of her right arm. "I just don't wanna become Gray Goo, that's all."

Two physicians were scanning her with Body Double Imagers. When her biometrics returned a Normal reading, Manning peeled her arm away from her frightened face. "See? Nothing. All your vitals are fine. The device is protecting you. Trust me!"

Maureen snuck through the hovering medical team and whispered to her, "Elisa—he's right, this time."

"Yeah, ya think?" she exhaled as a doctor instructed her to breathe.

Maureen leaned tightly into Elisa's right ear and whispered: "Since the device bonded with you, maybe the change is a good thing for you. It helped you before. It's helping us now. I don't believe Gem's bad at all. I'm your friend. You know I'd always give you the truth." She held her hand tightly. "I'm here with you."

Elisa slowly sat up straight. "Thanks, Maureen." Her shoulders slumped in an apparent infusion of peace as Manning directed others around them to back away, to give her some room to regain her composure, to get some air, and to get out of the way of Gem's photonic light exchange that resumed its surge with the screen.

"You're right, Maureen," she said, smoothing down her blazer that someone donned around her shoulders to warm her. "Besides, you can help me give myself a quick check up when we meet tomorrow at the lab before lunch. Can you also help me analyze Gem?"

"Sure," Maureen replied, patting her shoulder. "Oh-and-hey—I've got good news."

"What?"

"Terra streamed to me that I'm on The List. I'm going with you to Nelta!" Maureen had a weak but happy grin on her freckled face. Then, an Enforcer broke through, interrupted them, and escorted Maureen back to the far side of the room where the other scientists were working and requesting her help.

Helping Elisa sit back up on the stool as a Regent presented Elisa with a special platform onto which she could set Gem comfortably, Manning said: "Soon we'll have a picture of what happened on the moon and what's causing the disturbances here. Right now, we're still experiencing mild earthquakes and tidal disruptions. The Caryl Johnson Institute is predicting *two* tsunamis." Two, far-right hologram stages and several picture-in-a-picture wall-zones were imaging concerns from people around the globe. "Everyone's starting to freak out but because we don't have the *whole* picture," he continued. "We can't activate any type of alert yet 'cause we don't know the safest areas wherein people can seek refuge."

"Perhaps we can peek into The Future after the armband shows us The Past," Regent Sylvia Itonovich interjected. "I know most of us in this room won't be here if something horrible happens on Earth—"

"Damn right! You all *won't* be here! You're gonna launch off on your cushiony astrocity while those of us left behind suffer an extinction!" shouted someone deep in the crowd.

People broke out in gasps and cries: "Who's that!?"

"The spy!" Manning called. He had Terra light up areas with search beacons. "Grab 'im when you find 'im!" The spy had finally come out of hiding. That meant that he was streaming *everything* to The World. "Terra, secure the screens and stages!"

Terra holograms appeared and lined up around the room along the base of the towering wall zones. Everything extinguished, except for a few cone-shaped emergency lights, the rainbow cycling ceiling hubs, and the brilliantly humming screen.

Regents and Enforcers were dashing through the room. One cried, "Over here!"

"He's here now!" someone called.

"Grab him!" shouted another Regent. Enforcer firearms

were whining, powering up.

Manning said to his Terra, "Stop him from leaving!"

His Terra disappeared, but then quadrupled around the spy, haloing the intruder under a yellow floodlight.

When he tried to leave the confines of Terra's ceiling laser-net; his color-altering, face-morphing, nano-infused clothing caught fire and began smoking. He fell to the ground rolling and screaming. "Turn it off!" he kept crying.

Enforcers yanked him out of Terra's evolved Firewall hold and unfastened his wrist and neck processors responsible for generating his various disguises. Then they handcuffed him.

"A real chameleon," Manning said, walking up to him, the crowd parting.

"You *all* will *burn* in *hell!*" the spy screamed.

"Your name," Manning said, snapping his fingers and then tossing the processors on top of a hologram stage where Terra began an intense analysis.

"Figure it out yourself." The spy spit at him, the splatter striking Manning's black shiny shoes. The spy said: "What you're going to do—just take off—is damn insane! Everyone's gonna hear about the disaster. Soon, *everything* I got'll stream worldwide."

After wiping the spit on the spy's smoking pants, Manning pulled out his gun.

Jenkens ran up to him. "You're gonna just shoot him?"

People backed away, mumbling and shrieking, and began huddling for safety.

He could hear a few portable devices power down. That meant people were afraid of being shot as well. One reporter stepped on to a robot platform and showed him her Off-Mode wrist processor. "I'm not streaming *anything* to the public, Sir, per *your* orders. That was the condition when you allowed us to remain in here when the catastrophe erupted."

Pointing his gun so that its infrared target struck the defiant spy between his eyes, Manning said: "I *will* use this…and next time, *not* on the ceiling. Circumstances have changed." He had Terra show his face on two high wall-zones opposite the burgeoning IMAX screen. "Here what I said? If you didn't, listen up closely. Things have changed...circumstances *have* changed. I will shoot to kill if anyone jeopardizes our safety." He also opened the Enforcer Grid and said over his wrist device, "Lock and Load...and fire on anyone at my command." As people gasped and then quickly silenced, he deactivated the intensifying firepower. "Get *him* outta my face," he ordered the two Enforcers who were holding the spy. They began dragging his wiggling body toward a pair of double doors.

The spy shouted, "You *can't* leave people here to drown, starve or incinerate!"

"Sedate him," Manning ordered a physician.

"You might stop me," the spy shouted, "but I hope I got out enough info to let people know what you're going to do to them! You're all evil...eeeevvil." He collapsed, out cold.

Manning ordered Enforcers to take him to Station V. "Send him to Neuro Remapping not Rehab...and then give him a new identity, with three months to recuperate. If there's some memory of all this, let me know." As they complied, he had an idea for damage control, and then he told Terra, "Remember yesterday when you located that Tech-No commune?"

Terra streamed the show On Pause to him over his wrist device. "This was 7:10 p.m. to 7:15 p.m., yesterday, Executive Regent Manning," she answered.

Calling Jenkens over as people began returning to their work, he whispered to him, "We have to stop what just happened from spreading."

"Yeah, the guy said he was going to launch what he stole into the matrix," said Jenkens.

Terra's Firewall holograms had extinguished, and the standard numbers of Terras were assisting people throughout the room. His Terra said, "I am confining the grid that Regent Simon Helix utilized to record and stream information to major networks. He infiltrated the White House under that assumed identity; however, his real name is Terrance Zimmer."

Battlefield Matrix

On Stage-2 Right, she began showing them everything about the spy's real identity. "I am streaming this to Station V for analysis and countermeasures."

"And?" Jenkens asked, hedging his way right up into her holographic eyes.

"That grid Mr. Zimmer activated in here is expunged, Regent Jenkens," she replied. "I retained a cipher copy for archival purposes...for future safe perusal as per Regency Recon protocol dated—"

"Got it, Terra," Manning said.

Jenkens pulled Manning to the side. "We'll have mass panic worse than we had during the ozone attacks if people get ahold of all this scattered information that doesn't yet make sense." He pointed to some half pictures on the IMAX screen that still weren't coalescing into recognizable images. "It's as if several mixed up scenes are bubbling up on that thing...through Dr. Holton's device. The public won't buy what we're doing. That crazy guy was partly right." He was breathing as if trying to overcome a flood of carbon dioxide. "They'll blame us—us!—for not informing them. They'll storm the White House...*all* our Regency headquarters!"

"Anarchy erupting around the globe!" Regent Sylvia Itonovich interrupted.

We must counter the damage that the spy said could launch at any time into the matrix," Jenkens said firmly.

Manning fanned down their voices. "I have an idea."

"Whata we do?" Jenkens asked.

He had Terra begin yesterday's show of the assault on the Tech-No commune he had ordered from space that destroying their desert hideout. The entire cave-in of their community lasted twenty minutes. "Terra, stream *this* event to people whom the spy sent *his* information."

"How many people are we talking about?" Jenkens asked her.

"Four holosites at four major networks projected, Executive Regent Manning," Terra said, her eyes remaining green in the analysis. "I am now streaming that show to those hosts."

"We need to stop the spread of *his* data, Terra," Manning began, "so make the spy be one of those men in that underground commune who was hologram-shopping images, hacking into your matrix, and then generating deadly shows. Make *him* be the cause of those hovercraft crashes last month over Lake Michigan."

Jenkens eyes widened. "I remember that! Those pilots were coming in for a landing from several directions. They believed they were approaching a sky platform, but in reality, they flew right into each other. Oh...people have been *furious* over that hack that killed families."

"Messing with The Matrix and causing loss-of-life *should definitely* deem the guy in need of neurological intervention," Regent Sylvia Itonovich said.

In the aftermath of the spy's departure, all the wall-zones and hologram stages had reactivated. Views from around the globe appeared. Data from key science facilities and centers rematerialized. Again, the Press Room was bustling with people streaming information to Elisa and asking for help in weeding out irrelevant prices of The Past for Gem.

Manning's throat felt suddenly sore. He had strained his voice several times to make people listen to him. After Terra flashed his image on those same two screens he had used to threaten the spy, he tested their intercom connection and interrupted everyone. "Okay...the spy's gone. I'm streaming to you *everything* Terra learned about him. Be warned: If you had any part in his misdeeds, Terra will trace your covert grid, root you out, and I will sentence you to the same consequence...that is if I don't blast you first 'cause my patience is wearing thin." Most people were agreeing with him, some were cowering, and a few people reacted with angry hateful expressions. He noticed those disgruntled techs and researchers and gestured for his Terra to monitor them. "I'm sending you my reasons...but look around. We're at a tipping point here...with The Past about to come alive right in front of us. We can't—can't!—have spies, saboteurs and interference when we must learn what's causing our troubles on Earth."

"Yeah—no more power struggles," someone cried.

"Terra stopped the spread of Terrance Zimmer's information," he continued. The crowd settled like a wave of comfort. "Now, the question we need to be asking is this: Whatever show that screen finally gives us, can we stop the catastrophic effects? The earthquakes…the abnormal current patterns. *That's* the trend one probe is reporting early." Those statistics stood out like flares on the wall zones. "Regardless of *any* cause that the screen is about ready to show us, those are the catastrophes The World will experience. They could get worse…much worse. We need to prepare, now." After voices intermingled in a cacophony of wild speculations and ghastly cried of horror, he interrupted them and said boldly: "That spy *did* have a point. I believe all of us in here are on The List for *Sagan*." He stepped on a platform that Jenkens had used to reunite the scientist with his severed arm. Now, he could see over the crowd. "Am I right?"

Most people began agreeing with him, either nodding or saying, "Yes." The facility sounded like a thousand buzzing bees that abruptly silenced. There was not one, 'No,' not even from an Enforcer or a Secret Service Agent. *All* agents and Law Enforcement were on The List.

He continued, "We're looking at disturbances beginning at thirty-six thousand feet below sea level, people!" Through more gasps and mumbling, he said, his voice bellowing over them: "If this is an extinction-level event on the moon and heading Earth's way, it'll be a trickle up extinction instead of a trickle-down one—the opposite of what happened when the ozone depletion event occurred. Round up all the bathymetric charts of the oceans that Terra *doesn't* have. The old ones we can compare to our advanced oceanic maps. Terra can run a simulation of future tectonic activity, seabed and trench movement, and water flow around the globe."

His Terra and the Terra holograms interspersed throughout the room began activating locations where they could find outdated handcrafted maps.

"Stream that order to every oceanic and atmospheric site around the globe," he said. "Get archivists, librarians and curators to stream us *every* map they can find. Upon receipt, sweep them into the matrix. Then Terra can predict possible scenarios of destruction and consequences for life on Earth so that we can help people."

Several Regents and scientists plodded through the crowd and stopped in front of him at the base of the stage. One asked: "Sir, when should *we* leave? When should *we* pack up?"

Another asked: "When do *we* need to hightail it into space?"

"*Where* in space?" many began inquiring.

"Not just yet," Manning snapped. "We're getting some early results, but not conclusive results. Some images from The Past are abnormally mixing on the screen." He directed everyone to continue to sift through what the screen was imaging and that 9:05 p.m. start time. "Wait...just wait. About five more minutes and the probes, Terra, Dr. Holton's Gem, and time/space will give us the cause and effect of what's happening on the moon and the consequences for Earth. *Only then* can we decide what to do. In the meantime, Terra can begin to make a few valid speculations and at least begin to plot some solutions."

As scientists began streaming to one another data on the oceans and inter-planetary forces, Manning didn't even want to think of the possibility that they might not be able to do anything to stop what appeared to be a life-extinction event. He had always believed that if a person could predict a problem, he or she could prevent it from occurring. Obviously, not this time. No matter how hard he tried to allay peoples' fears, one or two would intermittently peek up from their work and yelling: "What if the moon cracks apart? Think that could happen?"

A few people kept dropping to their knees or heaving over wastebaskets, saying they were sick and in need of doctors. They couldn't stop vomiting. The instant they received medication, another would call out for assistance. He finally

Battlefield Matrix

told Terra that the moment she detected those types of abnormal biometrics, she needed to generate a noise-cancelling zone around the distraught person. Wafts of vomit interspersed with inviting smells of foods were circulating through their huge facility. He called in more maintenance crew to insert wall processors to vent in fresh oxygen.

Then he spotted a Regent who had just begun recording incoming images on a hologram stage. A Mars probe had self-repaired and was transmitting vital data. The images began streaming to Gem, which in turn beamed them to the giant screen. Quickly, he ordered an Enforcer to severe the Regent's grid.

"But the simulation is predicting that the moon could break into boulders and dust! I need my family to get to safety!"

Crushing the Regent's wrist device under his foot, Manning said, "You're a Regent...so I'll make an exception." He grabbed a handful of the Regent's shirt, twisting the ripping material in his hand. He felt his breath steamy through his clenching teeth as he lifted the leader to his face. "Don't you think that once we have *every* bit of valuable and necessary data that Second Regulate Jenkens and I won't act immediately to bring in your families and loved ones?"

As the Regent began crying and pleading sorrowfully to him, Manning pushed him away. The Regent slipped back into his work.

"Wow, I thought ya mighta killed Regent Pervis on the spot!" Jenkens handed him an energy drink. "He was just voted in. Poor guy didn't know what the job entailed," he laughed.

"He has much to learn," Manning said, and then he gulped down some of the drink. He said aloud so that the wall-zone blasted his voice, "God—I'm sick of having to fight everyone!" He threw the empty bottle on the floor that a small robot server pinched up in its tiny claws. He felt as if the air in his chest was seeping through his ribs, and he turned and faced Terra. He knew her gaze wouldn't leave his line of sight until he'd direct her next move.

J.P. Osterman

"Executive Regent Manning? Do you have a directive?"

He thought: Do you know what a lunar disaster might do to humanity? Call Ambassador Shaesar! Now!

He then realized that the quantum jingle-line to Nelta had severed, and that the Neltans were most likely slumbering in stasis pods. No way to reach them. And Terra couldn't be a bodily comforter. The matrix just processed facts, projected holographic responses, generated predictive algorithms, emitted intelligent-but-oblique Neltan dialogues and translations, incited human hoopla, and was always providing people with archival database of every movie, stored conversation, scanned word, and recorded human experience that had found a cloud life preserver, independent database, scanner, integrated circuit, or server farm. That's it. Then again, that seemed like everything! This new Terra-III appeared to be everything…except human, what he really needed right now.

Turning away from her, he reached inside a glass, grabbed an ice cube, rubbed it between his hands, threw down the thawing block and started tapping his face with frigid liquid until he could see clearly again. When Jenkens walked up to him with another in-flood of probe images, he told him to add his info to the screen, and then said, "After all *this* mess is over, Steve. I'm heading to *Sagan* to sleep off this nightmare. We'll just have to postpone *our tour* we had scheduled for another day."

"Fine with me." Then Jenkens said: "General Rand and The Manager on Station II said their grids are streaming everything they're receiving into the screen. Look at it now! In a few minutes, we'll have results, and *you'll* have to address The World. After all, *you're* Executive Regent." He exhaled a huff. "I must admit, I don't envy you now. Did yesterday, but not now."

Manning felt like slugging him. Without his "campaign Terra" coaching him on maintaining the proper image and generating a good spin to the public, Jenkens lacked people skills. And now, he was instilling more harm than calm. Then he remembered how to deal with him: give him a task that he could work on, a long task.

More puzzle pieces were flowing from Elisa's Gem to the screen. The radiating light images were now bluish tinged. He overheard a few scientists tell her that they had sifted out problematic images that weren't making sense with that 9:05 p.m. time. Now, a more recognizable show was manifesting. They had solved the problem! They could all see a real lunar picture.

He felt the cold lunar darkness slink through to his muscles. They had just needed more quantum-filter capability. "Steve, as Second Regulate, I'm authorizing you to contact *every* CEO harboring any kind of experimental technology and have them pack it all up."

"*Every* CEO? Pack up *everything*?!"

"Yep—we need to inform *every* private organization what we're discovering about the moon, but only in a Confidential holosite world and without all the drastic scenarios that Terra's running," Manning began.

"What'll I tell 'em?" Jenkens asked, suspiciously. "Why *that, now*?"

"Several of those companies have hardware and software that could help Earth. We don't want people believing we're undertaking some type of conspiracy to keep knowledge from them purposely," he answered.

Jenkens leaned into him a bit and whispered, "But Thornton...we are."

Manning folded his arms. "Some portions yes, but for safety and security reasons."

"And?"

"Some CEOs have been working on *Sagan*'s construction for quite some time," Manning began. "Besides, the more designs we can stream to *Sagan* right now, before we learn of any type of catastrophe, the more technology we'll have that people stuck here won't have. My motive is twofold. It's difficult to keep technology out of the eyesight of The Matrix, but a few companies might just be doing that. We *need* what *they've* got."

Jenkens activated a grid and asked his Terra to interface with him through a holosite projector so he could send out the Call for Technology. "But what information should I *keep* from them?" he asked through an expression of alarm. "As you can see from that wall-zone displaying the White House's main entrance, media crews are at the security barriers, begging Enforcers to let them in. They want personal interviews. They want immediate answers to the king tidal fluctuations and earthquakes. Giving them placating words isn't going to satisfy them when they know something big is occurring." He walked away, dictating the orders to Terra.

Manning realized the gist of what Jenkens had said. Those orders were indeed behaviors reflecting a full-blown governmental conspiracy, but he had no other choice than to begin to speak in terms of survival rather than altruism. Then, he spotted a reading of the Pacific's hadalpelagic zone coming in from one of the many Alvin submersibles. The sudden ebb in current added to the IMAX screen. People around the globe were receiving the interruption in tidal flow because the Caryl Johnson Facility distributed that information worldwide automatically as dictated by the *Transparency Clause.*

Several Regents groaned and gasped at the abnormally rising sea level and currents.

Regent Sylvia Itonovich stepped up to him again. At this early hour of the morning, she looked tired, worn out, and scattered. Her cheeks were flushed and blotchy. She was tapping the area over her heart as if she might have an attack. The hair looked flat and dull like a dyed bright yellow helmet. "Thornton, what if we *can't* contain *the, problem*?" she asked.

Manning put his palms in front of her face. "Let's not go there yet, Sylvia." He repeated that to others who were battering him with the same questions.

With a dour expression on his face, General Rand's image reappeared on Center Stage in front of the screen that was now showing a lunar landscape, a star-filled cosmic quadrant, and *The Spider* in the foreground. A complete show was almost

Battlefield Matrix

finished.

The General said, "Ladies and Gentlemen of The Regency, we are receiving more probe readings from the site where the terrorist's wormhole and the Neltan/Earth wormhole collided." He called open a large hologram that appeared on the stage next to him. "You can see that there is a one-hundred-mile-wide debris field. That's *all* our astrofighters."

People groaned in lament, and Terra began showing the scenes that the probes were transmitting from space. His words were like clickers changing slides. He continued:

"The enemy craft that the wormhole crushed are not—I repeat *not*—among our findings contributing to the lunar fissure. Their craft were utterly destroyed. I just wanted to provide you with proof that this anomaly was not responsible for the disturbances on Earth. However, we are detecting nano-organics in that debris field that The Matrix is gradually gathering into salvage. As soon as we receive the materials on Stations II and III, sift through all the parts, perform an investigation, and replicate all the craft, we *will* present a detailed report."

"That will take days," Manning said.

General Rand agreed.

Then Manning asked: "What about the quadrant in space where the Tech-No Protesters' wormhole went wild...teleporting Coflin's body to Nelta? Is *that* wormhole responsible, in any way, for the king tides and global-wide earthquakes?"

The General panned over to the furthest quadrant in space from Earth that Terra's matrix eyes could illuminate: 51 Astronomical Units. "Nothing's emanating from there either, Sir." He directed the probe's projector to skip towards the sun like a rock bouncing over water at every ten Astronomical Units. "All the experimental Hardware Stops that the Neltars helped us develop, that allowed us to bend space like an accordion so our craft could practice spacefolding, are stable and interference free. No radiation...no gamma...no pulsar, no black hole graviton readings detected that could be hurting

Earth." He stepped away, allowing the elderly Manager on Station II to take Center Stage. "Go on, Dr. Quafah."

A hologram of her appeared next to General Rand's image on Center Stage. "Our two probes in that Tech-No quadrant where *The Heed* activated its wormhole unleashed particle bursts long ago. Yes…energy waves hit the moon, but not with the intensity that could cause such a lunar fissure as we're seeing now. More probes just materialized in stable orbit around the moon and are activating their matrix connections. In two minutes, we should be able to add their data to Dr. Holton's Gem device and Terra should be able to stream them into the screen."

When Terra's eyes flashed green, Manning said, "Terra just included all your data with the show that's forming on the screen."

The forming hologram resolved into a large view of *The Spider*'s interior navigation center. A time stamp appeared as Captain Bartlet's fear-filled face materialized. Then it blurred and dissected into multiple tantagram pieces like a Chinese puzzle.

"Bring that back!" Manning shouted.

Elisa repeated his command into Gem.

Gem responded with one of its tiny blue facets emitting a beam of blue light at the screen. The light began pulsing.

"I believe it wants me to go over there and do something," Elisa said.

Manning and a few Regents ran over to her. "Proceed with caution, Dr. Holton," he said, guiding her slowly toward the currents cycling around the screen.

Her friend Maureen Strickler dashed over to her, raising Elisa's arm by her fingertips as Gem's pulsars intensified. "I got your back, pal."

"Thanks…I sure need you," Elisa sighed.

A gust of static hit them, and Manning yelled over the crazy wind: "We should be inundated with heat, but all I'm feeling is a cool chill. Where's it coming from?"

Terra had been walking behind them but then materialized

Battlefield Matrix

alongside them. She was radiating an orange and indigo glow—a new type of security intervention. "I activated the Shield Protector to cover you. The four forces are circulating around a powerful soliton. That stable soliton wave is the opposite type that opened the portal to Dimension 8." Terra began dividing and then reuniting.

Maureen said: "Space/time is slicing her in half. *Two* realities are vying for her."

"We have to keep moving to the screen," Elisa coached, "or who knows *what* could happen to Gem. It's lining is thickening…it's sharpening too…stinging my arm."

"Gem is being attracted and altered by some interaction between it and the screen," Manning said. "It needs to make direct contact with the screen to stabilize a force that could go rogue and turn catastrophic." He felt his eyes blur through the cool dry wind that appeared to be attacking his very cells. "This flow…I don't get it!"

While dividing and reuniting in intervals of two seconds, Terra said: "The breeze—*breeze*—is the fabric, *ric*, separating—*sep'ing*—you from points—*oint*—in space/time—*ime, ime*." She was talking in a musical round and obviously fighting Time that was like a body stretcher pulling her apart like putty. "If I do not intervene, *vene*, with a photonic Shield, *ield*, Protector, *ector*, The Past, *st*, will sweep—*eep, eep*—you up, *ppp*—"

"Where we could be lost and irretrievable in *any* space/time," Elisa said, pausing, catching her breath, lifting up her left arm into the bottom most portion of the humming and droning screen.

When Gem reached the screen, one of its mounds stretched out like rubber and touched it. Gem blasted several green flashes of light into Terra's white eyes. Her doubles united, and she returned to her solid virtual form. "No, Dr. Holton," corrected Terra, "*I* am here."

"Thanks…thanks." At the base of the giant screen, Elisa stopped and let Gem rest on the frame, where an infusion of particle brilliance appeared to rejuvenate the glowing armband.

A glowing yellow facet slurped out of the bronze gilded

armband into the screen. The long base began illuminating cycling rainbows, and the screen returned the slices-of-life show from The Past.

"*The Spider* and Captain Bartlet!" cried Elisa as colors on the frame danced with dazzling intensity.

Guiding her and Maureen back to the safety zone, Manning said, "At any moment, we should have an entire episode of what occurred on the moon that is causing all these earthquakes and king tidal disturbances."

From Military Station III, General Rand and his team were still appearing on Center Stage. Their voices filled with celebration. "The lab probes are in place above the far side of the moon...finally! They're now transmitting data to us that we're streaming into the new military-research grid for your Confidential viewing. All probes are working in unison, and analyzing *everything* on the moon and within 1 AU around it, including cosmic noises, topography, geometric statistics and temperature variations."

Terra said, "I am conducting a comparative analysis."

Elisa again extended Gem toward the large space/time screen. The breeze generating from the energy exchange was making her hair and clothes wave. Maureen rushed up to her, steadying her. Pieces of their sleeves and the hems of their clothes began flickering in and out of existence. Elisa called: "Gem, you did a good job sifting out everything irrelevant. Now show us what happened. But this time, give us an inside perspective from *The Spider*'s navigation."

When a fuzzy show began playing with a tiny spider as a stowaway inside a craft, she said, "No—not this, Gem!"

"That's from the 1969 Sea of Tranquility landing," Jenkens said.

"A spider was inside the lunar module with Armstrong and Aldrin?" a Regent asked.

When the room stilled—except for the droning screen currents—Elisa repeated the important day and time into the green, glowing, crinkled patch covering her pulse point. It was the location of Gem's nano-organic cerebral processor. "I need yesterday, on the far side of the moon, February 27, 9:15 p.m., EST." As Gem responded with a radiance of cycling rainbows, she added, "In a few moments, everything that began occurring at *that* time and at *that* location inside *The Spider* we should begin to see on the screen."

"All the new probe data should be incoming to you," General Rand said.

Over several stages, images appeared of various perspectives of the lunar fissure.

"Could this be terrorist related? Some last resort they left when they escaped...to kill us, General?" Manning asked.

The screen was showing an enemy craft landing on the moon with the stolen tropopause panel under its turret.

Manning felt hot anger. "That theft almost caused the tropopause shield to fizzle—"

"Yesterday, at 4:02 p.m., EST," Terra said.

"Faster, Gem. That's not the occurrence either," Elisa said, and then Gem radiated another string of rainbows into the screen.

The show began fast-forwarding.

"No way and in *no* form, Sir, could terrorism have caused the lunar fissure," General Rand said firmly. He looked determined to fix past mistakes by responding to Manning's questions rapidly. "Our engineers—"

"And *our* researchers," added Dr. Quafah from Station II.

"Yep," General Rand snapped, "*All* workers at *Station X* inside Olympus Mons broke through this nasty interference that been holding us all back from communicating. Everything they have is streaming into the screen. All the messages we received during the time before the wormhole collapsed— killing the terrorists—to the time our Stealth Force craft escaped. We've even locked on that Dimension 8 from where that Halite Being emerged."

"Don't' even touch that force!" Manning shouted.

As General Rand agreed, Terra stepped up and said: "I have included all that data, images, and instrumental reading for the space/time screen." More Terras appeared in front of the screen, their eyes turning on Gem, shimmering through a steady flow of puzzle pieces interlocking on the screen. "I am adding processing power," Terra said.

The screen's fast-forward began intensifying.

The green, crystalline Halite Being appeared briefly.

Elisa Holton told Gem: "Rewind. You've gone too far!"

The flow reversed—the images sliding backwards in time.

As the stream of 3D information slowed, General Rand said, "When CERN captured enough negative matter and bombarded it with a neutrino burst, scientists *safely* reactivated Dimension 8."

"What'd ya get outta doin' that!" Manning gasped.

"We realized that an inter-dimensional disturbance had nothing to do with the fluctuation in our ocean currents," Rand replied. "Dimension 8 did *not* cause the disturbances on Earth." He shook his head in apparent frustration. "Thus far, we've found *nothing* on Earth or in those quadrants in space that could have instigated earthquakes or king tidal disturbances. I'm sending everything to you from where we saw the Halite Being again."

"And now the screen has what *we've* gleaned lately," Dr. Quafah said from Station II.

General Rand gave a hard tug to his green uniform. "Ladies and Gentlemen, I am confident that whatever is occurring, we can attribute to some type of horrible lunar event."

Manning said, "Keep our probes analyzing the moon then, General." After General Rand and Dr. Quafah agreed, he turned to everyone in the room and shouted, "People!"

The speakers echoed his voice.

Everyone stopped and stood statue like. Only the swishing and gliding sounds of streaming images were resounding, as from a continuous autumn gust.

"Something caused that disturbance, and we need to know how to stop it," Manning began. "If we have nothing concrete to present to the public, soon, people will assume that the moon's ripping apart, or might blow apart. There'll be an insane rush for *every* shuttle to hightail it off Earth. Global chaos!" He told Terra: "Holosite all the owners of astrocraft and all astrocraft companies. Direct to send all their orbit-equipped craft to maintenance sites. That way, people will think something is wrong with the craft and leave them alone. *We* decide who needs to leave and when...everyone in this room will though, of course."

Another Regent yelled through the mayhem, "I own a renovated craft that can hold ten people and remain in orbit with gravity flooring for three months without needing fission rod refueling or food restocking." Several others echoed the same. They were people of wealth.

"Good...get 'em ready and on standby," Manning said, opening views of several old helipads, airstrips, and small airfields. Send 'em to the secure airport outside of McLean. That's the closest one. But keep them in secured locations." On their portable devices, they began following through with his suggestions. General Rand and Dr. Quafah began collaborating on survival protocols and emergency accommodations on their space stations.

Manning put them on total Lock Down. More now than the past few days, he felt helpless. All the previous events that had occurred had homed in on specific people, direct targets, specific locations, but not the entire Earth!

The Neltans were gone. Help from an advanced alien civilization was gone.

Most dreadfully, whatever was occurring had the potential to incite unobstructed chaos—even more so than the terrorist bombs of 2057. There weren't enough craft to launch and house the 2 billion off-Earth. There weren't enough space stations equipped with the power to sustain an entire 2 billion! Or subterranean safe havens on Earth, or Martian colonies...as if *anyone* would want to live for long periods underground on Earth or off-Earth, to push their limits over harsh terrain, or endure survivalists conditions with limited gravity that could fail at any time, with limited evacuation plans, food and drink.

He realized that Humanity could be at its ending point...even for most on The List of Survivors who would remain on Earth in secure quarters. When the survival instinct would kick in, people would surely storm every craft capable of sustaining life in space to ditch a flooding, freezing, or careening Earth that might leave its Green Zone for a rogue, black course in space…if, *if* such a catastrophe was in progress.

Then, he realized he might be engaged in hyperbole—exaggerating an innocuous lunar event that their new technology could easily mend: high-yield augers and nickel core infusions, to name a few. When all the virtual pieces of *The Spider* and the moon would unite in one coherent starting point—soon—the screen could begin showing with the facts. He gulped huge draughts of cold air. He felt dizzy. The objects around him appeared marvelously sharp and clear. Some thing, particle, or energy in the screen had triggered an ability to tune in brilliantly with all the objects around him. The new ability was energizing him—giving him the drive to accumulate facts while blocking off his emotions. Nothing predicting certain-and-utter devastation was in front of him. A feedback loop began cycling through his thoughts: Every problem, no matter how portentously disastrous, has a solution. I just gotta keep hunting for the causes then find solutions. Think solution!

Suddenly, on the screen, a cloudy view of the lunar surface materialized.

Elisa said: "Gem, where's *The Spider*? And fine tine the show, please."

When the screen stopped scrolling fuzzy foreground pixels, *The Spider* materialized. Behind the astrofighter, extending to the left and to the right, were multiple reflections of *The Spider* that seemed to extend into eternity.

Manning said: "The picture reflections to the left appear to be moving into The Past and those to the right leading to The Present. They're facets in space/time."

"Real slices of actual events," Jenkens added.

Manning stepped on top of the robotic platform that lifted him into the air. Two high wall-zones were projecting him so everyone could get a good view of him and the burgeoning show. "We're recovering what happened on the moon. We're re-cementing a *true* reality." He ordered Terra to activate her new yellow/indigo protective barrier in front of the screen. "I want to take no chances that something might come out of this situation and strike us."

"'Cause no one'll be able to retrieve you into The Present!" a reporter shouted, and then two Regents gave him permission to begin recording the event for the matrix archives.

Jenkens said, "This is the time before Captain Bartlet fired the Globule weapon."

A scientist in the back jumped on top of a robotic platform and yelled: "I don't know about all of you, but I can't look when that enemy craft shoots down *The Spider*. I can't watch it. I just can't." She jumped down, crying, and her colleagues began comforting her.

"Our best and brightest was surprised and killed by our *own* technology that the enemy stole and used against us," shouted another.

"Yes—*The Spider* exploding was awful," Regent Sylvia Itonovich began. Others rallied with her in agreement. "And people around the globe are still in shocked and bewilderment that our heroes are dead. We need to make this a tribute…for them…for all our fallen heroes." Some people asked Manning if they could record the show to use only for memorializing or eulogizing their dead heroes.

Manning knew a different possibility for The Captain and his crew. They were now on *Sagan*, and his Clone Techs on Stand By, waiting for further orders that he'd deliver to them later when he'd meet them on the astrocity.

Terra's voice resounded on a loud speaker: "9:15 p.m., Eastern Standard Time, February 27, 2068."

Manning checked the current time, and Terra showed him some events that had occurred on Earth at that same time. "That was over four hours ago, everyone," he began, his voice echoing through the darkened room. A few people clapped and moaned in relief—cathartic gestures and expressions. He continued: "The small interval between then and now means we should get a good read on what happened. I do know that I had ordered *The Spider* to hunt down that terrorist cell that had been in hiding beneath the surface. So *this* 9:15 p.m. time *is* the moment…and *this* location on the moon *is* the site where some type of disaster occurred."

"A catastrophe had to happen here somewhere," General Rand maintained, "because it's nowhere else."

Manning said, "Okay, Dr. Holton, order Gem to start the show." Before he hopped off the robot platform, he said: "Everyone…you can make a personal recording of this, but don't stream it outta this room without my approval. Yes, you may use snippets of the show in a memorial, but only after I approve the edit." Through an exceptionally large drone from the screen's stabilizing frame, he whispered to his Terra: "I want this entire show classified Top Secret. Interfere with their recordings and make them unrecognizable. But *you* capture and store the show in your *Sagan* matrix."

"One new grid…grid 84 activating, Executive Regent Manning," she replied.

After the room stilled and the resonating sounds of portable tablets subsided, Elisa said softly and slowly into her glowing Gem, "Presentation-mode, begin."

The wall-zones rippled into the most advanced acoustical speaker system as the ceiling and floor morphed into a virtual black-and-white grid.

"Elisa inhaled and exclaimed, "This is like standing in my own virtual grid, except this feels like we're about to be swept right inside *The Spider!*"

People quickly gathered in stalks of huddling bodies. Some began holding hands; others were grabbing onto clothing as if clenching survival ropes.

Beyond the astrofighter, a view of the Earth materialized; and behind the Earth, the sun. Below *The Spider* appeared a long flat enclave in the lunar surface. To the distant far right of the location and hidden inside a camouflaged precipice was a small, concealed enemy craft.

"Stability holding in quantum relativity," Terra announced

Battlefield Matrix

after a rainbow exchange of light information from Gem.

The facility stilled, and the time stamp appeared at the base of the screen: 9:17 p.m., EST.

He could see from some dust and debris kicking up from the lunar surface that *The Spider* was in the midst of a cosmic battle. Gem's focus fixed on the interior of the astrofighter.

Chapter 17

Grand Descent

Captain Robert Bartlet, Commander were the words that appeared on the entryway to the astrofighter's grand Navigation helm. Gem had rendered the entire live-stream scene of The Past on Pause-mode. The towering wall-zones were streaming live lunar scenery, environmental stats, and The Spider's biometrics. The giant hologram stage was displaying the un-camouflaged surface area under which the matrix had indicated the last terrorist cell was holding up. Around the stage, Robert Bartlet and his First Chair Crew appeared shock-frozen in time—their bodies and faces radiating their last profound expressions as they stood motionless at the threshold of exhaling their last moments of life.

Captain Robert Bartlet's uniform was Stealth Force starch perfect—beige with shiny brass bars on his collars. He had wet creases in his shirt, under his neck and armpits...unusual for him. Overseeing his entire crew, he was standing between his high-tech chair and the Glow Frame of *The Spider*'s

Battlefield Matrix

hologram stage suspended beneath Terra's beehive ceiling hub. The screen's Still-mode had halted the powerful, rainbow processor now displaying the sheen of one solid beautiful rainbow throughout the helm, giving the sterile Navigation zone a majestic aura. In the background, Terra's many helpful forms were yellow streaks of processing lights suspended in midair like ministering angels waiting to whisper messages to the crew.

Robert Bartlet's short black hair shone with smooth gel slickness over his ears, except for the few sweat-laden stragglers that looked like frayed strings on his forehead. With a look of cold surprise in his frozen blue eyes, he had his arms rigidly extended outward in anticipation of holding or clutching someone or something close by but out of reach. He had a longing aspect about him, with a slight pinging of teary-eyed redness that appeared ready to release all his memories in one final battle cry of, "Try harder—again!" His entire body exuded regret and accomplishment: his empty arms revealing a life void of intimacy yet fulfilled with a steady flow of respect from his crew. Situated around the Glow Frame, he had his First-Chair Crew in sight: Beth Tufter, Bill Wallum and EJ. He had handpicked his "Knights of his Round Table" as he often called them. Now, in their final battle moments, they all appeared bonded to one cause: to protect *The Spider* and win World War III. Far behind him below all the wall zones were his Second Chair crewmembers, appearing to be surrendering to an impossible and overwhelming force. They had their heads bowed over their tilt-n-rock cubicles, their hands clenched to miniature Glow Frames and their lips devoted to obvious prayer.

Still camouflaged, *The Spider* was experiencing trouble even though the matrix was showing amble processing ability. That intensity was deceptive. Obviously, surging plasma energy from the fission-fusion turret rods was depleting living conditions and matrix flow to hold the astrofighter's position. Clad in her Standard Image of the androgynous, brown-haired, athletic presence, only one Terra was processing. Her eyes glowing dull green, she was standing alongside Captain Bartlet, her *Proceed with Caution* assessment of the lunar landscape flaring at the base of his high-tech station. Behind her, the grand hologram stage had displayed its final virtual rendering of the lunar surface that looked like the gently rolling bed at the bottom of a sandy ocean. In reality, that deceptive cold landscape with its subtle surface bumps was the enemy's subterranean hideout. The frozen information hovering behind Captain Bartlet on his high-tech station indicated that he couldn't connect with General Rand to collaborate but he believed he could kill the enemy...

"Something *awful's* about to happen here!" Manning proclaimed, bowing his head at the show as a shot of despair overwhelmed him. "Let's not stall here...proceed, Dr. Holton, go!"

Pointing Gem at the interactive screen, Elisa Holton ordered, "Play, Gem," as she touched two, bright crystalline processors on the armband. The imaging puzzle pieces on the screen broke apart but reassembled into a new picture after a flash of Rewind. The combined energies reached into the past and captured the entire space/time sequence of the entire lunar disaster. The show began again...

Captain Robert Bartlet motioned for Beth and Bill to synchronize the Globule weapon with the fission-fusion rods. Informing the rest of the crew of the impending weapons fire, EJ began streaming icons throughout the astrofighter. Over the hologram stage, the crew was monitoring everything happening outside. *The Spider* lurched slightly over the gray lifeless terrain and stopped over a green biometric zone that Terra had outlined as the target. At her Captain's battle call, *The Spider* was in position to fire on the enemy. Like the sleek predatory nature of its arachnid namesake, the ship continued its surreptitious descent.

Captain Bartlet directed, "Down...a little more...one yard more—"

The Spider's camouflaged pace was unrelenting in the -153° Celsius vacuum of space.

Battlefield Matrix

He began talking into a Recording beam that illuminated on the side of his Glow Frame. "In forty-five seconds, we'll activate the Gamma Globule weapon for a full-scale assault on their hideout. We've finally managed to locate this bad terrorist cell through the plasma emissions the others left behind when they escaped. I ordered other craft that were supporting us to leave and hunt them down. We can take out this thieving murderous crew for good!" With a hateful and revengeful expression on his face, he exhaled—his fists clenched, his eyes squinting into the visuals of the lunar terrain illuminating in holographic rhythms like a poem. "Terra just picked up and isolated an outmoded, Linux SIGINT interruption signal in the Neltan/Earth wormhole vicinity. The terrorists are definitely congregating there, planning a mass exit outta the solar system. With us destroying this cell here and our best astrofighters taking out the forces there, we believe we can kill their entire army and end this war for good." He had a happy optimistic expression on his face, a tomorrow-will-be-brighter smile. "Finally—Terra lead us to this place. Her matrix was *finally* able to unmask their demon Terra and locate biometric vital signs right below us. We've got human bodies down there—the enemy for sure! We're certain of it this time! We're gliding in to take 'em out in Stealth-mode; but before I give the order to fire our new globule weapon, I'm double checking a few things. Terra is measuring high-particle radiation readings. The Chinese were doing some catalytic cracking on the south basin, but Terra shows that industry stopped when their colony found nothing. Firing the globule weapon with lanthanides bleeding out around us could blow the moon to smithereens and we don't want that!" He laughed through an expression of facetious blundering.

Lieutenant Bill Wallum interrupted: "Sir, the spectral analysis of this area projects no contraindications for firing our Globule weapon."

Bartlet replied: "Good, Bill. Increase its intensity to maximum."

J.P. Osterman

EJ sent him a tiny icon of the Globule weapon that looked like a shimmering, emerald-cut diamond on the turret of *The Spider*. The tiny model materialized alongside The Captain who enlarged it for the recording. "This is what it looks like, but it's true scale is five feet, by two-by-two. Its gamma power is in the embedded organics that'll release on my command. Beth Tufter sent you the specs so our additive manufacturers can produce more the future."

"Sir," EJ interrupted, "xenon and helium ionization surrounding the gamma processor are at maximum."

"Globule is ready for fire, Sir," Bill announced.

"Beth—are you streaming this recording to The Regency as well as to General Rand?" Bartlet asked.

She showed him Navigation's green Record-icon. "*Everything* we're doing *should* be streaming to both. Whether they're receiving this, Terra isn't registering Reception, so I can't know for certain whether we can image the firing of the Globule weapon to them."

The navigation stage was displaying the site of the Globule's projected zone of impact—two miles long and a quarter-mile wide, but the depth read, *Unknown*. The terrorist cell appeared to sink deeply, like termite tunnels, and widely, like a long Air Lane Skyway.

"Sir—I'm receiving an escalating cosmic disturbance," Beth said, her eyes reflecting the light blue waves of interference.

"Where the hell's *that* comin' from?" EJ scoffed, "'cause I'm getting a sorta whipping wave translation. I've never heard anything like it in my life!"

"Hunker down for impact!" Bill shouted, strapping himself in.

Pacing in front of the hologram stage depicting close-knit frequency waves akin to a racing heart, Bartlet said: "Break the whipping motion down. Let's see it…see if the incoming force has the potential to interact with the gamma aftermath of the Globule weapon burst."

"I'm trying, Sir, but this energy's way outta our scope and off the charts." Bill had the Sloan Sky Survey panning zones around Mars and two quadrants beyond the red planet.

The waves suddenly slowed and combined into 2D readings than began pulsing in a high-pitched musical tune of high C minor.

Bill's shocked face was reflecting the shine of the white readings. "Terra is indicating that the noise is most likely emissions resulting from our forces in a heated skirmish against the terrorists alongside the Neltan/Earth wormhole."

EJ interjected, "I bet Regent Manning's sure pissed at that!"

"The wild wave configurations are the massive numbers of hulls un-camouflaging for battle," Terra said, multiplying into several various forms to assist the crew. "But the high-frequency signal is a different power...a pulsar power that could blast the solar system with destructive radioactivity."

Everyone in the helm gasped, and Beth sent out a warning to Earth and the space stations. "Even if they can't hear us, I'm streaming down a protective measure for Earth into the tropopause shield. Whether they know it or not, they're gonna get hit by radioactivity, but this command to reinforce the shield should reach Earth before any terrible radioactivity can undo the good that The Matter Stream Sample has done."

Bartlet ordered: "Send an Echo, RFC code into that quadrant in space so we can receive a true picture of what's about to occur. I don't know *what* this means for our lunar Globule assault though." With a skeptical look pinching across his face, he appeared to doubt Terra's most recent repair on Station III to expunge all harmful matrix viruses and update to the most advanced Firewall version. After Terra complied, he returned to his Recording beam and said: "We're streaming all this through SpyWare to you, but we've heard nothing in return. I can't wait any longer to attack. We risk losing the enemy and this last cell returning to Earth and attacking you...right at the onset of the most important meeting with the Neltans." He pulled forward a small hologram of the Neltan/Earth wormhole that was quantum streaming from Nelta to Earth through spacefolding intergalactic connections. "We must act. We need to hold constant this quantum-communication wormhole. We *must* fire the Globule weapon and destroy this bad cell before they can interfere and stop Final Communication...*now*."

Beth enlarged a communication icon—amplifying *The Spider's* reception in space. She swept the icon toward the ceiling hub above the hologram stage where the matrix processed it. "I'm streaming these topographical scans, spectroscopic readings, cosmic surveillance readings, and biometric readings from the lunar surface with your recording, Sir. Thus far, on the surface, *The Spider* isn't detecting any enemy craft that could be aware of us or our messages. We're creeping up on 'em, Sir. I'm sure we'll down 'em for good this time, with *no* escapes."

"Yep—this time we're gonna blow 'em into the cosmic vacuum, Sir!" EJ clapped excitedly.

Beth added: "Our Camouflage-mode is holding...but I'm showing that the static's beginning to reveal *The Spider*...oh no."

Damn!" Bartlet exclaimed. "Terra, reinforce all communications grids. We can't have Terrorists know our directionality or breach the matrix."

"What is this darn new static? Bill—ya able to translate it into any frequency visuals?" asked Beth.

Bill stopped from manipulating the Rainbow Interpreter responsible for rendering all things cosmic and nanoscopic, visual and verbal. "Nope—but the dark energy the hull is soaking up to help protect the ship is emitting a lot of power and—"

The walls began crackling.

"What the heck!?" Bartlet bellowed.

Terra's rainbow-cycling hub began vibrating. Electricity arched through Navigation like active Tesla coils zapping at full blast. Extinguishers popped. The hologram stage hissed like water extinguishing flames.

"This is high electromagnetic interference!" Beth said, holding her ears, and then she activated another noise reducer. Two maintenance personnel with robotics dashed in and began making repairs. "Wow—could all this wild activity and radiation be originating from the Decagon system that's capturing and processing the Earth/Neltan wormhole?"

"Do something to counter the wave, or graviton influx, in case the source *is* the Decagon, or *we* could go down with the terrorists," shouted Bartlet. "I don't wanna make *us* the weapon."

The navigation stage suddenly darkened, its Glow Frame brightened to an intense green. In the center appeared the white-bright image of a flashing thread of light.

"Wormhole whiplash incoming," Terra's voice resounded. "Retreat recommended, Captain Bartlet." She materialized alongside him, her green eyes dimming.

"What the hell?" EJ screamed.

"No way, Terra!" cried Beth.

Bill turned abruptly in his chair—his face white, his hair tossed by angry strokes of his fingers. "A wormhole whiplash? Must be several conduits converging! Hell—we're dust if *that* thing hits us!"

Captain Bartlet shouted: "Terra, spacefold us outta here to avoid the conflagration."

"That blinding cosmic rip looks like friggin' lightning in space!" Beth said, tapping up icons over her station that they might be able to activate to shield themselves without retreating.

"Minutes away...*minutes* away," EJ said, her petite shoulders sagging.

"We can't leave, Sir," Bill said, "we just can't." He was swiping through virtual icons in search of another solution.

"Terra—*move* us behind the nearest crater containing the highest concentration of titanium and iron," Bartlet ordered. "And I don't intend to leave, Lieutenant Wallum. Not yet."

As *The Spider* ascended and redirected, Terra appeared on stage next to the image of the whiplashing wormhole. "Captain, an engine boost to spacefold from *this* position will interact with the sun's helium and boomerang into Earth's atmosphere." She showed the aftermath and then extinguished it, but the aftermath of the Globule weapon firing during the wormhole whiplash appeared worse: dust and particles erupting from the far side of the moon.

Beth was sweeping icons into *The Spider*'s weapons section that was blaring a red warning. "I can't shut down the Globule weapon. We have ten seconds before it fires on the target, Sir. I can't stop it from spiking…can't…trying but can't."

"Then pull the damn plug!" Bartlet grabbed the plasma gun from his chair and fired a burst of energy at the Gamma weapon's green Ready ignition bar. Smoke and flames erupted at several cubicles and Glow Frame stations. The extinguishers unleashed their waterpower. The crew began coughing and wheezing.

"The Globule weapon's firing! Take cover!" Bartlet shouted.

"We could destroy Earth!" EJ cried. With several wrist processors gripped tightly in her hands, she began running toward the hologram stage, appearing ready to hurdle over the frame into the yellow projector light. The processors looked like long colorful ribbons, but they were really icons of countermeasures she had conjured but lacked the time to fling them at Terra one-at-a-time for analysis.

Then, her image froze in space/time: 9:30 p.m., EST. Gem put EJ on Pause-mode.

Meanwhile, as the drone of the gamma Globule weapon resonated as it activated, Lieutenant Bill Wallum had managed to strap himself into his hover-tech station. Several Matrix Techs had their arms around him, their cheeks pressing into his back and shoulders. He had them tightly enmeshed in his care while breathing in their gathering breaths.

Gem put his image on pause and panned over to Beth Tufter.

As Bill had yielded his last exhale to the yellow explosion of oxygen unleashing throughout the great astrofighter, *The Spider*, Beth had been running toward Captain Bartlet and had almost reached his requited outstretched arms. With tear-filled eyes and a longing expression of love glowing across her aching

Battlefield Matrix

face, she was an inch away from his arms; but Terra—standing alongside The Captain with her weak green eyes—had linked their touches in a final burst of blue explosive light.

Then, the entire show stopped with glaring light and metal shards bursting through the Navigation center. Gem changed perspectives to the outside lunar surface.

The terrorists' subterranean hideout burst wide-open, pelting dust and rock into space. The pummeled ground appeared like an outstretched canyon—its long narrow bottom a river of floating and spinning metals, plastics, and pieces of jagged furniture. Now and then, a few torn and mangled body parts hit *The Spider*'s fading electromagnetic shield, disintegrating even the bones. The lack of atmosphere began twisting the debris and water from the stronghold into a coalescing icy ring around the moon.

The terrorists' destroyed bunkers lay in a concave mess of shards on the lunar surface.

"Captain Bartlet killed off this entire terrorist cell," said Jenkens, "except for one small enemy craft he couldn't see...the one that fired on *The Spider* and downed it." He pointed at the nose of a small triangular vessel jutting out of a niche in a mountain of trash that the Chinese Excavation Company had purposely launched to the far side to spare resources.

Manning groaned. "Looks like that's where the terrorists situated their craft on purpose, between the time I spoke to The Captain yesterday and the time he returned to wipe them out. They concealed it among some rare elements so *The Spider*'s matrix would distinguish it from the surrounding lunar terrain."

General Rand appeared on Stage-1 Right. He asked that Gem continue the show but on slow motion. As the live-stream event activated onscreen, he began to narrate *The Spider*'s fall from the vacuous lunar skyline:

"As the Gamma Globule weapon fired, the small enemy craft fired four plasma bursts into the base of *The Spider*. That last strike took out Navigation, but not before *The Spider* automatically countered with torpedo fire that struck the enemy vessel...a coup de main."

"Enough talk, please, General. Let's just watch the end in silence. Dr. Holton, please have Gem continue the show but on normal display," Manning ordered. "Anyone who doesn't want to watch or see...too bad. This astrofighter and its crew meant—meant a lot to me."

Through whimpering and thick laments resounding through the room, processing lights from the stages and ceiling hubs once again ignited, and The Past resumed its normal Live Stream-mode...

The base of *The Spider* flared yellow and white as its fission-fusion chambers and oxygenated rooms unleashed their matter. Bleeding out wavering, hot plasma fuel, the mighty astrofighter began its slow glide-of-death toward a lake of unstable stones. They were voiceless erosions of jagged millennia, perhaps harboring alien life, but now the gravel beds of ancient comets. Among them crashed *The Spider* in a silent burst of metal obscured by the rising view of Earth eclipsed by lunar dust. In the background, streaks of lunar dust were erupting.

Interrupting several expressions of despair and grief, Elisa said softly, after a hologram message arrived over Gem from Station II: "An expert in simulations said that Captain Bartlet and his crew died well before *The Spider* crashed. When we saw body parts, they weren't from anyone onboard *The Spider*. There are no survivors on the moon."

Gem had the show paused on a long jagged crack in the lunar landscape. An energy force beneath the moon's surface was venting dust and rock like slow-moving conveyor.

Battlefield Matrix

Chapter 18

Smoke Screen

Inside the Press Room, the giant screen hissed and went blank in preparation for the next space/time command. Terra counteracted the intense round of static as Regents and scientists began moaning and lamenting the loss of *The Spider* crew.

"Dr. Holton, is that the end?" Manning asked.

Jenkens plopped down in a front-row chair. "That was the end." He had an expression that implied he'd never recover.

Elisa said into the armband device, "Stop, Gem, but hold and prepare to start after you receive and process more data."

Several scientists ran up to Manning and a few Regents. They showed them blueprints and specs they had received from Station III and those Terra finished processing on the Research Station. Fanning through a few quickly, Manning said: "We finally received the statistics on the Gamma Globule weapon that Ms. Tufter said they had streamed to us from The Spider but that got lost in interference. Those will add to the show and tell us exactly what happened at that moment the explosion occurred outside The Spider."

Lights in the room brightened. Several hologram stages burgeoned with graphs, frequencies, date-and-time signatures and spectroscopic readings.

Jenkens called over a scientist whose advanced tablet was receiving quantum light beams. "What's this?"

Elisa glided Gem over the scientist's portable q-pad.

"This is interpreted data from the matrix and the screen," the scientist replied.

A close up image of matter spewing out of a giant fissure appeared on the IMAX screen.

"It's the moon! Looks like the Grand Canyon opened up there!" Manning cried. "See these results? The moon looks cracked the entire way through to the core!"

Jenkens said, "The Spider's matrix predicted this…but the crew couldn't stop or adjust the weapon's intensity."

A scientist called: "They were focused on exploding that subterranean hideout."

"They eliminated the terrorists, but now we have a bigger problem," someone shouted.

As everyone in the room gasped in fright, horror and dismay, Elisa ordered Gem: "Display all lunar statistics in ninety-degree increments."

The screen began imaging four separate views of lunar fissures. Dust and rock were erupting, or trickling, or drizzling out of each one.

"The Moon will self-destruct if this reaction continues," Terra said.

"When!?" hollered people.

"I am measuring and calculating," Terra responded. Through gasps and shrieks of fright, she divided into four forms and reappeared in front of the four displays.

Several Regents shouted, "The public!"

"Whata we do?" cried others.

"What'll we tell people!?" Several scientists began calling out solutions.

Battlefield Matrix

Manning blasted out one order: "Terra—block all communications!" Through laments and a cacophony of chatter, he said, "Nothing streams outta this room. Lock the doors, except for those I allow in and out."

Wall clamps burrowed into the doorjambs. The weather-stripping sealed. Bounding for the double doors, some people began quarreling, screaming for help and punching one another.

"Let us outta here! Now!" cried several people.

"No! Stop!" Manning countered. When no one complied, he pulled out his gun and fired into the ceiling, again. After the turmoil and confusion halted, he said: "Terra, prepare your Standard Emergency Alert to the public. But we need to add to the protocols already in place. That's what we're going to stream to The World, our Take Shelter in Your Designated Safe Haven broadcast, but add another condition: "Be prepared to seek refuge deeper underground." As some people knelt in despair and shock, others plopped down into the plush red chairs like falling dominoes. Manning called Security to send away all the reporters who were holding up in the corridors and waiting for interviews. He directed them to gather in the White House's main reception arena where he was planning to live-stream his updated global broadcast after Terra inserted additions. Then he jumped on the robotic platform and said so that everyone inside the locked-down Press Room facility could hear: "I have an idea that'll buy us time to leave while the matrix runs several simulations on the lunar event. But speaking impulsively and leaving here on wings of fear will only get us killed."

"They wouldn't dare do that 'cause they need us," called a Regent.

"That's right," he affirmed. "They need us to get to Nelta on *Sagan*—on *Sagan*." He pointed at the star-like object in the sky. "A fully constructed Sagan that someone can't blast to smithereens and destroy. Then we need to return with technology that'll save the moon, possibly save the Earth and humanity."

"That's if people'll be here when we return in two thousand years!" Regent Itonovich exclaimed. She was assisting Elisa and Gem's interaction with the matrix to form various predictive calculations of the lunar catastrophe. Several Terras had copying like dividing mitochondria as lunar data continued to collect from the past and present. The Standard Terra was taller among them all. She was at the center—the obvious conductor of correlations and differential comparisons.

As people began bombarding him with more questions and angry expletives, he ordered four Secret Service agents to activate four robot-projectors and expand the center wall zone. That improvement would create one, large, emergency live-stream network with matrix power capable of interrupting each individual's holosite address on-Earth and off-Earth. Immediately, the zone flashed an outline of its history—from its inception as The Emergency Broadcast System, to its expansion as Station WBET after First Communication, and its matrix update as The Emergency Alert System.

Manning shouted, "Quiet, everyone and listen to me."

As he continued to still the restless crowd, Jenkens ordered robot servers to pass around food and drinks. "Eat something and drink plenty of water," Jenkens prodded, making his way through several rows of people. "We have to keep up our strength. We all have a long night—I mean morning—ahead of us." He was panting, his face red and his droopy eyelids gray from lack of sleep and mounting stress. As everyone continued to lament, worry, and sicken over the moon's calamitous condition, he shouted: "Everyone! Hey!" He whistled like a hunter-master retrieving his bloodhounds. "We all know that Executive Regent Thornton Manning is the World's best impromptu orator...that he's always managed to de-escalate public panic, or nip-it-in-the-bud." All heated discussions stalled. "So let's calm down and hear his address to The World." As virtual Terras began disappearing in automated response to peaceful conditions, he continued: "We're all in this lunar disaster together. And you're realizing now, as I am...and I'm completely in a state of shock like all of

Battlefield Matrix

you...that we are about to embark on a new mission. Conditions have gone south, and only we know about the widespread catastrophe happening on the moon." He repeated those words forcefully, pointing to the many gathering images on the IMAX screen. "Only we know that Terra has projected that the moon might rip apart." He gulped dry air and wiped his sweat-dappled forehead. "Let Executive Regent Manning direct us on our new mission and informing the public. Let's hear his idea."

"The mission's definitely changed beyond just helping the Neltans!" several people cried.

Jenkens exclaimed, "Yes—but I trust that Thornton Manning will lead us in that new direction." As a host introducing a performer, he gestured in introduction towards Manning.

Manning felt the ceiling light strike his eyes—a floodlight of inviting leadership. He stepped up to the calling.

Jenkens said, "Now, let's support him as he gives a speech to The World."

Through a brief silence and thanking Jenkens, he called for Terra to alter the wall-zone network to generate a fifteen-degree view of him and hide everything else in the expanded bustling room. The zones' photon-crystalline borders flashed green to indicate Live Stream-mode. He checked the time under his tiny Beethoven avatar that he opened up in Teleprompter-mode on the tip of the robotic projector stand that glided upward in response to his hailing hand. After he swept his avatar into a virtual status bar, it directed him to smile, breathe and begin his speech. The grid light illuminated, On...

"Citizens," he began, "I want to thank you for electing me as your permanent leader until *Sagan* launches for Nelta. Your vote is a serious and a special calling for me to represent your desires and the vision you have for our healed ozone as we venture toward the final twenty-five years of the close of this century."

Pausing, he felt a brief sadness that he swallowed down like a large pill. He might not ever see anyone's face beyond the Press Room again, might not ever hear another global wave of excitement or touch Earth or ocean water again He gathered his thoughts that felt like damned up water and continued:

"As my Second Regulate—"

He waved Jenkens to join him and then gestured for his Standard Terra to join them.

"Regent Steven Jenkens will be assisting Terra and me in compiling your top ten priorities since Terra announced the end of World War III. Again, our sympathies are with the men and women who died in that cosmic tragedy." He activated designs of several memorials that a Regent had streamed to him after they learned of the loss of life. "These are some of the monolithic designs several architects have presented to us for immediate construction. You can cast your votes now for where you'd like us to erect this memorial of valor." He then tapped open a hologram of *Sagan*, still in orbit. "On *Sagan*, we intend to honor the brave heroes who died in in the war with a smaller memorial. For now, we, as well as you, are in deep mourning. For this reason, as your governing body, The Regency needs a brief period of time to recover and assess our future role as global leaders." He tapped open the Global Constitution and Global Laws. "We need a few hours to consult with scientists on Earth, researchers and engineers on Station II, and our military on Station III. We need to gather all new information streaming in through the matrix and from space, consolidate all this data, ascertain our damages, and assess the Tech-No protesters, their current numbers, and the threat level. Our terrorist enemies are dead; however, the Tech-No threat is still quite real. Expect more illegal matrix-shopping of your holosites, as we ourselves have intercepted and expunged out of our own Regency holosite." He jiggled up over his wrist device a small hologram of the moon's fissure, but quickly extinguished it. "Tomorrow, The Regency as a whole will announce our findings and propose solutions on which you can vote." Terra opened up her palm, and a virtual clock appeared that automatically adjusted to the holosite participant's time zone. "I have the speech scheduled for 10:30 a.m., Eastern Standard Time."

Then a column of new concerns appeared in the Popularity Bar on his left-hand side. They were statistically significant comments Terra's matrix had correlated.

"Yes," he began, acknowledging The World's Live-Streaming worries, "we have been encountering coastal tides and mild earthquakes." He gestured toward ground-shaking images coming through to him from around the globe. "For those of you affected by coastal abnormalities, or for those of you who live in or around fault zones, immediately obey the emergency icons that Terra is streaming to you and take refuge in your designated safe havens. We believe these light global disruptions are only the result of the 9:30 p.m. cosmic hit that the tropopause shield corrected. Again, at 10:30 a.m. tomorrow, Eastern Standard Time, we will have all the data and be able to announce what is occurring, how long the aftermath of the cosmic event will endure, and solutions to stopping it...which should be simple." He gestured toward the sky and Jenkens opened up a view of the shining tropopause shield array. "That's saved us so many times before, with solar infusions, and we're confident that this slight cosmic aftermath will be over soon."

After motioning for other Regents to add to his scientific information, he continued: "As elected officials, our jobs are to serve you to the best of our ability and to the standards of our Global Constitution and Global Law. For that reason as well, I am instigating a six-hour, Roll Call sequestration for The Regency...a six-hour period of isolation to evaluate our new positions and how we can better serve our constituents...you, The World."

He swiped up an image of an old Congressional and Senate meeting, wherein representatives and senators of the United States of America locked themselves in The Capital for an entire day after 6/20/2057 to assess the widespread destruction throughout the U.S.A.

Manning said: "As at that time, now such a Roll Call is

necessary and needed, to debate and come to a consensus on vital legislation and new threats to our safety. Now, this Regency must begin this necessary sequestration. That means that all of us, individually and collectively, will be completely Off-Matrix." He extinguished his Beethoven connection to The World's matrix communication grid. As the downturn hummed slightly in Regency Only-mode, he continued: "In the interim, Enforcers and community agents will act as mediators and legal intermediaries until we return to our positions at 7 o'clock a.m., Eastern Standard Time. When our sequestration is complete, we will resume all our connections. At that time, we should also have increased matrix capacity through which we can address your concerns, provide you with solid facts regarding Earth's status and begin conducting funeral services for our fallen heroes. At 10:30 a.m., in my Acceptance Speech with The Regency alongside me, I will outline your concerns and worries for humanity and how we can all work together to solve them. Until then, please research all information and cast your votes. Until then, God Be with Our Globe. Thank you, and good night."

The robotic projectors extinguished. Everyone in the room began discussing the speech as Regents congregated around him.

Jenkens slid through them and said: "Thornton, your Roll Call sequestration is not gonna work for long. Look at the night sky!"

Battlefield Matrix

Chapter 19

Fissure

Viewed from Earth, the third-quarter moon looked like a half-deflated ball surrounded by a white halo.

"Already the press is postulating that this is no Tech-No hack...that something terrible happened up there," Jenkens began. "And during your speech, I received several urgent prompts from astronomers and astrophysicists demanding that I break the silence you're imposing and discuss the abnormalities they're seeing through all their telescopes."

Several Regents were glancing at the abnormal celestial site through high obscured windows. Terras were showing the other Regents and scientists images of dust streams cascading from the epicenter of the fissure. Sunlight was illuminating particles like incendiary phosphorous. Only the matrix had the close up view from probes and repaired lunar robotics.

Manning designated all such images Top Secret/SCI and then he asked, "Terra—what's the composition of the particulate matter?"

J.P. Osterman

His Terra closed the giant screen's paused program of The Past and activated a Spectrum app that began analyzing several images, measurements, and frequency data streaming into them from the various probes. The screen morphed into a field of bas-relief, displaying six zones of lunar radial readings. Beneath each zone, scientists began consulting with their Terras.

"The lunar composition is ten percent iron," his Terra then said.

"My God!" Manning exclaimed, feeling faint. "That's core material! The terrorist bastards *were* lunar boring. Is that what happened that created all this mess?"

Terra re-materialized next to him. "Not entirely, Executive Regent Manning. The lanthanides from the drilling process are acting as an acid, changing the lunar iron composition."

"I bet that's how they were planning to take out Earth if their cause failed," Jenkens added. "Captain Bartlet was right."

Manning didn't want to focus on the past. He walked up to Terra who downsized at his eye level. "How bad is this fissure, Terra? How bad!"

Standing in place, she divided and then virtually stepped into one section of the show playing on the giant screen that continued to flash and scroll down lunar statistics. "In two minutes, I should have the exact parameters, the damage, projected ramifications, and several simulations of its future effects on the Earth. The Globule weapon *did* cause the fault, but only after several other forces were in place that exacerbated the weapons fire. I am waiting for Station II and all probes to finish gathering data. I need that information to run a comparative analysis on all the forces at play in our solar system. Only then can I generate future scenarios and postulate implications for Earth."

"Still, I bet they're not gonna be good!" a Regent called.

Regent Sylvia Itonovich ran up to them and linked her wrist device with Stage-2 Right beyond Center Stage. *Holosite ABC* appeared, streaming its *Living Wellness Today* show. The host was pausing for an emergency news flash. Terra was beginning

Battlefield Matrix

to stream the new *Emergency Protocol* to The World, but in segments, based on specific concerns that Matrix Techs had programmed the matrix to respond.

Regent Itonovich said, "People are aware that there's a big problem now, Thornton, and soon they'll realize our sequestration is only a time-stalling smoke screen."

Jenkens said: "Not only is *this* holosite station, but also *every* network is focused on the moon. And she's right. People *are* hailing us in spite of the sequestration. If we don't provide them with answers other than blaming Tech-Nos, soon we'll have global bedlam and chaos at our double doors. It'll look worse than the riots that nearly leveled Cairo way back in 2013."

On their wrist devices and portable tablets, Regents began viewing global-wide broadcasts in several languages. Circumventing the sequestration without making appearances, they directed scientists to answer questions through their scientific communities and holosite worlds. Astrophysicists and theoretical cosmologists began requesting access to lunar data from Station II, but Manning ordered Terra to generate solar interference and call the corrective measures they were using to resolve the difficulty: "tropopause shield, protective influx of energy." Then he messaged the scientists on Station II, telling them that he was receiving data indicating that the tropopause shield was in danger of being hacked. It too needed a six-hour inaccessible period to repair and re-energize.

Outside the White House, another type of crowd was slowly gathering—restless packs of jittery and agitated spectators. Some were shining icons into the Press Room. A few boisterous people were holding up signs that Law Enforcement Zeppelins were illuminating. Stealth Force officers inside the craft were trying to coach people toward safe havens. One Zeppelin had its bullhorns on full blast, its automatic program threatening one protester with arrest. It had loosened its ropes and nets from the hull in preparation to round up violent or aggressive protesters. Secret Service and Enforcer troops began keeping them at bay, but they were also hailing The Regency on its Secure Military Com grid for more orders in case violence might erupt and people react in panic or hysteria.

"I thought this was *aaawwl* over...but I was wrong," Manning said through feelings of hostile surrender.

"What's that?" Jenkens gasped.

Another Regent said: "The emergency status is turning out to be the new normal. That's what he's saying. People will most likely be living with friggin emergency icons all the time."

"And automated Terra guides!" a scientist shouted.

"They'll all be directing peoples' lives worse than eating on schedule," someone yelled.

"I have a temporary solution until Terra can run the full gamut of possible scenarios," Manning interrupted. He gathered the twenty-member Regency team who had managed the integration of the nations after the terrorist ozone attacks. "Using our new Emergency Broadcast, tell people that we're looking into the cause of the lunar fissure. Acknowledge it isn't a matrixshopped image. Give them a morsel of truth."

"We can't do that!" Regent Itonovich cried. "We don't have all the facts!"

"People need to know the whole truth right now though," another Regent demanded.

The room resounded into a heated, angry debate.

"No—we must hold back most of the information and only divulge a small picture," Manning countered. "Do you want what we talked about earlier to happen? Stampedes to every shuttle? Terra beginning a count of dead bodies?"

When most Regents stilled, a woman shyly stepped out of a group of white-coated scientists and said: "Sir, what do *we* do? What's gonna happen to those of us who are sequestered in here with The Regency? Should we stay, or go?"

Jenkens waved over his Terra. "You're staying, of course. Don't worry about your safety. We'll work out the details as soon as The Regency decides what we should do...where we should go."

"Thirty seconds, Ladies and Gentlemen," Terra said,

Battlefield Matrix

gesturing toward the IMAX screen flashing six lunar images in bas-relief.

"Terra," Manning began, "in the Emergency Broadcast, include that our best scientists are working hard to pinpoint the source of the lunar disturbance. Keep repeating that speech I just gave. Tell people to obey the new emergency protocols and head to safe havens."

"Some people are still in those locations since yesterday when the ozone flared," Regent Sylvia Itonovich said.

"Open all food-and-beverage storage facilities," he ordered Terra.

"And prepare your matrix to process through maximum photon crystals so you can accommodate a comprehensive, live-stream broadcast everywhere tomorrow," Jenkens told her when he showed everyone Terra's current output of weak energy. "The center wall-zone's functioning at max, but the matrix facilities need more crystal infusions.

Terra suddenly appeared in front of Center Stage. Behind her, on Center Stage, were two background views of Stations II and III. Techs and military personnel inside those facilities were responding in Alert-and-Analysis modes. "Ladies and Gentlemen of The Regency," Standard Terra began, "should I prepare a continuation of the *Emergency, Stage-1 Alert* for tomorrow?"

"And tomorrow and the day after that—"

"Forever!" someone lamented.

Through crying voices, Terra stretched out her virtual hand and a white piece of paper appeared over it.

Walking up to her, Manning noticed the new center wall-zone interfacing with holographic lights and the paper. The link looked like globules of nanobots that could circle Earth at near speed of light. Terra was ready to take dictation for a historical document.

He said to her: "Use parts of our new alert and blend it with the old one from WBET-TV. When I give the signal, send it to the Smithsonian. Make the last words read, "We are so sorry."

People began asking, "Sorry for what?!"

His gut aching in quenching the denial, he told them he'd tell them the answer to that question later. He already knew it: They had to leave, soon...abandon Earth.

On the paper, Standard Terra began compiling words into several languages, and then she commenced reading: "The Regency will be your liaison between all science centers, Enforcers, Security agencies, artificial street guides, and the public. Your elected Regency team, now including Executive Regent Manning—"

"I added that, Sir," she said softly, "since your title altered."

"Go on, Terra, we'll make more revisions later if we need to," he said.

She continued to read the new protocol: "Enforcers, guards, icons, and avatar guides might require you to vacate your home or business if the matrix detects an impending disaster."

Regents sent their avatars to the right of her—streaming that they were agreeing with her wording and adding suggestions, which she swept away or incorporated into the historical document. The tiny avatars looked like small kernels popping up and then disappearing around her holographic light.

"My God," shouted Regent Ruth Stein, "what does this mean for all of us?" She was desperately tearful—the first time he saw her stoic nature reflect the image of the delicate Hollywood icon, Marilyn Monroe whom she always dressed to imitate. Others around her were weeping and sobbing, their faces buried in Kleenex and their forearms.

"Calm down, Sylvia...everyone, just calm down," he said tenderly, giving her a glass of cold water. Then he ordered robot servers to do the same for the others. As they quenched themselves, he said: "We must remain focused on solving the problem when Terra comes back with predictive simulations and worst-case scenarios. We can't get caught up in the chaos and have the public see us as confused, unstable, unfocused and just plain out of control and disheveled...like some of you are looking right now. We have a speech to make tomorrow. 10:30 a.m. Remember that, and start getting yourselves together. Breathe, and move on." As Regent Ruth Stein continued gasping for relieving air, he began to incite other Regents into action. Noticing two, idle Matrix Technicians, he ordered them: "You two, come here—I have a job for you in the Bottom-Level Bunker."

"But *people* are *all around* down at the Security Kiosks, Sir," one shaking man challenged, in a Southern drawl. "What if the crowd thickens and Enforcers can't hold 'em—"

"I'm letting them know you're coming and Terra will shield you with her evolved application," he answered.

"Whataya want us to do, Sir?" the female tech asked, standing at attention.

"At the Center Lobby, take the far right elevator to the bunker. Get to the two matrix towers. You'll see the photon processor fully powered up. But it needs someone to manually input *my* Regency code to expand Terra's matrix through the covert site on Easter Island."

"Good thinking, Thornton," Jenkens whispered in his ear, "that's the *least* thing we can do for people if we have to leave Earth."

Quieting him, because Jenkens obviously had the same "escape" plan in mind, Manning had his Beethoven avatar duplicate a String File into the technicians' avatars. Then he said: "After you input my code, go to the roof where Terra's indicating a few craft have landed to evacuate people on an emergency basis. I'm telling the pilot that you're coming in fifteen minutes." As they scampered out the door, he called out to everyone: "That Pacific facility can't remain Secret any longer. People are going to flood us with questions that we're gonna have to answer from space…through a tight window in the tropopause shield."

"Whataya mean answer from space?" someone shouted sternly. Others parroted the cry.

"We're heading to space, everyone. Start packing' up, now!" he yelled. Jumping on one robotic platform and then another, he repeated the order, trying to round everyone up and energize them. "Come on…Move! Now!" When a few people fainted and doctors began assisting them, he said to Jenkens, after Jenkens asked him what he could do to help: "General Rand has a perfect view of Earth from space and can monitor all activity. Have him direct all the space stations to increase orbit. Take them *way* high above the shield…at a safe distance where he can intercept attacks from Earth or prevent all craft from approaching and landing."

"What?" Jenkens cried. "People will surely panic when they notice those stations increasing their orbits. All five of 'em look like stars. That increase, with the resulting diminutive reflective-light will spook everyone…almost like First Communication."

"Another mass panic for sure," Regent Sylvia Itonovich interjected.

"God—*where…how* do we begin to pack up all this stuff!" several people cried, glancing around the room like frightened prey.

Manning silenced them to a low continuous mumbling. "We have to reposition the satellites and leave Earth. I just set the matrix to Full Power, so it shouldn't crash, and General Rand can monitor everything from biometrics to crowd organization so we know what's happening while we're holding up in space. Whether here or on *Sagan*, we can still lead and help people. Besides, if Terra predicts terrible consequences, everyone…hear that?…*everyone*—will go into hysterics. Who'll they come for? Us. What'll they want? Astrocraft, or retrofitted hover craft—anything they can modify that can launch for the space stations and—"

"They'll attack 'em and take 'em over!" shouted Regent Ruth Stein. "No!"

Manning consoled her. "With some preventative action, that can't happen."

Meanwhile, Jenkens had asked several people, including Elisa Holton, to be in charge of directing people to pack up the Press Room facility. "Don't forget…we have to find a way to damage all the spacefold technology 'cause if the underground safe havens and surface beehives become overcrowded, people will add the technology to any old astrocraft and use it without accounting for the harmful boundary effects," Jenkens said.

Manning ordered Terra to search out all facilities harboring any spacefolding technology and insert their organic programs with viruses. As she showed him several such crowded facilities, he said: "You know, people will soon detect all our precautionary measures, head for the White House when they can't reach us personally, and storm this place…along with the rest of our other global headquarters."

"Yeah—they're gonna be want bloody revenge on us!" shouted a scientist.

A Lead Enforcer stepped up and he said: "Ladies and Gentlemen, you also have to consider those people who are wealthy and own private astrocraft. They'll not condescend to serving positions in The Mountain or Southern Silo Center. They've already told us that before in another mass evacuation we had to implement months ago. When they learn of *any* type of forced confinement, they'll head to the stations with their families in the hope of *buying* refuge."

"He's got a point," Jenkens said, sweeping up a few images of famous wealthy people who were now CEOs, dignitaries, activists, social figures, or Holosite celebrities. Some had distant ancestors who were prominent political figures or who had developed technical innovation. "Some of these individuals have been funding research projects on Station II. How do we turn *them* down? We might need 'em, even if the euro becomes obsolete and we re-instate the bartering system as people did after the ozone attacks. If we *do* take their money in exchange for squeezing 'em in on a station, how do we explain our decision to everyone else—the common person who is forced to stay here on Earth and weather out the destruction?"

"He's right," called another Regent, "we just won't have room on *Sagan* or the other stations to accommodate *everyone*…even those on The List right now."

"And don't forget our limited provisions," said a scientists, somberly crying.

"She's right, supplies on *Sagan* won't last," Regent Sylvia Itonovich stepped up and shouted. "The astrocity's not prepared to sustain everyone right now on The List for Nelta." Being a member of that committee responsible for stocking *Sagan* with supplies and animals, she showed them the ship's current cargo and percent needed. "We're only at ten percent capacity to sustain us all for the voyage...and months away from completing the food and storage centers on Level 3 and the planting and grazing zones on Level 7. Yes, the Neltan *Breath* is working to enlarge the astrocity. But supplies? *The Breath* program can't physically reach down to Earth and gather everything we need."

"Check and see if The Helm Facility picked up on what's happening on the moon," said Jenkens. "If it's as 'smart' as the Neltans claimed, the ship itself should 'see' the catastrophe and be responding in its own unique way to help those on The List."

In the meantime, Manning had Terras materialize throughout the assembly to direct peoples' attention to him at the center, from where he was striving to spread calmness into those who couldn't stop screaming, shouting, moaning, and sobbing. "We'll address those issues after we leave, but for now, we need to get off Earth ASAP...*now!*" He shouted the directive several times through more Terras that multiplied two-fold—popping up in front of peoples' faces. "Pack up. We're heading to *Sagan*." He had his reverberate the command in echoes as through an ancient acoustical coliseum.

Finally, people silenced when Elisa activated her GEM armband that spread a red, laser-light, spider web above their heads.

Thanking her while heaving in breaths, he added: "Don't you want to be off-Earth if Terra presents us bad scenarios? Don't you want to make sure we protect our best asset— *Sagan*?" As people shrieked replies of affirmation interwoven with words of disapproval, he said: "Now! We're movin' outta

Battlefield Matrix

here. We can figure out all the details as we move from here to our secure departure pad at Dulles. I think Station II and Station III can accommodate us if we can't all fit on *Sagan*—including whoever else will be joining us from Earth." He directed them to continue to check their messages in their wrist devices. He had Terra re-stream them *Sagan*'s latest construction news. The terrorists had fired on it yesterday, and builders and engineers had the construction labeled: *75% complete; 82% matrix efficiency.*

"Of course, we need to evacuate," Jenkens began, "but—"

"But nothing, Steve," he countered, then he shouted at the top of his voice: "Come on, everyone! Pack it up! We're leaving!" On his wrist device, he called out a command for astropilots within a two-hundred-mile radius to divert their craft to Dulles and land. "I'm not telling them why. And we have several craft at our disposal since I put out that last call for emergency support. When we get closer to boarding time, I'll tell them to set a course for the space stations."

All the Terras that had multiplied through the room suddenly disappeared, and Terra in her Standard Form appeared in front of Center Stage that was teaming with background images of bustling and frenzied personnel onboard Stations II and III. "I have the lunar statistics, Ladies and Gentlemen," she said. Everyone stopped and opened up their wrist device apps to receive her information. Terra added: "My predictions will follow."

Lunar statistics and measurements began streaming from the ceiling hubs to the large screen. All the while, Terra maintained her straight, serious face—the expression scientists had programmed into her back in 2062 before she began quantum streaming.

"Ladies and Gentlemen—"

"Wait!" Manning gestured for Terra to stop the presentation.

The data-stream froze, and her eyes flashed yellow for Wait-mode.

He said to everyone downstreaming the information into

373

wrist devices: "If you stream what's happening in here to *any* holosite, I'll arrest you." After gesturing for the Lead Enforcer to step up with his small team of officers, he looked around at the frozen people the room, his eyes feeling like zooming lenses on their terrified faces. They were swallowing hard, and some of them were shaking through their tears. "Keep everything you see and hear to yourselves, as information to use and help us compose a presentation later on for The World."

The room turned eerily quiet. "Arrest," meant a fast ride to Station V for neurological remapping, as what happened to the spy who had threatened to divulge some of The Past.

"Good—I'm glad we're in agreement. Go on, Terra," he ordered.

As thermal images of the moon and its spewing particles began coalescing on the IMAX screen, he spotted the giant astrocity—*Sagan*. It could be finished and fully stocked in a year—maybe a few months!—instead of twenty-seven months *if* builders, engineers, matrix techs, and physicists would intensify their work without the phenomenal cost increase…and with *The Breath* infusion. How could he make people speed up their work?

Concurrently, Terra had stepped into the huge screen. The moon enlarged as the dominant object in her presentation. She said: "The moon is in synchronous rotation and orbit with Earth. It has an orbital tilted of 5° from the ecliptic while Earth's orbit has a tilt of 23.5°. On the far side, where the terrorists maintained their subterranean stronghold, they implanted lunar bores composed of lutetium-176 and yttrium."

Several Regents gasped, and groaning scientists stopped gathering boxes, bundling hardware and wrapping delicate objects.

Terra continued: "These two elements combined as catalysts and interacted with the Gamma Globule weapon's dispersion during firing. This intense nuclear reaction caused a 1.2-mile fissure, 1.5 miles in length." She displayed the moon as pie segments. The far side portions were comprised of a long giant crack.

"Terra, how long before *this* section breaks away from the whole?" Manning asked.

Several predictive models emerged—each simulation worse than the previous.

"Ladies and Gentlemen, the South Pole-Aitken Basin could split to the Mare Moscoviense region in two days or two hundred years."

"Those are some wide-varying predictions, Terra!" Regent Sylvia Itonovich shouted through a flood of sickening moans and shrieks. Several scientists congregated, running algorithmic solutions. Elisa Holton began leading that small team of solution-driven innovators.

"Can't you be more specific?" Jenkens asked.

"Definitely, Sir, my highest probability scenario shows the fault dividing the moon within two to three years," she answered, showing images of various types of lunar catastrophes: from the moon breaking into two, giant jagged sections, to the moon gradually disintegrating into rocks, boulders, and several large asteroid-type bodies. In all predicaments, Terra was displaying various types of particulate storms raining down death on Earth.

"What are your projections for humanity's survival?" Manning asked her.

Terra displayed images of tidal waves. Various seismic readings appeared around several rotating models of the Earth and the moon in centrifugal motion. On the giant screen, she showed six simulations of various orbiting, celestial bodies throughout the solar system—all gravitational forces adhering the moon and the Earth in orbit around the sun. She predicted the moon's orbit and its effect on Earth, *unstable*, and their interacting forces, *weakening*.

Her eyes flashing green laser-lights as pointers into all of them, she began six shows of six complete forecasts: "The hadalpelagic zones will eventually alter. All life in the oceans will gradually change. I project a steady decrease. Thus all life will alter. Into what? I am unable to extrapolate. Earth's ozone has healed; however, any centrifugal change in orbit between the Earth and the moon…and the Earth, moon and sun…will trigger a ripple effect that will generate a wild wobble of Earth's axial precession. Should a major portion of the moon become dislodged from its current orbit, it will very likely crash into earth with the result being a complete, life extinction event. I recommend immediate preparation to either fortify safe havens or evacuate Earth."

"The time for all this to happen, Terra?" he asked…several people asked.

"Two days to several hundred years. Either a gradual lunar disintegration as in the first scenario, or an abrupt lunar divide as in the last scenario," she replied. "I recommend immediate preparation to either fortify safe havens or evacuate Earth, in mass."

Chapter 20

The Regency Stampede

As per the new Emergency Alert, Terras appeared alongside everyone, providing their holosite hosts with survival-affirming data, medical advice, and calming icons.

"All life could start collapsing as early as tomorrow!" a scientist shouted as everyone either returned more diligently than before to their work or began panicking. "God! Get me outta here! I gotta get my son!" The scientist lost his glasses, trampling them asunder as he raced to the double doors. Two others followed him.

Manning ordered a Regent, also an MD, who always carried medical supplies: "Helen, sedate anyone—anyone!—who tries going out the doors. Round up some others to help you."

Throwing off his jacket in an expression of being on overload, a Matrix Tech called: "The Earth's going to change. What are we gonna do about it? Just listen to and leave? Hell, I'm no coward!"

Suddenly, ring tones pierced through the air. The

J.P. Osterman

automated intrusion was a heightened communications grid through which Enforcers, Secret Service, the media, and astropilots were interrupting the Roll Call sequestration.

Jumping again on the robotic platform with his image blaring on two wall zones so that everyone could see and hear him, Manning waved Jenkens close to his side and said: "People! Attention!" After a few agents fired shots into the ceiling, everyone stopped to listen through panting breaths of hot intensity. He continued: "*We* have the only permanent-way out—that's space. As I said a few minutes ago, you need to calm down and keep a level head." He felt his beating cheeks and wild breaths finally decelerating. "Gather whatever you brought in here with you, whatever you were asked to pack up, and line up at my desk. There's an exit behind it." Terra highlighted the outline of the escape portal behind the illusion of a landscape mural. I can open it up to get us outta here fast. Later, on the other side, we can take care of minor details. But for now, just go. Follow Regent Steven Jenkens' direction. He'll open it."

After Jenkens acknowledged the order, he told Terra to stream each person the map of the subterranean exit, and he called for more Terras as guides to illuminate everyone as far as matrix power could process through the long passageway.

Then Manning realized that before he could leave, he'd first have to dismantle some Oval Office technology to take along with the—vital hardware he dare not leave because if anyone had the technology, they could expand it and win any type of war. Terra had advanced his experimental gamma-burst app in his ceiling hub into a small-scale version of Bartlet's Gamma Globule weapon when Dr. Coflin and the Halite Being had infiltrated the Press Room. Along with the Neltan's Encantado, shape-shifting program, the new gamma-burst app harbored disintegration energy. They'd need the hardware for implementation on *Sagan*. He called to Jenkens, "Keep people back!" He activated a yellow circle of privacy. Still, people were clamoring through the yellow light, break his circle of seclusion, pleading with him—the shield stinging their flesh and smoking clothing—to allow them to contact their families and friends.

Continuing to order them back into line from inside Manning's personal space, Jenkens whispered to him: "I just called my wife, told her to drive as fast as she could, but calmly, to Dulles and leave her hover car in Lot F. I told her I was taking her for a surprise holiday—the contest I entered for that free vacation to the Lee Lunsford Rim on Mars. I told her I'd meet her at Lot F in about an hour, but to wait for me 'cause I'm on my way, incommunicado. That's the time it'll take for us to get all these people out and through the passageway…that's if we can ever stop all this grumbling, crying and groaning…a waste of time."

Thinking that he was glad he didn't have a wife or kids, Manning said: "Fine, but don't spread that around…that you talked to her personally. I don't want the others going against my order to maintain silence and do the same thing. If that happens, word'll surely leak to the public that we're leaving 'cause something's terribly wrong." Then he saw lines of Regents and scientists lamenting over the plight of their loved ones. A few were about to fistfight with two burly Enforcers because they wanted to retrieve their families. After breaking up their argument, he told them that Terra had streamed an evacuation protocol to their families, providing them with a rendezvous. "Most likely, Terra has them on The List for Nelta because you're all on it. If you designated them, they're included with whatever we do and wherever we go. They'll soon be receiving instruction to meet you on astrocraft, a space station, or *Sagan*. Terra's figuring out the details. She'll stream them to your families via a Confidential grid after she does."

Regent Sylvia Itonovich ran up to him with eyes like hailstones. "We should head to *Sagan*, Thornton? I thought we were going to space stations? What's going on!?" She started long-winded whispers of confusion that rippled down the long lines to the escape portal. People were waiting for the hatches to desynchronize. Some glitch had them interlocking.

Now he too felt confused—caught up in the hurricane of

questions. "Terra, what do you think? Can we all fit on *Sagan*? In its current unfinished status?"

Everyone calmed down to a snail's pace to eavesdrop—even those packaging scientific instruments, wrapping hardware, and encasing ceiling hubs processors. They were also intermittently discussing the statistics that continued to project scenes in and around the White House. Those images and environmental stats were blaring yellow/orange on several wall zones—the orange the next warning before Red Alert 1...a White House attack indicator.

Terra opened last minute's viewpoint onboard the astrocity, *Sagan*. "The small Living Cubes on Level 2—the aft-portions—are complete and seventy-five percent furnished. The current RSVP response I am receiving from family members indicates that The Regency and their families occupy those rooms. The others can board as *Sagan* expands and completes."

Regent Itonovich stepped forward with an argumentative expression on her face. "Terra—as I said earlier, *Sagan*'s not stocked yet with food, and its circulatory water system's not complete. And there are only enough provisions on *Sagan*'s construction station for the designers, engineers, and construction workers."

After Manning was able to corral their attention back to him again because they began wandering off in speculations about running out of supplies, mobs stampeding craft, and angry citizens plundering their homes because Terra hadn't chosen them, he shouted: "Your homes? *That's* what you're worried about?" He laughed in frustration. "Come on, people!" He paused, feeling disgusted. "If all this hadn't happened, you woulda had to let go of your homes, gold, silver...*everything* before the June 10, 2070 launch date. So, just let everything go now. We have an entire manufacturing center almost finished on Level 7. It's an augmented world we're about to transition to, so start designing new things to replace the old."

"Hey—that's right!" shouted a Regent. "I guess the

realization hasn't sunk in 'cause this is all happening so fast…that we'll have everything new and we can start over on *Sagan*." People in the exit line began excitedly repeating renditions of that same sentiment.

Manning added, "So okay…great…now that *that's* resolved, get moving." He kept swooshing scientists toward their stacked boxes and cumbersome carry cases. The clamps on the exit portal were halfway unpeeled, and Enforcers were continuing to blast them to unclamp. After taking out a few important keepsakes from his desk, shoving them into a small box, and handing the taped box over to a scientist for transport out of the facility, he suddenly wondered if they had enough craft to carry them all off-Earth. Breathless and drinking water, he hailed General Rand on Center Stage and said to him, "I know I said to put more distance between all space stations and Earth and to clear craft away from the moon." Rand looked as exhausted as he felt, and he told him that as he streamed him all Terra's predictions, calculations and worst-case scenarios. "Send as many craft as you can right now—now!—to pick us all up at Dulles. Terra's giving you our count. Don't dally 'cause you have to make our evacuation from Earth appear as inconspicuous as possible."

After General Rand complied and left—the background of Station III's navigation facility remaining on Operational-mode until the hologram stages powered down upon the last Regent exiting the escape portal—several tiny avatars managed to stream through the communications grid. They all began asking simultaneously: "What should we pack? Where do we go? Who'll be there? What about school? What do I tell my friends? What about my portable matrixware? What do I…who do we…"

"Stop! You all sound like a deadly hornet's nest!" he cried. Glancing at the line, he called over his Terra to begin to buffer them out of the room. Then he said, "How the hell did these people hack through to the Press Facility? God not another one…another damn spy!" He yelled at the avatar messengers before giving Terra the Okay signal to Red Flag them as possible Tech-Nos at the rendezvous site: "You have thirty-minutes to pack—*seriously ONLY* thirty minutes. If you don't arrive at the designated rendezvous that *my* Terra streamed to you in one hour—one hour!—we *will* leave you behind. We *will* launch in one hour!"

He had Terra stream a timeframe of escape to *everyone* she had selected for The List, as well as those strict guidelines. Those people not present but on The List, Terra was setting timeframes to commence within the next two hours to take them off-Earth. He glanced at the time: 2:10 a.m., EST. That meant that the launch from Earth would commence at 3:10 a.m.

General Rand's image reappeared on Center Stage. "What are your orders should anyone object to the time constraint? We're setting up space up here right now to accommodate them."

"Tell that person goodbye. Someone else will take his or her place on *Sagan*. They'll never see their loved one again. And if they are left behind, I predict they'll have thousands taking them hostage or torturing them in order to secure a seat on the astrocity or one of the space stations."

"Yes, Sir—I'm going on Avatar-mode to answer all questions so I don't have to keep repeating myself to scientists streaming in and wasting my time. I need to continue to direct expansion up here and make room for about forty thousand. The Project Managers on Station II have locked down their com grids and are evolving the matrix there. They told me to tell you that they're making room for people, so Terra can send people on The List there as well." He patted sweat off his short forehead. More officers fed his fingers with projected population growth on his space station. In the background, the new *Emergency Alert* was forming on a giant hologram stage, along with the various lunar statistics preparing to downstream to Earth upon The Regency's orders. "I'm sending craft in orbit just below the tropopause shield. They'll hold position until Terra directs them to retrieve the rest on The List." Images of red dots forming long lines appeared in radar form in a hologram next to him. "Craft are on trajectory to Dulles to pick your party up. While they're camouflaged and waiting, they'll load up on dark-matter plasma rods we need up here. I have cargo filling with alternators we'll also load up on so we can reinforce on asteroids and on Mars. Most tourists there are indicating they're staying there until the alerts subside. Of course, they don't know yet that those alerts'll probably be going on for quite some time."

"I'm sure those people will help us, and we'll help them, until we launch out of the solar system," Manning said.

Then General Rand faded, but Station III's background continued imaging its standard flow of energetic military personnel and Black Ops lunar images.

Manning waved over Terra. "When we're gone, have robotics move all plants, animals, soil, and fertilizers into automated astrocraft. I'm sealing and setting up the tropopause shield to fire on anyone who approaches those sites within a half mile. Make sure *each* space station receives a double supply of seeds, livestock, fish, and so forth. In between now and the time *Sagan* launches, we'll slowly bring up and incorporate everything that's on The Noah's Ark list on *Sagan*. Still, I know I'm forgetting some things. I hate this!"

His Standard Terra divided. "Sir, I am searching the matrix for all consumptive and non-consumptive items humans need for the journey to Nelta. I will compile that list for your perusal later, as you requested of the other details you believe you omitted."

As Terra re-united, Jenkens appeared alongside him and began hurriedly waving. "We can return for supplies and take care of missing details later, Thornton. Come on—let's get outta here. That escape door's almost open—damn that Coflin disabled it and jammed it with organics!" Creaking vibrations resounded as the nano-organic seals strained to let go of their tight grasps in spite of Terra's, and strong Enforcer, intervention. The seals were acting like anti-gravity shots toward anything trying to penetrate the materials. Several objects were hovering above people, flying at them or striking at them. The two physicians and three available nurses were attending to the wounded.

"Details are important though, Steve," Manning replied. "Realize that some people will launch an attack to take possession of the space stations...except the prison station—which, by the way, we should unfetter from its tropopause connections and send somewhere else. We don't want people getting hit with a double whammy: a lunar catastrophe *and* violent offenders, including terrorists." After he appeared to the warden, whom he offered several seats on *Sagan*, he ordered Terra: "Release Station V." The ten-mile-wide station unclasped and began a slow drift into space. Over the course of the next hour, Terra scheduled three large astro-gliders to launch from the station to transport the warden, administrators, guards, physicians, robotics and vital supplies to Station II.

Then he remembered another vital detail. "Damn that I that slip from my mind!" he self-chastised. "Calculate a new launch date-and-time for *Sagan* and let me know it ASAP. And position Construction Station I and Warehouse Station IV as close to the *Sagan* as possible so off-Earth workers can have easy access to it as well as the building materials and interior furniture. Bribe workers with seats to Nelta in exchange for overtime and QA." He felt lightning proud that he'd finally figured out a way to get Matrix Techs, architects and manual laborers to work double and triple time.

"Thornton," Jenkens whispered harshly, pulling him aside, "you're offering *way* too many seats on the astrocity in exchange for silence and work. We can't do that!" He activated a statistical program of living condition onboard *Sagan*. "Terra selected the crew and calculated capacity based on *months* of accumulating data, predicting changes due to long-term, spacefolding, and all of us regenerating. The extra seats *you're* offering are becoming variables in her complicated algorithmic calculations, not outliers. Slight deviations will affect the astrocity's spacefold capability and counteract *Sagan*'s dark energy, lift-n-glide motion through wormholes. We could deviate off course like a wave unraveling to an undercurrent! We don't want that, Thornton. Shaesar warned us—"

"*Shhh*!" He saw Elisa Holton gesture at him happily, showing him that she had finally discovered how to unclasp Gem: with her line of sight positioned in the middle of one of the armband's right lower, golden-glowing processor streams interacting at just the right angle with Terra's flashing green eyes. The armband was matrix-interfaced, Neltan infused, and human-hardware optimized. She said she came to that conclusion when a portion of the screen began showing a scene from her childhood after she made an offhanded comment about her mother to her friend, Maureen Strickler. She told Manning that she believed Gem would perform in the same manner with anyone who'd have the courage to don the armband technology.

He discretely ordered Terra to usher Elisa to the end of the line, and he streamed Elisa not to remove Gem for good just yet. "Who knows what obstacle we'll run into." From the fast manner in which people were packing up and leaving, he realized that he was going to be last in line, behind her. Then he received a new update from a crew working on *Sagan*. He said to Jenkens, "I've got the extra numbers of accommodations covered, Steve."

"Huh!—how?"

He gestured with a tilt of his head toward the ceiling processor that was gliding back to its normal position in the Oval Office. The walls in the Press Room were slowly realigning to Standard-mode just as they were before Final Communication. Donned in thick white suits and working with special scanners and spectrometers, scientists and engineers were on ladders disassembling and packing up wall zones and Terra matrixware and then handing the hardware to Enforcers and agents who then raced into the exit line. One Matrix Tech hurled a robotic platform on his back, bundled wire around his shoulders, and tucked in a cerebral interface cap around his thick belt. He called others who were carrying the same technology to hold fast along the wall and wait.

Another tech was lugging two power packs over his arms and a tightly wrapped beehive ceiling hub on his back. Everyone was ready to move out...if only the portal would deactivate and unclasp.

"I'll handle the extra body count, Steve," he told Jenkens. "We simply get rid of 'em right before they believe they're boarding *Sagan* for good. Until then, we need those builders, construction workers and techs to speed up the job and finish the astrocity ASAP. If that means telling 'em what they wanna hear to get the job done....that's what we do. Later, they're gone." He smacked his hands together like washing away crumbs.

"You mean, *kill* people?" Jenkens' voice cracked. He pulled Manning further away from the exit line. "I could understand killing terrorists and the Tech-Nos who hacked Terra and endangered peoples' lives—but regular people? I can't do that—*nooo*, no way. I'll stay rather than be involved in cold-blooded murder, Thornton. I want *nothing*—"

He sidled up close to Jenkens' ear. "You'll help me, Steve...you have to, especially since leaving Earth means staying alive. Because if you don't leave, you stay...and if you stay, you'll have world-wide chaos on your hands." He showed him images streaming into them from around Earth. "See all those people assembling? And a few crowds have noticed that the stations have ascended in orbit. Newscasters are seeking out scientists who've obviously been ditching their questions. Any minute now...all the seconds we're wasting getting outta here...and the media'll start inciting panic." He gestured toward a few shows depicting people responding to Terra's new emergency alert and entering safe havens. "It's only been a few hours since the moon began spewing dust, and the public's just beginning to realize the images are Tech-No generated or matrixshopped from some covert hovel. People aren't stupid! And look here at all the transport stats coming in." Part of the room's Security Grid System, a wall-zone in the northeast corner of the room, was flashing subway occupancy numbers. Manning called open the Blue zone

Battlefield Matrix

depicting travel on the East Coast. "Terra's showing that every subway ticket to D.C. has been sold. People are on their way…here…now." He opened up the Sky Lanes in the Midwest. They were showing airway travel congestion. Usually void of hovercraft during the middle of the night, now people were on their way to D.C., their craft outpacing one another like bees and wasps competing to reach a small pollen field. "You wanna face all these people? Angry people, most likely. Without support? Answer *all* their questions, *alone*? Who knows what they'll do to ya alone!"

"*Aaaa*," Jenkens grumbled, "my damn back's against the wall…as is *always* the case with *you*, Thornton. You owe me. *You* owe me."

"Steve…you'll do what needs to be done when the time comes, just like me," he said. "We've got no choice but to do what it takes to build *Sagan* and then launch the hell outta the solar system. Sticking to *Sagan's* old launch schedule could make us become part of humanity's extinction. If speeding up construction means manipulating people and eventually killing people so that many in the future can survive…then we *must* do just that. Our mission's changed."

"I know." Jenkens' shoulders sagged, as did his baggy tired eyes. "We're setting our sights on more than saving the Neltans. Now, our mission is to save Earth. In Space Fold time, a year is like a month. Returning to Earth ahead of time—any time—could mean the difference between arriving in time to healing Earth or arriving in the thick of all Hell breaking out." He chuckled facetiously and tilted his wrist to display the time on the Smart Bar. "Just think…six hours ago you were worried about how we'd ever convince people to keep their promise to the Neltans and give up bundles of money to finish *Sagan*. You believed we'd have a global fight on our hands to make people adhere to *The Pact* and let people on The List leave Earth. Now, you can build a solid case to finish the astrocity as quickly as possible." He streamed that new quest to everyone on The List.

Manning added: "When we arrive there, we need to ask the

Neltans for technology that'll save Earth. If they're still in stasis when we arrive, 'cause I intend to get there much earlier than when they're scheduled to wake up—we drop off the DNA, look for the technology, then head on home. *That's* what I plan to announce to The World in a few hours after we're safe on *Sagan*." He synchronized his calendar app with Jenkens' when he offered it to him. Meanwhile, he continued: "It's ironic but true...that leaving will help humanity. Although, I bet most of them here won't see the solution in that light, especially during the next few days after we abandon Earth. Their fight-or-flight reflexes'll kick in, and they'll naturally come after us on the space stations and *Sagan*...wanting to save *their* lives by doing whatever it takes to take the places of those people on The List. Having shields powered on maximum and firing on all foreign craft should remedy that and allow us to complete the astrocity quickly. Then we can launch quickly. Hopefully, in between the two-thousand Real-Time years that we'll be gone, people will find a way—if Terra's worst scenario occurs—to save the human race. Somewhere some safe place."

Jenkens perked up. "*Hopefully*—after we arrive on Nelta, we can access the Decagon system, communicate with someone here, and find out what's happened during the time we were gone." His face reddened—as if the pressure of a one-hundred-year, Space-Fold, time constraint pumped a sudden flow of blood to his heart. "You make answers sound so easy, simple, Thornton." He gestured at the long line of people at the exit. They were positioning boxes at the entryway, some of them pushing and shoving, arguing over priorities, time, their dire situation, and various solutions to problems. He continued: "You and I *both* know, however, through the hard knocks of life, that whatever can go wrong *will* go wrong. There is no such thing as a failsafe plan." Jenkens' face appeared paste white. "You're right. We will do everything *and* anything—sickening or evil—to speed up *Sagan*'s launch and leave fast." He wiped his eyes and softly said, "God help me...'cause I never *ever* believed I'd resort to

Battlefield Matrix

murder." His Terra materialized alongside him with a Regeneration appointment that had downstreamed from *Sagan*'s Level 5. He said to the virtual specialist, "Affirmative—I'll be on time." The Regeneration Specialists then streamed him a youthful image of what he'd look like after undergoing the two-hour life-enhancement procedure. "Not bad. It'll take off fifteen years!"

"You mean *give* ya fifteen," Manning said, encouragingly.

Then Terra urged him to speed up the evacuation. Problems were brewing in piping numbers outside and beyond. The Smart Bar was recording twenty-thousand people on the Mall. Icons, miniature avatars, and laser emoticons were flaring at the White House.

He still felt safe behind Terra's Roll Call illusion. "For everyone who doubts that leaving is the answer, here's a taste of what awaits you if you decide to stay," he said to everyone.

He had Terra activate images of confused and terrified people all around the world. They were beginning to congregate in city-dome plazas, subterranean malls, and cluster worship centers. Sky Lanes were backing up with hover-car traffic. Around old airport sites—now hovercraft parking facilities—and space launch fields, people were having to power down their hover vehicles in a mid-air gridlock. Astrocraft were landing, but none launching. Hover-gliding beyond the legal speed of 120 mph in their black-and-whites and white-and-reds; Enforcer and Secret Service craft were racing against time like blackbirds outpacing falling snow to guard all the launch fields, inspection hangars, and astrocraft shelters. Stern reporters on holosite stations were showing images of the moon, the space battles that had occurred between Stealth Force and the terrorists, the wormhole that had whiplashed beyond Mars, and static images from space colonists and planetary settlers trying to transmit messages. Then, they displayed the spewing lunar fissure.

Obviously, there was a leak in the information he had ordered Top Secret because reporters were live streaming a few more of those events. Global Enforcer facilities were filling with people who were receiving Top Secret information and demanding answers.

Jenkens groaned and Manning said: "We're receiving a million calls a second. This has to be the work of another damn spy…recording from somewhere in here." Searching the long exit lines, he had Terra activate a tracer to track all secret data. After a second's scan, she said that the spy was holositing on skip mode; but she was probing each individual's wrist device and holosite signatures. She believed she'd soon mark the spy. He glanced at the tiny, green tracker light Terra just streamed into his wrist device. His small Beethoven avatar appeared and began hovering with a yellow aura as its shadow. Then he ordered Terra to stream back The Regency's Standard Busy Response to everyone hailing them, requesting they break their Roll Call sequestration. "Terra is returning calls with that Busy Response and our new Emergency broadcast. Even so, anarchy is about to erupt like a volcano." He ordered Terra to contain all the outside images for His Eyes Only. "We don't need people in line knowing more…recording something more that'll only make the spy somewhere in here angrier." Then he grew angry that the experts were experiencing so much trouble opening the escape portal. "What the hell's going on there! Ya got lasers and blasters. Ya can't blow the damn hatch, clasps, whatever!"

Two matrix techs folded down their white hoods. Their white-gloved hands were coated with translucent goop. "We're trying, Sir, but these microscopic seals are viral based with vortexes that act like skin eaters if we don't contain 'em properly. The creepy crawlers come to life at any foreign intervention and then go anti-gravitational! We haveta keep the temp around the tiny hinges at zero."

"Five minutes and we should neutralize this portal to open, Sir," his partner said. On the floor around them, engineers had cordoned off the section and were paralyzing bouncing goop with liquid nitrogen and then vacuuming the breaking falling pieces.

Meanwhile, people began a cacophony of low chatter.

Battlefield Matrix

Someone called, "You think the Neltans might have particle accumulation technology to help us?"

"Don't know," Jenkens answered sluggishly, "but it seems that *that's* what the moon needs to re-cement itself. Some type of particle acceleration would increase the intensity at which the moon could re-assemble and heal."

A scientist shot out of the exit line and called, "Little *that'll* do us anyway 'cause we're looking at two thousand years before we can return." Crying people pulled him back to his spot, and they began consoling one another.

"Yeah, that time-frame sounds a long way off…and returning to help people who are living now but who'll be dead in two thousand years seems useless, but it's not," Manning said.

"Those people will be our relatives!" someone shouted.

"And we'll be dead by then too, right? 'Cause Regenerating on *Sagan* isn't meant to keep us alive that long, right?" another asked.

Through exasperated and frightening speculations, Manning countered their fears. He was imbibing energetic oxygen while volleying answers to their questions, until he finally had Terras multiply after he silenced the crowd. "But at least someone'll be returning to Earth, even if it's not one of us. In whatever state we find ourselves in, we, or our offspring, *will* return in two thousand years."

"You mean we *hope* to return," a Regent called. "The people who'll be coming back'll be like aliens and stranger."

The Regent's Terra laid her virtual hand on her host's shoulder. "Days are like shadows without hope. You told me to always remind you of that famous quote."

Manning said: "We might not know who, or what, will be greeting our *Sagan* crew when we return to Earth. But we can promise people whom we're about to leave behind that somebody *will* return to help them." Several frosty portal seals burst open. "First, we have to get to *Sagan* and begin to follow through with our mission. So all of you…begin thinking about your jobs up there. Start preparing mentally for the transition."

"Maybe, by then, the people here, or the Neltans, will have a wormhole network that might return us faster," a Regent shouted.

As were most people in line, Regent Sylvia Itonovich had been in Record-mode with her wrist device and neck-disc connections streaming live to people on her Contact List—all of them growing impatient to enter the escape portal. She appeared Viking strong and ready to meet the challenge. "*That's* what we tell people in the speech we broadcast tomorrow. I know the Neltans have technology to re-energize stars. If they have that, and are using advancements in combination with their Matter Stream to create habitable atmospheres and alter rogue planets, they must have *something* that can repair our moon."

Elisa Holton stepped up with a small image of a glistening triangular astrocraft hovering over Gem. She explained that because Gem was Neltan-based, its programs contained a few sophisticated, but rudimentary, blueprints. "Here's a technology from their Advancement Committee. Thousands of years ago, they reined in a rogue planet ten light years away from them after they discovered that the iron ball was in direct collision with the planet they were exploring," she said. "They saved a primitive race from annihilation. I'll send you the info."

Manning quickly replied, "Don't do that, please. It's too confusing giving everything we're going through. Stream it to that grid I gave you the password to access on *Sagan*. Right now, we gotta get moving outta here."

Jenkens had washed his face and was wiping it with a white towel as he dashed toward the beginning of the exit line when a row of hinges on the portal opened. The techs and their white vacuums backed up and parted ways, leaving an open pathway toward the smoldering wall. Enforcers ripped away red tape, and the virtual yellow roped off zone disappeared. People at the starting point cheered. Enforcers began heaving boxes on revving robots and robotic platforms.

Battlefield Matrix

"Let's go everyone!" called Jenkens, gesturing for people to rush out the portal. "Out...out! The escape door's open!"

Chapter 21

John Baston's Warning

A hard chill and a slight fungal stench swept through the room. A low hollow reverberation and steady breeze were cycling through the tunnel like ghosts swirling from an ancient mining accident. As Engineers renovated the White House decades ago, they also transformed the old mine into an evacuation passageway to protect the leaders in case of another terror attack. The tight passageway extended from the Oval Office to a short, L-car ride under the Potomac to another climbing pathway leading to a discrete surface exit.

People donned jackets and raised their collars. Everyone at the front of the line began asking where the passageway ended.

Manning answered: "It leads to a concealed access outside D.C."

Several people gasped in complaint. That exit point meant they'd have to carry or push their loads a long way after exiting the L-car.

He responded: "So? You leave with your life, or ya stay.

What is it?"

They didn't answer. They began following Terra guides and illuminated their personal avatars or icons as they stepped out of the room into the frigid exit way and began navigating through the stone tunnel passageway.

Jenkens kept shoving people out the portal. "Come on! Move out!" Sending a *Farewell* emoticon to Manning through his tiny Jackie Gleason avatar, he slid behind a scientist who was in need of some intense prodding.

When Manning activated Jenkens' avatar, it said to him, "See you on the other side!"

Manning tried to catch a last glimpse of him at the front of the long line, but the evacuees looked like burdened refuges weighted down by their towering possessions. They were huffing and struggling, complaining that everything in their arms was necessary and that they couldn't part with anything that might save lives and ease their lives on *Sagan*. They were so frightened of their future living conditions even though Terra had been providing them with simulations of their future accommodations. Every packed box, wrapped tube, bundle of valuable wire, nano-organic fabric, software, matrixware, pencil and paper were like life preservers.

One person yanked open a drawer on an end table and crammed paperclips into her shirt pocket, saying: "I don't think additive manufacturing can replicate these exactly. What if the machines break down simultaneously? No way do I trust that self-repairing ship one-hundred percent. Everyone—take what you think we'll need. It'll have to last us two hundred years!"

A few Regents were discussing the sudden change. The departure for Nelta had always seemed to be a distant event. "God—we might never see this place again," one Regent declared.

"Hell, you know we'll never see Earth, at least not with the bodies we got right now," another shouted.

"What the hell's going on here?" Manning asked. "These people are completely losing it and in no way can I be their psychiatrists! They just can't seem to get movin' and accept the hard facts."

Terra said: "They are grappling with death and experiencing the anxiety that comes with the crisis of confronting a new worldview. You yourself once said, Executive Regent Manning, that change is the one constant that takes people to frightening places in their minds."

He felt a light-bulb moment rush through his thoughts. "Thanks, Terra. Now please stream your analysis to them. And stay on that analytic mode. We all need that type of reflective model right now." Bathroom doors at both ends of the room were still swinging—vomit and urine smells wafting in their breezes.

"Keep moving, everyone," Manning motioned. "No time for lamenting what once was...save it for later! Listen to my Terra. She's streaming some sound advice to all your avatars and Terra guides." He ordered two engineers to usher bewildered and panicking people to the exit. Glancing at the security wall zone next to a set of double doors leading into the corridor, he saw red-and-white flashing Emergency poles.

That meant trouble outside the White House, and Terra's evolved matrix was streaming two-fold through the historic building to fend off a perceived assault. Terra-III had learned and altered its Attack/Recon/Defend program after Dr. Coflin's strike, the Black Photonic Centipede virus, and the Halite Being's infiltration into humanity's space/time.

Tiptoeing to get a small view, he noticed the top of Washington's Monument cut off by a spotlight image. Someone had replaced the standard security floodlight with a large display of the moon that looked comet-stricken and exploding. Jagged, broken pieces of it were streaking toward Earth. The flashing icons on the wall zone began beating red, signaling that they were now under an Emergency, Stage-3 Alert. Calling for Terra to turn down the shrill warning sound, he told everyone in line that people outside were filling the perimeter. People weren't buying that The Regency was sequestering for a simple Roll Call. At any time, angry, confused, and frightened people would be overpowering Secret Service and Enforcers—who would be abandoning their posts anyway. Crowds would be stampeding through the White House, flooding the Press Room, tearing the place apart and looking for anyone who could grant them rides to space stations—to anywhere off Earth.

Manning cried: "Move! Go—get out, everyone! We're gonna have pandemonium in here soon. Armed guards at the entrances can't continue to placate people for long without committing mass murder. We need to get to *Sagan* and address The World so that won't happen." Again, he glanced at the time and had his Terra repeat, and stream, the countdown every five minutes: 2:20 a.m. Terra calculated a new time for all of them to catch astrocraft off-Earth. They had an hour and twenty minutes to elude the people they'd be leaving behind and launch from Dulles to various off-Earth destinations, or *Sagan*. As Terra's holographic form stood alongside him, coaching him on where to place boxes and packages for Regents to haul out the small passageway, he ordered her: "Terra, have retrofitted vehicles scattered at irregular points around the indirect access point on the other side of this tunnel."

She showed him the proximity of the secret access point inside a large park. "However, Executive Regent Manning, as per safety protocol, I cannot divulge that exact location until the last person completes his or her travel under the Potomac."

Then he also recalled another lucky factor in helping them avoid detection upon stepping onto the surface: a veil of darkness as they emerged from the passageway. "Still, I want air traffic conditions appearing as normal as possible on the way to Dulles and when we launch. Scatter our crafts' departures and trajectories so people can't tell it's us leaving in mass and where we're heading if someone sights us and streams a disproportionate amount of astrocraft launching off-Earth. Furthermore, I want no flags or emblems on any of our craft."

Her eyes flashing a green signal of compliance, she imaged

J.P. Osterman

several craft that had landed in the concealed field. Their crews and robotics were loading and arranging supplies. Terra was altering the crafts' paint jobs.

He wonder how he could give them all more time to escape. He whispered to her: "When the last person exits the Oval Office, have the server robots unleash some of the contaminated materials those tech extracted off the escape portal. That should buy us more time." But when he noticed the mass of congregating crowds, almost at half the intensity of Final Communication, he realized that a little time wasn't good enough. Those mad crowds pushing at Enforcers appeared treacherously mad, dangerous, and vehement. He needed to do something much more drastic than a simple microbotic invasion. On a small wall-zone at the back of the room, he saw an old-Earth drone attack on terror from 2012. "Got it! Terra, I didn't want to resort to this...but I must. *Sagan*'s priority. We must all arrive there safely."

"Yes, Executive Regent Manning?" she said softly.

"When the last person reaches the section of the tunnel beyond the Potomac, I'll program a drone to cave it in. Map that location, Terra." As she began a perusal of the L-car's path under the Potomac, he gained access to the nearest warehouse of counterterrorism weaponry, tapped on one of the drones, and synchronized it with the L-car exit under the Potomac.

Responding to each of his miniscule swipes, the drone powered up in Silent-mode, maneuvered out of its line and began a slow glide toward the exit. Then it camouflaged via a link with the tropopause shield.

"I need to do this carefully...exactly...so none of *us* gets inundated with water," he whispered to Terra. Anyone following them in the tunnel would die in the flood. He didn't want to make the strike appear as a murderous plot. That would definitely incite a war against everyone who had left. "Set a trip-light at that section underground so that when I pass the trip-light, the motion will trigger the drone to fire."

Terra faded and then reappeared taller in front of him.

Battlefield Matrix

"What's this?"

"Another protocol, Executive Regent Manning. A Second Opinion protocol."

Under exasperated breath, he said: "Just arm the damn drone. There's no need for a consultation at this point in the game. I know the body count's gonna be high. But I have to do this. We're going to have stampedes of angry people at our heels," he shouted. "We can't have that, Terra…I told you that!" He felt his stomach burn. He grabbed more water and gulped it down. "The flood needs to look like *their* fault. I know. After the collapse occurs, make it a consequence of too many people inundating such a small mining area. "This must be, Terra. To ensure our safety and arrive safely on *Sagan*." As Terra complied by circumventing the tunnel's capacity and inserting weak zones into the blueprints of the Potomac's surrounding grounds, he added: "And oh—stream to our Dulles guards that we're coming. Have them ready to receive us at the Big T at Launch Site 5. Close Air Lane 267 leading to that launch site now." She showed him the sky freeway that contained a few flying hovercraft. "Our escape craft need Direct-and-Covert access to Site 5. Contrive a diversion so all other hovercraft will keep away from Air Lane 267. Then, after we board our craft and launch, you can re-open the Air Lane."

"Yes, Executive Regent Manning," Terra said. Each word she spoke, his orders materialized in images over his wrist device. "I am raising the barricades ten miles prior to Air Lane 267 to read, *No visibility! Detour via Air Lane 257*. From the tropopause shield, I'm projecting Air Lane 267 with a haboob illusion."

"Good use of that Vision Matrixware we used to outsmart terrorists," he complimented.

"For the next two hours, Sir, no one will even consider approaching Air Lane 267 without believing they will hit a severe dust storm and collide into a hovercraft pile up." She also added the haboob illusion to the new Emergency alert streaming in everyone holosite around the globe and off-Earth.

J.P. Osterman

"Good," he began, "everything we're doing will ensure the safety of our lives, Terra, and ultimately, the future of everyone here...even though they don't realize that right now. Just *you* don't forget that."

"I won't, Sir. I am retaining everything in your *For My Eyes Only* grid, Executive Regent Manning."

In between moments wherein he directed her to store other information in that grid, he shouted words of comfort to angry and impatient individuals, saying to them: "It'll be alright;" and, "Just keep *your* avatars and Terra helpmates streaming to my Terra for updates;" and, "No—don't *at all* inform best friends and that *extremely* close relative. Only tell immediate family whom Terra has on The List. That's it! That's all Terra designated for you. Those are the people *you* agreed to accompany you on *Sagan* when you accepted your position;" and, "Nooo...you can't go home, or to your company, and get *that* to take along with you. There's not enough time. We told you that already. Damn—are ya deaf, dumb and blind to what you're avatar and my messages are streaming to ya!? *Ahhh*— you're exasperating the hell outta me. Leave it! Forget about it! It's gone! You can order a *new* one on *Sagan*. There is a manufacturing facility on Level 7, remember?" He was running out of breath and sweating. After five minutes of coaxing and pushing people, he called on more Terras to assume the job.

One Regent in front of Elisa Holton and Maureen Strickler began pacing the floor while obviously mulling over leaving-or-staying. "Go to *Sagan* right now? Live there? Now? Oh my God...my relatives! I just can't leave my dog!"

Manning repeated several times to others who began taking the man's side: "You have to go into that tunnel now. You'll have everything—and more—once you're up there. You'll see. It won't be any type of simulation. Money's not an issue. You know that. We're implementing an entirely new exchange system on *Sagan*. And pets are a no anyway. Virtual pet, yes. But put in a request to my holosite and I'll see if I can get your dog into one of *Sagan*'s zoos. And those who are joining you know the same thing. They signed the *Acceptance Document* agreeing to those terms and conditions of the voyage. Haven't ya ever said goodbye to anyone or left anything before? Just think of this exodus as a death and move on with your lives, 'cause you have a real long life—a different life, totally different—ahead of ya." Then he told Terra to make virtual copies of himself, and to stream his image and those words to everyone inside the tunnel. She notified him that at the point of embarking on the L-cars scheduled to transport them beneath the Potomac, she would lose her connectivity until they would disembark on the other side. That trip under the Potomac was ten minutes. Travel time from there to the exit portal entailed a ten-minute walk. He ordered her to have everyone stop there and completely fill up all six L-cars so that not one seat remained vacant. Calculating the intervals, Terra activated another six L-cars in a distant mine, directing them to break through a *Hazardous, Do Not Enter Zone* and coast to the location under the Potomac where another wave of weighted down individuals could board more L-cars and move toward the surface exit. As she did that and then triggered that *No Enter Zone* to quake and collapse, Manning said, "Staying together as much as possible needs to be our priority until we're on *Sagan*. Stay together once you arrive on the surface! No wandering off!" He told her to deliver that directive to everyone through his Virtual Copy, which began materializing in front of people in line like an extending reflection.

After delivering the message, Virtual Copy continued to bounce onward and then disappear down the tunnel.

In another discreet area, several scientists and Regents were arguing over how to handle overcrowding on *Sagan* and whether they might experience claustrophobia or island fever in spite of the controlled field experiments that statistically disproved incidents of claustrophobia while spacefolding. Manning ordered Terra to holosite the results of the experiments to them, which then appeared to ease their fears. Seeing outcomes seemed to be affecting everyone in a positive manner. He ordered Terra to attune to more arguments, process variances, and refute the argumentation by immediately streaming data and results.

No matter what he did or said, he noticed that one scientist's terror couldn't be assuaged. When he forgot about the frantic man for a while as he was paying attention to other important details, the scientist managed to sneak around the guards who had finished taping the last package. Other Enforcers were busy directing and transporting the IMAX hardware out the portal. Suddenly, the scientist unclasped one metal housing for the screen, grabbed a shimmering Gem program that began smoking in his hand, and sloshed the glowing nano-organic hardware into his wrist device. The device turned blue and purple like a horrible scab as it wound around his wrist into dark chains.

Wild-eyed, the scientist shouted, "Any time...and this'll infiltrate Terra's matrix! Everyone will know what's goin' on in here and what you're doing, Executive Regent Manning." He glanced down at his arm, at the dark armband's black glow. He blinked wildly, obviously in denial of the armband's pernicious cellular-invasive properties. "I know...I know what you intent to do with that tunnel."

Several Regents waved for the line to move to the side, and Terra ignited the yellow, laser-light shield, protecting them.

Manning ordered her, "Counter what he's saying with a noise cancellation app!"

The whites of the scientist's eyes yellowed and his hair began whitening. "That won't stop what I'll do as soon as this tech indicates I can use it!"

"And what exactly will you do?" While waiting for an answer, Manning asked Terra to give him an ID on the changing scientist. Most people were now in the tunnel. He could hear them prodding one another through their terror-filled voices.

"I cannot generate his identification," Terra began. "His genetics have altered. I am reversing biometrics for an identity, however."

Meanwhile, two scientists broke through the yellow shield,

joining the man in his revolt as Enforcers heaved a long tall box into the exit passage and returned to assist Manning.

Manning said to three individuals who left the line to help him as well, "Just go—get back in line—leave!" He told Terra to tell the Enforcers inside the tunnel who were busy hauling the IMAX components toward L-cars: "Prioritize it all to the front of the line, load it, head to the access point, and launch it all to *Sagan*."

Elisa dashed stealthily out of her place in line, stretched out her arm, and offered a glowing Gem to counter the scientist's threat. "I can help, Sir. Two crystals are emitting recognition rays. That means I have to act now, fast, for Gem to stop the man's disastrous morphology even though I have no idea how Gem will do it or what the man might look like when Gem's done with him."

He told her: "No—just go! You're almost at the portal. Get the armband the hell outta here. What this guy has on is altering into a weapon of some type or virus, Dr. Holton. Terra and I'll take care of him and his idiot colleagues who've chosen to join him." In reality, he didn't want her to hear the scientist's accusations.

As she left, he turned his attention back to the jiggling, glowing, black-and-blue, nano-organic armband device. In ten second's time, it had grown to twice its size and had the potential to alter and damage the matrix. He knew from yesterday's bad events that anything Neltan, and uncontrolled, could unleash ciphers, viral organics—anything *unknown* or *alien* from another world even. That IMAX Encantado matrixware was not quantum connecting with Nelta and under the Advancement Committee's delicate supervisory touch. Death by moon strikes was nothing compared to what the scientist's ghastly black and purple arm chain was about to unleash into him, morph him into, or discharge around the globe…and possibly into *Sagan*.

"Idiot!" Manning shouted. "Peel it off while ya still can! It's killing you! It'll kill us!"

Their T-shirts blotchy with sweat, the scientist and his two colleagues began debating whether to surrender or to discover another way to leave the Press Room.

Remembering that his gamma weapon was gone, Manning decided to try one last thing before prying his gun out of his belt and shooting them. "John…that's your name?" he asked when Terra imaged the scientist's identity. The white-haired, gray-faced scientist nodded in affirmation as his friends continued, although in vain, to help him work the glowing black-and-purple kelp-looking armband winding under his armpit. "Terra says you're Dr. John Baston."

He backed away, along with his two friends.

Manning streamed for Terra to dim the lights over them. At his back, he could hear a few people in line shouting expletives of terror and possible solutions to disarm the three rebels.

John Baston raised his monstrous arm high in the air. Grimacing in obvious pain, he was about to whip his hand as hard as he could at the door. "Some of this should slip off and hit a wall zone! People'll get the message loud and clear that diabolical things happened in this facility, Manning. They'll *know* you're a murderer." He had the dry heaves, his chest bulging as if something were settling inside him.

"Stop!" Manning reached under his shirt and touching the gun. "John—whoow, hold on now. You're a scientist, so let's talk common sense…facts, logic. Wait until we're on *Sagan*. We'll create a well-thought out plan with disaster preparedness for people we're leaving behind. But first, we gotta get to *Sagan*, alive…and that might mean that I have to do a few unconventional things to get us there. Understand?" Shaking his head no, the scientist collapsed, kneeling on the floor. The floors counteracting agents began unleashing a white repellant on the scientist's exposed flesh.

As hissing white silk began eating into the fabric of the man's pants, Manning said: "We have no idea at this exact moment about tidal motion or centrifugal changes in orbiting bodies. Terra's still analyzing data and configuring algorithms to provide people with cohesive images that can generate

Battlefield Matrix

sound holosite experiences. We need matrix stats and parameters of each person's holosite in order for Terra to generate simulations so we can start helping people. So, in light of what I just told you, I'm giving you one more chance to let Terra help you disable that armband and surrender. Let's not endanger all of mankind any further 'cause that's what you're doing with that thing and you don't even realize it. Come on—John...I need *you* to help me." He held out his arms, waiting. The Smart Bar flashed the next minute: 2:35.

His crying female friend who had been shielding him ran toward the exit portal. "I'm sorry! I changed my mind! I thought he was saying some things that were true." She stopped abruptly at the yellow, laser-light shield line, begging: "Please let me back in. I'm sorry! That thing on him's making him *crazy*...taking over his insides even. Any minute and he's gonna explode! Let me back in, *pleeeze*!" When Terra deactivated the yellow shield, Elisa and Maureen grabbed the woman's shaking body and pushed her toward the portal.

Meanwhile, John and his other colleague had been debating whether the armband had the capability to break through an even stronger shield at the double doors.

Feeling frustrated but not wanting to shoot the men just yet because the ghastly armband could infect Earth's matrix, which in turn would affect *Sagan*'s matrix, Manning thought of an idea and a plan. He streamed to two physicians to crawl around upturned chairs and tables, surprise the two rebels and sedate them. He gestured for his Terra to reproduce right in front of the men once the docs were about to pounce on them. As the armband crept around John Baston's thick, red-veined neck, Terra appeared and divided in in two in front of the men. Reacting in outcries of shock, they ducked. With sedation patches in his hands, a doctor sprang up and slapped the patches on their necks. Instantly, the rebels collapsed—along with the armband, that slurped off Baston's arm and began spreading purplish thick strings of nano-organic ooze like viscous oil floating on top of water. Where the ooze touched down, the floor bubbled. Robotic cleaners, roving on their lift-

and-glides, scurried to the site, where they sprayed the rampant compound with microscopic generics that created an antidote on contact. The substance hardened, but appeared malleable, like shiny stiff glue—now and then still jiggling. The cleaners began scooping up the lines of puddles that chunked when the substance reached their backpacks. The unstable foreign presence obviously needed more treatments so Terra could render it *Hazardous but Disposable*. One of the skilled technicians who had blasted open the exit portal directed the robotic cleaners to dispose of the material at Langley's Research Site after they had all evacuated the Press Room. Before their containers flashed green, indicating, ready for immediate removal, Manning directed the techs out the portal and rendered the contents, *Decorative Solutions*.

A portion of the foreign goop had missed their detection, slinking into a Terra hologram.

Terra's image began turning to paper-thin stone as the black/purple ooze altered the projection light into crawling particles with microscopic irritant hooks. They sounded like billions of communicating ants.

Manning ordered two scientists who were almost out the portal to help him search for instruments to analyze and destroy the entity. Others in line began screaming at the burgeoning infection as more Terras replicated around it, cautiously scanning and analyzing the alien virus that was obviously working hard to recognize, or capture, or kill, or investigate its new host. Those were the various assessments from people inside the tunnel. They were streaming advice on how to neutralize the invading entity. In the interim, a few globules broke loose and began floating out of the Terra structure—dividing now and then.

Elisa Holton ran out of line and through the yellow protective shield. Gem was glowing brightly around her arm— a few, small mound processors sparkling like crystals under heavy light. "Gem's indicating she has knowledge of the attacker, Sir. It's prepared to launch countermeasures to stop the foreign presence. I know you told me to get out of here fast, but Gem's acting on autopilot. I can't stop its reaction to the matrix attack." On her way to the infected Terra, she dashed around tables and chairs, avoiding a cluster of purple transparent bubbles that appeared attracted to her. As she maneuvered through a small, packaging debris field, she pointed Gem at the purple, shiny hovering orbs.

Immediately, they rolled backwards in the air like marbles cascading over a table. Stopping next to the infected Terra statue, they hovered together—darting around one another with energized activity—keeping their distance from Gem and Elisa.

His Terra said, "The entities are sizing up their new environment." They were spinning in place, surging up, and then inching down, as if in Inquisitive-mode.

"Gem's able to repel them...keep them at bay." Elisa crawled toward them, gradually backing them into a corner. "I'm sending these critters towards your instruments so you can contrive some sort of antidote or weapon that can eliminate them. I'll work here to interface with some other technology that might help us. Right now, I'm having Gem access the room's magnetic field...see if the things respond to electromagnetic forces."

As she said that, Manning noticed a small line of luminescent substance rushing towards him on the bubbling sizzling carpet. Racing from it, he headed toward the exit line and jumped through the yellow shield when his Terra deactivated it. Terra's laser-light protection stopped a smoking, rolling, purplish thread from clasping his shoes. Standing back in relief, he ordered Elisa: "Dr. Holton—take down these damn rolling things! They pack a mean wallop!" From his wrist device, he kept retrieving ideas from people in the tunnel on how to destroy the invaders.

Meanwhile, the doctors had managed to pull the two sedated rebels to safety on top of several rising robotic platforms. Four purple, shiny, nano-organic, floating balls were approaching them. They appeared to be evolving in intelligence, developing small cognitive abilities, as their round bodies moved whenever the doctors gestured to assess them. They were also forming anthropomorphic appendages on top of their sleek reflective surfaces that appeared mirror-like, soaking up images and wall-zone scenes throughout the room.

The doctor called: "This intelligence is functioning as a community. I just saw one of them morph into a swinging pendulum of a clock. It stopped in front of a wall zone that was showing a clock commercial, and then it shape shifted back to its original round form."

Elisa accessed the commercial and then swept the pendulum into an X-ray diffraction program Gem was running on the shape shifting entity. "I have the matrix synthesizing more info with Gem streaming Terra results. Just a little longer! The best I can do right now is to divert their attentions away from people in the exit line."

"Good thinking," Manning shouted, "because these things soon will be after us!"

A scientist ordered several Terras to stay put as she began running solutions whenever her small gas chromatograph yielded results of the creatures' composition. She said: "If we don't disintegrate the substance, I'm receiving indications that they'll *soon be* be*yond* killing!"

In spots, the floor was white, glowing, bubbling, and smoking—rejecting and countering the alien substances that periodically showered down on the carpet. The remaining ceiling processors were at their brightest intensity. Terra's matrix was at peak performance in its fight against the intrusion.

Elisa's Gem armband activated another brilliant set of attack lights that struck each shiny globule in midair. "The green beam that Gem's emitting is a Thrive program," she said. "Now let's see what happens to Gem's nemesis. That's what Gem is indicating in a swirling analysis she's showing me. These creatures in here *are* enemies of the Neltans. Millions of years ago, they rained down a contamination on Nelta that caused a planet-wide alteration in their genetics. These entities will annihilate humanity if they propagate."

Battlefield Matrix

Gem's powerful, electromagnetic light pulses began disintegrating a purple root inside the Terra statue that the entity had taken hostage. The popping and hissing caused a slight ionization of pungent onion quality.

A high-pitched, A-minor frequency resounded.

Several people in line began coaching Elisa: "The substance is dissolving! Keep firing!"

"All Neltan-based, photon interfaces harbor the same, basic, light-fractal layering," Elisa called. "With a boost from the matrix, Gem is blasting the entities with Synchrotron light to eliminate them."

As those forces continued to strike and pummel the hardened statue and hovering alien entities, the floor altered into a shiny crystalline surface, absorbing the attackers after they melted and rained down on the carpet.

Finally, Standard Terra was free. The matrix's photon projection light was back at its yellow holographic intensity. "Normal," Terra said, appearing and disappearing throughout the room as if on Test-mode. "Normal processing in progress," she said, and she began pointing at a few areas in the air that needed a pinch more of medicinal photonic intervention.

Noticing that his Terra had a look of relief on her smiling face, Manning felt a sudden burning sensation strike the center of his chest. "Ouch—damn!"

His Terra appeared in front of him with scanning eyes.

Elisa ran to him, pushing aside his arms. "Sir! Don't touch it!"

A tiny shard of the dead statue substance had ricocheted off the floor, hit him, burned through his white shirt and left a smoking residue of sizzling scab. The physician ran up to him with his Body Double Image scanner as an Enforcer dropped a box at the exit door to help him sit up. In the background, Terras multiplied and exploded the last of the hovering orbs. After Gem interfaced with the BDI, Elisa explained the results. Illumination-ware, like tiny bioluminescent ocean krill, were now on his skin and reacting with his cells. Composing of anomalous leptons, the dead substance had resurrected and were now trying to read him, clamp into him, and synchronize with his biology—obviously to alter him.

"What the hell kinda sick technology or alien identity is this!" he shrieked. He was drinking water and the doctor and physician were showering him with an aerosol spray and dipolar magnetic currents that were sloughing a layer of skin off his entire body.

As the doctor returned to his positions in line and the Enforcer moved out the last of the boxes, Elisa said, "Gem's assessment showed that Dr. Baston's errant technology was indeed an alien meteoric cell of ancient origin whose genetic material was trying to seed on Earth."

"However, your Gem acted as an antidote for the alien infection, Elisa," interrupted Maureen, "otherwise, it would have spread and perhaps eventually conquered Earth." Over her wrist device, she had images of two the scientists who had helped them resolve the problem.

As Elisa also showed him the results of Gem's conquering capacity, the floor returned to its normal carpeted state, and Terra had activated air vents that were gushing with fresh oxygen. "Terra's streamed the entity's genetic makeup to Station II's Secured Neltan grid, Sir."

"And the antidote I hope," Manning added, tapping off a bit of blood with a Swath-Heal pad. With the shield off and the room back to normal, he raced to his desk, pulled out a tourist T-shirt and changed shirts. Carefully unpinning his Executive Regency's gold stars, he secured them in the small gift box and then stuffed the box into his shirt pocket. Feeling anger biting through him from the place of his sore chest, he hollered orders to two Enforcers who had dashed into the room to report on the blaring alerts resounding through the White House. "Take the two rebels to *Sagan*. I'll decide their punishment there." He pointed sternly at the two sluggish men, adding, "They've lost their right to bring family to *Sagan*. And don't give them Face Time to say goodbye either. I gave them a chance to surrender and help us before this disaster happened," he snarled. "They didn't. Now they pay."

Dr. John Baston's colleague grimaced and said, "One day, I'm *killing* you, Manning."

Manning unleashed his gun and pointed the barrel into the man's face. Walking close to his eyes, he slapped him instead. Then he ordered the Enforcer who had handcuffed him: "Drop this one on the prison station that's on a trajectory to that rogue planet beyond Pluto. When you're through, transport Dr. John Baston to *Sagan*. If Intracranial Intervention doesn't change him in the next few days, we'll ship him off to Station V as well." He told John Baston, who was still in a state of delirium and half-unconscious from the experimental failure: "I'm keeping you only because you might be valuable to us in the future...your new genetics might be of some help to us on *Sagan*. But that's it." He nodded at the Enforcers: "Take 'em both out."

"What? No!" John Baston's friend countered. He began kicking the Enforcers who were struggling to restrain him. He stopped recoiling and said: "Hey—I'm no criminal! I just had an opinion!" He pointed at the simulations Terra was projecting for the moon.

One scenario showed it busting apart like a popped balloon. Another showed debris orbiting Earth's Roche limit but eventually falling to Earth in the ultimate meteor shower. In both cases, Earth was taking a cosmic thrashing, its life span extinguishing into a red/orange lava bed, or an everlasting ice age, or two jagged half-planets resembling two halved eggs.

"What you're about to do is wrong, *Executive* Regent Manning." He said that with contempt. "Transparency *is* the law. The public should know *everything* we know right now concerning the moon. I saw Terra's plan to use the tropopause shield to stop people from leaving Earth." Then he whispered through purple fear-colored lips, "I know your plan...your kill plan." He swallowed hard.

Manning then realized that the man and Dr. John Baston were the spies who were leaking information to the public. They were skilled matrix hackers...most likely Tech-No

Protesters who had long ago infiltrated the Regency's special science team to spy on all secret conversations during all the Neltan/Earth Exchange of Information segments. "Damn! How could I *not* have realized that! I didn't think to consider that! How could they have fooled me for so long!?" Thoughts of self-blame and self-loathing began cycling though his mind.

The last people in line along with Elisa and Maureen quieted down—their movements halting like cold atoms.

Manning folded his arms, opened up his secure com grid over his wrist device, and said so that everyone in line and in the exit tunnels could see and hear him: "There are new rules for *Sagan*, and I'm instigating those laws right now. Protecting the astrocity for launch to Nelta *is* priority. Any spy, hacker, rebel or dissident I find among us, I'll instigate the maximum sentence." As he closed the com connection and people returned to stepping out the portal, he felt his mind flashing all the horrible catastrophes that could befall *Sagan* in between the time they'd arrive there and the time they'd leave Earth. "Terra," he began when his Terra appeared beside him, "direct the tropopause shield to turn on Earth...to keep all craft here. Only de-activate the shield when *Sagan* launches and for craft transporting people on my Instant Contact List, which is everyone escaping from here. Stream this order to General Rand. I want to make sure there are no strikes or attacks on the astrocity or the space stations."

"Huh?! Manning—you can't do that!" The young rebel called for people in line to help him. "Come on! See this guy for what he is...a monster! You *sure* you wanna be trapped on a ship with 'im for a hundred years?! *Be* with *him* when he meets the Neltans? God—who the hell ya lettin' represent Earth!"

Manning saw that the last in line looked confused. Obviously, with the protective shield standing in between them, they couldn't hear the man's words, especially Elisa Holton who had Gem clutched tightly against her chest. They quickly snapped back to exiting the portal. Almost everyone was out of the Oval Office, and Terra announced that the first

Battlefield Matrix

individuals who had exited the Oval Office were approaching the first set of L-cars to transport them under the river. At the other side of the Potomac was the trip-light of destruction. He double-checked to make sure the trip-light wouldn't ignite the flood until it recognized *his* biometrics. After that point, he'd have another ten minute walk to the discrete surface access.

Manning checked the time: 2:59 a.m. Because of Dr. John Baston's rebellious stunt, the evacuation was taking longer than he had planned. He was pissed. He told the Enforcers who were scooting away equipment in preparation to lead their prisoner to a craft landing on the roof: "After you put John's friend here into the bay compartment on Station V, sever the compartment from the station. Sever all *four* compartments." They glanced at one another and straightened up in gestures of obvious discomfort. "We want no one *ever* leaving Station V to try to spacefold outta the solar system."

The man dropped to his knees. "You're kidding, right? Manning—you're joking...you must be. I'll be among mean prisoners...ruthless criminals and terrorists! I don't deserve that!"

Manning backed away into a shadow, leading to the end of the line.

"Okay, I'm sorry," pleaded the man. "I spied...but I'm sorry...really sorry!"

"Take 'im outta here," Manning ordered.

Lifting the man off the floor, The Enforcers began dragging him toward the double doors, but they appeared disturbed as they paused and one of them asked, "Sir, where should *we* go after dropping 'im at Bay I on Station V?"

"To *Sagan*, of course." When they left, he thought of the trip-light of destruction that would unleash a portion of the Potomac into the escape tunnel. It was becoming like a sick signal between his brain and nauseous stomach. As he heard the craft launched from the roof, he thought of all the law enforcement personnel outside in the corridors and at each security enclave. He noticed their images on the security wall-zones. They were like armed tungsten rods, holding people

413

back from charging through the White House. But their buffered protected bodies wouldn't survive down there in the entryways for long. The crowds would soon become like wind in a blizzard against the barrage of their protective laser fire. They were always operating under Orders to Shoot. But hurricanes of human flesh and raining blood-and-bones couldn't fend off stampeding masses from reaching the Press Room for long. Those officers and agents would soon have to abandon their posts, and angry and frightened people would be scaling the slick security walls of the White House. Soon, those officers would be inside the Oval Office in mass, seeking the escape tunnel. They'd befriend people. They'd take refuge in the tunnel as well. After they would enter, others would follow.

He felt suddenly panicked. He had to leave…get out. The portal was like a glowing black diamond in his line of sight. I have no choice but to kill these people, he thought. Besides, the craft waiting for us on the opposite side can't even accommodate a tenth of those military personnel. He realized that all those hard-working agents and military personnel now protecting *him*…believing that they'd receive safe passage to a space station…would soon die. No choice, he kept telling himself. No choice. He had Terra stream a pattern of interference through their com grids so they couldn't communicate with anyone on the space stations upon entering the tunnel.

Battlefield Matrix

Chapter 22

Pyrite Tunnel

He saw his shaking hands after Elisa Holton waved for him to join her as last in line. Even Terra was coaching him at twice her automated, encouraging intensity to leave his Oval Office. She had re-activated the partition dividing the two rooms— now imaging its previous illusion of destruction to anyone barging into the Press Room. On the wall zones, she was displaying environmental stats in the lobbies, driveways, booths, and entrance kiosks. A great tide of people were about ready to press inside—his nightmarish imagining about to come true.

"I predict twenty minute until violence erupts, Executive Regent Manning...plus-or-minus two minutes," his Terra told him. "Your last plan of arriving on *Sagan*, gathering all lunar data in a cohesive presentation, and then launching a Preparedness Plan into every individual's holosite address has the highest probability of assuaging the anger people are beginning to display through their actions."

He then thought of a bigger problem that felt like a

dragging dismal weight. The sacrosanct White House would soon become a ground zero location—a dead zone—and go down in history as the place where The Regency abandoned everyone for safety. Try as hard as he could to prevent another war, most likely, a new war would ensue at some point between the time people would realize that he had reversed the directionality of the tropopause shield—which would keep everyone from launching off-Earth—to the time *Sagan* would launch for Nelta. He streamed his fear of an impending attack to General Rand and ordered him to fire on all the technology they had used on Earth to fight terrorism and to transfer all Tropopause Shield settings to Station III. Running to the Smart Bar flashing red shield stats over his desk, he called in his secure code to change the shield settings on Earth to alter only via Station III. He shouted at the Smart Bar avatar that popped up in retaliation, demanding that he seek further consultation. The skinny scientist-caricature said in his high-pitch voice: "The only way such a global alteration can activate is to destroy the sites on Earth responsible for operating the shield. That can't be done, Sir."

"Damn it, do as I say!" he screamed. "I gave ya the damn codes! That's all you need."

Terra intervened in duplicate and magnetically streamed a disruptive current into those facilities, assisting him. The Smart Bar avatar gradually disintegrated like virtual foam from his toes up to his bald shiny head. When the countdown would reach 0, the tropopause facilities would annihilate, transferring all the shield's control to Military Station III.

The Smart Bar flashed: *Earth-Mode on Destruct, 15 minutes.*

He shortened the countdown. "Make it ten." As the countdown altered, he told General Rand to de-activate the shield array only when the evacuees streamed him their codes on the way to their final destinations. He had already ordered the shield to reverse from Outward-mode to Inward-mode. That energy transfer would be an advantage—giving everyone living on the stations and *Sagan* a solid defense. Then he accessed Station III's military grid and checked the amount of troops at his disposal. There were over ten-thousand military personnel trained and prepared for astro-battle. But they were psyched up to battle terrorists, not their fellow human beings. Still, combined with the technology already in space, on the four stations, and *Sagan*, that number should suffice to protect everyone until *Sagan*'s new launch date and time.

With a friend in line ahead of her and the both of them approaching the small exit portal, Elisa Holton said, "Sir, I'm receiving word that we must seal this portal now!"

"Yep—everything's taken care of in here," he said, taking one long last look at his Oval Office. He remembered the last President who had occupied the hallowed ground, Patrick Murphy, before the 2057 attacks. He died while at a meeting in China after a nuclear detonation in the lower atmosphere killed three fourths of that country's population. Now all the famous brave executives seemed to be standing in a succession of sprits behind Murphy—their small virtual portraits rotating in an historic presentation in front of the Press Room double doors. Ordering Terra to seal the partition, he motioned for Elisa to keep up her fast pace through the exit door while remaining at his usual eight-foot distance behind her and her friend, Maureen Strickler. Before stepping into the tunnel, he wondered if *they* had overheard what had he had said, and he checked the ratio of noise to sound reducers on his lopsided virtual Smart Bar. He sighed in relief when Terra immediately streamed the results: 20 Hz, the lowest sound wave measured by the human ear.

Because of Terra's continued noise-cancelling tunes and window illusions, he believed that no one could have overheard his conversations and the stern sentence he imposed on Dr. John Baston's ill-mannered, defiant, spy colleague. At that time, the people in line and observing the event had complained that Terra's sound reducers were giving them headaches and that they were feeling nauseated by the matrix too frequently altering the wall décor in order to keep up the Roll Call façade of pensive activity to the public. No one could anyone have eavesdropped on his tunnel flooding plan—or hacked through to his wrist device grid—to glean details of his confidential discussions with General Rand concerning the reversal of the tropopause shield that would stop any craft the instant they'd come within a quarter mile of the array. He'd make sure at least to put out a warning of instant incineration the minute they'd pass through the shield array themselves.

As he walked over the portal's threshold into the dim, chilly tunnel, he heard the portal seal shut behind him and the zapping and hissing sounds of small robots sealing the clamps. Terra was intensifying the materials, thickening the portal. It would take anyone who knew what they were doing five minutes at least to break through, and Terra told him that people were coming. He had a ten-minute walk to catch the L-car and a ten-minute ride beneath the Potomac where he'd then disembark off the L-car and then activate the trip-wire for the drone to fire down a laser strike. By that time, Terra predicted that the heated crowds coming after them would be at the beginning of the tunnel. Gasping, closing his eyes, and keeping in close range of Elisa's voice in front of him; he imagined the screams of everyone drowning. They were trusting people he was about to betray in the worst possible way. Maybe they were entering the tunnels believing it was their duty to save The Regency who they believed had been taken hostage and unable to send out a Call for Help. His new *Emergency Alert* streaming through the Center Wall Zone Network was now streaming to everyone everywhere! He felt his muscles numb, his stomach sicken. He thought: after it's don't, it can't be undone. At one point, he stopped and inhaled deeply. He hated the feelings, and he hit the slippery cold wall to make them stop.

Halting her fast pace, Elisa turned around quickly and asked: "Sir—you alright? Need help?" Gem was glowing strange colors. "It's guiding us and adding processing power to Terra who's experiencing a weak connection the farther we descend into the tunnel," she said. One of Gems crystal mounds flashed like a pulsar, and she turned it away quickly.

Battlefield Matrix

He noticed a look of terror in her brown eyes. She backed into her friend, Maureen, and then she flinched.

"No, I'm fine, Dr. Holton. Move on, go ahead." As she walked on with her friend, almost at a jogger's pace, he sped up to keep up with them. He wondered if, through Gem, she had acquired covert information because she appeared so afraid. Then again, perhaps he was wrong. No way could he be reading that type of profound fear in her. She had to be just tired, like everyone else, and in need of sleep and time to adjust to a new way of life that'd soon be thrust on them all. *Everyone* had been under Type-A, electrified stress for hours. Everyone was flinching, shaking, vibrating and wobbly. He was too, although he'd never admit it, and he'd never admit that he might need some help too.

Continuing through the dimly lit tunnel, he said into his wrist device—a message that would stream to everyone inside the passageway and on The List: "Now that most of us are on our way off-Earth, I believe this is the time I need to put everyone on warning." He paused to let people acclimate to his echoing voice. "We almost had a catastrophe occur in the Press Room, and Terra is sending you a shortened clip of what just occurred." He noticed that, intermittently, Elisa Holton was glancing at him over her shoulder. He didn't know whether she wanted to say something to him but was feeling apprehensive, or if she was just concerned about her friend Maureen who at times couldn't stop coughing and whose condition seemed to be deteriorating. In case it was fear, he believed that if he'd explain, in segments, his part in what happened to Dr. Baston and his colleague, that Elisa Holton's demeanor would calm and she'd warm up to him eventually. As well as other physicians, he needed her...needed her skills *and* trust on *Sagan*.

He continued: "I had to take drastic actions against those dissidents. To prevent such an incident like that from happening again, after leaving here—after launching from Earth, specifically, leaving the atmosphere—there will be *no* returning to Earth. I repeat: no return to Earth. Coming back to rescue people or recover possessions is out of the question. Furthermore, due to issues surrounding security, you cannot have, nor maintain, any face-to-face contact with anyone *not* onboard *Sagan*, even though they are your friends and relatives on Earth, and even if they secretly attempt to contact you. Later, after we present to the public our Preparedness Plan, that I hope will generate a positive response and not World War IV, we will meet at *Sagan*'s Central Platform on Level-1 and discuss any problems you're experiencing, how to solve them, and how to maintain silence with people you're forced to leave behind so suddenly."

He realized that he was leaving no one important to him, and he hated having to coddle people who were; but he had to foster camaraderie and community by continuing to use the plural 'we.' He continued:

"I have instructed Terra to disable *all*—all—external communication for every one of us space-bound. In addition, I'm instigating an initiative that I am calling the *Leave Behind Law*, effective immediately, which I am streaming to you and military personnel on all stations and *Sagan* will enforce. No communicating with anyone. That's the basic tenant of the *Leave Behind Law*. But to allay your fears of never seeing your families or partners ever again, in a matter of hours, everyone you designated for The List will be joining you on the astrocity from which there *will be*, *no*, exit—no exit! And *no* holositing *anyone* who's not onboard the ship. If you believe you have an exception, you may contact me through The Regency's holosite, which Terra has already redirected to *Sagan*. You can access it through your wrist devices until we can activate astrocity-wide matrix streaming."

As he listened to relieved responses echo back to him from long distances in line, he felt less tense and defensive. Now, this was his chance to win them over to *his* team, to convince them to trust *him*, and to inspire them to loyalty.

"Ladies and gentlemen…I'm giving you one chance to stay behind if you decide right now that that's what you want. Think it over. You have the next half hour or so—from the tunnel's entrance to its ending—to decide your future and the future of those you designated for The List. Remember: you must consider them and their well-being and safety here on Earth should you decide to eliminate yourself from The List. But if you think about what I'm asking you to do right now...leave everyone else behind and all your possessions, ultimately, that's what you would have had to do anyway at some point in the future. We're just leaving a little earlier than anticipated. And remember, after *Sagan* launches, we'll experience a one-hundred-year Dead Zone of Communication inside the wormhole network. Until we arrive on Nelta—and who knows what we'll encounter there that might not permit communicating with Earth—you can't contact anyone here anyway."

When he heard gasps and painful emotional cries, he interrupted their responses and said, "I know this is hard. Several of you have streamed your fears and frustrations to me, saying how emotionally important it is to say goodbye while being unable to do so." At a distance in front of him, he saw Elisa turn and glance at him wearily. She was one of those individuals. He couldn't afford to have her rescind her position and leave his Regeneration Team on *Sagan*. Again, he realized that he needed her. Her expertise in cellular nano-organics and genetics were vital.

Not wanting to lose her—or any other scientist—he thought of a gentler way to cement a positive public image while drilling in his new *Leave Behind* rule. "I'm sorry. I truly am. But know that *we are all* together in this great escape off-Earth. We *are all* about to venture on a new mission...to a new planet...a spectacular voyage...if you could only overcome your fears and see the potential of our future cosmic landscape on *Sagan*. We'll be together in our sorrows and joys...not on Earth, but on a *grand* astrocity, *Sagan*, for decades. Just remember how excited you were when you applied for The List. Keep in your minds the positives. Force out the negatives. I've asked my Terra to help you change your perspectives. We have several helping professionals on the astrocity right now who can help you if you need extra emotional support other than that available from family and friends. Seek out those professionals. Tell Terra, or have your avatar tell someone, or stream a Help emoticon to someone. Anyone will help you…if you need it. I'll be there for you…The Regency…and Terra's augmented, version-III matrix. Meanwhile, later on this afternoon, after we situated ourselves on *Sagan* and The Regency has presented a Preparedness Plan to people on Earth, we will meet. At that time, I will explain the rationale behind the new *Leave Behind Law* which I believe will help you adjust to our new way of life."

After he spoke, several Regents began streaming to him versions of the following: "This is the law *YOU* instigated;" and, "When are you going to include *me* in the legislative process?"

Sweeping closed their interfering avatars, he transmitted another order through his tiny virtual Beethoven. "I have the time for today's communal meeting…three o'clock p.m. We can map out and prepare to vote on more rules and laws. These will change I'm sure as our experiences evolve on *Sagan*. Until we meet, after you get some needed rest, be thinking about what rules and laws *you* believe we need to instigate in order that our voyage to Nelta remain safe and successful."

He sent another message to stream through his *Contacts on The List* when suddenly the feet of his Beethoven avatar began flashing a yellow indicator light. He was two minutes away from the wooden L-car platform where matrix reception would experience a power outage. His Beethoven avatar said: "*Last Message.*"

Before he extinguished it, he added: "One last thing. If you choose to stay behind, I will not permit you to board *Sagan* later. The tropopause shield is reversing directionality. After we launch through it, the shield will achieve Inward Function through Station III. Actually, the tropopause shield is currently on Inward Function. This extreme measure will ensure our safety and the safety of those you designated for

Battlefield Matrix

The List."

Someone far ahead of him called, "That means people will fry if they even approach it!"

"Don't you think that's cruel to do to someone?" Those words echoed back at him.

Another person called: "True—they'll die if they reach the two-hundred foot energy rim, but they'll also receive an Approach warning. I helped assemble the thing up there. Don'tcha see this *has* to be done for *our* good? Our survival?"

"Yeah—our protection and *Sagan*'s safety!" another shouted, agreeing with some others farther inside the tunnel.

He called over a challenging person's voice: "I'm still waiting for your decision if you chose to stay on-Earth. But be forewarned: That choice will immediately eliminate your position on The List open it up for the next in line." With the L-car platform almost in sight, and hearing creaking axels and grinding wheels, he continued to peer at his wrist device, waiting for someone to stream to him that he or she was remaining on Earth. Thus far, no one. He added: "We have plenty of people who would be glad to have your job and your living quarters. I'm having Terra stream you just how many people were on The Wait List *before* we learned of the moon's dire condition. Just imagine how many people *now* who'd give *anything* to be in your place." He breathed out a long relieving exhale when he still noticed not one Leave request. "That's it then. I'll see you on *Sagan*."

Picking up the pace because he had fallen so far behind Elisa and her friend, he could see a line of bobbing heads disappearing into the blackness of the tunnel. He suddenly felt lost. He had been in this exact spot before but couldn't remember. He remembered a team of bodyguards escorting him through after engineers had renovated the mine and concealed it, back in 2058, after he left Lynn for The Regency. Every Regency center had an escape tunnel—from this one to China's Zhongnanhai Headquarters. At one time or another, he had walked them all.

Why...*why* can't I remember *any* of them completely? he

thought. While trying to recall the details, he began comparing himself then to how he believed himself to be now. He suddenly felt changed—no longer young and naïve. It's because Lynn's still in my head, he concluded. Darn memories are still twisting through my head like badass tornadoes. Damn regret and continuing to pine over what can't be. I hate it...wish I could just get 'er outta my head and move on like she never happened. I was *waaay* too soft and vacillating...smart but senseless, and clueless as to how to separate myself from attachments, bonds, places and things. Survival means being tough, downright hard, *and* driven. I've got to suppress this damn guilt that keeps boiling up or I'll *never* be able to instill determination and drive into people on *Sagan*. Then he realized that some people would most likely cause problems. Maybe bad problems. There's going to have to be some little changes to our human nature if we're ever gonna survive the voyage and bring back technology to save Earth. And people don't change...the matrix will *make* them. Then he felt flooded by gratitude. *Thank God* I'm where I'm at! If not for being a Regent...I'd be here if, or when, the moon explodes and people go nuts. I'd be stuck with them...most likely be killed, or killing, or fighting to eat, or on some raft, drifting—ahhh! He almost stopped and vomited, but held back the instinct. Yep, thank God I'm Executive Regent. Now I need to keep it.

He asked his Terra who was fading in and out: "Does this passage end in a storage unit? A corporate basement? Can you tell me now?"

In front of him, he saw bobbing heads and heard shoes *tap-tapping* across the long Xylophone of rocks and cobblestones as people walked quickly to the L-cars. He could also hear people shrieking now-and-then whenever someone accidentally slipped on a mossy stone like ice skaters losing their balance. The deeper into the tunnel they walked, the more intense the darkness. Compensating for lack of light, the matrix activated more Terras, but the processor couldn't maintain its subterranean connection for much longer through the all the rock, concrete and rebar in spite of those two Matrix Techs increasing its processing power in the bunker.

Over his wrist device, Terra finally popped up the image of a large bronze sculpture in Langley Fork Park. After taking L-cars under the Potomac and then walking another ten minutes, they'd arrive at a slippery narrow stairway leading into the very early dawn of Tuesday, February 28.

He ordered her to activate the imagers in the bronze eyes of the Fallen Heroes Memorial. "Stream to *Sagan*'s archival grid everyone's reactions and conversations as people leave the passageway, congregate, and embark craft to *Sagan*." After the imagers activated, giving him the view of the outside, he noticed a snowy-white wintry view of the park. The ground looked crackled, like dry grass peeking out of an icy blanket. The barren shaking trees appeared defiant in the face of Earth's rotation to dawn. "This is the first snowfall since 2057!" he marveled.

Continuing to approach the L-car platform but still far enough behind Elisa Holton so that no one could hear him, he said to his tiny, Beethoven-smiling avatar: "You'll be recording me now, so here's all the details I'm leaving behind with you." His little avatar bounced up and swirled in the air, and a 3D-box emoticon appeared, showing him how much storage capacity was available in this current communication: one minute. Whispering, he began: "Today is Tuesday, February 28, 2068. I'm in the escape tunnel. It's 3:08 a.m., Eastern Standard Time, and these are my last moments on Earth." Terra's matrix was continuing to waver in-and-out of power. Tapping his wrist device in the hope of adjusting for the decrease, he realized he'd soon be on Portable Tablet Storage. He whispered faster: "I may never see Earth—breathe this clean atmosphere again. So sad...no, terrible. Earth's ozone's finally healed, but now there's a lunar catastrophe looming, and we can't do a damn thing to stop it. We can only hope for another saving grace from Nelta in the future...but that's two thousand years away. We're heading for *Sagan* and will be living in Space Fold Time after we launch to *Sagan*; but that huge number's I just mentioned is Real Time, the time it'll take our crew to get there and get back. I feel up against a horrible adversary, Time...no, Death. This recording holds *everything* I, or someone will need to know, in case I somehow forget or can't return. There's vital info in here...data existing in places that might help people, or save humanity. For example, a modified Gem armband Duke's been testing but that's now in a deep freeze where I stuck it until we could get our hands on more Neltan technology. I've been...well, secretive at times. I'm also including the location of a covert area in this recording. Like an old 1950s fallout shelter, the place has been *my* shelter that I've used to wind down in between traveling to *Sagan* or campaigning. When you find this, go there. I hope it'll be *me* who comes back here to retrieve this miniature time and data capsule...but maybe it might not. Goodbye."

After he ended the 3D-box emoticon recoding, he unstrapped his wrist device and tapped a section of the smooth back. Out popped a tiny glowing button that deadened. "You're my time capsule. A little bit of lasting me," he said to the small button. "Hopefully, I, or someone else I designate, will return to retrieve you and view you." Picking up a long stick, he set the small button on the tip of it, set his tiny time capsule into a deep crevice high in the rock ceiling, and covered the time/data capsule with a smidgeon of Sealant that Jane Dirk had given him yesterday. "Terra, remember this spot," he ordered her, when she reappeared for a second. As she complied and her eyes opened a connection in Record-mode, he saw his reflection and felt as if he were watching someone erect his living tombstone! In two thousand years, most likely, he'd be dead and gone—his only hope of returning to Earth was either through The Matter Stream's creative and regenerative powers, a clone, an ancestor, or some other form of technology. He left the spot, and Terra's hologram pointed at the L-car platform.

At the wooden edge while others ahead of them began boarding L-cars, Maureen Strickler began gasping for air and coughing. Elisa had a look of anger on her face as she said to

Battlefield Matrix

her, "It might be the right thing to, do but *you* can't do it! We'll figure out another way." She grabbed Maureen's arm and began pulling her toward an L-car for boarding.

"What's going on?" he asked.

Elisa's eyes were like bullets of brown fear as she swept her fingers through her stringy bangs and sipped some water. "Sir, we overheard what you just said and Dr. Strickler thinks she has a possible solution. I disagree."

As they began a small cycle of debate, he didn't know whether to push them forward or order them and move on past them. They'd catch up. But he didn't want to risk saying or doing *anything* that might make Elisa leave because his brazen honesty and hot temper had made people quit before right on the spot. He remembered what Jenkens had said about her when they were viewing her resume. In the last few years, Dr. Elisa Holton had received awards for community service and diligence on her job. She had close ties with Hampton jet-setters, but her humble demeanor and keen ability to study her environment—softly and quietly—and not make enemies helped her procure funds to treat indigent people in medical domes who were still suffering from the fallout of 2057. Elisa Holton was everything good, reliable and competent; yet she had been stuck for most of her career in a lab conducting research.

Acquiescing, he said: "Dr. Holton, go on, but make it fast. The last L-car's almost ready and we gotta be on it."

"I need to give this to you now, Sir. You decide." It was the armband device, lifeless, with its gems glowing in residual Off-mode. Shakily extending Gem farther into the dark space in front of her, she wiped tears from her eyes on her shoulders. Parting from Gem appeared like experiencing a death of a loved one.

"Decide what?" He gestured for her to keep it.

"Maureen—I mean Dr. Maureen Strickler—can't go on any more, Sir. She's my friend, you know. She wants to take the armband back, Sir. Back to the Press Room."

"What!?" He thought of the crowd that was most likely

breaking through the portal behind them, the time and the trip wire. He swooshed them onward. "You can't do that. Keep moving." After she coughed violently, he asked, "What's wrong, Dr. Strickler? If you are ill, a doctor can see you when we get outta here. This tunnel will flood with angry people at any second. They want rides off-Earth. Now go!" Another "flood" was sloshing through his thoughts—the one the small drone hovering high and undetected would soon unleash into their very spots. He had to get them moving. "We have another ten minute L-car ride under the Potomac and a ten minute walk after that. Go!" He began walking past them, his eyes glued to people stepping into L-cars.

Driven acoustically by the wet slippery stone, he could hear faint voices. They were coming from a multitude of people behind them.

Wheezing, Maureen pushed Elisa aside and took Gem. "Executive Regent Manning," she began, in a gentle voice, "I can't go. The medical facility isn't fully up and running on *Sagan* to help me. I've already had *three* stem-cell treatments but I'm not cured—"

"What!" Elisa shouted.

"*Shhh*," Maureen began, "Sir, I can take this armband back to the Press Room." Obviously experiencing intense pain, she bent down but quickly stood up so that air could penetrate the passageways of her injured lungs. "I have enough energy to make it back. You said yourself, Sir, that this armband—Gem—is one-of-a-kind. Maybe, while you're all gone—" She had tears on her white cheeks as she glanced upward with the expression of a saintly vision. "Someday, some brilliant mind might come along and find a solution to the lunar problem using this Gem technology from Nelta," she said. "Hell, who knows, maybe *I* my*self* can work some magic with it." She laughed then coughed.

Terra briefly illuminated as a slight outline in her obscure processing, and her eyes flashed a dim green in Scan-mode. "Dr. Strickler does present a feasible solution for the Gem device, Executive Regent Manning, and I am receiving biometrics diagnosing a cancerous condition from the 2057 poisoning. However, I included her on The List per Dr. Holton's request for a Designated Friend." Terra appeared alongside Dr. Strickler with her virtual hand on Maureen's hand—a Care Taker app. "Her suggestion to return to the others with Gem is the most practical and hopeful for her and humanity at this moment."

"No, Maureen!" Elisa cried. "We're supposed to work together on *Sagan*! Sir—isn't there something we can do for her?"

Manning closed Maureen's arms around Gem. "It's yours, Dr. Strickler." As Elisa tried to intervene, he gestured for her to stop talking. "I have two shape-shifting prototypes on *Sagan* but they weren't infused with the Neltan Encantado program from the screen. They aren't capable of accomplishing what Gem has the potential to do. You have it, Dr. Strickler. Now to and do some good with Gem. I'm sorry for you loss, Dr. Holton." He felt his guilt a tad bit assuaged, but still not enough to stop his hounding headache. "On one condition."

"What's that, Sir," she inhaled.

"Get it to the Oval Office immediately...now. There are several techs there who'll tell you where to take it. Ya hear? The Oval Office...now!"

Her cheeks appearing white with shock, she said, "Yes...yes, Sir. To the Oval Office."

"Bypass everyone. You'll have a chore breaking through them, but do it. They should let you through when you show them Gem." The armband began to glow—the crystal mounds shine and shimmer—when she slipped Gem over her arm. "Tell them the armband's Black Ops and needs immediate supervision. They'll know that from what happened in the Press Room."

"Yes, Sir." Maureen quickly hugged Elisa. "Bye pal." Coughing, she turned to leave.

Elisa slipped her friend the small container of Kleenex. "I won't forget you, Maureen. Never." Maureen covered her mouth, waved goodbye, and began walking back to the exit

J.P. Osterman

portal. Elisa added: "You do something good for humanity with Gem, ya hear?"

A bright shine reflected off the cold stone—Gem's farewell.

"Dr. Holton," Manning began, prodding Elisa to step into an L-car that had creaked to a halt. "Get in, now, please!"

Maureen's steps were almost inaudible. Elisa hollered, "I'll contact you later to make sure you made it back safely!"

"*Fiiine Byyyye…*"

Manning was pulling Elisa by the handfuls of her shirt. "Dr. Holton, come on. I'll make that exception and let you call her. Time's running out! We haveta make up time and that means I hope Terra can speed up our set of L-cars!"

Elisa's words sped out in shouts of curling cold breaths: "Maureen—check my station at Duke! There might be a source there that might help you!"

"*Wiilll doooo…*byyyyye." Maureen's sounds were gone.

Battlefield Matrix

Chapter 23

Tripwire

After their L-cars stopped and they disembarked, he spotted the red, laser-light tripwire. Stepping through it would set off the drone strike. He could hear faint sounds of people shouting from the direction in which they had just escaped. Terra's connectivity was still gone. He had to manually power down the L-cars.

"Sir," Elisa began, "sounds like thousands of people are coming after us!"

She was obviously about to ask, "How many?" to her weak avatar, whose presence was only a grim outline, but he interrupted her and said: "Just go. I need a minute to power down this transport system. Tell the others I'm *right* behind you. Tell them to keep quiet while they wait for their craft. I put in those orders, but Terra's temporarily disabled and the commands won't stream until her connections back up and processing. Go!" When he could no longer hear her echo, he stepped past the red trip-light indicator that activated the drone

J.P. Osterman

strike. Then he sprinted to the slippery stairway below the exit. Behind him and at a great distance, he could hear roaring water squelching the screams, shouts, and cries of dying men and women trapped under the Potomac.

As a smokescreen for their safety, before he left, he asked Terra to proclaim that the flood was a response to a shift in the earth deep inside the mines. He ordered her to tell The World that the subterranean collapse could unleash toxic fumes into the new ozone. He programmed the flood to end when a hologram stage in the Press Room would measure the two mines as *Nontoxic*. The flood was an automated neutralizing agent and standard protocol, although rare.

Bounding up the stairs and stepping into the star-waning yawn of dawn, he inhaled the fresh air that The Matter Stream sample had healed. It felt like new life as he heaved in another gasp of cold oxygen. He hadn't been outside since…since he could remember. When his Terra flared on beside him, he ordered her: "Seal the exit and give the area around it the illusion of overgrown ivy until real ivy covers it. I want the place around the memorial where we just came out thick with it." He stepped over a row of landscape stones that was a barrier to the public. "Increase the size of these pavers, and engrave each one with the words: *Eternal Growth and Permanent Rest.* That'll keep visitors off the sacred grounds."

As she complied, and the Smart Stones began gradually rising and engraving, he noticed the congregating people who had been waiting for him. He felt suddenly reenergized. They were all about to step into a vastly different way of life. Then he heard the muffled sounds of hovercraft whirring in the distance. Search and Rescue was over the Potomac, their floodlights wildly scanning the frigid water. In a hologram, Terra showed him the prerecorded explanation of the tunnel accident that was thus far claiming the lives of over two hundred people, including law enforcement personnel. The matrix was receiving no signs of survivors and the water valve had closed when measurements inside the mines rendered conditions safe for future excavation. In the distance, he saw

Battlefield Matrix

Elisa Holton take a new wrist device that someone had offered her to replace Gem. She donned it and activated the report on the accident after a Regent gave her permission to view the catastrophe for one minute. She was obviously searching for Maureen. Then Jenkens hailed him, telling him he was bypassing the matrix and putting Terra on Silent-mode. They had to remain undetected and keep matrix illuminations at a bare minimum. Everyone's wrist device icons, avatars, and personal Terra guides extinguished.

After his Terra left, he felt a sickening startle reflex in his stomach. A thought occurred to him and he believed it to be quite innovative. If guilt was still attacking him like arrows, he'd ask his Regeneration Specialist, who would be giving him his Body Regeneration later on today, to expunge the select images from those selects moments using the new Cognitive app. The app had just passed the initial experimental stage as demonstrated by the returning clones. Receiving *that* treatment would be worth not remembering and feeling the aftermath of what he had just done. Expunging and purging through Deep Brain Access was proving to be as effective as Image Creation/Enhancement in correcting extreme moodiness and violent tendencies. After tomorrow, I should have no guilt, he thought, and I'll see if I can get rid of memories of Lynn as well. They're just dead weight in my mind…holding me back…dragging me down.

As he walked to meet Jenkens, he looked back at the giant bronze memorial that reminded him of Lynn's small statue at Duke. He spotted the green-eyed imagers that were still recording everything they were doing and saying. That meant that he'd be in Terra's archives forever—this moment always alive forever. At least that's what Ambassador Shaesar had told Humanity several times whenever someone had discussed the human condition of death. But with Terra alongside him, and his re-scheduled Regeneration approaching, he scoffed off death anxiety to take one last look at Earth…the very early morning mottled sky and his breath curling over his nose. Dotted in several sections on the crispy ground, he noticed distorted slush angels from children having played in the snow. On pathways in front of them were tall, new matrix poles emitting light through crystal mounds. Yesterday, people had ventured outside to experience the new atmosphere and begin reconstructions. He wondered, what are they going to be doing here today? What'll this place look like years, decades, centuries after we're gone?

As he continued to stay behind the fringe of lights, he saw that the old desolate times were everywhere, especially in the background behind the people who were waving for him to hurry up and join them. When he grew tired of feeling the incoming calls vibrating on his wrist, he opened up the communications grid, and his tiny, smiling Beethoven avatar appeared, its cartoon little legs motioning like a roadrunner. "Pick up the pace, please, Executive Regent Manning," was the message someone was streaming to him. "The shuttles are here, their doors open and waiting. Someone soon will notice us...hurry!" The damn little thing just kept on smiling like that old outdated Energizer Bunny.

After he streamed back, *I'm right in front of your eyes!*, he paused and breathed long lasting breaths of Earth's new crisp air. He wished he could encapsulate some right now...but wrist devices were useless in that. He called in a brief reminder for later...to have someone sneak down and somehow absorb or copy the energizing oxygenated mix. Meanwhile, beyond the large park, he noticed haunting estates, their castle chimneys at one time puffing out warm curls of smoke. People had vacated them after 2057. The water was poison; the ground deadly. Still, their shattered windows and acid streaked facades told the story of that terrible day that changed everything. If not for the ozone bombs, he wouldn't have promoted that intense cosmic beacon that resulted in the Neltans receiving their Cry for Help and answering it. I hope I made a positive difference here, he thought, in spite of what might hit Earth. I hope people will remember that I, Thornton Seth Manning, did do something good that benefited people.

Noticing one decimated home, he recalled his childhood

Battlefield Matrix

home in San Diego. That place was now in a Dead Zone as were his parents' burial sites. Contrary to the others on The List who'd soon be having friends or family joining them, he had no one designated as *Special* or *Immediate Family*. Once, he had someone. But Lynn Altmin's atoms were now part of the atmosphere that was also harboring the murdered occupants onboard *Greeter*. When he inhaled again, he believed he was breathing in just a little bit of her. So unfair...so damn unfair!"

"Shhh!" whispered people.

Looking up, he spotted *Sagan* with its Construction Station I revolving like a shining Oz in the early dawning zenith. A cold breeze stung his eyes to watering and pinched his lungs. He felt suddenly free—like a titanium cable untethering a barge of space junk. He breathed again, deeply, feeling new energy percolate through his brain. Approaching Jenkens, he noticed peoples' reactions as he joined them under barren trees branches and alongside bushes crusted with tiny icicles. He touched a piece of bark. It felt as if each hard crease and corky epidermis was speaking to him. "Jenkens," he whispered to his distraught Second in Command who was tapping his feet in place like a restless performer. "We gotta stop all this. If people keep crying and grieving, we'll get stuck here. Help me round everyone up and evacuate. That's what you were hounding me to do!" He felt the elements of the cold bark impress on his hand until his skin hurt. Feeling as if all eyes were on him when he groaned in pain, he quickly brushed himself off. Terra appeared, scanning him. After informing him that a heal patch would fix the cut, she disappeared again on Silent-mode, but streamed that all craft were ready to launch. He picked out a piece of bark that looked like a large Indian arrowhead. "I know, Terra. I'm moving." He thrust the bark into his pocket and wiped his hand on a T-shirt that someone had thrown to him.

That's when several Regents planted their feet in the snow, informing him that they wanted more time to say goodbye.

That pissed him off. It wasn't contrary to the *Leave Behind Law*, but still defiance. He said: "You've been chastising *me* for taking too long. Hypocrites! Get the hell to your designated craft. Now!" He had just killed hundreds of people, for them...but he couldn't move these Regents? Their lamenting hot breaths were stretching into several branches. They seemed powerful enough to dislodge icicles that could strike them down dead. Then he noticed that each of them was holding on to something. One person had dug up some brown grass and was clutching it in his muddy hands. Another had pulled up a bunch of dead flowers to study on *Sagan*, so she said; and Sylvia Itonovich was whistling and then crying because she wanted to see a bird, but they were rare sightings under normal conditions. A Global Intelligence Agent resorted to activating a noise reduction shield. Several doctors were about to sedate several kneeling grieving people, and Enforcers were alongside them, ready to haul off the bodies.

Manning picked up snow and began flicking it in their faces. "Come on! Snap out of it!"

Startled and shocked back to reality, they gasped and listened.

"Now...I want you to get the hell up, and walk quickly, calmly *and* quietly to your assigned shuttle or craft. We have to remain undetected and leave, fast. You're going to get us killed doing what you're doing. I'd kill ya myself and leave ya right now. But you're Regents...normally smart, especially you, Dr. Itonovich. What you're doing here surprises me...makes me change my opinion of you."

She stood up, wobbling a little. "Sorry, Regent Manning." She looked embarrassed in her disheveled hair. "I mean, Executive—"

"Just go...all of you...get to your craft. We'll talk about this later. You can make up for your mistakes later," he huffed. As they all left to their designations, he said to Terra who appeared in a mellow outline, "Finally—we corralled 'em al. Give them guides as icons, but on Low illumination. Soon we'll be on our way to beginning new lives."

In the distance, over the Potomac, Search and Rescue craft began launched from the area. Obviously, someone had called

Battlefield Matrix

off the search for survivors. It was over. But not in his mind.

It was 3:41 a.m. when he checked the time. The park was closed until dawn, but Terra was about to lift her deadly haboob allusion in the Sky Lane. Above the yellow tropopause shield array, *Sagan* and its Construction Station I were shining white and hourglass shaped. They were like an island in space and enlarging by the hour with polymorphic nanomaterials as *Sagan* continued to increase in size and capacity. Engineers were obviously working overtime. *The Breath* was still infusing the giant astrocity with its own unique life force.

Walking behind everyone, he paused, inhaled and exhaled, and said: "I want one last look. One last breath."

After he boarded his chauffeured hovercraft, Terra appeared in the back seat alongside him. Their craft suddenly accelerated, deviating from a long line of other speeding craft leaving the outskirts of McLean. Entering Air Lane 267, the driver began a fast glide southeast. Air Lane 267 was wide open and empty, with flashing guide beacons directing them to an open portion of the tropopause shield. In fifteen minutes, they'd all be on *Sagan*, for good.

Yawning and fighting an invasive sleep that even caffeine candy couldn't stop, he told Jenkens, "Who would *ever* believe circumstances could change so suddenly, that the unexpected could happen so quickly. Life's sure filled with uncontrollable twists and turns!"

Jenkens replied, *"My* experience at *my* company..."

Manning sighed, again, feeling an onslaught of boredom. Jenkens would be pontificating over his past until after they'd dock. Blocking him out by looking out the window at a bowl of soft golden sunlight hugging a clear, cold, silver horizon, he listened to the high-pitched sound of their craft's fuel rods intensifying. The craft pitched upward, accelerating. He felt his eyes sting and his skin tingle. But it wasn't backlash as in those months after First Communication when astropilots first began testing spacefold rims and turrets. They had mastered gravity a long time ago, thanks to the Neltan; and now they'd soon be using it to glide through wormholes. Hover travel was like navigating regularly through life.

"How do you think we'll measure time when we're up there," Jenkens asked. He had stubble, and sewer breath, and lower eyelids shaped like soggy rinds. He pulled out a snack bag and began unfolding it.

Cringing, Manning scooted gently as far away from him as he could until the armrest descended. "I don't know. We'll have to discuss the options at this afternoon's meeting. Then I have a Regeneration scheduled. Can't wait. You ought to get yours done ASAP." He coughed. "You need it. Gotta keep up a good appearance, Steve. We talked about that. It's important. We have to be the examples and show people they have nothing to fear."

Jenkens slid over until his side reached the window. He tapped open the beverage compartment in front of him and took out a small bottle of liquor. "Yeah, I'll schedule mine right now." He contacted the Regeneration Corridor.

Glancing out the window as they approached the tropopause shield that had parted for their approach, Manning saw a shield panel fire a burst of yellow plasma, disintegrating a meteorite that exploded like a firecracker.

He thought, more of those are coming...glad I'm leaving 'cause it's gonna be hell later on to prepare those who're staying for a lunar disaster. Damn, so unfair!

He called for his Terra and asked her, "Do you have a new launch date yet?"

"November 29, 2068, Executive Regent Manning," she answered. "Perhaps sooner. I am unable to predict *The Breath*'s cumulative effects as it expands within the astrocity."

"Great! That's half the old time," he exclaimed, streaming the new date to the others on The List. That made him curious about something that he had noticed about her but was too busy to ask her inside the tunnel. "Terra, why do you sometimes address me as Sir and sometimes as Executive Regent? I don't think I programmed any commands for various greetings or closings, although I remember asking you to round numbers."

Battlefield Matrix

She disappeared and her body rematerialized on the small hologram stage over his beverage compartment and tray. "I extrapolated the manner in which others have spoken to you, and reconfigured the options. How should I address you? Do you prefer I call you Sir, or, Executive Regent?"

Jenkens' drink sprayed out of his mouth. "What'd she just ask?"

Manning coughed. "An evolution in matrix application. *Hm*, this is gonna be an interesting voyage to Nelta!"

###

J.P. Osterman

Battlefield Matrix
Timeline Of Events

November 23, 2030 Regent Steven Jenkens' birthdate.

January 9, 2033 Regent Thornton Seth Manning's birthdate.

May 1, 2035 Elisa Holton's birthdate.

July 7, 2057 Thornton Manning meets Lynn Altmin at Duke University.

June 10, 2057 The Ozone Attacks.

June 17, 2057 World War III erupts.

January 2, 2058 Global Vote uniting *all* nations in a new United Global Democracy.

March 3, 2058 Global Vote establishes The Regency; Global Restructuring of nations.

April 1, 2058 Establishment of Global Enforcer Agency: Earth's Law Enforcement.

April 8, 2058 Global election and Constitution approved.

May 30, 2058 The World elects Dr. Thornton Manning as Regent.

August 23, 2060 Wormhole activates in the mesosphere: First Communication with Nelta.

August 24, 2060 *Greeter* explodes near the Decagon Satellite Accelerator, killing ten.

October 10, 2060 Second Communication with Nelta.

December 11, 2060 Third Communication – People first hear and see the Neltans.

February 24, 2061 *The Need for Advanced Technology* Vote.

March 26, 2061 Fourth Communication – first quantum visual exchange.

April 5, 2061 *Project Go-or-No* debates on WBET-TV.

April 24, 2061 The World approves *The Need*.

July 1, 2061 Fifth Communication.

July 2, 2061 Television broadcast of *Scenic and Serene Contemplations*.

October 4, 2061 Humanity bargains with the Neltans for The Matter Stream sample.

Battlefield Matrix

January 1, 2062 Tropopause shield activates with Research Station II, protecting the ozone.

February 4, 2062 Nelta sends life extension technology to Earth.

April 11, 2062 Implementation of Stealth Force, Global Earth's astro-Armed Forces.

April 21, 2062 Earth receives The Matter Stream sample.

April 23, 2062 Terra-I, Version I, Earth's quantum-computer matrix activates.

August 8, 2062 Terra streams global.

September 19, 2063 Terra-II streams on Earth.

August 30, 2064 The World approves *The Pact*. Construction of *Sagan* begins. The Gift.

November 11, 2064 Thornton Manning records his account of First Communication Day.

July 17, 2065 Space Stations I through V synchronize.

September 18, 2065 Global financial systems unite into one Terra grid.

September 25, 2065 The Neltans clone an interspecies human/Neltan, Mercy.

March 20, 2067 Elizabeth Tufter becomes the only person whose mind teleports to Nelta.

July 7, 2067 Robert Bartlet hires Marty Hernandez as Lead Drive Room Technician.

October 8, 2067 Bill Wallum reports as Navigation Matrix Specialist on *The Spider*.

October 10, 2067 Captain Bartlet hires Emma Jane Wright – EJ – as Matrix Interfacer.

January 15, 2068 Captain Bartlet names *The Spider* that launches from Space Station III.

January 18, 2068 Bartlet hires Beth Tufter as Nanoengineer.

February 22, 2068 University of Chicago students become trapped in near-fatal augmented world experiment.

June 10, 2070 *Sagan*'s projected launch from Space Station I for Nelta.

J.P. Osterman

About The Author

J.P. Osterman was born December 21, in East Chicago, Indiana.

Writing Career: As a futurist and serious Science Fiction author focused on future space travel, J.P. Osterman became an Independent Research Scientist studying the laws that govern space and issues relating to space travel, exploration, and colonization of Mars and exoplanets. In addition to the physics of long distance space travel, J.P. studied the necessary computational theories necessary to control of the physics of space travel and extreme time-space compression; optical quantum computing, quantum communication, and AI Computer intelligence reaching well beyond the "Singularity" with organic quantum level human neural interface and exchange.

J.P. Osterman was a reader and writer throughout her youth. She graduated from University of San Diego with a B.A. in English (with an emphasis in writing) and later a Master's degree from Azusa Pacific University. In the early 1990s, she met Ray Bradbury who inspired her to write science fiction. "I felt that something strange and wonderful had happened to me because of my encounter with Mr. Bradbury, he gave me a future...I began to write every day."

She has written seven novels, mostly science fiction: from exploring Mars, to spacefolding to an ancient alien world. She has won several awards, including the prestigious Rupert Hughes Award at the seminal Maui Writers Conference for her sci-fi novel, The Matter Stream, which she is transforming into her Nelta Series of novels. She won First Place for her play, The Man Next to Me that was subsequently published in the San Diego Writer's Monthly magazine.